To Love, Honour and Betray

(Till Divorce Us Do Part)

RIES

N

ALSO BY KATHY LETTE
FROM CLIPPER LARGE PRINT

How to Kill Your Husband

To Love, Honour and Betray

(Till Divorce Us Do Part)

Kathy Lette

W F HOWES LTD

This large print edition published in 2009 by
W F Howes Ltd
Unit 4, Rearsby Business Park, Gaddesby Lane,
Rearsby, Leicester LE7 4YH

1 3 5 7 9 10 8 6 4 2

First published in the United Kingdom in 2008
by Bantam Press

A CIP catalogue record for this book is available
from the British Library

ISBN 978 1 40743 986 0

Typeset by Palimpsest Book Production Limited,
Grangemouth, Stirlingshire
Printed and bound in Great Britain
by MPG Books Ltd, Bodmin, Cornwall

FSC
Mixed Sources
Product group from well-managed
forests and other controlled sources
Cert no. SGS-COC-2953
www.fsc.org
© 1996 Forest Stewardship Council

For my sister Liz, with love

CHAPTER 1

FISH OUT OF WATER

Like all prisoners, I feel the presence of my captor like tentacles reaching down to where I'm cowering at the bottom of the stairs. The house is hushed. I take a deep breath, as if I'm a diver going under, and peek down the hallway. Empty. A rustle of leaves outside the window startles me. The nerves in my body contract as I move gingerly towards the door. I bump into something in the dark and jump as if bitten, but it's only the fronds of a pot plant I've forgotten. I wait an agonizing eternity to see if I've been detected. I shuffle forward, apprehension dogging each tentative step. Finally, I can see the outline of the front door, but the sensation that I am being watched intensifies. Goosebumps rise on my neck and arms. Adrenalin slams through me. I tell myself to breathe, then inch, one painfully slow tiptoe at a time, towards liberty. The door handle is almost within reach when a mutinous floorboard creaks. I hear the running thud of feet, and fright licks like flames all over me. Trapped, I wheel around to face the furious countenance of my captor. The hall light snaps blindingly on.

'What the *hell* do you think you are wearing? You are not going out dressed like that. Go back to your room and change immediately!'

I glance down in abject humiliation at the Wonderbra-ed cleavage semi-draped in one of her sequinned tank-tops, and the vertiginous stilettos I've stolen from her wardrobe. The top is not quite long enough to hide the fact that I haven't been able to do up the zip on her denim mini.

'I don't know how to break it to you,' her voice is metallic with scorn, 'but your chances of becoming a famous cat-walk model have kinda faded, you know.' The next word she utters, dripping with contempt, is '*Mother*'.

I sag into myself. 'Oh spare me the third-degree sarcasm, Tally, please.'

'I mean, look at yourself! You're forty-two. When are you going to start acting your age? You really are pitiful,' sneers my fifteen-year-old daughter, with a sucked-on-lemon expression. Her sun-kissed hair streams back from her face like a Viking warrioress. 'If you think you are going to win Dad back by dressing like . . . like *that*,' she makes a moue of disgust, her lips as pursed as a cat's bum, 'then you're even more deluded than I thought.'

'But I can still wear short skirts, can't I? I mean, my legs are all I've got left.'

'It's not the legs. It's just that that skirt doesn't go with your face.'

I wilt like day-old salad. 'Oh.'

'You think you're funny, but the sad thing is,

you're really not. If you'd been nicer to Dad, he never would have left.'

I've read articles about the psychological impact of marital breakdown on teenagers, and this isn't how it's supposed to pan out. My daughter, Natalia, should have been blaming herself – not her shell-shocked mother. When my husband walked out two weeks earlier, I'd told the kids that their dad was away working. But my endless sobbing – and the post-it notes stuck to my forehead asking passers-by to please apply alcohol intravenously – told them otherwise. Tally was adamant that I'd driven her father away with my endless niggling about where he was going and whom he was with. Even though it's pretty clear that Jasper has officially forfeited his chance of winning Dad of the Year, I say little in my defence, not wanting to badmouth him. I just take it on the chin . . . OK, the double chin.

'Gosh, Tally, if only *I* were young enough to know everything.' But pain and anger bubble beneath the flippant surface of my words.

'OhmyGod. Is that my *top*?' Tally regards me with slant-eyed hostility. 'How *dare* you borrow my clothes?' She hisses, so as not to disturb her ten-year-old sister Ruby, already asleep upstairs. 'If I've told you once, I've told you a million times not to go through my stuff. It's pathetic.'

Until Jasper walked out on me, I'd tended to wear the kind of baggy dresses you could use to slip-cover a small island. My wardrobe, mostly bought from catalogues, comprised vast shirts to cover up wobbly bits (I was planning, one day, to have my buttocks taken in), and pedal-pushers to hide leg stubble. But this was the third time in a week my teenage daughter had found me squished into her clothes, setting out to the city to win back my absentee husband.

'I mean, just look at yourself.' Tally is standing to attention, one foot turned out like a ballerina. Her hands move agitatedly at her sides, as though ruffling an invisible tutu. 'It's, like, beyond sad.'

I glance into the mirror above the hall table. What I see makes even my passport photo look good. My hair, dull blonde and centre-parted, curves around my jaw like a pair of parentheses – making me the unessential aside. My once-pretty, pale-blue eyes are pink and red-rimmed, like a laboratory rabbit's. Livid semicircles under both eyes give me the appearance of a neurotic possum. My hastily applied lipstick has bled into the tension lines around my mouth, and there's a dismal dab of it on my eyetooth. Mirrors can't lie – but they can be smashed to pieces once the kids are at school, I decide, flicking my gaze floor-ward.

My daughter sighs, 'I don't know what I'm going to do with you.' Her voice is clear and adult and self-assured as she turns, disgusted, on her Ugg-booted heel.

Sheepishly, I trail Tally to the kitchen of our rented surfside accommodation in a south Sydney

4

beachside suburb. It is vintage *Brady Bunch*, with breakfast bar and cheery tiles and kangaroo clock whose rotating tail points to 9 p.m. She's been making biscuits. Since her dad's unscheduled departure my oldest daughter has taken to obsessive baking at all hours of night and day. One morning in May, over breakfast in the leafy London suburb of Hampstead, Jasper had announced he'd been offered a job opportunity in Australia with the Football Federation, coordinating coaching for the international and youth teams. He would move to the Antipodes for a year while I stayed in England with the kids. But I insisted that we let out the house and travel with him. The experience would be enriching for the girls; we would be part of a trend. I told him how nearly two hundred thousand British citizens had packed their bags for Australia in the last year alone, the highest number to leave since the heavily subsidized mass emigration down under in the 1960s. Jasper tried to talk me out of it. But our marriage was curdling, like milk on a stove – and there was no way I was going to take my eyes off the pan.

And so we'd decamped in July, at the end of the English school year. Our oldest daughter, Tally, detested her posh North London private school and was happy to uproot. Our younger daughter, Ruby, was passionate about animals so Jasper rented a house on a Sydney beach, close to a national park, packed with cockatoos, wallabies and goannas. (I like animals too. Right there on the plate, next to the couscous and carrots.) The clincher for the girls was that their new school would be co-educational and the curriculum offered surfing lessons. The place sounded idyllic – even if our marriage was not. We left Heathrow forty pounds overweight – and that was just our emotional baggage.

A month into our Australian adventure, Jasper departed the family so fast he left skid-marks. He moved into a hotel overlooking the Harbour Bridge, to 'find himself' he said. But we were the ones who were lost. If only there were a psychological satnav: 'You have taken a wrong turn. Go back to your wife. Cerebral cul-de-sac.'

'You should have been less critical.' Tally snaps me back to the present. 'And why didn't you diet? You were, like, a size ten when you married Dad. I've seen the photos. Now, you're, what? A fourteen? I don't know how many articles and ads I cut out for you all year about how to stop pigging out.'

Biting my lip, I try to remind myself that a child is for life, not just for Christmas. The best way to do this is to open the fridge and pour a hefty glass of wine. 'You have let yourself go, Mother.'

Her words hit home and I wince at the blow. Why would Jasper want to get into my pants, when even *I* can't? It had taken me half an hour to stuff myself into my daughter's most voluminous skirt – and even so the zipper is wedged half-way up my pudgy flank. No wonder for the last six months

6

our sex life had been like trying to thread a darning-needle with spaghetti. No doubt he worried that if he climbed aboard he'd burn his backside on the light bulb.

'You're right, Tally. Hell, if I left my body to science, science would contest the will.' I could hear my own voice, falsely cheery. 'I'm so out of shape that men in lap-dancing clubs would pay me to put my clothes back *on*.'

I wait for her to contradict me, to say something conciliatory, but her silence knifes me. When Jasper walked out, I had screamed at him: 'You brought me to a foreign country and then dumped me where I have no friends or family. How could you? I don't even know my way to the city.'

His reply still rattled around my cranium. 'Well, just make sure you leave a trail of crumbs so you can find your way back. Cake-crumbs, I expect. Have you noticed how much weight you've put on, Lucy?'

'Hey, when depressed, it's important not to skip a meal. You must eat something . . . even if it's only three or four courses an hour,' I'd retorted with mock-nonchalance. But what he said was true. Since our marriage had started to sour, I'd done nothing but eat. My only criteria for dinner was that there be a lot of it. I was considering putting speed-bumps in the kitchen to slow down my progress to the refrigerator. It wasn't my fault. As any woman can tell you, 'stressed' spelled backwards is 'desserts'.

'Well, why didn't you *do* something about it?' Tally demands, fractiously. She is eating raw cookie mixture off the wooden spoon, a childish gesture at odds with her severe demeanour.

A dull throb makes my temples ache. My oldest child is starting to give me a migraine. No wonder the Panadol bottle reads: 'Dangerous. Keep away from children.' I kick off Tally's high heels and glug back more wine.

'And you're drinking way too much.' Tally snatches the bottle. I notice for the first time that my daughter is taller than me, by at least an inch. When had that happened? She is so lithe and light, my darling girl, yet weighed down with worry. 'Every night since Dad left you just drink yourself legless. How many mornings have I found you passed out in the living room?'

'Hey, walk a mile in my stilettos and then you'll know why I need to lie down. Well, *your* stilettos.' I am trying to sound buoyant, but can feel the abyss of misery beneath me.

'And I just can't believe you're smoking again. You're so weak.'

'I am not smoking . . .'

'I found the packet in your bag. I wasn't born yesterday, you know, Mother. You must think I'm retarded if you believe you can get away with that.'

'Smoking helps me think. And I need to collect my thought,' I attempt a feeble joke.

Tally just rolls her eyes, declining to be cheered,

and angrily shoves her tray of cookie dough into the oven.

'And my thought is that I need a drink,' I add, pinching the wine bottle from the draining board where she's deposited it.

'Well, *my* thought is that I'm, like, adopted. At least, I'm praying that is the case.'

In a rush of nostalgia, I think back to the time my daughter adored me. It was all hot hugs, fierce kisses, her face a warm smudge against my neck, her little fingers coiled tightly around my own, as I rocked her with lullabies in the enclosing dark. I can still feel her arms wound around my neck, dreams skitting across her flickering eyelids, her skin smelling of vanilla and sunlight. Handmade Mother's Day presents, cups of luke-warm tea and cold toast in bed on Saturdays . . . Now it's just disdain, contempt and sarcasm. But how can she respect me when she keeps catching me trying to grovel to my runaway husband in clothes half my size, made for a female half my age?

'The truth is,' I confess, hovering near her, 'your father's brought us to the other side of the world and just walked out. I don't even have a bank account here. I need to see him about practical things, like, um, starvation. If he doesn't give me some housekeeping money, Ruby will have to start wearing your hand-me-downs – while you're still wearing them.'

Once more, she refuses to be amused. Tally has perfected a look of aloof insolence which implies that she is just too cool, too suave for mundane emotions like humour. And she is looking at me that way now.

'Don't you have your own money?' she says, accusatorially. 'I would never, like, give up my career for a *guy*. No woman in her right mind would do that.'

Another body blow. 'Honey, I had a mind once. Now I just have offspring. But whatever your dad is going through, this midlife crisis of his, he will get over it and come to his senses. But in the meantime, he can't leave us poor.'

'Nobody calls people "poor" any more. You call them deprived, underprivileged or disadvantaged,' she bridles.

'Oh great.' I take another slug of wine. 'So, we're still poor, but our vocabularies have been enriched. That's helpful.'

I feel a wave of nausea wash over me, and sink down into the nearest chair. It's fear. Jasper and I have – had – a very traditional set-up. I gave up work as a physiotherapist when Ruby was born ten years ago, and devoted myself to the cooking, cleaning and child-raising. My husband had always been the chequebook-balancer and smoke-alarm battery-changer. He was the one who made sure the house insurance was up to date, the private health-care paid and the radiators bled. He was always on hand to fix things that leaked, fumed or boiled over. He knew where the fuse-box was situated and what to do when he got there. How would

I live without him? What would I do about vehicle maintenance and shifting heavy objects and Allen keys? Who was going to open the honey jars? Who was going to take all the holiday snaps and never be in them? Who was going to shine flash-lights around in a manly way, or drive to the all-night chemist at three in the morning?

I stare at the alphabetized spice rack, consumed by my own bleak thoughts. How will I cope, Jasper-less? I call every gadget a 'thingy'. My only DIY procedure is the highly technical art of whacking the crap out of any electronic device to make it work again. Thank God wine bottles now have twist tops, because even a corkscrew is probably beyond me.

Cold panic curls around my gut. Not only do I not know how to live without Jasper, I don't want to. I have loved him since we lay naked on a beach in Greece in our early twenties, and I traced the constellations of freckles on his broad shoulder blades. I knew them all by heart. I still do. Even during the last year, when he'd been callous and neglectful, paying me no attention except to put me down. Even when I found a love bite on his ass, which he dismissed as a tennis injury but I hoped was leprosy or the Black Death. My best friend, Renée, had told me to kick him out. 'Why are you allowing him to corrode your confidence?' She told me to be a 'glass is half-full type'. She told me to look on his betrayal as the catalyst for fashioning a new life. I could refurbish my personality and redecorate my dreams. It sounded no more difficult than one of her interior decoration jobs. I'd first met Renée when she'd saved me from the renovation from hell. Our bed was in the hall, the dishwasher was in the bathroom, the fridge was in the garden . . . and the builders were on holiday in Ibiza. Renée knows about integral showerheads, dual-action flushes and the swan-necked versatility of taps – which is all Sanskrit to me.

Although I'd come to depend on Renée for much more than tiles, taps and terracotta – taking advice from a childless woman on marriage seemed like taking tap-dancing lessons from an Ayatollah. Although Renée pushed and pushed for me to see a divorce lawyer, I stayed right on loving my husband. 'Jasper and I are entwined, Renée. We've been married so long our wedding certificate should be in hieroglyphics,' I'd remonstrated.

But what I meant was that Jasper was the first man I'd ever loved. The first man who'd found my G-spot without a map, a compass and a list of edible berries. Tanned and sinewy after a lifetime of football, he has deep-set eyes slightly slanted, the colour of dark honey, close-cropped hair and a handsome, chiselled face which wouldn't look out of place in a shaving ad. He'd been there when our babies were born. He'd been there when they took their first steps. We were just woven together; knitted by domesticity, daily little kindnesses, in-jokes, in-laws . . . OK, he isn't perfect. He doesn't walk like a puma, regard a woman's body as a revered classical instrument, or wash-up naked having cooked a gourmet extravaganza. But he ticked so many other romantic boxes – intelligent, capable, handsome, athletic. And above all, *mine*.

Slurping back more Riesling I determine to see him, no matter what Tally says. I am the adult here, I remind myself. Why am I taking the advice of a teenager? What would a fifteen-year-old know about the complexities of love? Do you know what comes out of the mouths of babes? Weetabix.

'Tally, if you ever fall in love, try to wipe it off your shoe before you walk it all over the carpet, OK? It's a messy business.'

Tally confiscates the wine bottle once more. 'Don't you think you've had enough, Mother?'

'Of sobriety? Yes.'

I rummage in my handbag for the cigarettes I am not allowed to smoke.

'What are you looking for?' she tersely interrogates.

A loophole in your birth certificate, is what I want to say when I realize she's hidden my fags, but I reply instead, 'Car keys. Watch Ruby for me, will you? Once I explain to your father the chaos he's caused and how much we need him, he'll come back.'

Tally bars my exit. 'Have you, like, *no* self-respect?'

Self-respect? I muse silently. I don't know if you'd categorize my condition as chronic low self-esteem, but I definitely have an inflated idea of my own irrelevance.

'I thought the good thing about being an adult is that you get smart enough not to, like, do dumb stuff,' she admonishes, making a grab for my keys.

'I thought the good thing about kids is that you keep your parents too busy to break up,' I hit back, wrenching the keys from her hot little hand.

Tally's eye-roll is full of contempt. Our fight is about to escalate, when Ruby suddenly appears in the doorway. 'I wet the bed,' she mutters. The face my ten-year-old turns up to me is a blur of despair. The look of her tear-stained visage tears at my heart. Her big, blue eyes are now nothing more than crescents, from a week of crying. For a minute, I feel paralysed by love, and then I curl her into the circle of my arms.

'That's OK, honey. It's no big deal, darling.'

'Has Daddy come home yet?'

A question like that should be stepped around as carefully as a dozing crocodile. So I did . . . For the first week of Jasper's absence at least. But when I eventually tried to explain that Daddy was very tired and needed some time on his own, Ruby had started crying and hadn't stopped. 'Doesn't Daddy love me any more? Was it because I lost the hamster?' As well as crying herself to sleep every night, she'd also started wetting the bed. Jasper walking out on us was a cataclysm on the scale of an emotional tsunami. My daughters had

14

responded in different ways. While Tally remained closed-off, her eyes slits, mouth zipped, feelings tourniqueted, Ruby had gone into meltdown. But either way, the tectonic plates of their infant world have shifted, opening up a bloody great fissure of uncertainty and angst. I feel a sudden stab of love for them both. The pain of it takes my breath away. How can I have let this happen to my family? Tally's right. It *is* my fault. I gulp oxygen to try to hide the harrowing sob which is about to burst from behind my tonsils.

'Why don't you just ring Grandma?' Tally asserts.

I recoil from the idea. The glacial condemnation of my twinset-and-pearls mother from her heritage listed terrace house in Wimbledon; the 'I told you so's' raining down on my head like hailstones. No, thank you. My mother had always said that Jasper was a man of straw. And my dad? Well, he knows all sorts of fascinating and useful info, like the correct tyre-pressure for long-haul trucks in Alaska and how to fix a fan belt with your pantyhose. But not what to do when your heart has broken. I cringe from the public humiliation, just as I would from a communal mirror in a bikini changing-room. I can't even ring Renée as she's gone on a diving-trip to some remote part of Madagascar. 'There's no point worrying Grandma because I am going to patch things up with your dad. We just need to hold the fort,' I say, rocking Ruby in my arms. 'I don't want everyone from home calling Daddy and demanding explanations.

15

He's obviously in a fragile state. We just need to hang in there, kids. Carry on as normal.'

'Normal!' Tally seethes, shaking her head emphatically as she looks me up and down with disgust. 'Yeah, right. *You* being normal.'

'Why *can't* we just be normal, Mum?' Ruby asks, sleepily. They both crave the dutiful domesticity and matrimonial longevity of my mother's generation, something I am starting to view with a nostalgic awe, just as I find myself amazed by the valour of the Spartans or the ingenuity of the ancient Greeks.

'And I don't want you girls emailing anyone at home in England about this, either. Not after all those farewell parties and going-away gifts. It's just too embarrassing. Besides, it's only a momentary blip.' I try to smile, but it makes my mouth hurt.

Tally opens the oven and removes the biscuit tray. The smell is homey and warm – the only thing in this rented, modern brick house which is. She slams the tray down on the slate bench-top. 'A *normal* mother would know what to do. A *normal* mother would never have let this happen. A *normal* mother wouldn't have told her husband to go to hell.'

'Hey, living in Cronulla, hell would be a step up,' I retort. Now that Jasper has left us, I'm starting to have suspicions about why he'd rented a house as far from the city as possible. Cronulla is the last stop on the rail line. Mind you, as I'm

16

now suicidal, at least the segue from Cronulla to death will be pretty effortless.

'As your sister has grounded me and I'm not allowed to go to the city tonight,' I rally for Ruby's sake, 'what say we all have warm biscuits and hot chocolate? Are you going to dock my pocket money too, Tally? Ah!' With glee I find a hidden packet of cigarettes in the back of the pantry and light one up with desperate relish.

'I can't believe you think this is funny. Why do you have to make jokes about everything? Dad's, like, *left us*. How can you make a joke at a time like this?'

'How can you *not*?' I respond dismally.

'This is all your fault. I hate you!' Tally spits at me. 'I wish you'd just die!'

I take another swig of wine, draw back on one of the cigarettes I stopped smoking ten years ago, and reply, 'I'm doing my best, darling.'

CHAPTER 2

BEWARE OF SHARKS

Living with a teenage daughter is like living under the Taliban. Mothers are not allowed to dance, sing, flirt, laugh loudly or wear short skirts. Let alone stalk absentee husbands – which is why I was climbing out of my bedroom window at one in the morning.

The drive to the city at that time of night took half an hour, along the lip of Botany Bay and past the glittering tarmac of the International airport. Getting into his hotel room was even easier. I was his wife, after all. Tottering on heels so high I resembled a toddler taking to the ice for the first time, I explained to the receptionist that I had been on a Girls' Night Out with pals and was very late (cue tipsy giggling) and it would be best if I didn't wake the hubby. The receptionist chortled conspiratorially, looked at my family name on a credit card, and made a duplicate key.

The speech I'd prepared about how much I loved him and how much we all needed him choked in my mouth when I switched on the lamp of room 156 to find two bodies in the bed. I desperately

18

hoped I was in the wrong room, but my throat was on fire with misery.

'Jasper?'

His head, crumpled with sleep, emerged from under the duvet cover, wincing from the light. But it was the second head I was focused on. The smile the woman gave me was more transparent than a window. 'Oh, hello,' she said.

I clutched my arms around myself to try to hold the terrible hurt inside. The room pitched like a boat caught in a gale. I needed a life jacket, or a buoy – as there were no men in the room, my best friend Renée would have quipped caustically. Except that it was Renée lying in my husband's bed.

'Renée?' I shook my head as if tormented by bees. Everything hurt, as though all my nerves were peeled and exposed to air. I started to cry without any noise. Until, finally, an urgent, choking sob burst out of me.

Jasper lurched up to his feet, moving towards me, arms open. 'Shit. Shit. Shit. I'm sorry, Lucy. There was just no good way to tell you.'

'Yes,' Renée added, 'we're both devastated.' But there was nothing apologetic in her voice; and her stare was like a laser.

It was as if a pin had been pulled on a live grenade. Reflexively I took a step backwards. My husband put out his hands to me in a conciliatory gesture, but I shrank away, ambushed by painful flashes of memory: of Renée probing me for information about my marriage, Renée comforting, consoling, concocting an exit strategy for me, Renée telling me to be a 'glass is half-full' and not a 'glass is half-empty' person, and reinvent my life without him. The woman was a graduate of the Mata Hari Charm School.

'How . . . how long?' My voice was a miserable whisper.

Jasper's expression was as blank as a broken clock. When we'd first met, my beloved's face had flickered with every feeling; his supple body had been pure athletic energy. I used to think of him as solidified light. But the man who stood before me now was anchored down with remorse. He hastily knotted a towel around his waist. 'Ren, I mean, Renée, came to do up my offices, do you remember? After she'd done such a good job on our house . . .'

I felt as though a bucket of ice-cold water had been tossed over my head. That was just over a year ago. Like a kaleidoscope, all the pieces suddenly fell into place – the coincidence of my best friend and my husband often being away on business at the same time. The late-night consultations at his office. And all along, she, Renée, had been coming around to coax confidences from me – which I had given freely, trusting her so completely. And all the psychological ammunition I had equipped her with she had then used in the heat-seeking seduction of my husband.

And seducing is something at which Renée excels. I had seen her in action many times at parties – the light touches on the man's arm, the big, moist eyes looking up at him as she asked: 'Are you happy?' Men don't take their emotional temperature as often as women. This is not a query which crosses their radar.

'Ah, yeah, I guess so,' he'd invariably reply.

'Really?' she'd pout, compassionately. '*Really* happy?'

Then her prey would stop and think, and look down at her luscious breasts, breasts which had never suckled a squalling infant – and he'd begin to have doubts. 'Well . . .' He'd take a moment – right before he took her hand. And oh, how delicate her hand would seem in his big strong paw. Her French manicure had never been sullied by a vegetable peeler or a garden trowel. It had been twenty years since she'd washed her own *hair*.

I'd watched her go through the same coquettish manoeuvres with endless men over the five years I'd known her. The woman took the adage 'there are plenty more fish in the sea' so literally, she should have applied for a commercial fishing licence. I just couldn't believe she'd ensnared my own darling husband. Or that my darling husband had fallen for her, hook, line and sinker.

'And then, well,' Jasper was talking again. His voice seemed to be coming from a long way off. '. . . then we really got close when she was advising me on updating my computer.'

'Yes, I'm sure she's very user-friendly,' I shot

back, having located my tremulous vocal chords. My husband had told enough white lies to ice-skate on. But it was the thought of my best friend's breathtaking betrayal which made my blood run cold. She was Iago to my Othello. Brutus to my Caesar. And how it made me blush to think of the secrets I had told her about our sex life.

'Look, Lucy, you and I, we've become like brother and sister, anyway,' Jasper said, wretchedly.

'Where? In *Tasmania?* A brother and sister who have sex and make two babies?' I said incredulously. 'I think that's illegal, actually.'

'Adultery is not the cause of marital breakdown,' Renée piped up in her polished purr. 'It's only a symptom.'

Rattled, I interrogated my memory. When had Jasper started to withdraw? Exactly a year ago . . . exactly when Renée had started working for him. He'd become brittle and snappy and increasingly absent. At first I'd suspected it was work pressure, but then there were the gaps in his life, the time he couldn't account for. I should have seen the signs when he gave me a bread-maker for Valentine's Day, instead of the Agent Provocateur lingerie I'd asked for. He started faking it in bed, too. Faking sleep, that is, to deter nocturnal gropings from my side. All he'd given me between the sheets of late was an anti-climax. Oh, we still made love occasionally, but whereas once he would look deep into my eyes and tell me how much he loved me, he now kept his eyes closed or stared at the pillow.

And it wasn't just sex which had lost its intimacy. Post-coital cuddles had become a thing of the past. Whereas once we'd snuggle on the couch and he'd kiss me for no reason, I suddenly found myself suffering from an affection deficiency. He stopped doing the crossword with me, too, which meant I could never solve any of the sports questions. When he gave up bringing me tea in bed on a Sunday morning, I'd felt a sense of doom, but just tricked myself into thinking that this was a normal transition, now that the children took up so much of our life. With the brilliance of a twenty-five-watt bulb, I had believed it when he had told me that his second pay-as-you-go mobile was back-up for work, and not because he didn't want me to see the bill. My attitude had become ostrich-like. Hell, I would not have looked out of place on the plains of the Serengeti. How had I allowed myself to be so stupid? It was as though I'd been bungee-jumping without a rope. But no longer. I steeled myself. Times had been tough before and we'd survived. Hell, we got through the eight-week-old-baby-with-colic ordeal, so we could get through this, goddamn it.

For a moment I forgot that I was dressed like an ageing prostitute on the brink of a nervous breakdown, my wobbling stilettos the most stable thing about me. 'You,' I yelled at Renée, jabbing my finger in her direction, 'You, I never, ever want to see again. Jasper, you've been an idiot. You allowed this, this . . .' I couldn't think of the right word for her. 'This *monster* to seduce you and take you from us. But I forgive you. It's a midlife crisis. That's all it is. The kids . . .' Thinking of Ruby and Tally I welled up, but stopped when I realized my husband might be tempted to wipe away my tears with a divorce petition. 'The kids and I love you. I'm so sorry if I've let you down.' I looked at Renée's slender arms propped behind her head on the pale linen pillow. 'I'll lose weight.' The woman's dedication to being thin meant that she wouldn't even read a fat book. Although she was a product of England's best boarding schools, the books she did read were condensed, and her CD collection was all compilations.

'Jasper, we have a whole history. We have so, so much in common. And not just our kids. I can make you happy again . . .' I blurted. 'I promise. Just get your things and come home to us.'

'Lucinda.' Her voice was as crisp as the sheets my husband was paying five hundred dollars a night to soil. 'Jasper and I are moving in together. He's been trying to tell you for ages . . .'

The job opportunity in Australia with the Football Federation, I painfully realized, had been his escape strategy. His departure from the family was planned to coincide with this new job. That way he could sidestep any scenes and recriminations. He would leave us, ostensibly for work, and then the separation would just become permanent. When I announced that we'd move with him, lock,

24

stock and two smoking children, I'd obviously scuppered his evil plans.

And perhaps Jasper really had thought better of ruining his children's lives? Except that Ruthless Renée, having pretended to me she was on that Madagascan diving holiday, had followed. The brutality of her actions took my breath away. In my reflection in the hotel mirror above the bed, I looked like the victim in a horror movie who has just seen The Creature. But instead of screaming, my anger began to boil over, hissing and spitting on an invisible stove. I started hurling cushions, books, shoes, whatever I could find, at Renée, until my husband strong-armed me into submission.

Renée gave no reaction. The skin on her smooth cheek merely twitched once, and she ran her mani-cured fingers through her ebony, Louise Brooks bob. 'I think you should go now,' she said tightly.

And then the absurdity of the situation struck me and I laughed out loud. I was doubled up by a paroxysm of hilarity as startling as it was unanticipated.

When I had exhausted myself and was limp with drained emotion, Jasper pulled some clothes on and led me back to my car, with promises to come out to see us for lunch the next day, with prom-ises to make it up to me, to talk things through. On automatic pilot, I fired up the engine and drove, numb with shock. But on the long journey south, the image in my mind was of Renée, looking cat-that-swallowed-the-canary-ish in her self-satisfaction.

My glass wasn't half-full or half-empty. It was just not what I'd bloody well ordered in the first place.

CHAPTER 3

BEWARE OF CLIFF EDGE

A woman's work is never done. Not by men, anyway. Sweeping a woman off her feet is the closest Jasper has ever come to housework, besides leaving a roasting pan to soak. But I didn't resent it today. I whirled around the house like a demented Doris Day, sweating over a hot cookbook. I was so happy I couldn't bring myself to beat the eggs for the crème brûlée. I just spoke to them with stern affection and encouraged them to fulfil their potential. Ruby made cards and banners reading 'We Love You Daddy'. Tally picked wild flowers. I conditioned my lanky locks, tweezed renegade chin hairs, layered on eyeshadow – then rubbed most of it off again with my finger in a feeble effort to 'blend'. I moisturized myself until I was slicker than a used-car salesman. The kids excitedly set the table. And then we just waited for our prodigal patriarch.

By two o'clock, I was starting to feel anxious. By four o'clock, I was starting to feel ill. By seven o'clock, Tally had started baking again, Ruby was crying as usual, and I had started drinking. When Jasper didn't answer my hundredth call to his mobile, I drank even more, wandering around the untouched banquet in my best dress like Miss Havisham. When I rang the hotel and discovered that Jasper had checked out, I emptied the rest of the bottle. It wasn't until Monday that the FFA confirmed he'd taken the week off work and was holidaying somewhere near the 'Top End' – wherever that may be. It was clear that I had chosen the Road Less Travelled . . . and now had no bloody idea where the hell I was. Marooned, in an unfamiliar country, I had no family, no job and no friends . . . In truth, my husband had run off with my best girlfriend . . . and I really, really missed her. I had lost the two people I trusted the most, in one fatal blow. And all emotional equilibrium had gone with it. On those forms where it said 'In case of emergency, please notify . . .' I suddenly had no one to call.

I had always admired Renée's sloe-black eyes, so full of Machiavellian mischief. But now, how they mocked me! Thoughts of the way she'd wheedled classified information had me gnawing my teeth all night, chewing on my pillow, staring bug-eyed at the ceiling in a fugue of horror at my own gullibility. Whenever I edged towards sleep, I would see Renée in my mind's eye, her falsely concerned face rather too close to mine, her teeth small and pointy, her duplicitous, solicitous smile lipsticked bright red. But there was no point going to sleep anyway, as the kids insisted on having their 'I miss my daddy' crying nightmares at different hours of the night. If only their melt-downs had coincided I might have snatched the odd hour. The worst feeling in the world is to see your children in pain when there is nothing you can do to alleviate their suffering. The kiss-to-make-it-better technique favoured by mothers worldwide just wouldn't work. Nor would a Band-Aid or treat. A lullaby couldn't lull them to sleep. Sleep? Huh! I lay awake all night only to plummet into deep slumber minutes before the 7 a.m. alarm had me dragging myself out of bed to get the girls off to school.

In Australia the sky is a blatant, euphoric blue. Even in September, which is still winter, the clouds skid across the horizon, as if skylarking for the sheer fun of it. They seemed to scoff at my misery. Our rented brick bungalow was at the southern-most tip of the Cronulla peninsular, with the Pacific Ocean on one side and the Port Hacking River on the other, across from 154 square kilometres of national park. The area seemed to be throwing some kind of architectural fancy-dress party. One house had come as a Spanish hacienda, another as a palatial Texan ranch homestead. Competing for attention was a Swiss chalet incongruously situated next to a Japanese pagoda, nestled beside a modern glass cube jutting over the sea. Our house was all Italian tiles and big windows. The rooms were seared with light. Each morning I drew the blind, convinced that the best way to start the day was to go back to bed.

You know you're depressed when you feel like the day after the night before . . . and you haven't even been anywhere. All I could manage was to climb into a tracksuit occasionally to tend robotically to my children's breakfast, sandwich and homework needs. As the best-known cure for insomnia is sleep, I started taking pills. Munching on tranquillizers meant that I was soon napping between naps. I was full of so many pills I needed to put a childproof lid on my mouth. I planned to join Narcotics Anonymous just so that I could get more pill prescriptions under another name.

For Ruby and Tally's sakes, I tried to maintain that I had a twenty-four-hour virus – OK, a twenty-four-hour virus which was lasting their entire spring break. As for housework, apart from looking thoughtfully at the washing-up now and then, my only cleaning technique was to light a lot of candles, so nobody would see the dust. When the kids came looking for clean clothes I attempted joviality, explaining that doing housework when you live with kids is as pointless as washing the car when it's snowing. I did try to cook dinner at night, but often only managed to smear congealed peanut butter on to three-day-old bread. I told myself that when depressed it's dangerous to operate heavy machinery – like a vegetable peeler. One night I was so out of it, I rolled Tally's socks in breadcrumbs and baked them until golden-brown. After that, the kids lived on Chinese takeaway and McDonald's. Until the night I was unwrapping the fish and chips and came face to face with a photo of Jasper and Renée on the social pages at the Governor's garden party.

My thirst for revenge became unquenchable. Haemorrhoids, cystitis, typhoid – I wished them all on to Renée. The woman should have come with a 'buyer beware' sticker on her forehead. Couldn't Jasper see that? Renée is the type of label snob who turns over the plates to check if they're Wedgwood. The water in her cistern is baby-blue. Her shrubs are miniature, as is her schnoodle (a cross between a poodle and a schnauzer.) In the end, I comforted myself, living with perfection would become perfectly horrible and he'd come back to us. To *me*.

I would have moaned about Renée's shortcomings – hell, I would have vilified the evil bitch to anyone who would listen – except I knew no one. Loneliness consumed me. Even my imaginary friend got bored and went off to play with someone more interesting. Cold-calling telemarketers started writing *me* cheques, just to get me off the phone. There was a huge Jasper-shaped hole in my life. But humiliation kept me from calling home. And it was impossible to go back. Our house in Hampstead was rented out. The kids were enrolled happily enough in beach suburb schools, and were flatly refusing to return to grey and grimy London. So, I just clung to the wreckage.

When I finally tracked Jasper and Renée down

31

to an apartment overlooking the harbour and rang them in the middle of the night, hysterical, Renée quickly lost patience. 'Pull yourself together, Lucinda,' she scoffed. 'Giving up a man is easy. I've done it thousands of times.'

Easy for Attila the Best Friend. I, on the other hand, needed some kind of patch. A husband patch to cure me of my obvious addiction. Unable to move forward, I could only go back – to the time when we were all safe and happy, before Jasper fell in lust with Renée Craven.

Parent–teacher night gave me an excuse to get in touch without looking desperate. I rang Jasper at work. When he agreed to attend, my emotions yo-yoed. I so longed to see him . . . Yet was horrified by the thought of him seeing me like this . . . I wanted to look sexy . . . No, I wanted to look destroyed and on the point of a breakdown. On the day of the school meetings, I dressed one minute in a basque – and the next in sackcloth and ashes. I went from wanting to kill Renée for betraying me – to wanting to kill myself for being so naive.

Welcome to the brain of the newly abandoned woman. I was lonely, yet afraid of company. I wanted to ask for money . . . And yet I didn't want to look needy. But if I didn't get some house-keeping money soon, what would I say to the kids? 'Sorry, but due to a downturn in our economic situation, I'm going to have to let one of you go.' At lunchtime I found myself pirouetting around

the kitchen making home-made bread. By one
o'clock I was curled up in a foetal ball, sobbing.
Which of these moods would be more likely to
bring Jasper back to me? I loved him, I hated him,
I loathed myself and I really, really detested *her*.
But if anyone had told me I was being hysterical
or contradictory I'd have scratched their eyes out.
As the hour of our school appointments
approached, my nerves shrieked like the unoiled
hinges of a screen door in the wind.

Sitting through the consultation with Ruby's
teacher, I heard nothing as my eye was constantly
on the door. If Jasper didn't turn up I would kill
myself – except the only weapons to hand were
Ruby's compass and protractor. (Finally, a use for
them!) At the meeting which followed with Tally's
teacher, I gnawed my nails to my elbows.
Desolation clung to me like a wet raincoat. At
least it numbed me to the principal's address,
which received a few desultory claps from the one
or two parents who had somehow managed not
to fall into a coma. Over refreshments afterwards,
when there was still no sign of Jasper, I did what
all women do when traded in by their husbands –
I made a misguided lunge for the wine bottle.
Next would be the peroxide bottle. As long as I
didn't get them confused.

For the next week, the world became a blur of
gloomy shapes and noises. I gave up eating. Or
rather, eating gave up me. I was often so drunk
that the fork just never reached my mouth, making

33

catastrophic contact instead with ear, nose, throat and, occasionally, the forehead. In the mornings, my teeth were all furry, as if wearing little coats. I was so hungover, I could only eat soup – everything else was too noisy. And who wants soup for breakfast? My head thumped so badly I wanted to ask the lady next door to keep her needlepoint down. It was all I could do to hoist my eyelids, get the kids out of bed, and make the sandwiches without getting marmalade in our hair.

Tally was scathing. 'You're pathetic. An old alkie. Obviously if you hadn't drunk all the way through your pregnancy with me, I'd be, like, *so* much more intelligent now. I'd have about six billion more brain cells. But *no*. You had to eat soft cheese, sushi and drink alcohol. That's how selfish you are!' She gave me an exasperated, judgemental look which screamed, 'Raising parents these days is not what it used to be.'

And she was right. My life had become a bad country-and-western song. In fact that was my theme tune – 'If The Phone Don't Ring, You Know It's Me' – as I waited and waited for Jasper to call. I fantasized about how vile he'd feel at my funeral after my liver had given out. It wasn't like me to be so useless. Any day now I would wake up, take a good hard look at my situation – and fall back into an alcoholic coma again. I knew I'd reached rock bottom the night the doorbell rang, and when I tried to struggle to my feet they turned out not to be where they are normally situated.

34

Lying there on the cold kitchen terracotta tiles, I remember noticing through half-closed lids that there was a dribble of chocolate on the floor. It struck me that if I wiggled my body a fraction forward, I could probably lick it. That would be dinner taken care of.

And this is how my neighbour Susie found me. When she received no reply to the doorbell, curiosity propelled her over our communal back fence and through the open kitchen door. Her curly head appeared, inverted, above mine.

'What the hell are ya? A bowling ball? Then I suggest you get up out of the gutter, girl,' was what she said, or something like it.

The fact that I was only wearing a bra, Jasper's boxer shorts and a cardboard tiara probably hadn't escaped her notice, either. 'OK, love, what's the story?'

I prised my tongue from the roof of my mouth and managed to utter, 'I think I must have tripped over the phone.'

'The cordless phone. Right,' she replied sarcastically, hauling me up to a sitting position. 'Where's your old man?'

'My husband . . .'

'Yeah. Where is he?' Her voice sounded galaxies away.

'He needed more space,' I sobbed.

'Who is he? Captain Kirk? Come on, darl.' She tried to manoeuvre me to the living-room couch, but movement made me nauseous.

'I'm like a good wine. I don't travel well,' I tried to explain, although it sounded more like 'Likkkggg azzzz sine tttvvegghggg'.

And then I vomited all over her. It was the beginning of a beautiful friendship.

'I'm s . . . s . . . sick,' I stammered, somewhat superfluously.

'Was it something you ate?' my neighbour asked, cleaning me up.

'Yeah. My wedding cake.'

CHAPTER 4

SWIMMING PERMITTED

'Your interior decorator? You're kidding me. I think your old man took the expression "*Once it's in, you'll love it*" a little too literally.'

'He's definitely decorating *her* interior now. He hired Renée for a job and . . .'

'Ha! Sounds like the only job that bitch is good at is the one with the word "*blow*" in front of it.'

Susie poured me another cup of coffee, strong, black, reviving. She opened my fridge to scrounge for milk and came face to face with a bowl of old Chinese takeaway, growing fuzz.

'I hate cleaning the bloody house. No sooner do you finish than you have to do it all again, like, two lousy months later,' she joshed. 'But *this* is disgusting. Bloody hell. No self-regarding cockroach would enter here.' Snapping on rubber gloves, Susie tore through my kitchen, bagging and binning everything. The woman vacuumed so thoroughly, she practically sucked the skirting boards right off the walls.

When she'd finished cleaning up, she scrutinized my pantry, her curvaceous arse swinging back and forth like a denimed pendulum. 'Um, Miss Lucy-Lou, you seem to have travelled all the way from Britain without realizing the importance of adequate provisions. Just ask Burke and Wills . . . The famous outback explorers,' she explained to my bemused expression 'who perished in the desert through lack of food and water. Doan worry about it. I'm popping down to the late-night supermarket.' She waved away my feeble protest. 'You can pay me back later.'

The first step in befriending an English person is to let them thaw out. You should allow at least ten years for this. Australians, on the other hand, are, in general, so open and warm-hearted, so frank, that you find yourself putting your foot flat to the floor of the friendship accelerator.

When Susie found me again the next night in a drunken sprawl – 'I'm not drunk. I'm just hanging on to the floor for a while' – in lieu of a reprimand she offered coffee and comfort. 'You've been dumped. It's normal to be lying drunk, sobbing. It's normal not to eat or sleep or make a decision. You'd have to be insane not to go a bit bonkers, darl.'

Susie's husband had left eight years ago when their daughter, Matilda, was two and their son, Heath, was eight. 'When I went to see this solicitor bloke about child maintenance, he asked me in a routine way whether or not I had any convictions. I told him, "Yeah, I do. That all men are bastards." "No," this pinstriped solicitor reiterated, "I mean *prior* convictions." So I said, "Yeah, that all men I met *prior* to my husband were bastards, too! I just didn't bloody well know it!"'

Susie threw back her head and gave a hearty, deep-throated chuckle, before cooking chicken schnitzel for dinner and calling all the kids, hers and mine, to join us. I tried to help but Susie pointed out, in her dry Aussie way, that in my present state she wouldn't trust me to organize a polar bear cull in the tropics.

'Just make sure you only get drunk with people who won't let you dance naked on a table-top or do the school run topless. People like me, OK, Lucy-Lou?'

Susie's daughter, Matilda, was the same age as Ruby, so, while I convalesced, the girls had sleep-overs and went to the beach. Susie started cooking meals for all of us on a pretty regular basis and bringing around necessities like choco-late and vibrators.

'This is the ultimate in vibrators, darl. It can do everything imaginable.'

'Oh great – can it bake fairy cakes for the school fete and complete a project on igneous rocks whilst unpacking the dishwasher?' I replied, from my prone position on the couch.

'Well, well, well. *That's* a good sign.' My new friend beamed, hands on her shapely hips. '*It* has a sense of humour. Are you glimmering back to life then, Miss Lucy?'

More restorative than the meals Susie made were

her funny stories to snap me out of my self-indulgent miseries.

'When I found my husband in my best Dolce & Gabbana skirt, I was gutted, furious and profoundly mortified.' She paused for dramatic effect. 'He was wearing stockings with sandals! How could he *do* that? I mean, how naff!'

It was only when the children were all asleep and we were sitting on her veranda, nursing cups of hot chocolate and watching the midnight moonlight shimmering on the sea, that Susie admitted how shattered she'd been when her husband had left her for a man.

'Mind you, I should have guessed the bastard had gone gay. The sex just got pathetic. It was like being ravaged by a tree sloth.'

And I reciprocated with tales about Jasper. How we fell in love when he was a football player and I was the team physiotherapist. How we met when I treated him for groin strain . . . And if he wasn't all that badly strained before, he definitely was when we finally got out of bed four days on. We married three years later and had Tally straight away. Jasper had to give up playing football after he suffered another groin injury. Not his own. He kicked the team manager in the balls over some negative comment he made about a treatment I'd administered. The club let us both go, and he'd been coaching ever since. 'And we were so happy, until Renée made her move. *Apparently* the affair's been going on for twelve months. Jasper obviously

40

didn't tell me till now so that I could have a heart attack at leisure.'

Susie couldn't understand how I had become friends with such a man-eater as Renée in the first place. I explained how my best friend since university had died of breast cancer six years ago. When Maggie went bald from chemotherapy, I shaved my head so she wouldn't feel alone. 'This turned out to be a mistake,' I admitted, taking a sip of hot chocolate. 'As *she* just looked like an extra in a Sigourney Weaver sci-fi thriller and *I* looked like a distressed egg.' Susie's laugh encouraged me to elaborate. I explained how Renée had come along when I was grieving, and how her sheer chutzpah and no-nonsense style had buoyed me up. She had taken me shopping for the kind of clothes I had stopped wearing, as well as done up my house. I had come to rely on her opinion about everything. With heartbroken hindsight, I could see now that it was an unlikely friendship. Renée was chic. I was cheap. She wore Prada. I wore Primark. She had dinner parties where she served woodpigeon with Cabernet Sauvignon, walnut oil dressing, parmesan shavings and frisée. My recipe for dinner party success was to leave Get Well cards all over the mantlepiece, so that people would imagine I'd been too ill to cook, which was obviously why we were ordering takeaway.

'Jesus, hasn't the stroppy bitch seen the sitcom? Friends come first!' Susie scolded. 'Hasn't she read the *Divine Secrets of the Ya-Ya Sisterhood*?

41

Friendship should be the brolly you use when it's raining shit.'

But watching Susie expertly packing kids into her car, naturally assuming responsibility for household DIY, balancing a chequebook with one hand and changing a light bulb with the other, I didn't think she would ever need an umbrella. The woman could whip up an entire gourmet meal for all the children plus their friends and any handymen around the place, even though the larder was bare and all she had in the fridge was thrush cream, wart medicine and half a bulb of garlic. Whereas I was over-compensating for Jasper's departure by kowtowing to Tally's every mood, Susie was wearing a T-shirt which read: '*I had sex with my husband and all I got was this lousy kid.*' Although scouring my house top to bottom in an attempt to bring it up to minimum health standards, Susie's cleaning technique in her own home was to feign a migraine whenever she needed anything done. 'Kids must be exploited. That's what they're bloody well for. Hey, I drive my offspring crazy, but I also drive them every-where. So they've gotta be nice to me, right?' she Winked.

Whenever Tally snapped at me, or rolled her eyes in horror as she flinched from my embrace, Susie assured me that all teenagers were like that. 'I'm taking out a restraining order on my kids so they won't bloody well visit me in the old people's home. I'm booked in to a maximum security retirement village. I also tell them over and over that only children who are adorable to me will be in the will. Where there's a will . . . your kids don't have to be in it. *Being of sound mind, I have spent all my moolah on myself.* You are just too bloody nice to that Tally of yours. Toughen up, woman.'

'I can't, Susie. Their father has left them. And it's all my fault.'

'Yeah, right, because you're married to a bloody saint. I'll send away for the necessary paperwork to have the bloke canonized the second I get the chance,' she said flippantly.

'It *is* my fault.' I post-mortemed. 'I did thoughtless, terrible things. I accused him of being lost when we were driving. I pointed out that his short cut added another hour to the journey . . .'

Susie feigned horror. 'Oh, call Amnesty International.'

'If I hadn't been so busy nagging, I might have noticed that my husband was becoming demoniacally possessed. And until the spell is broken, I have to coddle my kids no matter how difficult they might be.'

'But you've got to set boundaries,' Susie stressed. It was Sunday morning. Susie's sprawling cottage, crammed with cooking smells and domestic clutter, seemed, like her, happy with its lot in life. Susie was taking a pee in her hall loo, which bore the sign 'ancestral seat'. As usual, she'd left the door open. Aussie women are very relaxed with each other, especially about bodily fluids.

They're always peeing together or showing each other where the tick has got embedded in their labias when squatting in the bush. 'Kids want something to rebel against,' she called, above the gush.

'Their father has rebelled,' I said over the flush, shifting from foot to foot in an embarrassed English way, not sure where to look. 'That's enough rebellion for one household, believe me,' I sighed, my voice quavering.

Susie raised eyebrows the colour of caramel toffee as she washed then wiped her hands down her jean leg. But she zipped her mouth along with her fly. Although she was now a hairdresser with her own local salon, in her youth Susie had danced naked at fertility festivals on Byron Bay beaches, attended women-only workshops on the phallus-centricity of twentieth-century literature and given birth, naturally, surrounded by her poet pals in a fern-laden garden on a tropical island. She was so much more worldly than me. But I had to follow my instincts. And my instincts said to batten down the parental hatches and do nothing to further upset my fragile offspring. Settling into Susie's kitchen, I commandeered her laptop which was open on the table.

'It's time you got your sorry arse out of the house,' Susie decreed as she absentmindedly poked at her bolognaise sauce with a wooden spoon.

'Out?' I recoiled, lifting my head up in alarm. 'I can't go out.'

'Why?' she demanded.

'I just can't bear to see people happy. There's only one place I can go socially. Funerals.' I was only half-joking. My grief had no texture – it just simply cloaked me. Now that I was no longer drinking or sleeping all day, I had a terrible need to find out everything about Jasper and Renée's living arrangements – poring over his bank statements to learn what they'd purchased for their penthouse apartment on the harbour, where they'd stayed on their trips to Bali for the weekend.

'Oh God. Look at the website for this restaurant he took her to last week. I got the name off his visa bill,' I moaned. An instruction should have popped up on the screen. *Smash forehead on keyboard to continue.* I knew I was in the grip of an obsession. But Susie was the closest I got to a Rejected Wives Anonymous support group.

'Get over it, woman. You're contaminated by jealousy,' Susie said, snapping shut the computer. 'You must let it go or it will eat you alive.'

'I know, I know,' I despaired. 'Jasper says I'm a prying, interfering busybody . . . At least that's what it says on his emails to his lover.'

'You're hacking into his emails? That's it.' She turned off the spaghetti sauce on the stove. 'Come on. I'm taking the girls to the beach before lunch. I've told Tally to meet us back here to eat at one, no excuses.'

Tally had been making noises about becoming vegetarian but Susie believed you should offer your children a choice come mealtime – spaghetti bolognaise or adoption. 'Hang on a jiff, while I get my cossie on.' I watched as my new friend abruptly stripped off her clothes in front of me and struggled into a tight black Speedo. Although in her mid-forties, Susie's body was muscular and compact. She was always complaining about her bottom – 'Jewish arses are so big from centuries of having to flee carrying all our furniture on our butts. We just keep unpacking until the next pogrom.' But it looked perfectly peachy to me. 'Matilda's got Nippers in half an hour.'

'Nippers?' It sounded ominous. Everything in Australia was always trying to nip you.

'Junior surf lifesavers. They have swimming and running races, learn to ride boards and generally have a ball getting confident in the water.' She scooped her thick, dark curls up into a ponytail and lassoed it with an elastic band. 'And you and Ruby are coming.'

I looked at her as though she'd just asked me to split the atom. 'I can't go to the beach.'

'Why the hell not?'

'Here's an entirely random list of things I hate. Sharks, jellyfish, not being able to see the bottom, waves, big waves. Oh, and swimming. Besides, the beach will only remind me of Renée. And how much I wish she had crabs.'

Susie had a spirited face, made for laughter, an electric mane of hair and dark eyes, which glittered with intensity, especially when I said something

46

which annoyed her. 'Everything reminds you of Renée, you big boofhead. This has got to stop.'

She frog-marched me through our communal back garden and into my rental house, where she started rummaging through the laundry for some clean clothes for me.

Tally watched with disdain, slowly chewing on a strand of her blonde hair as she leant on the kitchen doorframe. During the last week she'd taken up with a surfie boy nicknamed Chook (because his last name was Hennessey) from the year above her at school. His only perceivable skill seemed to be his locust-like ability to strip-mine the weekly food shop. Dropping in after an early-morning surf, he was busily devouring anything in the fridge which didn't bite back. 'You're not taking my mother out, are you?' Tally deigned to comment. 'She hasn't shaved her underarms or washed her hair in, like, three weeks. Put it this way, if That Woman I'm Related To went to the House of Horrors, she'd come out with a job offer.'

Chook snickered, before recovering to grunt 'Ah, g'day. Gettin' heaps?' To experience Tally's boyfriend wrestling with the mother tongue was like seeing a Ming vase in the hands of a toddler. 'Top tucker.'

'My mum's given up on life,' my daughter reported, contemptuously. 'Like all losers.'

It was tempting to point out what I'd given up for her. My figure, uninterrupted sleep, privacy, my pelvic floor, the ability to wear bikinis, a top job as a physiotherapist, and, oh, just the best years of my bloody life. But I said nothing. Instead, spurred on by my daughter's derision, I prised myself out of my pyjamas – PJs which had been welded to me for weeks – and into shorts and a T-shirt, and said, 'Let's go, Susie.'

'Great! See youse!' Susie farewelled. 'We're off – like a male stripper's G-string.'

I feigned enthusiasm and strode after my new friend down the hall, while secretly wondering what had happened to me. If I met myself now for the first time I'd think I was a washout. It was as if I'd been taking Pathetic Pills. But no more! I grabbed my towel and sunhat, determined to be a better role-model to my daughters.

Little did I know that they'd soon be worshipping the quicksand I walked on . . .

CHAPTER 5

SWIMMING BETWEEN THE FLAGS

Australia is a place where you can enjoy the finest cuisine, exquisite wines, world-class opera and ballet, fine art galleries and museums – and then, merely by straying off a pathway, get devoured by a crocodile, python, dingo or great white shark.

The city of Sydney lies supine under a big, easy-going sky, with houses lazily laced around its many waterways. The seaside suburb of Cronulla sparkled in the sunlight. The light scalded me and I blinked like a newborn field-mouse as we strolled on to the four-mile stretch of yellow sand. The beach curves north into sand hills and south to the sandstone fore-shore, which lies like great slabs of golden cake. It was early spring, the day was bright and beautiful. The sea crashed exuberantly on to the sand while whipped-cream clouds scudded overhead. But just as I'd feared, the sight of happy families frolicking proved a torture. Big strong dads slathered sunscreen on to their giggling offspring whilst doting mums draped themselves attractively around their picnic hampers in their cheerfully coloured bikinis. Everywhere I looked,

I felt mocked by happy couples and their cavorting kinder.

Cronulla is a family beach. There are no His and Her chihuahuas being paraded by couples in matching lemon leisurewear, no men in glow-in-the-dark trainers with equally fluorescent teeth looking for the nudist section. No, it was all breast-feeding mums, fathers with babies papoosed to their bellies, toddlers squirming on teddy-bear-emblazoned rugs, and a cacophony of kamikaze kids, hurtling around on foam surfboards.

Ruby kept wandering over to the periphery of family gatherings. She would just stand there, hovering, as if hoping to absorb normality by osmosis. Waves of laughter rolled out from under sun umbrellas. My youngest daughter's longing was painful in its nakedness.

'I've ruined her life,' I wailed to Susie.

Susie squeezed my hand affectionately. 'A happy marriage is like an orgasm. Half of them are faked. Your trouble, Lucy-Lou, is that you take life too seriously. What you've gotta realize, darl,' she biffed my arm good-naturedly, 'is that life's just something to do when you can't go shoe-shopping.'

'What do you think I've done for the last year? I've got more pairs of shoes than the entire cast of *Riverdance*.' But what I was actually beginning to think was that reality is just for people who can't cope with hangovers. It was beginning to seem to me that the only reason to say no to drugs was that it afforded more time to drink. 'Let's go via the bottle shop on the way home.' Australians love their booze so much there are drive-through bottle shops, in case you're already too pissed to get out of the car. No wonder I liked it here. 'It's been a week, Susie. Only camels can go that long without a drink.'

Susie narrowed her eyes at me. Before she could deliver any kind of rebuke, a whistle blew and kids exploded from the crowd like champagne from a shaken bottle, squealing with delight as they streamed towards the North Cronulla clubhouse which stood squatly to attention on the hill.

Ruby's head emerged from her hooded sweat-shirt like a possum from a tree hollow. The bags beneath her eyes resembled little aubergines. 'Can I go, Mum?'

My answer was redundant as Ruby had already peeled off her clothes to reveal a polka-dot bikini. Without waiting for permission, she flung herself into the lava of limbs flowing towards their Nippers groups.

Although human beings spent millions of years evolving out of the ocean, Australians devote all their time to trying to get back in. Surf lifesaving is an institution. Bleary-eyed Aussie parents spend every Sunday morning trying to figure out which kid is theirs amidst the hundreds bobbing up and down in the breakers in their multi-coloured caps.

With one eye on Ruby, I joined Susie in the queue for hot coffee and meat pies. The women

51

managing the Nipper teams and running the café were gruffly no-nonsense in a Girl Guide kind of way. Sun-worn, with waistlines of Ordnance-survey dimensions, they didn't seem to care what they looked like. This was their moment of power, as they barked out orders about races and prizes and stopwatches. Everyone was intimidated, except for one man. He stood apart, hands on sturdy hips, passing caustic asides about fascist tendencies to anyone within range. As Ruby joined in a running race, I studied him from the side-lines. In his early fifties, match-fit, muscled, mahogany brown from the sun, his wavy hair was bleached at the tips by salt and sea. He was also so tall you could attach wheels and use him to breach a medieval castle. But there was something world-weary about him too, the way he leaned nonchalantly against the club wall. It was as though his face had been carved by a trainee sculptor, the features strong and handsome, but not quite symmetrical, giving him an offbeat charm. I suspected his nose was not the original edition but had been busted in some testosterone-related endeavour. He was wearing nothing but a pair of minuscule Speedos. Australians call men's tight swimming trunks 'budgie smugglers'. Well, this was no budgie. This was an eagle – a wedge-tailed eagle with a *Guinness Book of Records* wingspan.

'Who's that?'

'Who?' Susie followed my gaze. The man in

question was now being berated by a spectator, whom he was regarding with a sceptical eye. 'Oh that's Lockie. Jack McLachlan. Otherwise known as the thinking woman's Vegemite on toast. Except he's so antisocial. The bloke's harder than advanced trigonometry. His dream is to move to a deserted island and build a bar – with one barstool. But he's tied down by his boy. The big bastard's devoted to that kid.'

'And the mum?'

'Nobody's ever seen her and he's lying doggo about it. There's a rumour that she karked it.'

'Oh, how sad. What does he do?'

'Well, what we've sussed out is that he was a lawyer, in Melbourne. We reckon he gave it up when his wife passed away. He moved up here four years ago. Runs the local surf shop and takes people out whale-watching in the winter or on angling adventures outside Botany Bay. He also teaches scuba diving – the guy's a serious bubble-head. Plus he gives surfing lessons in the summer. He's club captain. Volunteer, of course. He also runs the surf lifesaving courses.'

'Isn't he too old to be in charge of surf rescue?'

'Hey, Lockie may look old, but he's still fast. As the boys say, when he turns off the light at night, the man's in bed before it's dark . . . Lockie!'

'Don't call him over! Oh how embarrassing.' The big man was now moving towards us with the understated swagger of a cowboy.

'Lockie, you old bastard. How's it hanging? What

53

did that pelican want?' Susie asked, pointing to the irate member of the public he'd just sent on his way.

'Just another nutter. Said he'd seen a flying saucer. I asked him if it was full of milk.' His eyes, I noted, were cornflower blue.

Susie gave a rich chuckle, throwing back her head to laugh. 'Did you find out if this flying saucer had a matching cup?'

I envied the way Susie could blend in so effortlessly. I stood apart, in awe of her ease and confidence. I suppose people left me alone because they could smell the grief on me. The sour, mildewed tang of my marriage was in my hair and clothes, like mould. Lost in my self-obsessed reverie, I took my eyes off Ruby for a moment too long. It wasn't until I heard her high-pitched squeal and wheeled around that I saw she was in the surf. Ruby had endured swimming lessons in a typically overheated, slimy indoor London pool, but was not used to the open ocean. I watched in horror as the foaming lips of the sea closed over her head.

My scream alerted Lockie. When he saw Ruby struggling, the man ran as though taking news from the battlefield to his emperor. He barrelled into the surf. The raw love of a mother for her child means that no matter how slothful, in times of emergency, mums can go from zero to a hundred kph in a heartbeat – which is why I was in the water, too, fully clothed. When I came up for air I saw that Lockie was already striding ashore with my darling daughter in his arms.

I spluttered back on to the beach, panting, and crushed Ruby to my breast. A triangular hulk of bronzed muscle stepped forward and jabbed a finger in my chest. I was expecting words of sympathy and assurance, but instead Lockie said in an accusatory tone, 'This kid can't bloody well swim. Where do you get off letting her go into the surf like that? You should join her up to Nippers, immediately. And get her swimming lessons. I can't believe you haven't,' he barked, seawater dripping from his hair and nose. 'Where do you live?'

'On the Point.' I gestured to the far end of the beach. I had never felt so hopelessly, autistically, parochially British.

Lockie flexed his muscles in irritation. Each bicep was the size of Arnold Schwarzenegger. 'You're living right on the bloody beach and your kid can only dog-paddle? Congratulations.' He shook himself dry like a wet animal. 'You were nearly up for a Darwin Award.'

'A Darwin Award?' I parroted, starting to shiver in my soaked clothes.

'It's awarded every year to someone who loses their life through his or her own spectacular stupidity. It's natural human selection through idiocy.' He noticed Ruby's teeth clicking like castanets and clocked her mottled thighs, blue-veined with cold.

55

'As you've narrowly avoided a nomination, I s'pose you'd better take a hot shower,' he said crustily. 'Come inside.'

Flabbergasted by his rudeness, but shivering hard enough to take up his offer, I stooped to collect Ruby's dry clothes from the beach where she'd left them, then scooped her into my arms, before following him into the club changing-rooms. As I buckled beneath Ruby's weight, Lockie thrust two threadbare but clean towels into my hands, plus some dry clothes from lost property, and pointed to a cupboard masquerading as a shower cubicle. I looked towards the men's showers opposite, a huge, tiled expanse.

'Women are a new addition to the club,' he answered my raised eyebrow. 'The laws in surf lifesaving are like sausages. You really don't wanna know what goes into making them.'

There was only one nozzle, so I showered Ruby first and helped her dress. When I emerged ten minutes later, wearing an old pair of tracksuit pants and a T-shirt which the Salvation Army would reject as too decrepit, Ruby was perched on a stool watching Lockie make toast. Next to her was a boy about the same age, his hair laced with algae.

'This is my son, Ryan,' Lockie said, although he didn't need to tell me. Ryan was his father in bonsai, except for a shock of red hair. His face was a miniature of his father's features, only made delicate, as though re-sculpted by a kind and artistic hand. When Lockie looked at his son, I watched fondness spill across his stern face. 'Ryan's in Nippers, which is why he's so confident in the water,' Lockie said, pointedly. He was fossicking at the back of the fridge and emerged with an old Vegemite jar. Australians use Vegemite as a toast spread, but I'm sure it could be equally effective as an industrial solvent. I watched as he held the jar under a stream of hot water, before knocking the stubborn lid loose with a knife.

'Mum! Mum! Can I join Nippers? Then I'll never nearly drown again!'

My immediate instinct was No! Being English, we just weren't at home in the water. Even when Ruby was in the womb I'd been worried about her putting her head under the amniotic fluid. But my daughter's face, so pale and traumatized five minutes earlier, was now vivid with excitement. I felt a fierce onrush of tenderness for my little girl. 'Of course you can, Rubes.'

'But . . .' Hair fell into her eyes like the mane of a Shetland pony. 'I'm terrified,' she said softly. 'Of the surf. It's huuuuuuge. Could you come out with me?' Her wind-tangled hair blurred wildly around her face. 'Pleeeeeeeeease?'

'Sure.' I shrugged one shoulder, whilst trying not to stare at Lockie's formidable package. His bathers were so skimpy I could detect the man's religion.

'No bloody way,' Lockie said gruffly. 'Nobody on this beach is allowed to swim outside the flags unless they're training for their bronze medallion, competing, or on patrol.' I watched him trowel the thick, black muck on to a slice of white bread. He spooned Nescafé into a cup, adding water and a squirt of long-life milk and sugar. He placed the cup in the microwave and hit ping. A gourmet spectacular.

'What's the bronze medallion?'

'Surf lifesaving techniques, resuscitation, first aid, board rescue. You'd have to enrol for classes before you could go out into the sea with your daughter.'

'Isn't that great, Mum! We can both join the club! That would be sooo cool!' Ruby's enthusiasm was absurdly touching.

'Um . . . Ruby, I, um, I don't join things.' I turned to Lockie, blurting nervously, 'I'm not saying I'm the timid type, but it takes me two Valium and a double gin to get up the courage to tell anyone how shy I am. Besides, I'm English. Meaning I'm only slightly more active than a pot plant . . . I get winded licking stamps.'

'Typical Pom,' the man said. In the same tone you'd say, 'Typical chainsaw-wielding psychopath.'

'Yes, but I'm learning Australian. It's like English, only there are fewer words for cold, wet and miserable.'

He didn't smile, but he did eye me more shrewdly.

'But being English, I really can't swim that well. Would I have to put my eyes under and everything?'

Lockie and Ruby exchanged a pitiful glance. 'Yet more reason why I can't get my bronze. I mean, I need a lifeguard in the bath.'

'So, what size flippers do you wear?' Jack McLachlan demanded, rummaging through a Perspex crate beneath a rack of wetsuits.

He might as well have asked me what size space suit I required. 'Um, what I'm trying to tell you is that it took a lot of will power, but I finally gave up feeling I should exercise to keep fit,' I bantered.

I felt sure Lockie's eye wrinkles crinkled a little more. Succeeding in slightly amusing this taciturn club captain made me feel I'd won some kind of medal.

'Goggles.' He pulled the equipment from different boxes, bumping the rack of wetsuits, which waved their liquorice arms and legs as though dancing.

'Wait. Stop. You Australians. Your love of swimming in the open ocean shows that prolonged exposure to the sun causes mental retardation. What is it? Proof of Darwin's theory? Natural human selection through idiocy?' I said, echoing his earlier barbed comment to me on the beach.

'And for you, young lady . . . Ryan?' Lockie said to his son. 'Would you mind kitting Ruby here out in some gear? It can get cold out the back.'

I looked at him in alarm. Even I'd heard that *out the back* was an infamous aquatic, Jules Vernish area way beyond the breakers referred to by the Aussies with sombre reverence. 'Ruby, I'm sorry.

But no way. You see, swimming "out the back" was not invented by sensible, rational people. It was invented by Australians. People who eat Vegemite of their own free will.' I turned to Lockie. He was so keen to push me into the sea. But it was my turn to test some waters of my own. 'Doesn't your wife worry about your son going out there?' I probed.

Judging by the slit-eyed look which came my way, I realized that I'd unintentionally accused him of either paedophilia, alcoholism or rampant homosexuality.

'Did I say something wrong?' I asked, coyly.

'You haven't been here long, have you? Australians don't like to be asked questions,' he barked back, shrugging on a T-shirt. 'It harks back to convict days when people had a lot to hide.'

And what, I wondered, did Jack McLachlan have to hide? Not his luscious lunchbox, that's for sure.

The risk of another brusque dismissal was avoided by Susie's flurried arrival. 'I heard you've been imitating a tea-bag,' she said, kissing my daughter's head. 'Dunking up and down in hot water.'

'Mum said I can join Nippers!' Ruby enthused. 'But she has to get her bronze medallion to come out with me.'

Susie waited for Lockie to disappear into the men's changing-rooms before raising a sceptical brow in my direction. 'Bronze medallion? You'd

60

have to learn mouth-to-mouth resuscitation. What a novelty, eh? To hear heavy breathing again!'

'Me? In a swimming costume? I don't think so. People will think I'm a whale, beached. I'm so fat I should wear a stretch burkha.'

'Um . . . have you actually *looked* in the mirror of late, Lucy-Lou?' Susie said, incredulously. 'You're so thin, your pyjamas have, like, *one* stripe.'

'Really?' I glanced down at my neglected frame. I hadn't eaten all that much in the last six weeks, come to think of it, except for my words. And I hadn't liked the taste of them much, either.

'Won't you come with me, Mum?' Ruby was licking the last trace of the vile Vegemite from her fingers. 'Pleeassse? Come on!'

I looked at the wetsuit arms, thick as eels, writhing on the rack. 'Let me get this right. You want me to get out of my nice warm bed at dawn and leap into the cold ocean where there are things that can eat me?'

'You can't spend your entire friggin' life procrastinating about when you're gonna start living it.' The deep, low voice, smooth as Burgundy, alerted me to the fact that Jack McLachlan had returned, dressed. His tone was curt, but he playfully cuffed his son Ryan across the top of his carrot head. Ryan pretended to punch his dad as they ambled for the door. 'I've got a race to judge. Lock up when you go, Suze,' he tossed over his shoulder. But almost imperceptibly, I saw his eyes flick back to me.

61

'OK, what if I joined with you?' Susie enthused, riffling through the wetsuit rack for something suitable. 'It could prove very interesting as a husband-hunting exercise. Have you seen how hot those young surfies are? Hubba hubba. That's my new motto.' She placed her hands over Ruby's ears. 'No pecs, no sex.' She heaved open the door of the surf club and Ruby ran ahead to fetch Matilda.

Susie paused to squash a huge, shiny black cockroach on the car park asphalt. Australian cockroaches are so big, so brazen, they practically cruise around in 4X4s with sub-machine guns, terrorizing locals. 'Actually,' Susie reacted to my grimace, 'I'd be more worried about husbands who go scuttling off in the dark.'

I was about to retaliate that it was Renée who had more in common with the cockroach (they both spread disease, scavenge other people's leftovers and are impossible to kill), when the cry of 'Mum! Mum!' had Susie and me wheeling around simultaneously, not sure which of our daughters was calling.

'Is it true that Ruby's joining Nippers?' Matilda trilled.

'Only if her mum will join the club, too,' Susie said.

'My only work-out is a daily three-hour worry about where my marriage went wrong. It's a mental and emotional marathon,' I replied to Susie. 'I'm sorry, Ruby, but there's no way I can go for my bronze,' I said, shamefaced.

* * *

That night Ruby ate little and went to bed early. After tucking her in, I sat for an hour, stroking her to sleep until her breathing slowed at last. From the lamplight sliding in under the door, I could see the glisten on her tear-stained lashes and my heart gave a wrench of protective love.

Tally was baking cookies again. When I entered the kitchen, she knifed to her feet, glaring hotly. 'Ruby told me how you let her down. Maybe Dad left you because Renée does exciting stuff. You, like, never take any risks. You're nothing more than a walking, talking vegetable.'

I wondered if it were illegal in Australia to tape your kid's mouth shut. I also reminded myself that teenage daughters have an '*I find my mother contemptible*' clause written into their contracts and swallowed my anger. 'Me? Surfing? I had no idea you and Ruby were so keen to be orphaned.'

In the morning, when Ruby said she felt too sick to go to school, I despaired. Ruby, a bright pupil, adored her new school with its casual curriculum and breezily informal teachers. With no temperature and no tummy pains, it was pretty clear that depression was setting in. 'You know I don't let any child stay off school unless green slime is oozing from a visible orifice,' I said, dragging her out of bed and dressing her forcibly. The effect Jasper's departure was having on our children was mortifying. Ruby was bed-wetting and having night terrors and Tally had shape-shifted into a growling, disgruntled, surly heap of hormones constantly embarrassed by her mother. I felt a sudden pang of anxiety that my second daughter would soon go the same way.

'What do you want for your birthday, darling?' I asked with fake cheeriness on the drive to school.

'The only thing I want is my daddy,' snivelled my little daughter.

That afternoon when I heard Susie's car pull up outside, I greeted her in T-shirt and knickers, as my fake tan dried.

'Well, I don't want to look like a Pom,' I told her.

My neighbour beamed at me. 'But first off you need a wax.' She pointed at my bikini line. 'The last time I saw anything that hairy I was being attacked by a herd of wildebeest in Africa.'

'A wax? No! The one time I had a bikini wax I sobbed and hollered . . . And that was just in the waiting room.'

'Darl, you're having a wax. Your pudenda looks like William Shatner's hairpiece. You'll have every Trekkie in town all over you.'

And so, hairless but happy, we signed up for our bronze medallion. It couldn't be that hard . . . *Could it?*

CHAPTER 6

BEWARE DEEP WATER

The waves slapped my face repeatedly. I felt I was being interrogated by the Nazis. No sooner did I catch my breath than another crunching shorebreak crashed down on me, each white crest a malicious sneer. As wave after wave slammed me on to the seabed, my feet pedalled frantically for purchase on the sandy bottom so I could propel myself upward again. I would scramble to the surface, gasp for oxygen – only to be chundered once more.

'Bloody hell!' Susie was wearing a wig of seaweed. She gave me a look fizzing with laughter. But the next wave's foam overwhelmed me before I could reply that I was going to kill her for talking me into this.

Just as my mouth broke the surface again, I was tugged violently left then right by the leg rope umbilically attaching me to my surfboard. Basically a leg rope is a good way of seeing your board close up. Then far away. Then close up again. Ad infinitum. Every time the sea swallowed or regurgitated my limp and soggy form, the leg rope had me ricocheting in the opposite direction.

This allows you to get water up both nostrils on the way in *and* on the way out. *Repeatedly*.

'Are you OK?' Susie panted when a momentary lull allowed us both to scramble back on to our boards, some fifteen panic-stricken minutes later. 'Are you in pain?' she called out, seeing me wince.

'Oh no. It's not that painful. No more than, say, LABOUR,' I screamed back at her.

Clinging on for dear life with one hand, I checked my body over with the other. Unfortunately no bones were broken so I had no choice but to face the next mighty wall of water. Our mission was to paddle our surfboards out through the breakers. A heroic feat like this required Olympic stamina even *without* a dining table attached to your leg, but in a five-foot swell, it was as plausible a proposition as Britney Spears in a nunnery or Bin Laden with a bar tab. I looked at the churning sea with terror. The most athletic thing I'd ever undertaken before now was to get the lid off a jam jar.

As the next sheer cliff face of green water reared up and I yo-yoed and cha-cha-ed on my leg rope, I vowed to take up some physical activity which didn't inflict bodily harm – say, hopscotch. Knitting, shopping, shuttlecock and rock, paper, scissors were also not known for their fatalities. It was becoming clear that 'surf lifesaver' was just a euphemism for organ donor.

The next descending wave loomed skyscraper high. Seven feet at least. It was what Lockie had referred to as a 'vomit comet' in the theory class I'd attended earlier in the week. Jack McLachlan had also explained that there are no atheists in big surf. I'd scoffed at him then, but *Dear God who art in heaven, bless me Father for I have sinned, and I was a heathen to think otherwise, oh keeper of souls, Amen.* The smooth wave rose insouciantly, scorning my panic.

The Pacific Ocean is big and blue, complete with rips, treacherous currents and man-eating monsters. Is it any wonder that each year thousands of tourists come to experience the surf lifesaver's superb rescue techniques? And I was about to be one of them.

The only trouble was, I was too winded from oxygen starvation to scream for help. I just squeezed my eyes closed as the engorged wave broke, tumbling and rumbling me this way and the other, like a human sock in a giant washing-machine. I spluttered surface-ward, blowing my nose with my fingers, while seawater streamed from every orifice. Tally's voice came back to me, 'You? A surf lifesaver? You, like, can't even save yourself.' I'd flinched at her words. But she was right. I was a paid-up member of Underachievers Anonymous. I'd become so dependent during my marriage, I'd wake in the mornings and say, 'So, how am I going to feel today, Jasper?' If I were Frank Sinatra, I'd be singing 'I Did It *His* Way'.

Exhaustion tugged me off the board and under again in a squall of limbs. I'd just begun to take in serious amounts of water when I felt a strong shove from the rear as two firm hands grabbed my ass and boosted me on to my board. I turned, in a mix of indignation and relief, to see Jack McLachlan sink below the frothy surface. He blew a vertical stream of water like a sperm whale, then emerged, beaming smugly. Those clear, cobalt-blue eyes sparkled with a mischief which belied his age. 'Don't mention it. All in a day's work. There just aren't enough humble heroes. I seem to be the only bloody one left.' He winked. 'I gave you girls surf-boards because they're easier than rescue boards. Just do what we practised in the pool and you'll be right. All you need is balance.'

'I can't even balance a chequebook, so that's a great help.'

'I thought you wanted to earn your bronze? Not put on a floorshow for the locals.'

'I do want to get my bronze, yes, but not *posthumously*.' Sensing there was something behind me, I glanced over my shoulder. A rogue wave which wouldn't have looked out of place in the movie *Deep Impact* was welling up. Its face was almost vertical. 'The waves are way too big to be out today,' I screamed at the lunatic who had got me into this.

'Oh you poor, weedy Pom,' Lockie laughed. 'Sure there have been some injuries and deaths in the surf, but none of them serious,' he joked. He then submerged the base of my board so that the nose rose easily over the top of the big white wave. He simultaneously grabbed my hand and yanked me under in an effortless duck-dive below the crest.

When our heads bobbed up through the foam, fear and fury made me splutter. 'At least I now know what happened to your poor wife. She drowned getting her bronze medallion, didn't she?'

Lockie's face drained of all expression. I couldn't believe what I'd said. It was just the terror talking, but I could have sued my own mouth.

'This is a pisspoor effort,' Jack McLachlan deduced tersely. 'You're not even half-way out the back yet. Now get stuck into it.'

'You want me to keep *going*?' I asked incredulously, looking ahead at the endless lines of breakers trundling towards me. The red buoy we were paddling towards bobbed into view now and again between the watery mountains. The surfers were so far out, bent over in their black wetsuits they looked like commas – and they were definitely giving me pause for thought. And what I was thinking was – *get me the hell out of here*. 'Gee. I dunno. I kind of like my body in its current configuration. I don't really fancy losing a limb from leg-rope whiplash.'

'I have two words for you,' my coach growled at me. '"Determination" and "perseverance".'

'I have two words for *you*. "Ego" and "maniac".'

Susie thought Lockie agreeably caustic, but I found him to be self-righteous and overbearing.

When I'd signed up to the bronze medallion class a week earlier, his opening line to the assembled throng had been 'G'day. Welcome. My name's Jack McLachlan. But as we Clubbies are quite informal . . . you may call me sir or Your Lordship. Actually,' he'd added, drily, 'Australians don't stand on ceremony . . . so why not just call me My Liege.'

But this was one serf who was sick of surf. The pun was nearly as weak as I was, but God knew what the man next had in mind for his trainees. Sky-diving without a parachute? 'I'm just not as keen as you Aussies to include blood-loss in my leisure pursuits,' I snapped at him. 'Goodbye, My *Liege*.' A tsunami-sized wave was bearing down on us, hissing spray. I was numb from the ceaseless ferocity of the ocean, so turned my board for shore, held my breath and just let the water hurtle me away from my tormentor and towards terra firma.

By the time the sea spat me on to the beach, both my ears were waterlogged. No matter how much I leapt about, shaking my head like an Indian chieftain, I could still feel the ocean swishing around inside my cranium. I dug my finger so far into my ear it came out of my mouth, but all I found was a mound of sand the size of, say, Hawaii. I also had sand embedded in my eyes, armpits, even in my fanny. Just as well I was celibate; a lover's penis would be whittled down to a pretzel.

'Are you OK?' Susie asked, surging in on a wave beside me.

'I can't stand that man. I don't think anyone should wear a Speedo man-pouch unless he's a world-class swimmer, won an Olympic medal and is about to race *right now*.'

'Um, Lockie *is* a world-class swimmer – he won a Commonwealth Games medal – and he *is* about to race again.' She gestured to a group of men in their forties and fifties gathering on the beach, wearing swimming caps, goggles and Speedos. 'He belongs to the Harold Holt Swim Team.'

'The what?'

'Harold Holt was our prime minister who mysteriously drowned at sea.'

'Oh great, so he's a cynical bastard as well.'

'They're part of the Last Man Standing Surf Team, for blokes who can still get it up and get on a wave,' she laughed.

'Be nice if he surfed one of his brainwaves now and then.'

That was it. I was done with surf lifesaving. As I peeled off the rubber limbs of the wetsuit, I noted how it tended to stay in the same shape whether or not I was in it. Maybe I could just send it out on its own? When Susie signed me up for the course, I'd assumed that gaining the bronze medallion would entail a small splash in the pool and a little light mouth-to-mouth resuscitation. It wasn't until I'd paid my hundred and forty dollars that I'd discovered I would have to complete a two-hundred-metre run, plus a two-hundred-metre swim in open ocean followed by another two-hundred-metre run, and all within eight minutes.

'You? Running?' Tally had scoffed. 'The only time you would ever run would be for your life, like in the path of an exploding volcano.' I was also meant to haul a victim from the water, then surf back to shore between the legs of the comatose patient. The only trouble was, I didn't like adventure. Even at Disneyland I only ever went on the teacup ride.

Fish have no alternative and therefore deserve sympathetic consideration, but I was determined to remain land-locked. No more kelp in my cossies. No more catching a wave, only to realize that my bikini bottoms had caught a different wave altogether. But, just as I was wrenching off the Velcroed leg rope for what I believed to be the last time in my life, I glimpsed Ruby. Her Nippers group comprised a gang of about fifteen kids. They were riding small foam boards in the shallows, sheltered from the big surf by a sand bank. Ryan was teaching Ruby how to catch a wave. She darted to shore, quick-silvered with delight. It had been an aeon since I'd heard her laugh like that. It made my heart flop about in my chest.

Resolving to try harder, I slouched up to the club for a shower.

Women had been banned from surf lifesaving in Australia until a few years ago. Our makeshift changing-room was so small even the cockroaches were hunch-backed. It had a crack-den ambience with veined and fractured cement floors and walls, and one bleak, bare bulb. It was also where the brooms were kept. Which is why, I have to presume, Lockie walked in on me some ten minutes later while I was towelling dry a rather personal area. As a married mother of two, I hadn't expected to be seen naked ever again by a member of some other major gender. I squealed like a raped piglet and rearranged the towel. Needless to say, there was a fair amount of throat clearing and clothes straightening going on at this point, but not quite enough for my liking. Jack McLachlan was so laid-back he had a tendency to erupt into great nonchalance.

Lockie casually took the broom off the rack, avoiding my eyes. 'Next class, Wednesday night. Eighteen hundred hours. Dress code – clothing optional,' he chuckled. 'See you there.'

Like hell he would. I think Jack McLachlan had seen enough already. One thing we underachievers have learnt in life is that there is no problem too complicated or too daunting that it can't be run away from. Well, walked away from, if you aren't the sporty kind. But at pace!

'I'm zorsted. Too zorsted to do anything,' Ruby muttered that night, crawling into bed about seven. After my pounding in the surf, I was so sore that I could only get into bed one section of

73

my body at a time. The only way I'd been able to brush my teeth was to place the toothbrush on the sink and move my mouth back and forth over it. I vowed to break the news to Ruby next morning that I was giving up, but then my dear little daughter slept through with no night terrors for the first time since Jasper had walked out on us. Nor did she wet the bed. Which is why I decided to continue getting up when the poison-green light of the digital alarm clock read 6 a.m., in time for our swimming lessons in the local Olympic pool at Caringbah. And so it was that on Wednesday night, I found myself sitting in Lockie's theory class. Gee, only nine weeks to go. What fun. I'd rather have my IUD extracted with barbecue tongs.

CHAPTER 7

SLIPPERY ROCKS

What happens if you get scared half to death twice? This was on my mind as I listened to Lockie talk about massive tissue-damage and severe blood-loss associated with shark and crocodile attacks or powerboat injuries. To distract me from his detailed instructions on spinal injuries (pack sand around the victim to stabilize) I examined my tormentor. At first it bemused me that he never sat down. He would stand at all times, even during casual conversations after class, when he would lean on a doorframe, one hand lightly on the handle, a boot levering open the screen door – as if always ready to make a get-away. He didn't give away a lot in his conversation either. Susie thought his humour drier than an AA clinic, but I found him abrupt and rude. Lockie's main response to anything personal was 'It could've been worse', 'You never know', or 'Fair enough'. That was the man's entire lexicon. Roast dinners, cricket, rugby, afternoon tea, *The Goons*, *Absolutely Fabulous*, *Monty Python*, George Street, Oxford Street, Hyde Park, King's Cross, it seemed that Sydney had everything in common with London except the language. Lockie felt that Yes or No were perfectly adequate responses to any question. Yet when Jack McLachlan talked about the sea, the air lit up with eloquence as his body, corded with muscles and sinews, grew taut with excitement. Susie also liked him because he treated everyone equally. 'Yes,' I replied. 'Equally badly.'

The clubroom suddenly reeked of stewed tea, the signal for break. The eating area, an assortment of ill-matching chairs and tables near the fifties-style kitchen, boasted the laminated sign 'You heave, you leave'. On the open club door another sign read 'Vandals always welcome. Shark bait is expensive.' The male and female toilets were marked 'flip dry' and 'drip dry' respectively. Avoiding the brown blobs of hardened sugar in the bowl, I examined the other class members.

There were about twenty of us in all. Susie and I were the only females. The rest of the pupils were mainly men in their twenties and a few teenage boys, who'd obviously been forced to join or face reform school. Seventeenish and Neanderthal, they referred to their manhoods as their 'man snakes' and their testicles as 'the boys'. Each one no doubt knew the taste of his own toenails. They drank beer out of their motorbike helmets and compared notes on how much they'd puked the night before. They wore board shorts with pictures of a rhino sloganed 'I'm horny', and T-shirts which read 'Official Bikini Inspector'.

'Hey, you got a licence for those tits? They're lethal,' one surfie addressed Susie's chest, killing himself at his own drollness. From then on they referred to her breasts as 'chesticles'. I'm afraid our fellow classmates were the kind of guys who flip to the B-side of their underpants and buy comedy condoms which glow in the dark. They occasionally used bits of their own bodies as ventriloquist's dummies. The highlight of the night was to Xerox their genitalia in Lockie's office.

Cronulla is the only Sydney beach on a train line, so locals have always felt invaded by immigrants from the city's teeming western suburbs. Susie had told me how it had all come to a head during the Cronulla riots in 2005, which started when some aggressive Lebanese boys beat up a couple of surf lifesavers, then escalated into a furious weekend of retaliatory gang warfare, flamed by irresponsible radio shock jocks. But an uneasy truce had been called. The Aussie way to heal wounds is with humour. Which is why my classmates referred to the one Lebanese male in our group, a thirty-year-old computer operator called Ali, as 'Al-Qaeda dot com'.

'You're *so* gonna win the running races up the beach,' Susie taunted Al-Qaeda dot com. 'I mean, you grew up in Beirut. The only trouble is, when you hear the starter gun, you'll just keep on running, right?'

Ali retaliated with a teasing comment about Susie's lack of fitness. 'If you break a leg, woman, don't come running to me.' He understood that in Australia, not being able to laugh at yourself put you just below leper and just above someone who didn't love rugby.

But not all Lebanese boys were as evolved. I had seen a gang of them kicking sand in the faces of some sunbathing girls on the beach and calling them 'Skippy sluts'.

I had basically landed on Planet Macho. Hailing from intellectual Hampstead, where men talked knowledgeably of scherzos and love sonnets, I felt like a zoologist who had dropped in on a bunch of gorillas, and had forgotten her tranquillizer gun.

When practising CPR on the training mannequin caused the dolls to expel air, the boys guffawed with feral delight. 'Hey, she fanny-farted,' one teenager elucidated, clawing at his groin with casual arrogance.

I hoped Ruby would one day appreciate what I was sacrificing on her behalf. The girl should personally offer to lick clean my jogging shoe inner-soles for the rest of her natural life. I then recalled how Susie had been hoping to use the lifesaving classes as a dating agency.

'So, tell me again, exactly, what kind of man you were hoping to meet here?'

'One who is doused in petrol and has a stake driven through his heart, preferably,' she muttered dispiritedly.

Lockie re-entered the clubroom then, face like thunder. 'Behave or I'll rip off your arms and beat you with the soggy end,' he fumed, confiscating the CPR training dummies. 'It takes a dedicated individual to gain the bronze medallion. But the rewards of the investment are truly worthwhile – knowing that you have the experience to help others and maybe save a life. I can't think of a more important skill for a man to acquire. Can anyone else?'

'Um . . .' I put my hand up. 'Washing-up, hoovering and monogamy?'

Lockie flicked his disapproving eyes in my direction. 'Oh g'day. I didn't recognize you with your clothes on,' he said, not missing a beat in his conversational stride. 'Now, back to work. Mass-rescue situations occur quickly and without any warning,' Lockie told us, picking up where he'd left off before tea break.

Oh, how true, I sighed, thinking of my own little family, cast adrift and treading water. Some nights my slumber was uninterrupted – apart from the 254 times Ruby woke crying for her daddy. (Except for the previous Sunday night, that is, when she'd been worn out from Nippers.) 'Is Daddy warm? Does he have food? He won't die, will he?' she'd sobbed all the rest of the week. Jasper texted the kids regularly to say he loved them but cancelled every reunion. 'Sorry, stuck in traffic.' 'Sorry, stuck in meeting.' 'Sorry, stuck finding a good excuse.'

I rang the doctor for advice. She said to time the night terrors and wake Ruby up half an hour before the scheduled attack. 'It's not your fault,' I told Ruby over and over. 'Daddy being away doesn't mean that Mum and Dad don't love you.' I said it to Tally, too, as she baked maniacally. Of all the joys of parenthood, stepping on to a cookie cutter on the kitchen floor and getting a permanent imprint of a duck on the sole of your foot – which means leaving very confusing footprints up and down the beach for ever more – was not one of them. Even though my reassurances sounded banal and Tally responded with her customary eye-roll, I just hoped something would sink in. 'Dad will be back soon.' But the thought that he wouldn't had me regularly waking in a sweat, too, swimming up from the submerged caverns of some black dream.

Lockie's talk had now moved on to anti-venom shots for stings and tetanus shots after standing on a sea urchin. I longed for an injection to make me immune to the pain inflicted on me by my husband.

'Arterial tourniquets are now recommended only as a last resort in shark or crocodile attacks,' Lockie advised.

But what about a tourniquet for the heart? I was slowly bleeding to death here. Only the shark wore Prada high heels and had carried off my beloved husband between her perfectly bleached white teeth.

The doctor suspected that Ruby might be suffering from bullying at school, and suggested

80

counselling. At Nippers that Sunday I asked Lockie to make sure that Ruby's English accent was not causing her to be teased. But his solution was to administer some survival skills of his own.

'If you ever get bullied, j'know what you should do, Rubes?' He squatted down to her level. 'Get the bully alone, pinch her ear lobes with your nails and whisper into her nostrils that you're the child of Satan come to claim her for Your Lord.'

'She can't say that!'

Lockie drew himself up to full height so that I was now addressing his belt buckle. 'Why the hell not? Otherwise,' he said to Ruby, 'get the kid on her own and let your big sister do something so weird to her that no one will believe her when she rats on you.'

Ruby giggled, as did Ryan who was pulling on his wetsuit beside her.

'Or if this bully hits you, just say something like "*It's really courageous of you to risk coming into contact with me after the diagnosis.*" That will definitely freak her out.'

Ruby chortled before running off with Ryan for their 'fun run' – an Australian contradiction in terms.

'Oh, and how many years of psychological training did it take to master those brilliant manoeuvres?'

'It's not as if Ruby's going to do any of those things. But it'll make her feel stronger to know she *could*.'

'You are such a bad parent,' I chastised. But was I doing any better? I wondered, when I got home at lunchtime to find my older daughter and her boyfriend doing their homework. Chook was seated at Tally's desk consulting the computer. Tally was also staring at the screen, but she was sitting on his lap, and only in her skimpy pyjamas.

'Ah, Tally, I think it's time we had a little talk,' I said, summoning her to my bedroom. 'I know you've done sex education at school, but I think we should go over the basic points.'

'You're so lame,' my fifteen-year-old daughter said, dry-retching.

'Well, now you've got your period it's quite imperative that . . .'

'Ugh. Ugh. Stop. Ugh.'

Any mention of the word 'period' in any context other than 'Jurassic' or 'Hellenic' met with derision and cringing. Teenagers, I was realizing, are obviously God's punishment for having sex in the first place.

'Look, my only aim in life is to stop anyone getting pregnant. That's all.' But my real fear was that Tally had a greater working knowledge of sex than I did. Hell, reclusive Trappist yogis living in caves could ring me up for tips on celibacy. I was so famished for bodily contact I was occasionally tempted to give myself a strip search. But whenever I tried to talk to Tally about sex, she suddenly had something vital to do, like file a nail or blow-dry a hair frond. When I tried to talk to Chook,

82

he replied in skidding, lazy vowels which I couldn't decipher, except for the odd 'toe-dully' or 'shanky spaz'. And I didn't know what that meant anyway.

The only comfort I took was that Tally wasn't yet using tampons. The sanitary towels she preferred were so big they didn't just have wings – they had wingspan. You could charter one to fly to London. But this knowledge didn't soothe me at night when she was, no doubt, writhing in the sand dunes (I'd read *Puberty Blues*) and ignoring my frantic text messages to: Come home right now! And it wasn't as though I could send her father out to find her.

Oh, if only I hadn't given up recreational alcoholism. When the grinding hollowness of the daily routine without Jasper forced me to ring his secretary, she always promised he'd ring back – but the blinking light on the message machine only held calls from boys for Tally. Calls for me? Zero. And I just couldn't bring myself to ring him at home, in case it was answered by the Whore with No Flaw.

By the end of October, I could avoid it no longer. Ruby's Nippers group were ready to go 'out the back'. All the mums and dads were coming to watch this rite of passage. A picnic was planned. There were going to be prizes for the fastest runners and swimmers. The fact that I had promised to paddle out with her had me only slightly worried. Well, it was nothing that couldn't be cured by an emergency air evacuation to intensive care.

'Dad will come, won't he, Mum?' Ruby turned

those huge eyes up at me and there was only one answer.

'Of course he will, darling.'

I felt nauseous about making the call. If Jasper answered, what would I say to him? What if he asked if I was feeling any better? Oh yes. I only feel like killing myself sporadically, now. I'd ring the suicide hotline, although, knowing my luck, the number would be engaged.

'Just call him, Mother. I call him all the time. God! You're the most immature woman I've ever met,' Tally said, dismissing me with a melodramatic gesture of her pale arms. The girl was so extremely slight in body, so still nearly a child, that her authoritative tone was like hearing a ventriloquist's voice through my daughter's mouth. 'No wonder Dad left you.'

Steeling myself, I picked up the phone . . . And there it was. Her post-coitally contented purr. 'Hello? Renée speaking.'

For a moment I couldn't respond. It was as if my lips were novocained. 'I need to speak to my husband.'

'Jasp? He's asleep.'

Jasp? 'Well, tell him I'm doing my bronze medallion,' I blurted. 'Because Ruby's scared to go out into the big sea on her own,' I rabbited on, tensely. 'This Sunday is Ruby's first ocean race. It's a very big deal and she'll be heartbroken if her father doesn't come. 9 a.m. North Cronulla surf club.' It all came out in a rush.

'Wait,' my arch-rival clarified. '*You* are training to be a surf lifesaver? You can't possibly. I mean, it's too dangerous. You're so unfit. I'm telling you this for your own good, Lucy, so I must be blunt. If you go to the beach, Greenpeace will push you back into the bay.' She was on a roll now, cloaking her condescension with concern. 'When you dive in, sailors will shout "Land ahoy!"'

I'd heard enough of what passed for her wit. 'Yeah, yeah. And when I put on that black wetsuit, English people will automatically shout "Taxi". I get it. Just tell him to call me urgently.'

Having ignored me for weeks, curiosity about my aquatic endeavours prompted '*Jasp*' to ring back within the hour. His mellifluous voice was like a caress.

'Lucy, sorry I've been hard to reach. Work's just frantic. I'm just going through so much at the moment emotionally and professionally. Thank you for being so patient. How are you?'

'Oh, OK. Mainly because I have a cyanide tablet ready to slip beneath my tongue.'

'Don't say such things, Luce. You make me worried. As does your latest endeavour. What's this I hear about surf lifesaving?'

'Well, I thought it might be good to show the kids that there is more to their mother than nagging about eating vegetables and teeth-cleaning.'

'But do you think this is wise, Lucy?'

I could hear Renée chortling in the background: '*She's so overweight. If she bungee-jumped, she'd take in the whole bridge!*' Even though Jasper put his hand over the mouthpiece and 'sssh-ed' her, the thought of them laughing together at my expense curdled my stomach. I couldn't believe I'd allowed myself to be best friends with the kind of woman who would have turned me in to the Nazis for eating a bagel with cream cheese.

I unkinked the telephone cord which I'd nervously knotted. 'I need some more money,' I said abruptly. 'I'm practically churning my own butter and threshing my own wheat.'

'But the rent's paid for a year and I left you enough in our joint account. You need to work within a budget, Lucy.'

'Jasper, when you have kids, a budget is just a more organized way of going into debt.' Even though Jasper had run out on me, he obviously hadn't forgotten his manners; when it came to destitution, it was still mothers and children first.

'We'll talk about it on Sunday. Meanwhile, keep calm,' he said, ringing off.

The only way I could keep calm was to undergo a lobotomy. But, come to think of it, I'd already had that, the day I invited Renée into our life.

The thought of seeing Jasper kept me awake the rest of the week. Sunday morning, I was up early, brewing coffee. The sea mist against the window was like milk. Perhaps it was a sign that some of the human kindness variety was coming my way?

'I'm so nervous I feel sick,' I confessed to Susie

as we waited on the driveway for Ruby and Matilda to get their wetsuits.

'*You* feel sick?' Susie scoffed, taking her son Heath's L-plates off her bumper bars. 'No woman should have to go through the menopause and teach her kid to drive in the same month. That can just never, ever work,' she groaned. At six foot, Susie's sixteen-year-old was like a large friendly dog in a small apartment. Every time he wagged his tail, he knocked over a vase. The thought of him behind the wheel had me reaching for a crash helmet. 'Let's get cracking, shall we?' Susie said.

The most embarrassing aspect of attending an Aussie get-together is the realization you only come up to the kneecaps of the male guests. Bronzed Aussie athletes loomed over me, wolfing down bacon-and-egg rolls with steaming mugs of hot tea. As more and more parents arrived, surf-boards, picnic blankets, wetsuits, snorkelling gear, collapsible chairs and card-tables were magicked from the boots of cars. The men gathered around the portable barbecues, greeting each other with the habitual incantation of the Aussie male: 'How they hangin'?' By 9 a.m. the beach was bustling with people, mainly the Nippers in their red, blue and yellow scull caps and the heroic Iron Men training on their surf skis.

'The only Iron Man competitions I'd like to see would involve the male of the species, some starch and a laundry basket,' I commented as Susie enrolled Matilda and Ruby for races on sand and sea.

'Bugger Iron Men,' Susie laughed. 'Mums are much bigger superheroes. Crikey, we should wear our undies on the outside of our clothes, goddamn it.'

Ruby was swept up into the noisy whirlpool of kids. As I hauled on my wetsuit I watched them tussle for a prime starting position.

'You'll have to excuse me now, Susan, as I have some death-defying to do,' I said pessimistically, tucking the surf-board under my arm. Club members, or 'Clubbies', refer to early-morning surfing as the 'monkey bath' because when you enter the water it's so cold you can't help exclaiming 'Oh! Ah! Oooh! Aahh! Oooh! Ahhhhh!' I was so terrified of the jellyfish and frostbite and things with fangs that I had kitted myself out in a cold-water, all-in-one arctic-diving survival suit I'd found in the bottom of a box at the club. I must have looked like an astronaut. All you could see were my eyes behind my mask, and, judging by Susie's guffaws, they were obviously terrified. In the past weeks, Lockie had attempted to bridge the yawning chasm between me and buoyancy, but it was still with great reluctance that I inched into the water. I'd tried to squirm out of my promise – 'What if a Chinese submarine surfaces beneath my board?' But Ruby accepted no excuses. I lifted my goggles and looked at the sea ahead. It moved like a silk cloth covering a writhing pile of snakes. Qualified lifesavers, including Lockie, sat impassively astride their rescue boards in nothing more than their budgie smugglers, guarding the route to the marker buoy 'out the back' – about a hundred and fifty metres out to sea. Ruby raised her head to make sure I was in the water, and waved just before the starter gun fired and the sea erupted into a churning maelstrom of kids, barging, wriggling and kicking to get ahead.

Resisting the urge to ball up like a petrified echidna, I pulled the goggles over my eyes. They immediately fogged up, thus rendering me legally blind as I paddled like crazy . . . For New Zealand apparently. It was only when I felt a tug on my leg and heard Lockie's amused voice, 'Hey, Gidgit, you really that keen on a close encounter of the Kiwi kind?' that I realized I'd paddled past the turning buoy. Without waiting for a written invitation, Jack McLachlan climbed on behind me and lay down, his face pressed into the crack between my thighs, totally oblivious to the fact that he was playfully cutting off all circulation to my legs and cavalierly arousing my reproductive organs.

'Classic surf rescue. Take up your paddling position between the patient's legs, trim the craft and continue with the rescue,' he lectured, turning my board towards shore with a couple of strong strokes.

'Call me bonkers, but I don't think you people have got a really good handle on tourism,' was all I could call back to him at the time. Ahead, I could vaguely detect the kids frothing up the open sea as they freestyled back to the beach. Ruby seemed to be coming last. I sprang out of the water then retracted violently, having forgotten to untie my leg rope, landing on my arse at Lockie's feet. It was only then that I removed my fogged goggles and realized I'd been screaming encouragement to the wrong child. Ruby was crossing the finishing line in third place. Lockie was beaming with satisfaction as he strode to the judge's table to hand out the awards. Electric with joy, I scanned the crowd for Jasper's familiar face.

'Oh God,' I said to Susie, peeling off my arctic-survival suit. 'He's not here.' I blinked water from my stinging eyes. 'That bitch has stolen him away again.'

'Stolen? What is he? A suitcase? It's not like she picked Jasper up off the baggage carousel of life and just walked off. An adulterer is a bloke who helps himself because he can't help himself. It's beyond me how you can diss her but still be in love with that dipshit.'

'Well, apart from the fact that he's the father of my children, and that his was to be the last face I saw on earth before drawing my final breath – you're right. Jasper doesn't mean that much to me any longer at all,' I replied, sarcastically.

'If Jasper's such a wonderful bloody bloke, then how could he have sex with a woman like Renée? Although, don't answer that. Men will put their dicks where women wouldn't put an umbrella,' she surmised.

Ruby ran to me, beaming. 'Did you see me, Mummy? I went out the back! It was soooo cool!' Her eyes, as bare and round as light bulbs, raked through the crowd. 'Where's Daddy? Did Dad see?' Ruby rubbed the back of her hand across her soft knob of nose. 'Dad did come, didn't he?' She looked up at me with those wide, dismayed eyes.

Even Tally had turned up, attracting the attention of all the fathers, with her high breasts and buttery blonde hair. 'Did you even tell him?' I heard the torn fabric of my older daughter's voice.

I fingered my rosary of guilt and then just lied. 'Dad was trying so hard to come,' I informed them both. 'Then he got stuck in traffic. He sent a message to say he loves you so much.'

Ruby's smile receded and her vibrant face faded to blank. Tally's expression, which had cracked open for the first time in months, slammed shut again like a book. I was terrified at the way Tally was bottling everything inside, only for it to no doubt erupt, aged eighteen, into a self-destructive rage of glue-sniffing and bank-robbing.

Just as all the happy families were settling down to picnic lunches, a text finally came through. 'Woke with terrible flu,' it read. For flu read mild sniffle. Jasper says that he is not a hypochondriac. But his neurologist, urologist, osteopath, heart specialist, immunologist and oncologist certainly diagnosed otherwise. 'Might make it later.'

And so we went home and then waited for the

rest of the day, all dressed up as if for a party. As neither Ruby, Tally nor I had any appetite, Susie's veal casserole and cheesecake remained untouched. By six I suggested taking the girls out to a fancy restaurant in celebration of Ruby's achievement. No. The cinema? No. Shopping? When I finally cooked them dinner at eight, both kids pushed their food away. Jasper had left his family to find himself, but there didn't seem to be any doubt about who got custody of the psychological fall-out.

Your husband walking out on you affords all the joys of getting your arm caught in the food-disposal unit. Only it's much more disabling. After all, you'd eagerly give an arm and a leg to get him back.

CHAPTER 8

SWIMMING PROHIBITED

Low self-esteem is hereditary. You get it from your kids.

'Oh dear God.' Tally's pretty mouth was held tight in disapproval, or perhaps disgust, when I appeared in the kitchen in high-heeled boots and a new size ten, skin-tight dress all of three inches above my knees.

'What?' I asked facetiously, having thrown out all my shaper briefs and control-top pantyhose weeks before. 'Does my bum look *small* in this?'

'Do you *have* a mirror, Mother?'

It would be churlish to point out to my daughter that she was wearing an outfit that needed only one accessory – a crack addiction. Her dress was so short I wasn't worried about people being able to see her pants. I was worried they'd see her ovulating.

'Well?' she demanded, confrontationally, when she clocked my censorious look. She was holding her jam knife as though it was a weapon.

I decided sarcasm was the least lethal option. 'So, where are you off to? Gospel singing?'

My daughter gave me a scalding look. If I'd been

an egg I'd have boiled. 'Anyway, why are you dressed up?' Barrister-like, she cross-examined me about where I was going.

'To see Ruby's teacher,' I ad-libbed, lowering my voice to a whisper. '*About her bed-wetting*. And what about you? Shouldn't you be in uniform?'

'It's mufti day. Could you, like, hurry up? I'll be late.'

It's a mystery of life that even though Australian teenagers spend all day windsurfing, hang-gliding, kayaking and abseiling, they still insist on being chauffeured four blocks to school. Driving all four kids was my job, along with picking them up and doing the joint food-shops, while Susie did most of the cooking. Susie and I worked perfectly in tandem, better than any marriage. When the kids had piled into my secondhand Holden, Tally turned on her iPod and slumped back into her seat with her eyes closed. As we waited at a red light, I attempted to immerse myself in the travails of the singer for whom life held no charm, despite the fact that he was, apparently, one of the richest musical artists on the planet.

'Could you please turn down your iPod? Do you actually like this rap music?'

'Yeah. Why? What's wrong with it?' my daughter challenged, defensively.

'Well, it seems to be all about macho black men demanding sex from women who are all hos.'

'You're so racist!'

94

'I'm not! I just don't want the children listening to this rubbish.'

'You're criticizing their culture. And their culture is black. Making you a racist.'

'Just because they're black doesn't mean they can oppress women, Tally.' I prayed to God to make me more patient – *IMMEDIATELY*!

'Oh, spoken by a woman who gave up work for her husband's career. And if you're not racist, then why don't you have any black friends? Answer me that.'

'Back in London I do. Lots.'

'Only Indian or mixed race.'

'OK, then, I have beige friends. Is beige so bad?' I looked to the heavens, praying: 'Gift of tolerance urgently needed, RIGHT BLOODY NOW.'

'So that just makes any criticism from you, like, totally hypocritical and condescending . . . Condescending . . . That means talking down to,' Tally condescended.

I thought of all the mornings she'd lurched to the kitchen table clutching her homework diary, pen poised, demanding to know everything about Minoan culture or Viking society or she'd be on detention. She hadn't found me stupid then. But I bit my tongue. Tally continued interrogating me on every aspect of my race relations for the rest of the journey. It was good for her to develop intellectual abilities and debating skills, but I also found myself thinking how much easier it is to love your children unconditionally before they learn to speak.

Back from the school run, I met Susie on the driveway. She also registered my appearance. 'Ooh-la-la. If you keep crawling to that hubby of yours, you're gonna get gravel rash on the knees, j'know that,' she said, in her laconic Aussie drawl. 'I mean, what on earth are you going to say to the bastard that can't be said by a divorce lawyer?'

'Um . . . what about "The proctologist called. He found your head"?'

Susie barked a laugh before adding, 'Talking of heads, Lucy-Lou, a marriage without a husband is like a chicken with its head cut off. It may run around in a frantic fashion, but it's actually dead.'

'My love's not dead, Suze.'

'You need a nicorette for love. A husband-ette.'

'I don't *want* to be weaned off. I want *him* to be weaned *on*. Which is why I'm wearing this ridiculous outfit.'

'He's not coming back, you know, Luce. They never do. There's no such thing as a retro-sexual . . . Unless you're watching a bad seventies porn flick,' she joked.

'Jasper is a gentle, good, loving man. Once he gets over the novelty of Renée's huge tits, he'll get a yearning for the greener-after-all grass of our marriage. Renée is like a Chinese meal – sweet and sour and cheap. He'll be hungry again in no time. And what he'll crave is the meat and two veg of family life.'

My vehemence told her I would not be swayed. A look of pity softened her eyes. 'Oh well, bugger it, then. If you're determined to humiliate your-self, you might as well look your best. Just 'cause you're a single mum doesn't mean you have to resemble one. Your hair is two months overdue for a cut. It's just sitting on top of your cranium like roadkill. You don't just wanna hairdo. You wanna hairdo which says, "I'm soon to be tousled by an obscenely famous Hollywood hero in his private jet as he whisks me off to his enchanted island in the Caribbean."'

'I do?'

'You bloody do. Now shut up and follow me to my salon.'

The highlights and lowlights plus a cut and blow-dry took two hours. Susie ordered for me as if I was to the salon born. Add to that a mani-cure and pedicure and it was lunchtime before I was ready to leave for the city. Susie stood back to survey me, smacking her lips with satisfaction. 'Here.' She fished into her receptionist's bra and removed two pouches of silicone. She then shoved the gel implants down my cleavage. 'Chicken fillets, for an extra ego boost. And don't worry about the sprogs. I'll pick up all four mongrels from school and feed them, OK?'

I owed my new friend so much. My first-born – at the very least. But, I shuddered, who'd want Tally at the moment? The English are not good at hugging. A handshake, a peck on the cheek, a wince perhaps – these are our farewell gestures of choice. But I now kissed and hugged Susie with promises to work in the salon gratis for weeks to pay back her kindness. Then, with my breasts pouting over the neckline of my dress like vanilla blancmanges, I headed off to stalk my husband.

When I saw a sports car with a 'Renée' personalized number-plate parked on the tip of Point Piper, a salubrious promontory with views of the Opera House, my nerves got the better of me. I was torn between revulsion at the thought of seeing Renée and a grisly voyeurism. I wasted so much petrol driving round and round their apartment block, desperate to catch a glimpse of them, that I had to detour to refuel. By the time I summoned enough courage to ring their bell there was nobody home. I found myself rummaging through the recycling bins getting clues as to where they ate and shopped – Armani, Versace, Moschino. They say it's lonely at the top, but obviously the shopping's better, I thought bitterly. Jasper's affair with Renée represented the gazebo extension I'd been planning for our home in Hampstead when we returned, the Caribbean cruise we'd picked out and the eye-lift I'd been saving up for to make myself so attractive my husband would never leave me.

I rang Jasper's office but his secretary told me he'd gone out for lunch. I checked my watch. Nearly two. He'd be back by half past. I drove to his office at the football stadium. Sport is a religion in Australia – the Sydney football stadium and the Sydney cricket ground sit side by side in

Moore Park. It is hallowed turf. The football stadium rises in all its glittering glory as not just a sporting complex, but as a shrine. I pulled into the car park with such ferocity I made the gravel ssshhhhish under my wheels like breakers on shingle. At half two exactly, a massive Range Rover cruised by and swung into a car space marked 'Reserved'. I couldn't believe Jasper would drive such a ridiculous car. In the old, pre-Renée days, he would have agreed with me that men only drove such huge cars because it's illegal to masturbate in public. But Renée was more worried about her butt buoyancy than the future of fossil fuels. If I hadn't been so agitated, I would have laughed out loud.

When Jasper sprang from the driver's seat, I immediately followed suit, as if pulled by an invisible rope. My husband stopped in his tracks as if stun-gunned. It had been nearly two months since we'd seen each other. I was thinner, blonder and tanner than I'd ever been in my life. He did the kind of double-take you see in cartoons. I felt a surge of confidence and hope – a hope which was dashed when I spied Renée. In leopard-skin trousers and Jimmy Choos, the maneater was alighting. When she saw the way Jasper was looking at me, her eyes glittered with malice.

'You've lost weight,' Jasper said, an astonished look on his face.

'Yeah, well, a nervous breakdown will do that to you.' My breath seemed too loud, as though I were scuba diving and running out of oxygen. My lungs were scrambling for air. He looked so handsome in his short-sleeved charcoal shirt and slim black trousers, a sleek Rolex on his tanned wrist, that if I looked at him a minute longer I would start crying. I focused instead on the chewing-gum splodges on the wall and nearby graffiti. '*If you feel strongly about graffiti, sign a partition.*' 'I need to talk to you, Jasper, but does it have to be in front of *her*?' I said to a crack in the cement.

As Renée was wearing a T-shirt which read '*Property of Big Boy*', I imagined that the question was somewhat redundant.

'Renée's come in to organize my office. Arrange the paintings and the desks and so forth. She's been very helpful.'

I bet she bloody had. I shifted my eye line to another scrawl on the wall behind his head which read, ironically, '*I hate graffiti.*'

'So, how are you?' he asked.

'Oh fine . . .' I lied, omitting the fact that if I'd been in hospital the wavery line on the terminal beside my bed would have been fading to black.

'It's great to see you, Lucy, but I'm, ah, a little pushed for time right now.' He looked at his watch sheepishly. As Renée was sticking to him like nylon underwear in a heat-wave, I would just have to talk in front of her.

'The trouble is, Jasper, every night, like clockwork, Ruby pees at 4 a.m. . . . Unfortunately, she doesn't wake till seven. And Tally? Our darling

Tally hasn't stopped baking cakes since you left. Sometimes at two in the morning. She's possibly about to have sex with a boy called Chook. *She*,' I hooked a thumb in Renée's direction, 'obviously doesn't care that she's devastated the lives of our children . . .' Renee sent a narrow look of contempt in my direction. 'But *you*, darling, you have got to understand that if you don't come home soon, the only time you'll see your kids is once a week for an hour – because that's the maximum visiting time in prison, where they'll obviously end up because of the psychological damage you, no, *she* . . .' I was shaking '. . . has done to them.'

Renée's hand tentacled on to Jasper's arm. 'Of course, initially this is going to be difficult for all of us,' she said in her angular, prodding voice. 'But an unhappy household is also psychologically damaging for children.'

A wire tripped in my brain and my temper exploded. I reeled around to face my ex-best-friend. 'You planned this all along, didn't you? The whole move to Australia.' My voice came out in an exhausted sing-song as I turned to my husband. '*Why*, Jasper? And *why* with Renée, of all people? How appropriate that she's in interior decorating. I mean, the woman's a door knob – everyone gets a turn.'

Renée regarded me with a vinegary expression full of spite, but in front of Jasper she tried to sound reasonable and compassionate. 'I know this

101

is just your anger and rejection speaking, Lucy. This is not the friend I knew,' she concluded, pseudo-compassion dripping from her voice.

'Friend? You're no friend of mine.' Tears started from my eyes. 'You are a pale reflection of a true friend. Hell, you don't even *have* a reflection, you vampire.'

'Well, *you* do. That's obviously why you're crying. Because you saw yourself in a mirror,' she bitched. 'Your marriage was over, a sham. You told me that many times, Lucy. Can't you see that I'm doing you a favour?'

'Renée has told me everything you said about me,' Jasper uttered, wounded.

I felt jelly-legged with shock. 'My marriage was in trouble because *you* were having an affair with my husband. Don't believe anything she's said to you, Jasper!'

Our raised voices were piquing the curiosity of passers-by. My husband put a restraining arm on to each of us. He spoke as slowly as speech therapy. 'Maybe this is not the best venue to talk. At my work place,' he said pointedly.

'Well, when? When *can* we talk? You never answer my calls. I need to talk to you now.' My voice was petulant but I couldn't help it. 'Even if she won't let you see your children, you still need to keep feeding them. At the moment we're eating cereal with a fork to save on milk. I need you to put some more money into our joint account.'

'I'd like to, Lucy, but, ah, well, there's just a

momentary glitch, finance-wise. The investments Renée and I have made haven't come good as yet . . .'

A cold chill crept up my spine. 'Investments?'

'Jasper and I are going into business together – a sport and spa scenario. The concept is *interior* decorating,' she tapped her head, 'via motivational talks and yoga retreats. Plus *exterior* decorating, i.e., fitness and beauty.' She gestured to her own slim form. I knew for a fact that no carbohydrate had passed her lips since her first communion wafer. The woman lived on air (unsweetened) and low-cal water.

'It's a very commercial and timely idea, Lucy. But we've just had a momentary monetary loss. There's been panic selling because of a fear that Britain will be hit by problems in the American sub-prime mortgage market. The investments will come good, but we're just waiting for the market to rise. Renée's been acting as financial adviser.'

I looked at my beloved husband, aghast. 'You lost our money on the stock market?' A convulsive start shook my frame from head to toe. 'To err is human, Jasper, but to really fuck things up requires a financial adviser.' I spat the words in her direction.

'I haven't lost the money, Lucy. I've invested it. I was doing it for us. For the kids. The investments I've made will save us money, long term.'

'It's certainly an interesting approach. Going broke saving money. And when exactly do you expect the promised land of skimmed milk and organic honey to make a profit so your family is no longer skint?'

'Skint? But where is all the money that was in the joint account?' Jasper quizzed.

'Gee, I don't know,' I replied sarcastically. 'I obviously spent it all on toy boys, masseurs, haute couture and vintage champagne . . . The rest I just frittered away.'

'Look, my wages kick in in a week, so I'll transfer some of the . . . Lucy, are you paying attention?'

'I'm too broke to pay anything,' I shot back. This was not my loving husband. This was a life-sized, battery-operated hand-puppet. 'Jasper, remember that little old woman who lived in a shoe and had so many children she didn't know what to do? Well, she was *rich* compared to me. I'll soon be living in a sandal. A flip-flop. The homeless will be offering *me* money. That's how destitute we'll be. We won't eat dinner any more. We'll just meet at the dining table while I read out the recipes.'

'OK, OK.' Jasper patted himself down, then fished into his pocket for his wallet. Realizing he'd left it in the car, he strode quickly back to the Range Rover.

'It must be degrading to have to rely on a man for money. Maybe if you'd had a career Jasper wouldn't have found you so dull,' Renée said venomously. At five foot eight and wearing high heels, the woman towered over me like Godzilla. 'Why don't you go back into the workforce and stop sponging off your ex?'

I seized her hand, flipped it over and peered at the palm. 'I'm just checking for credit card burns. Prada, Manolo Blahnik . . . How degrading to exceed the Bling-ometer with another woman's money.' I would have driven home my advantage, except, at that precise moment, the gel insert Susie had lent me popped out. It plopped on to the ground between us like a stranded jellyfish. I looked at Renée's breasts, which were as big as a garage. Every man she met wanted to double-park in that particular erogenous zone.

Jasper reappeared, wallet in hand. He, too, stared at the quivering silicone pouch lying at his feet. Renée smiled archly, then her body started to twitch with derisive laughter. I felt my face begin to burn.

'Um . . . Would you believe it's a stress-relieving squeezy executive toy? OK, my breasts might be small, but at least they're organic.' In a moment of childish rage, I lunged forward and squeezed the silicone tits of my adversary. Renée squealed, batting me away. 'Actually, Jasper, your new girl-friend and me, we have a lot in common. We've both had plastic surgery. She's had a boob job and I've had to cut up my credit cards.'

'Really, Jasper, how did you put up with her for so long?' Renée demanded of my husband, realigning her store-bought boobs in her designer T-shirt.' I just can't believe that a man of your style and quality ended up with a woman with so little sophistication . . . So little flair.'

'Oh, you have flair all right. All of it in your jeans

105

legs to hide your fat ankles.' It wasn't my best retort but the requirements of delivering a bitingly barbed riposte are limited when you're stooped at the feet of your rival, retrieving a plastic breast pad.

Renée took a threatening step closer to me. Jasper manoeuvred himself between us. He also defused the situation by peeling a dozen hundred-dollar bills from his wallet.

'I've got to get back to work now, Lucy. I'm sorry. I'm sorry about everything. Renée told me how unhappy you were in our marriage.' His gentle hand was so warm and familiar on my waist; the feel of it was so beguiling that I let him steer me back towards my car.

'But . . . but . . .' I was crosshatched with feelings – anger, guilt, remorse, jealousy. The warp and weft left me tongue-tied.

'You don't want me to lose my coaching job? On top of everything else? Tell the kids I love them very much and will be out to see them really soon. I'm just working things out. You look great, Lucy.' He opened my car door and guided me into the driver's seat. 'You also deserve so much better than this. I'm sorry I let you down as a husband.' He closed the door behind me. If he hadn't blown me a kiss, I might have protested some more, but, disarmed and emotionally exhausted, I just watched him follow Renée into the stadium. I might as well have dropped a feather into the Grand Canyon for all the effect I'd had.

And so I did the only thing a woman could

under such dire circumstances. I drove to the nearest pub. I'd never been into a pub on my own. I sat in the the Olympic Hotel, feeling exposed and alone. My protective shell, my husband, had been removed. Socially I was as peeled as a salad prawn. The gin felt so good as it coursed through my bloodstream that I immediately needed a second. Cradling my drink, I wondered what lies Renée had told my husband to sway him in her favour. I also wondered why it was that I allowed myself to wither beneath her contemptuous gaze. Renée was as sleek and smug and sexually satisfied as the cat who got the cream. *His* cream, I despaired. I was the scruffy alley stray kicked out into the cold, and left to moult and count fleas.

I rustled in my handbag for a tissue. By my third gin and tonic I'd decided to show Jasper that I too was independent and chic. Although I might need another steadying drink to do so. And then perhaps just one more . . .

Do you suffer from self-loathing? Do you feel about as useful as a chocolate teapot? If you answered yes to either of these questions, ask your pharmacist about alcohol. Alcohol is the natural, legal way to feel confident again. WARNING. Side effects may include nausea, incarceration, loss of motor control, loss of purse, loss of dignity . . . And barging into the office of the spouse who has dumped you in a desperate bid to beg him to come back.

★　★　★

'What are your long-term intentions regarding my husband?' is what I meant to say. Except that it came out as, 'One day your nipples will be on your knees, Renée, do you know that? You big fake-titted freak!'

The taxi had taken me back to the football stadium where I'd talked my way up into my husband's office. Jasper looked up in alarm from his ergonomically correct chair as I lurched through the door. Renée, who was up a ladder adjusting a painting, listed dangerously.

I ploughed across the room, pin-balling off furniture. 'Jasper, oh Jasper.' Every breath was a shallow, panicked little pant. 'We've been dangerous reefs to each other, but also lifeboats,' I gushed, the gin making me all poetic. 'What we share may look like a shipwreck, but we share it. We've survived it all – and that is worth something, darling, isn't it?' Jasper drew back. The man was so displeased to see me, you didn't just need a knife to cut the air, but a chainsaw. Wobbly and unwieldy, I felt like a stranded manatee. If only I could just flop into the water, which in my tipsy stupor was the comforting harbour of my husband's arms. Closing one eye to take better aim, I lunged for him, knocking a vase off the desk in the process. It toppled to the floor, splattering water and shattered glass all over my shell-shocked husband.

Renée flew to his side. 'Oh really, Jasper, this is getting embarrassing,' I heard Renée say superciliously. 'Where is your dignity?' she taunted me.

'Gee, I dunno. Maybe it got mixed in with Jasper's stuff when he moved the fuck out to live with you?'

'Lucy,' Jasper patted himself dry with tissues, 'I think in heated situations like this . . .' an unfamiliar frostiness had crept into my husband's tone, 'it's best to try to show some admirable restraint.'

'Admirable restraint? Yeah, that's what we dumped wives exercise right up to the moment when we shoot our marauding husbands,' I somehow managed to drawl.

'Shooting? Dear God. Do you think she's got a gun? That's it.' Renée picked up the phone. 'I'm calling security.'

Anger about my ruptured life consumed me. I wanted to cry Foul! I wanted to remind him that he was supposed to kick the ball, not his wife. I wanted to kick Renée right over the crossbar. 'You vile, lying witch!' I screamed at her. 'Look what you've done to me! To us.'

Rule 1 in How to Impress Your Husband's New Colleagues is probably *not* to appear in his office drunk, trash the room, then jump on to the interior decorator's back and beat your fists and scream till hoarse.

Once I was escorted off the premises, I waited for my husband to come after me. Was he really going to let me disappear into the sunset without calling my name, without taking me into his arms? Without prostrating himself at my feet to beg forgiveness?

Apparently, yes. I had a terrible feeling that I'd just given a penalty to the other side. It started to rain. I walked along the squelching streets, the pavements of Paddington undulating beneath my feet. The enormity of my situation hit me full in the chest. Jasper was actually in *love* with this woman. He had just fallen for her like a tree to the logger's axe. I must have walked for hours, as night had descended before I came to a street I recognized. It was William Street, the huge boulevard which swoops down to the red-light district of King's Cross. The whole road was a neon river of red, green and orange as the traffic lights changed. I just stood there, snapshots of memories strobing through my head: unstoppered laughter on our honeymoon; high-wattage beaming the day Tally and Ruby were born. On and on the memories scrolled: our arms wound fondly around each other at children's parties and family reunions; Mother's days and Father's days with bundles of badly wrapped presents on the bed. Passing sets of headlights slid over me like egg yolk. A bus blasted me with its foul petrol breath, waking me from my desolate reverie.

'Do you know where my car is?' I said to the taxi driver I'd hailed down. 'Because I may have to sell it to pay the parking fines I've probably accumulated. It's somewhere near the Olympic Hotel.'

Twenty minutes later, feeling sober but desolate, I was grasping the dashboard of my car with both hands, although it took me a while to realize that the car was moving and I was behind the wheel. I was driving by gin compass, the invisible device that ensures your safe arrival home, even though you're too hungover to remember your own name, let alone where you live. I nearly made it too, except for being pulled over for speeding. I was only doing thirty in a fifty zone. But it was in reverse, because, in my distress, I had taken a wrong turn into Sylvania Waters and got lost in a one-way system.

After a roadside breath-test which showed positive, I was arrested and driven to Cronulla police station. A further breath analysis showed I was just under the limit. 'Of course I would never drink and drive . . . I mean you'd only spill it,' I said to the officer. But my attempt to lighten the mood only made him more gruff. He ran my car through the computer and discovered Jasper hadn't paid the car registration or the third-party insurance. I was charged with driving an unregistered and uninsured vehicle. I tried to explain that it was my husband's car, but as the driver, the responsibility was all mine. I was bailed on my own recognizance to attend court a few weeks later. I would also have to pay for the car to be towed home, then spend the next two days organizing insurance and what Aussies call the 'rego'. Waiting to sign forms, I saw myself in the mirror above the charge desk. So much for my new look. I was no longer wearing my hairdo. My hairdo was wearing me.

I didn't want Tally to know I'd been drinking, or as she would put it, 'chemically inconvenienced', so I walked the four blocks to the sea. Was I really so far off Jasper's radar that he'd forgotten the basic practicality of insuring his wife's car? Or had he done it on purpose, to isolate me even further? It was late. The ocean crawled with whitecaps, like something alive. I stood on the bluff, watching the sea's hypnotic boil. Australia is the earth's oldest land mass. Its cliffs are pumiced by centuries of storms. Behind me the lozenges of light in the windows of houses along the point looked warm and comforting, increasing my feeling of alienation. An engine alerted me to a fishing-boat puttering around the point from the Port Hacking River. I watched until there was only the occasional muffled sighting above a crest as a wave troughed. I walked along the ridge, drawn to the vertiginous pull of the dark water.

Unnerved, I made my way shakily down to the beach and sank on to the sand to catch my breath. I had only vague recollections of what had actually happened but there were unsettling flashbacks to breast gel pads and smashed vases. Feeling giddy and sick, I lay on the sand but descended into memories so raw they made me shut my eyes tight against them. I couldn't go home like this. A swim would clear my head. South Cronulla is so safe, it's known as Coward's Corner. According to Lockie, the South Cronulla surf club is home to 'ponces' and 'poseurs' who hide behind their cappuccinos at the sight of a three-foot swell. I was obviously wearing what the locals call a 'white wine wetsuit' – the invisible outfit which allows you to plunge into the cold sea, naked, at night, with no qualms, because next thing I knew I was clawing off my clothing.

The jolt of the cold water fizzed straight to my brain. I dived under a wave and felt a surge of energy through my blood. Cleansed and revitalized, I swam further out and ducked under the next frothy line of foam. Each cold blast chased another demon from my head. Two more waves and I turned for shore. I swam freestyle for a few minutes before glancing up. But the shore seemed to be getting further away with each stroke. I paddled more determinedly. As my head bobbed up and down, I saw the cluster of houses on Cronulla Point. The lights coming through the windows were so far away they seemed like cut-out squares of yellow, stuck on to black paper. They were also getting smaller.

The awful truth of what Lockie had said in class hit me in the gut. Signs on every Australian beach advise all swimmers to swim between the flags, to make surveillance easier. Despite the warnings, English tourists were for ever plunging in, unaware of rip tides. The rip around Cronulla Point is known as 'the backpacker's express', because most drownings occur in the first twenty-four hours of tourists arriving. My regular swimming lessons had improved my speed. I'd obviously swum out further than I'd realized and been caught in the current. I had learnt in surf lifesaving class that the only way to survive a rip is not to fight, but to go with the flow, while all the time swimming on a diagonal into calmer waters.

Moving parallel to the beach meant that breathing on the right-hand side was fine, but trying to inhale on the left had to be timed carefully with each wave or risk swallowing a huge gulp of seawater. I kept my head down, resuming a steady stroke, looking into the void, the only distraction the bubbles of air made by my hands as they cut through the water. When I realized I was still being dragged out to sea I started to panic, which made me hyperventilate. It wasn't that the sea was all that cold – I'd had more bracing swims in the London lidos – but all around me was a heaving black expanse of gloomy, murky water. Who knew what lurked beneath? Hammerhead sharks had been sighted here just days before. Hammerheads use surfboards as toothpicks.

I tried to breaststroke over the swell, but felt waterlogged with grief. The deadening weight of my own failure was weighing me down like lead. I accidentally guzzled some seawater. The choking fit took so much breath out of me that the backpacker's express just swept me effortlessly around the point and into the Port Hacking River, a shark breeding-ground. I emitted a brittle sob of exhaustion which nobody could hear. I gasped for air one last time, pain flooding in like sea into a torn hull. Life, I then realized, is in two acts.

The trick is to survive the interval.

CHAPTER 9

TIRED SWIMMER TOW

'What the fuck are you doing?'

It was a question I'd been asking myself. And now it seemed to be hanging in the air. I thought I'd heard a boat mutter and groan against the tide. The muffled engine matured into a ragged beat, followed by a full-throated roar. It's only in novels that coincidences seem contrived. In life they happen all the time. Which is why I shouldn't have been surprised when Lockie found me, caught up in his fishing-net, not just half-drowned and hypothermic, but also in a lachrymose puddle of self-loathing.

The expression on the face which loomed over the side of the boat was as unfathomable as the sea beneath us. 'What the fuck are you doing?'

It was a totally understandable query, and one which I couldn't answer. Of late, my life had been proceeding with the same smooth efficiency of a land war in the Middle East. 'Hey, b . . . b . . . being uns . . . s . . . stable and unp . . . p . . . predictable is all part of my mystique,' I stuttered, as the big man disentangled me from the net, flipped me around so my back was to the boat, grabbed me under the armpits and dragged me aboard.

As I'd sobered up, the water had not felt so warm. The cold was now deep in my bones. My legs were so cramped I wasn't sure they could support me. Once on deck, I staggered and Lockie had to catch me, pressing my body up against his for support. I could see by the lamplight that dark crescents seamed the armpits of his T-shirt from the effort of hauling me aboard. He had a bitter-sweet smell of sweaty skin and hard work. It was then I remembered I was naked. *Again*. This was getting to be a habit. And it was so out of character. Appearing naked in front of a stranger appalled me. Even in the communal changing-room of a department store, I would loiter for the duration of what felt like three general-election campaigns, until the coast was clear and I could strip off unobserved.

'A towel. A coat. A . . . a . . . anything,' I stuttered, turning my back and cowering like some Renaissance painting of Eve expelled from the Garden of Eden.

'I was kinda wondering why you're starkers,' Lockie said, taking an appraising look at my white wine wetsuit before tossing a towel and jumper my way.

'S . . . s . . . swimming with your clothes on can lead to a rather alarming decrease in b . . . b . . . buoyancy, you know,' I said through chattering teeth. 'Well, that's what this bloke taught me in

116

surf life s . . . s . . . s . . . saving class,' I added, facetiously.

'I don't think you're all that bloody buoyant either way. Hurry up and get warm. Dress in the cabin.' Lockie flicked a switch to illuminate the small wooden cabin below. 'You need tea.'

'I need more than t . . . t . . . t . . . tea. I need jumper l . . . l . . . leads,' I said, shaking violently.

As I rugged up and turbaned my wet hair in a towel, I watched Lockie pour a stream of hot water from his flask into a chipped mug. He added three sugars, then worried the spoon around the cup.

'Drink this. And eat.' He rummaged in his shoulder-bag.

'Do you have a sprinkling of Valium and a heroin chaser?' My lips felt thick with cold, the words ponderous. I drew the sleeves of his jumper down to warm my hands, sat on the bunk, legs drawn up, and swigged from the mug with the tea-bag string still dangling.

'How the bloody hell did you end up out here at this time of night?' Lockie demanded, unceremoniously tossing a tin of sweet biscuits in my direction. 'Weren't you scared shitless?'

'No . . . only when I saw that bright tunnel with my dead ancestors waving me towards the light,' I replied between bites. The half-stale Anzac biscuits tasted better than a five-star Michelin meal.

'Pardon my French, but what the fuck were you thinking? What a time to go skinny dipping!'

'Don't yell at me! Do you think I wanted my life to turn out like this? If I'd *wanted* to be maimed spiritually, physically and emotionally, I'd have gone to Baghdad and made a day of it.' My voice was thick with self-pity.

'OK, OK.' The big man backed off. 'What else can I get you?' He opened cupboards, fossicking for food.

'Oh, I don't know . . . Do you have any strychnine? I know you don't like to ask questions, convict heritage and all that. But if you're wondering why I'm upset, it's because of my husband. He's so careless in his appearance.'

Lockie regarded me incredulously by the wan cabin light. 'Lemme get this right . . . You're half-drowned in the sea, stark bollocking naked, because you're worried about your husband's appearance?'

'Yes. He hasn't made one for nearly two months. You see, *I'm* happily married. But apparently my husband isn't.' And then my story poured out of me, just like the seawater streaming out of my nose. I explained how my marriage had been for better or for worse . . . but not for a prettier best friend. I told him that back at home we used to say that 90 per cent of men were unfaithful in Britain – and the rest were unfaithful on overseas trips. 'I probably sound embittered, cynical and twisted. That's mainly because I am,' I concluded, stifling a sob.

Lockie topped up my tea. I wrapped my fingers

around the mug, the warmth spreading through my fingertips and down my arms.

'It's not Jasper's fault. Obviously there was something seriously missing from our marriage or he wouldn't have gone looking elsewhere,' I said desolately. 'If I'm honest, if Jasper and I *did* get a chance to reminisce about all the fun times we've had in the last year, we'd be chatting for, oh . . . about 3.6 seconds.'

'Don't blame yourself. This has happened to you accidentally, like stubbing your toe. The pain will pass.' When he wasn't scowling Lockie had a thoughtful face. I studied it by the anaemic lamplight. 'The best anyone can do at a time like this is to just keep breathing in and breathing out and wait for the agony to fade.' There was some sadness straining his face. But I knew better than to ask. 'You can't blame yourself for the atomic bomb which has gone off in your family.'

I nodded wanly. 'I just feel so lost. As if I've sunk without trace.'

'Ah, but you didn't, did you, Lucy?' It was the first time he'd used my name. 'Bloody nearly, though, you mad Pom. Sounds like that husband of yours never exactly knocked himself out for you. Although, jeez, after the stuff you've told me, it's tempting to bloody well do it for him. The prick.'

I looked at Lockie's broken nose and wondered how many men he'd pulverized in the fight. 'Maybe Jasper doesn't have the best emotional responses, compared to other men, or even certain species of plankton. But I love him, Jack.'

'Still? Well, that settles it. You're obviously in shock. I'm going to take the boat back to my place where you can shower, and then drive you home. You're just so bloody lucky Ryan's camping with the sea scouts tonight, so I could go trawling.'

'Where do you live?' I asked, the chattering in my teeth easing off.

'Bundeena.' He pointed to the small cluster of lights of a seaside village, surrounded by the pitch black of the bush, the other side of the Port Hacking River.

'Isn't it lonely over there?'

Lockie hauled in his net, kicked the engine out of neutral and into gear. The boat strained against the tide to cross the bay. 'I downsized. I learnt to appreciate what I've got, instead of striving for more all the bloody time.'

'What did you do before?' I hazarded, slurping at my tea and cocooning myself into the blanket. I knew my rescuer could clam up altogether, but something about the stillness of the night and the gentle throb of the boat's engine must have lulled him into a more trusting mood, because he surprised me by replying.

'Lawyer. But then I got scruple-itis. Once scruples set in, it's pretty bloody incurable. I started going into every negotiation with a fixed determination to win or lose. Which was not the best for business,' he concluded, drily.

'And that's how you ended up here?'

'Yep. Avoiding what I call the effluent society – the stinking rich. My old mates think I've failed myself. But there's something more honest about failure, don't you think? Gallipoli, Ned Kelly, the Eureka rebellion, Dunkirk . . .'

'No! I'm furious with myself that I failed to notice Jasper getting such a psychological and financial hold over me,' I mourned.

'Maybe so. But killing yourself over a failed marriage is like using a guillotine to cure dandruff.'

'I wasn't trying to kill myself! I was just trying to sober up. Besides, the marriage hasn't failed. I'm going to save it.'

Lockie expertly spun the wheel to avoid a rock. 'Are you sure? Life is like surfing. You have to know when to get off the bloody wave.'

I looked at him aghast. I had loved Jasper since, approximately, the Boer War. And I would always love him. 'I'm sure,' I said, determinedly.

'OK. Then talk to the guy. Work it out. Don't go to divorce lawyers. As soon as each half of a couple has their own advocate, then the legal serpent whispers that they should go for more and the bile tap is turned on.'

I wondered if he were speaking from a personal or professional point of view.

'Divorce lawyers are greedy, malevolent and second-rate. I should know. I was one,' Lockie confessed. 'Put the kids first. It disgusted me when clients tried to take their revenge on their exes through their kids. Lawyers are so bloody unscrupulous. "I was just taking instructions," they'd say . . . the classic concentration-camp-guard defence. I couldn't stomach it. Walked away. So many solicitors screw their female clients. Literally. One of my colleagues, a real flash bastard, took a client to the opera, slept with her, then sent her a bill – which included the cost of the tickets and the time between when he left the office in the evening and returned next morning. "Divorce" is an old Aboriginal term for "*send your lawyer to a luxury resort in Bali*".'

'So, what do you think I should do?'

Lockie shrugged. 'Don't go swimming naked in the sea in the middle of the bloody night.'

'I really could have died out there,' I said and started shaking again.

'Ah well, yes, but just think of the tax relief.' The arm Lockie leant confidently on the boat rudder was brown and broad. The hand he put on my shoulder to steady my nerves was strong and experienced – the quiet, understated strength of a former athlete. My shaking subsided.

'Yes,' I rallied, 'and a sure cure for worrying about wrinkles.'

'Too right.' There was a smile in his voice so I moved more into the light to see him. Lockie didn't have the slim, young, handsomely chiselled qualifications normally associated with a romantic lead. But he was undeniably sexy. It had something to do with the way he moved. A masculine grace. As though totally at ease in his skin. The jumper he'd lent me smelled of salt, fish heads, cigar smoke and a manly, musky sweat. I snuggled down into it for comfort.

'I reckon contemplating suicide is nature's way of telling you to do more fishing,' Lockie added, flippantly.

I offered him a biscuit and, as he took it from my hand, I noticed there was soil beneath his finger-nails and there were calluses on his hands. It was strangely reassuring. 'Yes, drowning is definitely a breathtaking experience,' I replied jauntily.

His smile broke on me like a wave on a rock. 'That's the thing about life,' he bantered, slowing the boat as we neared the shore. 'You're lucky if you get out of it alive.'

The moon shone on the water with the bright-ness of a motorcycle headlight. It illuminated something bulky on the shoreline which made Lockie start to attention.

'Crikey! What's that?'

Its size and colour made me think shark. My blood ran cold to think of a creature that size in the black waters I'd just escaped. As Lockie brought the boat closer to the beach, I discerned the fin of the beast.

'It's not a shark fin. The tail looks like a dolphin, maybe?' As Lockie beached the boat, digging the anchor into the sand, I could see that the dolphin's distinctive snout was missing. The head was blunt.

'Baby whale,' Lockie clarified. 'Poor bugger.'

He held out his hand to help me leap from the boat. Catching me around the waist, he then lowered me gently to the sand. The big woolly jumper I'd borrowed rode up and I felt a blast of air on my bare backside. I also felt a furtive glance from my saviour. 'About two hundred and fifty kilograms, I'd say.'

For a worrying moment, I thought he was talking about me and instinctively held my stomach in. But he was already striding towards the whale. The dull impassivity of death was in the whale's eye, fixed almost nostalgically on the ocean. But then it blinked. I squealed in alarm, just as the vent on its head suddenly opened, blowing wet air on to my arm.

Lockie sprang to action. 'We have to roll it,' he ordered. 'Time it with the wave going back to sea.' He ripped off his cable sweater and put his bare back against the whale's side. The sinews on Lockie's straining lats reminded me of the roots of an old tree. I splashed towards him and added what strength I had left after my impromptu ocean ordeal. 'One, two, *three*,' he ordered, and then we heaved, bracing against the whale's bulk with all our might. After five or so waves, the whale began to inch ocean-ward. Once the baby whale was afloat, Lockie manoeuvred it into deeper water. He was up to his chin by now, but still steadying the creature on its course. The whale twitched its tail. We watched in an agony of anxiety. Elation surged through me as it started swimming – only for our hopes to be immediately dashed when the poor disorientated beast turned back to shore.

In my 'to do' list in life, saving a whale was curiously absent. A London girl, born and bread, there are some experiences you assume will never require your ingenuity. Floating over a desert, say, strapped into a lawn chair propelled entirely by balloons. Or finding yourself at a nudist colony with Johnny Depp. Or saving a stranded whale on the Australian coast by moonlight. I was ill-equipped for any of these eventualities, but positioned myself between the whale and the sand, desperate to stop it beaching once more. I could hear Lockie talking to the mammal – soothing, encouraging, reassuring words. He was beside me now and we both planted our feet firmly in the sand. As the baby whale surfed towards us, we shoved with all our might in the opposite direction. The whale submerged, then surfaced a few metres away, vertical to the shoreline.

'Come on, honey,' Lockie urged it. 'You can do it, darling one.'

And then, ever so slowly, the whale turned towards the sea, its tail steering it into deeper waters. Exhausted and exhilarated simultaneously, I let out an exultant cheer.

'You little beauty! Whaddaya know? We bloody did it.' Lockie touched me lightly on the arm, and his touch glowed briefly like a firefly on my skin. Some unspoken tenderness passed between us. The sky was purple-black like velvet. The Milky

Way was all diamantés sewn into dark cloth. The enormity of what we'd achieved eclipsed my angst.

Lockie's wooden, weatherbeaten house on the oceanfront was so dilapidated it was like an old ship, run aground. But inside I was pleasantly surprised to find plain floorboards, sanded back, a linen tablecloth and crisp white towels. I showered and pulled on dry clothes I presumed had belonged to the wife he never spoke of. While I drank a restorative hot toddy, I did a little light snooping around his living room. On the coffee table was a box of Bach's cello suites and a tattered hardback edition of Defoe's *Robinson Crusoe*, plus *Moby Dick* and books on Admiral Nelson and Grace Darling. Watching as Lockie hunted for his car keys, the lamplight behind him suddenly made him seem warmer, even enticing.

'Do you want to see my etchings?' he asked with no warning.

For a brief irrational second, I felt a spasm of something I'd long forgotten, but recognized, hazily, as lust. This was quickly extinguished when I realized that Lockie really did want to show me his paintings. The man did watercolours. And not bad either.

At midnight we drove in companionable silence, Handel on the radio, all the long winding way through the national park and back down what they called the 'insular peninsular' to South Cronulla, where I collected my clothes and bag from the beach.

'A slab of beer is the standard Clubbie fee for saving someone,' Lockie instructed, when he dropped me home. 'See yer later.'

Not even encountering Tally's new boyfriend, Spider (the bass player in a heavy-metal band, who smelt of dead rodents and seemed to have an entire eco-system under each toenail), was enough to capsize my calm.

'Mum,' said Tally, confrontationally, 'this is Spider. His band's got a gig on Friday night and I'm going.'

'Sure,' I said, thinking – sure you can go out with my daughter . . . *if you can get past the armed security guards around her bedroom, you vile, wretched worm.*

And then I crawled into my enormous, empty bed and slept the first long and lovely sleep I'd had in what felt like months.

I awoke with a new determination to win back my husband, and faith that I would succeed.

I knew I was on the right track . . . I just had to hope to God that this time there was no train coming.

CHAPTER 10

BEWARE OF STINGERS

The definition of a juvenile delinquent is a child who starts acting as badly as its parents. This is what I told Tally's head teacher when she was caught truanting. I suspected her absence had more to do with Spider's band rehearsals than with any allergy to education. When dating Chook, Tally had preferred the natural look. But she now guarded her eyeliner and mascaras with the ferocity of a Columbian drug lord. Her once pristine bedroom had become so dirty and unkempt that guests wiped their feet before *leaving* her room. Taking out the rubbish and emptying her bedroom now amounted to the same thing. With her pierced lip, black 'Placebo' T-shirt, leather boots, denim shorts torn around the ass and an overdose of black eyeliner, Tally was obviously attempting to dispel all rumours that she was a 'teenage tearaway'.

'Tally is just provoking arguments as a way of connecting with me, but also keeping her distance,' I explained to Susie over our regular hot chocolate on the balcony later that night. 'That's what the psychology books say. She's struggling with her love for me, and her desperate desire to be different, apparently, which is why I must be patient.'

'Really? I'd just ground the little mongrel,' was Susie's less philosophical response.

'If I'm judgemental, she'll just run off to join some strict religious order whose entire diet consists of woodchips, lawn clippings and the odd human sacrifice. I just want to keep open lines of communication.'

'Lucy, you big dag. Parents and their kids aren't supposed to communicate. It's a totalitarian regime. A parent needs hostility and resentment and terror to sustain command. Which reminds me, I'd better go untie the sprogs from the radiator.'

But it seemed to me that mothers and teenage daughters have more wars breaking out per day than in the Middle East. And I didn't want to start another. Tally's rebellion seemed pretty textbook. I was more worried about my other daughter. Of all the millions of brain-bending questions my children had thrown at me over the years – 'Why do clairvoyants have to ask for your name and profession?', 'How do eyebrows know to stop growing in the middle?', 'What if there were no hypothetical questions?' – '*When is Daddy coming back?*' was the only one to which I had no answer.

I was so sure that Jasper wouldn't turn up on Ruby's eleventh birthday that I told her he was out of the country on a business trip. Ruby's birthday coincided with the North Cronulla surf club's November fund-raising barbecue. Ruby wanted to join her friends at the sausage sizzle, and then have a cake at home later. I only realized that her errant father had deigned to make an appearance when every male optic muscle suddenly leapt out of its socket.

There's a lot to be said for being an idle rich Trophy Girlfriend. And Renée Craven intended to say it all. A member of the Glitterazzi, she was wearing Versace gold-embossed sunglasses, a see-through sarong revealing a skimpy scarlet bikini the colour of chilli peppers and high-heeled sandals. She looked as though she should have had a yacht surgically attached. And then there were her breasts. Basically, her mammaries were so big they really required their own radio transmitter so they could report back to the rest of her body on weather conditions up ahead.

Cronulla is a working-class beach. It is home to an oil refinery, sand mine, sewage treatment centre and proposed desalination and pesticide plants. The most elegantly dressed man at any social gathering invariably turns out to be the barman or a bodyguard for a famous footballer from the local 'Sharks' team. Board shorts and flip-flops are the norm. As the entire party swivelled to eyeball Renée, she stripped back her lips to show the perfect, yet gritted, dentition which passed for a smile. As the diamond-studded Delilah minced towards the bar, the sea of male guests parted in biblical awe.

I was gawping too, but at what followed hot on her four-hundred-dollar crocodile heels. The all-over tan and the tailored teeth were new, as was the coronet of newly streaked, highlighted hair. My husband was suddenly dressing like a lead actor in *Miami Vice* – obligatory white blazer with rolled-up sleeves over black T-shirt, white trainers, gold chain and dark shades.

'What the hell's the matter?' Susie asked, noticing that the colour had drained from my face. We'd been drafted in to help at the sausage sizzle and were attractively sweating over the barbecue grill on the veranda – our hair limp, damp patches under each armpit and eyes slitted red from the smoke.

'I can't believe he brought her,' I muttered in a tiny voice. 'For God's sake, hide me.'

'He brought *her*? NO! Where?'

'Just look for the woman who has stretch marks around her mouth . . . And not because she talks too much,' I explained.

Squinting through the barbecue smoke, Susie was obviously impressed by Renée's immaculate appearance, but said loyally, 'What's her job? Sniffing luggage at the airport? Because the woman's a dog!' She delivered this verdict in a whisper that could be heard in the Outer Hebrides. It caused Renée to break away from Jasper at the bar and sashay over in my dishevelled direction. She smiled hello but her look was one of glacial condemnation. 'So this is your little club. *Sweet.*' I felt my teeth lock

131

with unexpressed irritation. She looked me up and down with undisguised pity. 'And how nice that nobody here cares about appearances. Must be so . . . relaxing not to have to make an effort.'

'Yeah, we're very casual here. Why don't you make yourself at home, Renée, and seduce somebody's husband,' Susie retorted, wielding her tongs like a spear.

I would have given a retort of my own but was too busy trying to make my molars grind more slowly so as to muffle the sound of disintegrating enamel. I saw Jasper approaching, beer in hand, so made a surreptitious attempt to tidy myself up.

'Where are the kids?' Jasper planted a perfunctory kiss on my cheek. Well, it was perfunctory for him. But it sent my pulse racing. Whenever I saw Jasper I felt so at sea someone really should have lit a marine distress flare.

'If there's food, they'll be along soon,' I managed to say. 'You know kids. Their favourite food is seconds. Speaking of which . . . I'll be needing some more housekeeping money, Jasper.'

'I gave you enough money until the end of the month, Lucy.'

I felt his voice hit the pit of my stomach. 'Yes . . . unless I need to actually *buy* anything.'

'Emergency rations for you are wine, beer and spirits, aren't they, Lucy?' Renée gave a forced laugh, but her voice was chilly. 'Any more of your sob stories and you'll make the onions cry . . . Money isn't everything, you know.'

'Yeah, you're right,' Susie chipped in. 'It usually isn't even enough.'

'Renée is going to make us a lot of money,' Jasper mollified. 'I'm just waiting for the shares to go up. Who knew the American markets would go into free fall?'

'Renée is my husband's *financial adviser*,' I informed Susie, who was glowering at them both. She was now holding the sauce bottle like a handgun. I wouldn't have been surprised to see her fire off a volley of squirts.

'Oh really?' Susie gave the kind of cackle which was normally associated with a cauldron. 'I'm sure Renée's just the type of woman who'd stimulate a higher interest rate in a bloke's private sector.'

A truce was called in this conversational skirmish at the sight of Ruby rocketing across the veranda. '*Daaaaaaddd*!' Happiness spilt from her eyes. 'Daddy!' She leapt into his arms. The smattering of freckles dusting her little cheeks glowed pink with pleasure. Jasper swung her around while she squealed for joy. 'Aunty Renée!' Ruby burbled, excitedly, kissing my nemesis.

Humiliation was a wet, slimy live thing in my throat. But for the sake of my girls, I swallowed it down.

'Oh, Ruby, how simply *divine* to see you again.' Renée's smile was as sickly sweet as icing. 'Happy birthday.'

'Guess what?' Ruby gushed, not drawing breath. 'What do you call a fish with no eyes?

133

A fsh,' she giggled. 'Mummy's going to be a life-saver! Isn't she soooo brave?!'

'Yes, she's very *brave*.' Renée imbued the word with utter contempt, adding under her breath for Jasper's benefit, 'To wear no make-up at *her* age.'

'Mum makes the best sausages in the whole wide world, Dad! Try one! Ryan calls it snaffling a snag!' she giggled.

'I'd love to, Rubes,' Jasper said, taking the buttered roll she proffered.

Ladling a sausage into Jasper's bun, the gesture was so domestic, so reminiscent of our old life, that I was cross-eyed with the effort not to cry. 'Would you like the name of a heart specialist to go with that?' I said, breezily, to cover up my raw emotions.

Renée looked at the sausage Ruby offered her as though it were toxic waste. 'Are these organic?'

Susie and every other Aussie within earshot immediately fell about laughing.

Renée looked Susie up and down once more, lingering on her peachy nether regions. '*Some* of us like to watch our weight.'

I had seen Renée close a restaurant for serving whole milk in her skinny latte. 'Are you trying to *kill* me? The cholesterol. OHMYGOD.' For a real treat, the woman might lick a sultana. A spritzer for her would be half-Perrier and half-Volvic. The hypocrisy of only drinking flat mineral water to keep her inner self purified – while poisoning her system with collagen and Botox – seemed totally lost on her. Today she was as undressed as the rocket salad she would no doubt have for dinner. And my husband was looking at her ravenously.

'Renée worries about what she eats. I keep telling her that the worry in Oz is *not* to be eaten,' Jasper quipped. His charisma was melting all within charm range, as usual.

All *I* could eat were my nails, upon which I was gnawing ravenously. I must have sounded like a small, foraging rodent. 'There's a health food café on the boardwalk,' I said, helpfully, hoping to get rid of her. 'They have a wheatgerm kiwi-fruit smoothie to *die* for.'

It sounded like liquid lawn to me, but Renée's appetite was piqued. 'Ruby, will you take your Aunty Renée, darling?' she said with counterfeit kindness, her smile as lacquered as her nails.

I'd rather have force-fed myself a hemlock milk-shake than let my daughter anywhere near Renée, but I needed time with Jasper, alone. Emails, texts, faxes, phone calls, carrier pigeons, smoke signals; all my efforts at reconciliation had been returned, unopened. I was beginning to think that the only way of getting his attention would be to take out an ad in *Sports Illustrated*. I'd been on tenterhooks for too long. Hell, of late, I'd spent more time on my toes than a member of the Bolshoi Ballet. And so I nodded my consent.

'Jasper,' I whispered, urgently, once Renée and Ruby had left the club and we'd sat down at a corner table. 'Why haven't you answered my calls and letters? Everything Renée said to you about us was a lie. She was just manipulating you. I adore you. I need you. Do *you* still love *me*?' I asked baldly.

'Of course,' came his bland reply. 'You're the mother of my children.'

'Then why? Why have you abandoned us?' My voice was pitched two octaves higher than usual and my face was distorted with the effort not to blub.

'This is why I don't answer your calls. You just fly into such a rage.'

'Hey, well, I'd *like* to fly *first class to the Caribbean*. But I can't afford it.'

'I gave you this week's money, Lucy.' Jasper blinked neutrally. He wasn't himself. He seemed like a hologram. What had that blood-sucking harridan done with my real husband? 'You're obviously going senile,' he concluded, coldly.

'You're the one with a bad memory, Jasper. You've obviously forgotten the vows you made to me when we married.'

'You've obviously forgotten how many times you told Renée how miserable our marriage was! Hell, your memory is so bad, you forget that you have a bad memory.'

We would have gone on in this vindictive vein, except that Ruby suddenly slipped between us. She took our hands in hers, then ever so gradually moved them together until our fingers were touching. She then delicately extracted her own small hand, leaving her parents' fingers laced.

Which is how Renée, sucking her liquid lawn up through a straw, found us, five minutes later. Her eyes, cat-green from contact lenses, narrowed into sour slits. She immediately put out her manicured paw to Jasper, confident of his attention.

'Just a minute, Renée.' Jasper held up his free hand, traffic-cop style, while he took Ruby's gangly frame on to his knee.

Wearing the predatory look of a hungry fox, Renée loitered on the periphery. A bunch of hearty, horny dads immediately engaged her in conversation. 'Oh hello,' I heard her say in some kind of strained BBC accent. 'Extra-ordinary,' she said in a dull, bored voice. 'How very fascinating.' All the time, her eyes were fixed on the happy family tableau before her.

'Jasper, dah-ling,' she finally simpered. 'You simply must take me for a swim. Look at that ocean. It's just too, too cruel to make me wait a nanosecond longer.'

'Daddy, yes!' Ruby's face lit up with glee. 'I can show you everything I've learned. I'm amaaaaazing. Like a mermaid!' It had been so long since I'd seen her toothy geometry arranged into such a big broad beam that I didn't remonstrate.

'We'd love to see you surfing,' Renée enthused. The 'we' made my scalp crawl. Even though supposedly encouraging Ruby, Renée's smile was so cold that when she parted her lips I expected a little light to come on.

Ruby shot off Jasper's lap like a rocket. She was

tugging him up out of his chair and dragging him towards the beach.

'Mum, are you coming?'

Swimming with Renée would be an opportunity to drown my sorrows – if I held her head under long enough, that is. Still, Renée is the kind of woman who has a St Tropez tan before she goes to St Tropez and a man on hand to rub more in. Haphazard, one-handed suntan application meant that my tan had patches which were the colour of a milk bottle. Stripping down to my swimming costume would allow Jasper to make comparisons. No matter how slim I'd become, I had given birth to two children. How frumpy I would look in my sturdy one-piece beside Renée's teeny weeny bikini. 'No, no, you run along with Daddy,' I said through what was left of my dentition.

I then watched in horror as Renée captured Ruby's other hand in her own. My daughter was skipping along between them, oblivious to the way her mother's stomach was churning sourly at the sight. Numb with anxiety, I sat slumped, tearing holes in the paper tablecloth.

'I look a total boofhead, I know.' The voice was Lockie's. He was squirming in a starched white shirt which showed off his broad chest and chiselled musculature. His jeans, I noted, were ironed, and his hair uncharacteristically free of salt and sand.

In my short time in Australia I had noticed that Aussies, humble and self-deprecating by national decree, always run themselves down as a way of asking for praise. 'I look like a total dickhead in this, doan I?', or 'A total knob-jockey could have done a better job than me, right?' and, according to Susie: 'You've been to bed with much better-equipped guys, yeah?' This is the cue for lavish reassurance, which will then be declined for an hour or so.

'I'm sticking out like a dog's balls, aren't I?' Lockie tried again.

'No. *That's* what we call a total boofhead.' I pointed down to the sand where Renée was using the beach as a yoga studio. She splayed her legs in the Downward Dog and thrust her buttocks and groin about in the Sun Salutation. It struck me that the people who designed string bikinis have never studied anatomy. It's physically impossible for four triangles to cover anything bigger than a freckle. One thing was clear, there was no need for Renée to go swimming in the sea. The woman could just do laps in the drool deposited by passing males.

Lockie followed the direction of my gaze and peered at the semi-naked woman contorting her taut body though an origami of knots and stretches. 'Crikey. Do you think she's on something?'

'My husband's face, unfortunately.'

Jack McLachlan stopped squirming. He stood to attention, locating Jasper and Ruby in the crowd. 'I never comment on my friends' husbands, and I'm not going to break my rule for that piece of shit.'

'The science of beauty. Puh-lease. It's more like the science *fiction* of beauty,' I moaned as Renée crossed her lithe legs and placed her fingers in a yogic circle of energy. 'All of it's fake, you know. Looking so natural takes hours of maintenance,' I said, without conviction.

I watched as Jasper took Renée and Ruby's hands and they ran down towards the surf as though filming an advertisement for shampoo or life insurance. I could imagine the voiceover. 'You haven't lived until you've died with Mutual Life.' My facial features, reflected back to me from the club window, looked like the before advertisement for wrinkle cream. My husband was not coming back to me. I could feel the pressure of it, of my heart breaking, against my rib cage. I turned my head away so that Lockie couldn't see the tears. I had cried so much of late there was probably a water-proof mascara shortage in the southern suburbs. I still loved Jasper so passionately, but he'd consigned me to the box under the stairs where you keep old holiday snaps, and souvenirs which seemed a good idea at the time. I was nothing more than a sombrero or a Swiss chalet made from matchsticks. That's where he'd stored me in his mind, right next to the dust-covered rowing-machine.

'I think as surf club captain you'd better warn the jellyfish that Renée Craven is coming into the water. They could suffer from envenomation,' I said.

Lockie's calloused hand was warm on the back of my neck. 'I think you'll find that the main cause of death for vacuous anorexics is falling through cracks in the pavement,' he said, in a gallant effort to rally my spirits.

'Can't you take Renée to swim somewhere where there are stingers? She'd look so good with raised welts all over that fake tan of hers. I'd also get to piss on her to stop the pain . . . But would the poison kill her? What about stingrays? An unwary swimmer could hit one and the tail would whip up, driving in the barb, like poor Steve Irwin. And what about stonefish? They're camouflaged brown, aren't they? That tough, warty skin, covered in slime, has all those lethal spines. If she steps on one of those, the pain is not just severe, but she'll become frantic and delirious and could die . . . Or, better still, take her where she'll stand on a sea urchin. If the spine breaks off in the wound she could get tetanus, right? No, diving would be better. If you made her descend too quickly, she'd get an air embolism for sure, causing unconsciousness with a very high probability of drowning. Or, hey, what about sea snakes? It's a relatively painless bite but is often followed by drowsiness, visual disturbances and then breathing problems, correct . . . ? What are you looking at? You're shocked I could be so cold-blooded, right?'

'No. I'm shocked that one of my students has been bloody well listening in class!'

Dismayed by how the day was unfolding, but

masochistically drawn to the scene of the disaster, I found myself pushing up from the table and skulking towards the beach. Seeing two people so in love, so united in mutual adoration, made me experience something I'd never felt before – nausea to the point of projectile vomiting.

Tally had appeared on the beach, too, in time for Ruby's party. She'd broken up with Spider and was now draped over the arm of a rap artist called Fang. (Chook, Spider, Fang – my daughter obviously chose all her boyfriends from some maximum-security petting zoo.) At the sight of her father, Tally's brittle manner melted. She reverted before my eyes into a bubbly young girl. '*Dad*!' She flung herself at him as though he'd just come back from a ten-year imprisonment with FARC. Tally glanced from Jasper to Renée, her face flushing elusive expressions. But the chief emotion was adoration for her dad. As she hugged him, her thin T-shirt slipped, disclosing her pale and delicate shoulder. A sudden, sweet stab of love ambushed me.

Ruby bolted towards me. 'Mum. Guess what! Dad says I can go and stay with him in the city! He's living near where he works, which is why he's been away! And Aunty Renée is staying there! She's bought me an iPod and is going to make cup cakes! This is the best birthday ever!'

I put my sunglasses on, even though the sun had gone behind a cloud.

'Tally, dah-ling, you look fabulous,' Renée chirped. 'And who's your handsome young man?'

I looked at Fang's face, embroidered with acne. The swagger and grunting insolence, the nipple ring, the artfully revealed waistband of his undies and 'lick me' tattoo – I don't think 'handsome' quite captured it.

'You're into rap now, are you, Tally?' Renée said, nodding at Fang's Snoop Doggy Dog T-shirt. 'I have a leather jacket and some boots which would look sooooooooo much better on you.'

The woman should buy lip balm in bulk so she could kiss even more ass.

'If there're ever any gigs in town you two would like to go to, you'd be welcome to stay over.'

To me, Renée's wet, tangled hair resembled a writhing mass of eels. I told myself that it took forty-two facial muscles to frown and only four to stretch out my arm and bitch-slap the witch. Surely my clever daughter would see through her sycophancy.

Tally made a fist and jerked her elbow back hard, the miasma of teenage apathy momentarily pierced. 'Yes!' As she excitedly turned to me for an answer, I noticed that she was wearing a full face of foundation and her eyes were kohl-rimmed.

'Tally, I can't believe the muck you have all over your face,' I said without thinking.

'Oh, so I'm not allowed to wear make-up now? Why? Because you don't want me to be, like, hotter than you? It's my body and I can do what I want with it.'

'Darling, it's just that your skin is flawless. Why clog it with make-up?'

143

'It's medicated make-up for spots,' she hissed, confrontationally.

'Oh, OK,' I backed down. It was clear that my only use to my daughter was in the being born department. Oh, and that I'm the only one who always seems to know where the sticky tape is. Otherwise, I had dwindled to barely a blip on her radar.

'I like it,' undermined Renée, with the poisonous charm of a cobra. 'It's only bronzer, after all.'

'Mum, Mum!' Ruby squealed elatedly. 'Can we stay at Dad's? We can, can't we?!'

I thought of all the times I'd cleaned up their sick at two in the morning. The times I'd stuck out my hand in restaurants so they could spit out some offending vegetable. The peestained shoelaces I'd unknotted with my *teeth*. The number of times I'd taken the blame for the out-of-date letters scrunched at the bottom of school satchels saying how vital it was that I sign the permission slips for school trips that had taken place *weeks before*. The 1,095 meals I cooked per year. The six hundred packed lunches, the 3,764 snacks. The endless special banquets for birthdays. The flocks of sheep I'd roasted, the acres of toast I'd buttered, the five hundred miles I'd ironed – and then I took the cigarette from Fang's mouth and drew back on the foul fumes.

'Mum!' Tally scolded, belligerently. 'You can't smoke in front of Ruby. That is, like, so irresponsible.'

'Oh, OK. So can I take arsenic instead?' I could hear my voice spiralling up into a shriek.

'Can we stay at Dad's, Mum? Can we?!' Ruby's nose twitched eagerly. Tally clutched on to her father's arm ferociously, her knuckles strained white with the effort of not letting him go.

One thing was for sure. When fate closes one door . . . she crushes your foot in the door-jamb of another.

'I'll think about it,' I said. Meaning – OVER MY DEAD BODY.

CHAPTER 11

BEWARE OF SUDDEN DROP OFF

The trouble with saying that you'd only permit something 'over your dead body' is that a teenage daughter tends to take it too literally.

'I wish you'd just die!' Tally screamed at me when I told the kids they couldn't stay the night in the city with their father. She disappeared to her bedroom and, apart from the occasional raid on my purse or the fridge, I obviously wouldn't see her again until she was old enough to borrow my car.

I knew it was illogical. I felt furious that Jasper didn't see his kids. But then I resented him when he wanted to see them. Why was he suddenly interested in them *now*?

'Hey, want a child-friendly dad? Then get divorced. It's only when those dipshits can't have what they want that they realize they want it,' Susie advised. 'Blackmail the bastard. Tell him when he pays you some more maintenance, he can have some more kiddie time.'

'This weekend is not convenient for me,' I told Jasper when he rang, an hour later.

'I've been so busy getting to grips with the new job, co-ordinating coaching for all those teams. But now things have settled down a bit, I should be able to see my kids when I have time, Lucy. Not just when it's convenient for you. My access should be when it's convenient for us both.'

'Oh really?' I fumed down the phone. 'Well, it wasn't particularly convenient for me when you started shagging my best friend and moved out now, was it?'

I tried to explain to Tally that I couldn't let them stay with their father because Ruby was too young to understand that he'd left me for Renée. 'I broached the subject by asking your little sister if she knew what flirtation meant. And do you know what she said, Tally? That flirtation is how they make water safe to drink because it removes sand, oysters and kayakers.'

'You're just jealous because Renée is capable and interesting. That's what Dad says.'

Tally's words wounded me to the core. They also made me rethink my attitude to stem-cell research. As punishment for not allowing her to stay at her father's place, Tally stopped talking to me. She would only communicate by eyebrow movements. The girl was so morose and withdrawn, people presumed she was deaf and started frantically signing to her on their fingertips. 'Do . . . you want . . . cake?' waitresses would mouth, assuming Tally was lip-reading. She had dentists and shop assistants Marcel Marceau-ing their way through

147

conversations with her all over the Sutherland Shire.

I tried to ignore her and just get on with showing my girls how capable and interesting I was . . . a plan which immediately backfired when my car got a flat tyre on Kurnell Road.

'Speech happens not to be Tally's native tongue,' I explained to Lockie the first time he met my oldest daughter. I was standing there, car manual in hand, staring at the flat tyre (you'd have thought I was trying to teach myself how to dismantle a nuclear reactor), when Lockie cruised to a halt in his utility truck, called a Ute. (Abbreviation is the norm down under. Mozzie, cossie, sickie, brickie – it's just too hot to say the whole word.) I recognized him by the way he drove – one hand on the wheel, so that he could change radio stations, wave at people and ruffle his kid's hair.

'Of late, my daughter's got the communication skills of a shrub. If you put her in the sun, she'd photosynthesize,' I joked, embarrassed by her sullen silence, as Lockie jacked up our car.

Enigmatic emotions flickered across my oldest daughter's face, but it was certain that none of them were consolatory.

How many electricians does it take to change a light bulb? *Please continue to hold. Your call is very important to us.*

The other obstacle in my path to proving my capability was that everything in our rented house seemed broken. Including the real-estate agent, who was in rehab. Things had got so bad, I was defrosting frozen mince in the clothes dryer because my microwave was on the blink. My only DIY technique was to spray anything which didn't move in WD-40, whatever the hell that was. Or to just move house.

When the fuse box blew and we were reduced to feeling our way around the house by Braille, and not one electrician I phoned was available until, oh, the next millennium, it was Lockie who dropped by, torch in hand, to fiddle with the fuse box.

Tally's response to his kindness was to give the man a look which could freeze a melting glacier.

'She doesn't mean to be rude. It's just that teenagers don't speak our language. You need those little United Nations headphones to decipher them. "*You are just soooooooooo embarrassing*" means "I have a pimple and I'm mortified." "*I wish I were dead*" means "If I act suicidal I will get out of homework." And your basic "*EEEEkkkkkkkkk-urghh*" means "If you'd been nicer to Dad he never would have left us."'

Light flooded the house. It had been easier to talk to Jack McLachlan in the dark. I felt exposed, suddenly, and awkward. 'Thanks. I'll have to send away for the *Abandoned Wife Manual*. I'm sure it's full of handy DIY tips for those whose wedding vows said "From Here to Eternity . . . or Till Someone Hotter Comes Along".'

149

'Eternity? Now there's a bloody awful thought,' Lockie deadpanned. 'I mean, where's it all going to end?'

But when Ruby stopped talking to me as well, the stereophonic sulking made me relent. But I did take some revenge on Renée. I encouraged Ruby to leave her descant recorder at her father's place, so that she'd have something to play when she was staying over. Oh, and her violin, too. The bagpipes would be an excellent instrument to take up also, I recommended. I then gave Ruby a little lecture on helping Dad to set the table. Forks on the left and . . . knives in Renée's back.

The first Saturday morning I woke up without my children was the most wretched of my life. So often I had ached with exhaustion from doing all the cooking, cleaning, mending, house maintenance and homework. How I had pined for some time alone. But now that my nest was empty, I didn't know what to do with myself. I wandered around their bedrooms, touching toys and books. The silence roared at me. Is it any wonder that mothers find it hard to let go? For fifteen years I'd fed the girls when I felt hungry. Made them go to bed when I felt tired. Layered them in coats when I was cold, and stripped layers off again when I felt warmer.

I tried to distract myself with reading, but instead of devouring the Booker Prize shortlist, I invariably found my nose buried in tomes with titles like *Why Marriages Fail and How You Can*

150

Make Yours Last, Women Who Love Too Much, Opening Our Hearts to Men, Intimate Terrorism until my head was spinning. Was Jasper a New Weak Man or a Lost Warrior?

When my children finally boomeranged back to me on Sunday evening on the train from the city, I was ravenous for reports. I had to bite my lip not to cross-examine both my girls under a bright light with a stenographer. 'So . . . how was Dad?' I found myself asking in a thin, pathetic voice, as I peeled the spuds. 'What was he wearing?' Followed by a casual, 'Did he look tired?' And a more high-pitched, '*Did he look happy*?' I tried to read between their lines to discover if Renée was finally starting to annoy Jasper. The woman made Martha Stewart look slovenly. Put it this way – she washes soap. Surely perfection was beginning to pall?

As Ruby babbled about Daddy's beautiful apartment right on the harbour, I bit my lip. 'The roof has a pool and a Jacuzzi and there's a house-cleaner who comes every day!' At that revelation I nearly bit my lip right through. 'Mum, it's just like a hotel! There are ten pillows on each bed!' Surely by the time Renée took all the Italian linen pillows and lace throws and tasteful ornaments off the duvet, she'd be too exhausted for sex? I also seethed about the expense of such luxuries. Jasper had put me on the equivalent of a crash diet. It was financial bulimia really: he over-indulged while I threw up from stress. Jasper got to buy the girls treats – iPods and leather jackets – whereas I only got to buy them the dull daily stuff, like pencils, pasta and underpants. It made Jasper look so much more generous, whereas I was listing lopsidedly when I walked due to the 262 discount petrol vouchers in my handbag. As far as Tally was concerned, I was a stingy, mingy mum, hell-bent on ruining her social life because I wouldn't give her a proper allowance like, say, Paris Hilton. Whereas her father always turned up with armfuls of expensive presents and tickets to Cirque du Soleil.

After dinner, I lifted Ruby's suitcase lid gingerly, as if a hurried move could wake the terrible rage within me. And there were all her clothes, washed and ironed. I was aghast. Not just at the fact that Renée had shown a maternal instinct, but at the thought of my daughters' clothes swirling around in her high-tech, brand-new washing-machine with all those soiled sheets soaked in adulterous juices. I was appalled to think of my daughters' smalls mingling with the knickers of my nemesis.

When the girls wanted to go to their father's place the following weekend, I told myself over and over that their need to see Jasper didn't represent disloyalty to me. I chanted it like a mantra. Through gritted teeth. I didn't want the kids to have to take sides, so I didn't criticize Renée or Jasper in front of them. However furious I felt, I didn't sob and slam doors until they were at school. But, once they were out of earshot, my own house could have taken out a restraining order on me.

When Ruby started dressing like Renée and using her expressions, 'Dah-ling, I nearly *died*,' I had to pop a Valium. When I got a note from Renée ticking me off for having given Ruby a sip of my coke on the drive in to Point Piper, apparently the reason why she'd been too hyperactive to sleep that night, she made me feel as if I'd stuck a lighted cigarette into my daughter's mouth. I thought of writing a note back, but felt that a prod with a soldering iron might be a more appropriate response.

When Cronulla primary school wrote to Jasper, querying Ruby's erratic performance in school, the letter Renée wrote to the teacher, and which the teacher sent on to me, blamed an escalating incidence of childhood depression on the amount of junk food mothers allowed their children to eat. I wrote my own letter to the teacher. 'Ruby's depressed because her father left us for an anorexic harridan who doesn't eat but uses some kind of osmotic process involving only low-cal water and UV-screened light.'

But it was only when Renée dropped Ruby off one Sunday, and she, Ruby and Ruby's doll were all wearing identical Pucci dresses that I was really tempted to kill. I was supposed to be mastering DIY to look more capable and independent, but my only pressing concern was to wonder which kitchen appliance could be used as a deadly weapon against my husband's lover – and be made to look like an accident. Did the local hardware store sell a Shallow Grave Shovel? But even if such a tool existed, would I be able to afford it?

The battle of the sexes has always been waged in the economic arena. The novels of George Eliot, Jane Austen, Henry James and Wilkie Collins depict how women were traditionally kept in place by a lack of money. The plots of *Middlemarch, Pride and Prejudice, The Wings of a Dove* and so many others fall apart when you remove inheritance, property, money and wills. When I rang our accountant in England to discover that Jasper, in an adroit piece of financial machination, had spirited away our savings, most of which had been in his name and included the rent for our Hampstead house, I realized that I had now become a character in a Victorian novel. At charity fundraisers Jasper had always been the first to put his hand in his pocket. Now he just forgot to take it out again. If we ever did divorce, I had a feeling that he'd get the Wedgwood and the Royal Doulton. And me? The paper plates.

There was nothing for it but to earn my own money. Ten years out of the physiotherapy profession meant re-training. In the interim I would take part-time jobs. I drew the line at organ farming and prostitution, but apart from that I wasn't being particularly picky. When I leafed dispiritedly through the Work Wanted section of the local paper and found that the only jobs on offer ranged from Portaloo servicewoman to earthworm farmer's assistant or colonic therapist, the possibilities for feeling sorry for myself rapidly increased. Was I too old for a paper round? After being rejected from eight job interviews in a row because I was a single mother (the maternal wall is the new glass ceiling), car windscreen squeegee-ing on street corners was fast becoming my only employment possibility. I finally found a short-term job as a deodorant tester, which basically meant sniffing armpits for ten dollars an hour. Now I just had to find a way of asking for a five-year advance on my salary. While I was at it, maybe I could suggest to the research group that they run some experiments using snobby English interior decorators instead of lab rats – as there's so much less chance of becoming attached to them. Now that I'd pay *them* for.

'How you doin'?' Lockie asked when he found me lapping manically up and down the local Olympic pool.

'Oh, I'm coping. I really am. OK, I've been hiding under the dock beside my husband's harbour penthouse all weekend listening to Renée playing with my kids, and I've been through their garbage to see what they're drinking (vintage Krug) and what they're eating (lobster). But I haven't been given an injunction not to go within a ten-mile radius of their residence, so that's a step on the road to recovery, right?'

Lockie's solution to my empty nest despondency was to train me harder. With the first test for the bronze medallion in one week, he had me training in the water so often I could have been declared an environmentally protected wetland habitat. I wasn't what you'd call a natural athlete. I spoke about my two-mile jog, a soft sand run up the beach followed by a short medley of bench-presses, the way mountaineers talk about K2.

'Oh God, OK, so what torture have you got planned for me today, Jack?' I asked, when he appeared at my door early that childless Saturday morning. 'Windsurfing to Fiji? Abseiling Mount Kosciuszko? Walking on hot coals?'

'Scuba diving. I'm a dive-master.'

'Oh yes, what a joy! Dressing up in a rubber bat-suit, dragging twenty pounds of incredibly heavy equipment around on my back, before plummeting over the side of a boat into the black, cold, jellyfish-teeming sea, only to have to drag it all back up on board again an hour later. It's just way, way too much like marriage for my liking,' I explained.

But he press-ganged me aboard his beloved boat. 'If you do find yourself swimming with sharks, make sure it's out of preference rather than by misfortune. If it's by accident – make sure you are swimming like hell away from the teeth end.'

'That's it? That's your entire safety drill?' I asked, peering over the side of his boat, anchored in the mouth of the Port Hacking River.

'The sharks are more scared of you than you are of them. Humans are their only predator. Do you know how many people are eaten by sharks compared to how many are, say, electrocuted in their own homes?'

'That is *not* comforting. Since attempting my own DIY, I electrocute myself in my own home on a daily basis,' I pleaded, dismally.

'Well, if you're gonna panic, panic now,' Lockie replied, an amused twinkle in his eye. 'Because once you are under the water nobody can hear you scream.'

When we plopped over the side, at first I felt calm as I watched the silvery garfish, shimmying sea mullet, darting whiting, bream, flathead, leather-jackets, electric stingrays, and butterfly fish going about their day-to-day lives, without a care in their weightless world. I felt I'd merely dived into the fish tank in my dentist's waiting room. But when a huge groper skulked out of the shadows, I scratched Lockie's leg for getting me into this.

Lockie scrawled a sardonic message on his waterproof pad, 'You really don't want to scratch me as blood only attracts the sharks and you'll be eaten alive.'

I screamed, but, of course, nobody could hear me. Story of my life.

The day of the bronze medallion written examination arrived. I had pored over the sacred surf lifesaving texts as diligently as any Talmudic scholar. On our practice swim that morning, I was buoyant with excitement. This would show my girls that I was just as capable, independent and interesting as Renée. Nothing could dampen my spirits. Not even the four trillion gallons of the Pacific Ocean. Or so I thought . . .

It was the voice I heard first. Renée's voice could open a can of tuna. I jerked my head upwards. The brittle morning sunshine sliced into my eyes but I could still see my adversary. She was mincing into the sports equipment area beneath the club wearing an athletic two-piece swimming costume. When I realized she was carrying flippers and goggles, I did a double-take worthy of a pantomime dame.

'What the hell are you doing here?' Susie said on my behalf, as my own tongue seemed stuck to the roof of my mouth. Jasper was Velcroed to Renée's side as usual. He was wearing board shorts – a towel casually knotted around his neck. His toned body was tanned butterscotch brown. I ached to touch him. Whenever I saw his chocolate eyes and ready smile, I was suddenly wearing all my yearnings and desires on the outside, like the suckers of an octopus.

'I thought it would be sensible for me to take up surf life-saving,' Renée said, her absurdly over-sized sunglasses dwarfing her face. 'It will be a good way to bond with dear little Rubes, as I'll be seeing so much of her.'

There was a smug note of certainty in her tone which made my blood run cold.

'I'm so enjoying getting to know your adorable girls,' she said to Jasper in a piping voice laced with falsity.

'What a woman,' Jasper volunteered fondly. Renée smiled complacently at the compliment, as if it were her due.

I was very restrained. After all, I didn't stuff my surfboard up her nose.

'Um . . .' Jasper cleared his throat, realizing that I craved a list of Renée's attributes about as much as I longed for a George Bush and Robert Mugabe nude sandwich with me as the filling. 'That's very thoughtful of Renée, don't you think? She's already filled in the forms. As you know the club so well, do you think you could hand them in to the right person, Lucy?' He thrust the official papers towards me. While Jasper was reunited with a gleeful Ruby, I scanned the admission form. Renée had only partially filled it in. I grabbed a pencil and under 'profession' added *female impersonator*. Under 'sex', instead of ticking a box, I scrawled *only with other people's husbands*.

As I climbed the stairs to Lockie's office, I comforted myself with the thought that Renée would never survive as a club member. I mean, if the woman ever ended up lost at sea in a lifeboat, the other passengers would eat her on the first day, even if land was in sight . . . just because she's so damn annoying. But what was I worried about? Renée was English, making her as competent in the water as Robert Maxwell. She probably had an inflatable pool toy around her waist this very second . . . I looked out the upstairs club windows and saw Jasper frolic into

159

the waves with Ruby – where Renée was turning somersaults like a dolphin.

Despondent, I dragged myself downstairs to put away our rescue boards. Fifteen minutes later I headed for the shower room. Susie was already there, reciting radio calls in preparation for the theory test we were about to sit. I had just peeled off my one-piece, spraying sand and seaweed from my chafed body, when Renée stomped in. I lunged for a towel, knocking Susie backwards. Renée was clutching her sabotaged admission form, which Lockie had obviously rejected.

'Is this your idea of a joke? You know that Jasper is quite worried about your erratic behaviour. I explained to him that you are obviously menopausal. Is your friend going through the menopause, too?' She indicated Susie, who was picking herself up from the floor. 'Gives new meaning to the word "changing-room",' she chortled.

With the speed and accuracy of an Exocet missile, Ruby burst in and flung herself into my arms, making me drop my towel. 'Good luck, Mummy! In the exam!' My youngest daughter always talked in exclamation marks, although no grammatical term for punctuation could accurately express the beguiling blend of love and optimism in her sweet voice.

'Thanks, darling.' I groped for terry towelling as Renée appraised my body with a calculating eye.

'Can I have a chocolate milkshake and a burger with Ryan?'

'Yes, honey. My money's in my purse in the locker . . .' Ruby, bubbling with glee, had bounced out of the changing-room before I finished my sentence.

'Chocolate?' Renée reacted as though the request had been for heroin. 'Won't that put her on a sugar high?' She tapped her pedicured toes with irritation. 'Does she have many allergic reactions? I need to know, as I'll be making so many of her meals. I hope you breast-fed her, at least. *I'm* a total lactivist . . . Otherwise it increases their chances of becoming fat.' If Renée had her way, foetuses would be put on a diet in the womb. I would have said something along these lines except I was too busy concentrating on my Houdini-like contortions beneath the towel as I struggled to climb into my clothes unseen. 'As for all these reports of Ruby being disruptive at school? Well, she's obviously been watching too many cartoons. There's scientific proof that it will lower her IQ. Mind you, having a stay-at-home mother could also be what's made her clingy and needy. I mean how can a girl ever become independent with that kind of role-model?'

'Gee, it's a wonder I knew how to give birth. That thing YOU'VE NEVER DONE!' I snapped at her. In my agitation and distraction, I accidentally found myself facing her with one leg threaded through my knicker-elastic, balancing like a flummoxed flamingo.

Renée took in my unwaxed pudenda and baby-marked belly before answering tightly, 'You see? That's how little you know me.' Her fake smile narrowed. 'You have no idea how I've longed for a child.'

'Only when you needed your chimney cleaned.'

'You pretended to be my best friend, but you never knew me at all.'

I pretended to be *her* best friend? If table-turning were an Olympic category, she'd win gold. I felt I'd been doused in cold water all over again.

'You never asked me if I wanted children. You moaned and whined about how stressful it was being a mother, completely unaware that I would have given anything to have a child.' I withered in the splenetic stare of my vendettist. 'Especially a little girl. So I could love her the way I was never loved . . .' She suppressed a self-indulgent sob. 'But no, I was just a cliché to you. Successful, single career woman.'

Renée hadn't been a caricature to me once upon a time, but she was now. My loathing of the woman had turned her into Cruella de Vil. She looked positively under-dressed without a Dalmatian coat. It was hard to imagine her having any genuine emotion. 'You would make Medea look like good mother material.'

Renée's expression became vinegary. 'Still, why bother to breed when you've done it for me?' Her voice was high-pitched and brittle. Clichéd? No, my reaction to her was more extreme than that.

She was now a cartoon character – the Evil Empress of Planet Zardore. 'This way I get all the delights of a ready-made family without . . .' she looked my naked body up and down with repulsion, 'ruining my body.' Her toenail varnish was chip-free, her heels pumiced. Whereas I hadn't even shaved the hairs off my big toes.

She gave another cartoonish sigh. 'You know, Jasper hasn't found you attractive for years. He said that after sex he would roll off you thinking, "Well, there's plenty of room in there." It felt like an aircraft hangar. What did he call it? Oh, yes. "Touching the void." Whereas *I* am honeymoon fresh.'

Her words bit into me. 'Jasper would never say anything so horrible! You liar! You must really hate me, Renée. But why? What did I ever do to you?'

'Oh not much. Just flaunted your life in my face. Perfect house. Perfect husband. Perfect children. And look at you. If *you* could have it all, why couldn't I?'

The green-eyed monster had swallowed her whole and turned her into a Psychic Vampire. 'That just proves you will never be a mother to my girls. You're far too selfish. You don't have enough compassion to fill a . . .' I couldn't think of anything small enough. 'A gnat's navel.'

'Hey, Renée,' Susie added, savagely, moving to my side in a protective manner. 'If you ever do breed, may we have one of your puppies? I mean you're bound to have a litter . . . being such a bitch.'

Renée's eyes glinted like metal. She flounced

163

from the changing-room, swinging her pert derrière. Susie cheered, feeling we'd triumphed in the skirmish. But sitting in the examination room trying to concentrate on multiple-choice questions about sprains and strains, I had a terrible feeling this was just an initial exchange of fire in what was about to become a very ugly battle.

Renée Craven was the opposite of a cuckoo which lays eggs in another mother's nest. She'd not just stolen my mate and my financial nest egg, but was now determined to appropriate my chicks.

Q – Why did the menopausal woman cross the road?

A – To kill the chick who stole her bloody husband.

CHAPTER 12

BEWARE OF SHALLOW WATER WHEN DIVING

In the Top Ten Justifiable Reasons for Killing Your Husband, his turning up to your children's speech day with the woman for whom he left you is numero uno.

Presentation Day induces severe PDB (Presentation Day Bum) from sitting through the interminable assembly. This is an annual prize-giving for Most Improved Student, etc. Though more accurate categories would be Only Set Fire To His Farts Four Times In Science Class This Year and Best Excuse for Not Turning in Homework. ('Would you believe a super-evolved galactic being vaporized it?' had been Tally's most memorable effort.) As the ceremony dragged on, I pondered the fact that school speech days would be most effective in remote areas, like arctic base camps, when they've run out of sedatives and surgery is imperative. The threat of having to sit through a school speech day could also be used at Guantanamo Bay to obtain confessions. I'd take the blame for anything – assassinating Abraham Lincoln, even breaking up the Beatles – if it would get me the hell out of one.

One cheek had gone to sleep and the other buttock was beginning to prickle with pins and needles when I saw Jasper enter from the side door of the auditorium. My heart leapt against my Wonderbra and that familiar surge of electricity tingled through my body . . . Until I saw what he'd brought with him.

At the end of the ceremony, the parents mingled over cups of tea and cake. Jasper and Renée approached me. Renée was wearing a tailored Armani suit and non-prescription glasses for that sexy librarian look.

Jasper kissed me on both cheeks with the expression of a child rejecting Brussels sprouts. 'I'm surprised Ruby didn't win anything. She was always top of her class in England.'

'It's clear that your over-emotional response, psychological collapse, binge-drinking and refusal to deal with the realities is taking its toll,' was Renée's brittle précis of the situation. 'I'm sorry, Jasper. But that's what women in Lucy's state need – tough love,' she belittled.

'Maybe you do need a little rest,' Jasper said, gently, running his hands through his thick dark hair. 'I have put you through the most taxing ordeal. And I do feel so awfully guilty. You deserve so, so much more, Lucy. I can't believe how selfish I was, making you give up work when Ruby was born. You sacrificed your life for our family and

166

now it's my turn.' His face contorted with seriousness. 'I think it's only fair that the girls come to live with me for a while. You could have a break. Then you could get your career back on track. I do love our kids so much.'

The silence between us was so cavernous you could abseil down there with a miner's light. When I *did* find my power of speech, I burst out laughing. 'Yes, yes, you love your children so, so much that you'd do absolutely anything for them – except, of course, live under the same roof as their mother.'

I glared at Renée who was waiting in the conversational wings like a lipsticked raptor. '*She* put you up to this, didn't she?' Just as Renée had manipulated me without my realizing it, she was now puppet-mastering my husband. Yet he seemed to have no idea that he was in a relationship with strings attached.

'Renée feels just as bad as I do, don't you, darling? It's just that you've rung me so many nights, weeping that you can't cope on your own, and saying how exhausted you are and how difficult Tally has become that I feel it's my turn to take the load.'

'Oh, I see. And now, just when I'm starting to cope, you suddenly want more access. Great timing.'

'Not access,' Jasper's voice grew decisive. 'Custody.'

Now I really did guffaw. I was laughing so hard, Jasper had to steer me outside by my elbow. The school grounds overlook the shimmering ocean,

167

which was glittering in the sun as far as the eye could see. The tangy smell of salt filled the air. I took a few deep, restorative gulps before I could talk again. 'Jasper, you know nothing about children. When Tally was little and I asked you to take her to the nursery you went to a shop which sold pot plants. You've never made a crocodile head out of four egg-boxes or a space helmet out of loo rolls at short notice.'

'But he's never been arrested for illegal driving, either,' interrupted Renée, viperishly. 'Lucy, I don't think you've quite understood that when you get a note under your wind-screen saying "Parking Fine", this is not a complimentary comment on your driving skills.'

'Um . . . Yes, about that,' Jasper harrumphed. 'As the Holden was bought in my name, all the fines were sent to me.'

'But that was your fault for not paying the registration and insurance.' My voice went almost falsetto with fury.

'We don't live together any more. The car is your responsibility now. And just more proof that you're not coping.'

I gawped at Jasper. What was wrong with my husband? He'd obviously headed too many soccer balls over the years and got brain damage.

'Not to mention the near-drowning incident. Ruby told me how she had to be rescued.' Jasper folded his hands ministerially. 'I really can't have my children put in such a dangerous situation. It's not like you to be so negligent, Lucy. You're obviously exhausted.'

I felt translucent, like those pictures of magnified amoebas I'd seen on nature programmes. And just like a giant jellyfish, I felt sure that, despite my bravest efforts not to look terrified, Renée could see right through me.

'Negligent? Me? Who got up every two hours when the girls had fevers, to administer paracetamol? Who ran cold baths for them at three in the morning to bring down their temperatures? Who cleans up their projectile vomits at dawn? Who runs trays up to their bedrooms thirty times a day for a stubbed toe? Your solution to Ruby's colic was to buy earplugs! Can you tell their temperatures to within a .0001 margin of error by just placing your hand on their foreheads? No. But I can! You wouldn't even know they'd contracted a flesh-eating bacteria until their limbs fell off!'

'Forget limbs, it's Ruby's grades which are dropping off. I'm also worried about her diet. And then there's the amount of television she watches. Not to mention Tally's truanting.'

'Excuse me. But you've always been a parachute dad – cherry-picking the fun parts of parenting. *I'm* the one who's done all the grunt work. Whenever it was time to change a nappy or help with homework, you would disappear into the toilet with the entire *Guinness Book of Records Sporting Feats* in seven volumes. How many tissues do you have in your pockets, right now, for example?'

'What? None. Why?'

'Well, I have three packets, for runny noses and sticky fingers. You would just tell them to use their sleeves, am I right?'

Parents were beginning to trickle out of the auditorium so Jasper propelled me brusquely through the school gates and on to the pavement.

'I'm not saying you've been a bad mother, Lucy. But you've taken your eye off the ball. I know I'm partly to blame. And I'm sorry. But this is the reality of our lives now and we must put the children first.'

'Hello? Who gave birth exactly, you or me? Although come to think of it, men would be so good at labour. Your brain is so minuscule that you'd feel far less pain, like a prawn.'

Jasper glanced at Renée as if this were proof of my mental degeneration. 'A p-r-a-w-n?' he repeated, as though I were a toddler.

'Yes, you can boil them alive and they don't feel a thing, apparently. I mean, you obviously didn't feel anything when you left me for That Woman and abandoned your offspring.'

A dark car sharked around the corner of the boulevard on two screeching wheels. This hotted-up vehicle was as macho as an automobile could get without actually growing a penis as a hood ornament. All it needed was a gold chain, some chest hair, a few sideburns and a pec or two to win Mr Universe. The muffler was so unmuffled that one rev could blow out residential windows and cause shingles to fly off roofs. The car was crammed with dark-haired boys who were craning out of their side windows to wolf-whistle a stunning, blonde sex kitten in a tight black mini-skirt and low-cut T-shirt. I put on my prescription sunglasses for a better look. My heart skipped a beat when I realized it was my own darling daughter.

'Hey, Skippy, suck my cock!' one of the boys yelled out the window at Tally.

'Everyone is right! Your mother should have swallowed!' my daughter shouted back before giving him the finger.

Jasper winced. 'I had no idea when I rented here that the area was so working-class.' Squaring his shoulders he strode to his daughter's aid.

Renée's mouth was pursed with disapproval. 'If the girls lived with us, they'd meet a better class of people,' she said sniffily.

Renée grew up with people who pronounce off as awf and gone as gorrrrn. I'd met her family and awfullys and frightfullys detonated through their conversation like land mines. They said loo 'pepper' and 'abite the hice'. 'There's no loo pepper abite the hice, it's awfully frightful.' If my girls lived with Renée they'd be socializing with boys called Theodore and Enoch and Thisby – Peregrine – Fortescue – the Third. Suddenly Chook, Fang and Spider were looking a whole lot more attractive. At least Australians don't believe in class. Just ratbags and non-ratbags.

The car gave a low, sexual growl before disappearing in a fug of exhaust fumes. 'What kind of homes do these people come from?' Renée shuddered. 'I hate to think of the violent upbringings they've had.'

'Well, don't you worry, Renée,' I joshed. 'I only hit my children in self-defence.'

Renée looked down her nose-job at me. 'Oh, I would never hit a child,' she replied, scandalized.

If the woman spoke to me again I felt I would burst inward, just implode, like a diver crushed by the weight of the deep water. 'I'm joking. It's a joke. Tell her, Jasper. Have I ever hit either of the girls?'

Jasper was walking back to us, his arm protectively around Tally. He was looking at me as though he'd never met me before. 'I just don't know what to think any more, Lucy.'

I watched in pain as Tally sank into his fatherly embrace. She refused to hug or kiss me now. If she had to touch me at all, it was with as much enthusiasm as you'd embrace a plutonium-riddled Russian spy.

Renée beamed at Tally. The woman was positively floating on air, whereas I was scuttled, a sinking ship, a wreck. 'I will never give up my children,' I seethed quietly to her. 'My children are everything to me. They're my entire life. Isn't it enough you stole my husband?'

'The girls make Jasper happy. And what makes him happy makes me happy. Besides, I always knew I'd make a wonderful mother.'

I glared at her, aghast. 'You remind me of my old friend Renée, except she had a heart.' What I recalled now was Renée's trademark look of sympathy but also what I had occasionally glimpsed *behind* the sympathy but had chosen to ignore – a look of hungry anticipation.

'Haven't you hurt me enough? Do you think this is fair?' I gasped.

'Fair? No. But what's important is to win. If winning isn't the point of the game then why do they keep score?'

I saw Susie striding towards me then from the school auditorium. 'Get a wriggle on, woman. It's bronze medallion day. Don't tell me you've bloody well forgotten?'

In all the emotional upheaval it had slipped my mind that Lockie had scheduled Friday afternoon for our practical test.

'Oh Mummy. How exciting!' Ruby radiated enthusiasm like a heater. You could toast marshmallows on her. 'We can cheer you on! Can't we, Daddy?'

All I could think about was the horror of Jasper seeing me in the surf lifesaver outfit. The red and yellow patrol cap which tied under the chin was set off nicely by a matching lycra, long-sleeved top. The colours were so toxic it looked as though I'd fallen into a chemical spill. The sort of chemical spill which causes you to sprout an extra head. Renée and Jasper exchanged cynical glances. They obviously thought I knew as much about surf lifesaving as a fungus knows about nuclear physics . . . Or a married woman about her husband.

Anaesthetized with disbelief, I followed Susie to the club changing-rooms, regurgitating the conversation I'd just had with Renée and Jasper.

'What a joke! There's no bloody way that'll ever happen. He's talking out of his arse. Crikey, my old man was more worried about who would get custody of the dope plants than the kids. And the ten hanging baskets. Mind you, they were pretty, those geraniums and petunias. Should have been pansies, really,' she said in an effort to raise my spirits. 'Anyway, he fought me so furiously over custody of the flowers, it was the War of the Roses. Literally,' she snorted. 'My solicitor said that the paramount consideration should be the best interests of the plants. Did the defendant ever talk to the plants? No. Was he reliable or would we need to appoint a plant welfare officer?' Suzie placed a steadying hand on my arm. 'It'll be the same with your kids. There's no way that hypocritical ratbag will get custody.'

'I always thought Jasper would dispute custody of the cars and antique furniture. Not the children,' I muttered, shell-shocked, as we walked down to the water's edge to find Lockie standing firmly, his muscular legs in a V sign.

'I wish we could have reverse custody cases where my ex would take away that god-awful sofa his mother gave us. Still, one thing's for sure.

Do you know why divorces are so expensive? Because they're bloody well worth it.'

'Come along, girls.' Lockie tapped his stopwatch. 'You know the drill.' The drill was to paddle the board 'out the back' and rescue a volunteer.

The air had become very still, as if in anticipation. The inky sky in the south was bulging, fit to burst. I watched an incoming wave break at my feet, hissing like a snake. By the time the next one had reared up and collapsed in a spatter of spray, I could feel tears starting to well. The sea had turned snot green and choppy, as if it were being whisked from above by a demented, invisible chef. The wind carved huge escarpments before my eyes. I turned to see Ruby and Tally sitting on the hill with Jasper and Renée. Ruby gave me a cheering wave. Even Tally managed a half-hearted thumbs-up. Lockie blew his whistle and Susie and I launched our boards into the agitated ocean along with ten or so other pupils. The sand gave way to murky slate-grey water and then nothing but deep currents swirling beneath, full, in my imagination, of monstrous creatures with uncoiling tentacles.

There had been storm warnings on the radio, but no mention of the emotional gale which had blown me off course. No mood meteorologist had urgently interrupted the scheduled programme to forecast that Cyclone Renée was approaching. I had paddled far out where nobody could hear me have a category 9 meltdown. I was crying so much it took me a while to realize that the sky was weeping with me. The rain was torrential. Absorbed by my own anxieties, I paddled out too far and completely missed the poor man I was supposed to be rescuing.

'Hey! Front-bum! Over here!' My assigned volunteer waved his arms furiously in the air. I glimpsed him treading water through the forest of white crests as the dark waves curled and arched. I hate big waves. I hate big waves more than I hate terrorists. The turbulent tide was dragging me towards the rocky reef, which was no doubt made up of the skeletons of other English tourists who'd been stupid enough to attempt the bronze medallion. Stroking towards my target, I tried to ignore the lurching horizon and calm myself down. And maybe I would have rallied enough to complete the rescue. Except it was then I saw the fin. Panic constricted my trachea for longer than I feared healthy in a human being. The fin circled closer. Fishermen had reported seeing bull sharks and hammerheads further out. At least I had the rescue board to cling on to . . . A churning wave crashed down on me and, in my struggle through the squall of foam to the surface, the board was torn from my hands. I felt a tremor of nerves fizz along my spine. The only sound, my own stark, rapid breathing. Exhausted and treading water, I just froze. Oh well, at least I'd never again have to worry about finding the latest in shoe wear at a sale price, as pretty soon I *would have no feet*. As the shark torpedoed through the water towards me, I prayed to every God I could think of – Buddha, saints, Greek gods, Roman gods, Jesus, Hare Krishna, Muhammad . . . even, in my desperation, L. Ron Hubbard. If seeing a shark's fin slicing towards you does not make you wet your pants, then you have no pants – or bladder or brain, for that matter. What had I been thinking, hurling myself into a liquid environment known to be home to huge, irritated, aquatic entities with mouths the size of garbage trucks? Maybe Jasper was right. Maybe I *had* taken my eye off the ball? If I could put myself in such a dangerous position, what was to stop me doing the same with my two darling daughters?

When you're going to die, a lot of thoughts cross your mind. Firstly, the desperate hope that Shirley MacLaine is right about reincarnation. And secondly, all the things you've never done. My brain jumped from one missed opportunity to another. I'd never learnt a musical instrument. Well, not properly. Grade 1 glockenspiel didn't really count. I'd never read Proust. Or been in a threesome. God, I'd never even played doubles at tennis. I'd never had adventurous sex, say, in a broom cupboard. Or with a rock star. I'd never even been allowed backstage. Not even at Tally's eisteddfod, because my mobile rang during the performance. I'd never sky-dived. Not that I want to . . . But I'd like to think that I'd have time to at least chicken out of it at the last minute. I'd never gone on a protest march. I'd never tied myself to a tree or put a flower in a gun barrel, or burnt an effigy of a world leader. I wanted to learn astronomy and read the night sky. Hell, I hadn't yet seen the Aurora Borealis. Let alone a solar eclipse. I'd never ridden an elephant or swum with a dolphin. No, no. I just couldn't die yet. What about all the wonders of the world I'd never glimpsed? The Great Wall of China? The Taj Mahal? Machu Picchu in Peru? Brad Pitt naked? I wanted to stand on the International Date Line. Mind you, it'd be the only date I'd be able to get now that I was to be an amputee. Yes. A shark could really put a hole in your social life – not to mention your upper torso. It wasn't fair! I wanted to reach a hundred and get a telegram from the Queen. I wanted to live to be really old, so that I could get away with murder because I'm eccentric. And I knew exactly who I wanted to annihilate. That bloody, bloody bitch who stole my beloved husband and who got me into this bloody, bloody mess in the first frigging place.

When the flotation rescue device thwacked down in the water beside me, and club captain Jack McLachlan yanked me aboard the inflatable boat, I was expecting a Lockie-like telling off. But all he said was, 'We have to stop meeting like this.'

A swimmer who survives the ordeal of going 'out the back' is rewarded with the sight of herself vomiting up seaweed and extracting octopi from

178

her oesophagus. I had a raised welt the size of a fondue pot on my thigh. And my arms were rapidly turning the colour of an aubergine. I'd been in the water for so long that I was more wrinkled and bug-eyed than an extraterrestrial in a sci-fi movie. Oh, *that* would attract my husband.

'I'm afraid I have to fail you,' Lockie said, dejectedly, once we were back on the beach. I looked at the smear of sun block across the broad bridge of his broken nose. Whereas Jasper was lean, lithe and toned, Lockie looked like one of those heroes from a Hollywood epic – stern, tall, with muscled thighs, powerful shoulders and capable hands – a durable man. He'd stood by me – and I'd let him down. I breathed in shallow gasps. I wondered if this was how a fish felt, lying on the bottom of a bucket, mouth opening and closing, drowning in air.

The rain had blown north and the sun had burst out again. As Ruby left the shelter of the club veranda and pushed through the successful contestants to the inflatable boat, I felt humiliation staining my face and seeping down on to my neck. Renée was working her elbows like oars to get through the sea of people to my side, all the better to gloat. I figured now would be a good time to fake a terminal illness, say, Necrotizing Fasciitis or the bubonic plague. I tried to speak but I seemed to have a live eel half-way down my duodenum. 'But there was a shark . . . Didn't you see the s . . . s . . . shark?' I sputtered.

179

Renée canted an arched brow, her smile spackled on. 'Well, I had the binoculars and I think you'll find it was a fairy penguin.'

Ruby's face crumpled like a paper bag. Tally's lip was curling into its customary sneer. I was obviously a total disappointment to my children. I just hadn't lived up to my early potential. I was so embarrassed, all I could think of was which South American country I could flee to without a visa at short notice.

'Everyone else passed, even the Lebanese chappie. Never mind,' Renée purred, 'maybe we could organize a telethon to help you? Alcoholic failure needs a helping hand out of gutter.'

An English tourist out for a walk recognized Jasper from his old playing days and stopped for an autograph. Graciously obliging, Jasper quipped, 'It's been lovely, but I must get back to the team, to pass on some practical tips, such as . . .' he checked his watch, 'the fact that the game started five minutes ago,' he jested, dazzling everyone within earshot with his captivating charisma.

I hadn't won my bronze, but I'd definitely created a new world record for self-loathing. If self-assurance were elastic, I wouldn't have been able to make a garter for a canary. I felt certain I could hear the shark chuckling snidely through all seven million of its razor-sharp teeth.

'If it makes you feel any better, I failed too,' Susie placated, wringing out her hair. 'But only' cause I refuse to rescue any bloke who greets me with 'Tit's a nice day.' When the shit-for-brains patted my ass and told me it looked like I had a couple of wombats down my daks, I bloody well hit the bugger over the head. I bloody hope he *does* drown! Made me feel so much better. But what would make you feel better, darl?'

'Um, declare me legally dead and have my estate probated?'

I glanced up at my small family. Jasper had his arm around Ruby, kissing her goodbye, and Renée was rubbing sun block into Tally's arms. And they were all looking at me with pity.

And all I could think about was the need to invent a new Divorced Ken doll model. One who came with all of Barbie's kids.

CHAPTER 13

MOUTH-TO-MOUTH RESUSCITATION

There are four things you will never hear a teenager say.

1) I don't need money. I'm going to get a part-time job and be self-sufficient.
2) Can I get you a cup of tea after I've unpacked the dishwasher?
3) Drugs and sex are overrated. I'm going to pour my energy into learning Mandarin and algebra and studying the *Iliad*.
4) I don't want to go out with him again. An incredible physique, a Harley-Davidson and a recording contract are totally overrated.

What you will hear them say is:

1) If you talk to my boyfriend again I will kill you.
2) If you gave me a decent amount of

pocket money I wouldn't have been caught shoplifting.

3) I'm just having a few friends over. (Which translates as an open invitation to everyone under twenty-five in the free world.)

4) I HATE YOU. I hate it when you dance around the kitchen, singing along to songs you are way, way too old for. I hate it when you say 'cool'. It is *not* cool to say 'cool', OK? You are far too old to watch *America's Next Top Model*. It's sad. You are sad. Face it. You're old. I hate you. Why couldn't I have been born into a normal family? (Etc, etc, ad infinitum.)

An innovative parent resorts to different creative steps to deter male suitors. I played Bartók and operas, loudly. I kept the television welded to history and gardening programmes and hid the remote. I stocked the fridge with organic mung beans and urine samples. Basically I was armed with every kind of deterrent bar a short-range missile. But nothing would deflect Fang. He was as adhesive as a stay-fresh minipad. My dislike of Fang was subtle at first. I'd merely trip him backwards down the stairs and accidentally stand on his thorax whilst 'helping' him to his feet. But the trouble with flinging mud is that you only lose ground – the more I mistreated the creature, the more Tally adored him. I had no choice but to put out the welcome mat.

Even more hair-raising than her boyfriend was her shoplifting. As we waited outside the store detective's office at Miranda Fair shopping centre, I tried to convince myself that this was merely a sign of my daughter's assimilation to the convict capital of the world.

'At Sydney airport, when the customs official enquires if you have any prior convictions, that's just to ascertain whether you're criminal enough to be allowed in, right?' I beseeched Susie who was waiting with me.

'*Teenagers, are you tired of being harassed by stupid mothers? Well, act now. Move out! Get a job! Pay your own bills,*' Susie said in a mock voiceover. 'Lucy, I'll arrest *you* if you don't ground the little brat.'

'Believe me, I'd like to ground her until she hits the menopause, but I'm not going to be angry, Suze. My parents were strict, and look at me. My confidence is so minuscule you'd need an X-ray to locate it.'

Susie scrutinized me. 'You think Tally going off the rails is your fault. And it's made you stop trusting your mothering instincts. Well, it's not your bloody fault, yer big dag. It's *his*. You don't need a *How To Be A Good Parent* booklet; Tally needs a *How Not To Be An Annoying Teenager* manual.'

'Oh, Susie, who am I to give advice to anyone? My best friend was sleeping with my husband and

I was too dumb to notice.' I tried and failed to disguise the tremor in my voice. 'I need to take a course – Your Ass From a Hole in the Ground – A Comparative Study.'

Susie squeezed my hand affectionately. 'Actually I do have a convict ancestor, did I ever tell you that?'

I shook my head. 'What was he guilty of?'

'Not running fast enough,' she said.

Susie and I drove home from a school meeting the next night to find my house throbbing and shuddering with heavy metal bass and drums. Tally had asked if she could have a few people from Fang's band around to listen to some music and it had turned into a house-trashing party for the Satanic masses. The hundred or so kids inside had drunk so much beer and puked so many pizzas that the living room now resembled a Jackson Pollock painting. What was the point of calling the police? A zoologist was what I needed.

The house was chock-a-block with inebriated teenagers, dancing like demented chickens, twanging imaginary guitars. Tally's dance movements were so violent that I began to wonder if there was epilepsy in the family tree. In desperation I decided to deploy Parental Emergency Tactic A by dancing along with them, lip-synching to whatever monosyllabic drivel was oozing from the speakers. Some quintessential Mum Dancing

Manoeuvres refined during the 1980s can clear a room full of teenagers faster than a fire alarm.

As the screen door slammed on the last retreating head-banger, my daughter screamed at me, 'YOU ARE SO EMBARRASSING. Why can't you just grow up?' before executing a very mature flounce upstairs and a petulant slam to the door.

As I mopped up Vesuvial amounts of vomit and jack-hammered grime from the bathroom sink, I couldn't help but reflect on why I'd had children in the first place. I'd had kids because they give love and joy and purpose to life. But then again, so would a King Charles spaniel.

'There are worse people I could have mothered.'

'Who?' Susie asked, helping me rattle beer bottles into the recycling bags at one in the morning. 'Himmler?

'Yes. Or Nero. That wouldn't have been good. Pol Pot would have tried my patience a tad, too.'

But Susie would not be won over. 'That daughter of yours is like a giant toddler, throwing very messy . . .' she paused to peel pizza crust off the chandelier '. . . tantrums. Cancel her pocket money. And if that doesn't work, I have access to more persuasive techniques involving a taser.'

'If I crank up the anger, she'll rebel even more. Best to let her unwind on her own,' I said, scraping sick off an antique ornament.

Susie opened the drinks cabinet and held the gin bottle to the light. 'Water. And your vodka is cold tea.'

I shrugged. 'I suppose it's not a successful party unless you have at least one police raid and someone gets caught trying to have sex with an inanimate object.' But when I trod on the balloon condoms which were batting around my ankles, the ensuing squish burst my flimsy bravado. 'Her father would know what to do.'

'Lucy, I'm telling you this as a friend,' Susie said, washing-up-gloved hands on her shapely hips. 'Even your pot plants will file for divorce if you keep whining about how much you miss that snake-bellied, two-faced bastard. Your old man has left you. It's a big bloody pain in the ass,' she lectured. 'But you've got to start living again. Living . . . you know, the bit between being born and death? A gang of us are off camping down the coast this weekend. We go every few months. It's fun. Why don't you come?'

'Camping is nature's way of promoting the luxury hotel business,' I shuddered, remembering the music festivals of my youth. I knew the true definition of a campsite – a nettle-riddled, insect-infested, leech-laden area, enclosing nostalgic, competitive men and pissed-off, cold women who are secretly planning a mass exodus to the nearest shopping mall.

'Sleeping rough, living off the land, using candles and eating by firelight . . .'

'You have just described fleeing the Taliban over the Afghanistan mountains.'

'The kids will bake damper,' she enthused as we dragged out the garbage.

187

'Damper? That dough bushrangers once used to bake in the fire ashes? It's disgusting.'

'Look at it this way: if nobody eats the loaves, we'll use them to tile my patio.' She gestured to the cracked stones of her front steps. 'You could always sleep in Lockie's Kombivan,' Susie suggested.

'Oh yes, that sounds great,' I said, sitting her down in the kitchen in front of a cup of herbal tea and some halva, five minutes later. 'Why don't I leave behind my lovely warm duvet and soft mattress for a freezing cold, uncomfortable tin can? Not to mention becoming an all-you-can-eat diner for sand flies the size of sumo wrestlers.'

'OK, OK. To be honest, I'm not bonkers about the great bloody outdoors either, with all its multi-footed insects. Ugh. I only like getting bitten all over by eligible blokes . . . But unfortunately the best place to find eligible blokes is in the great bloody outdoors. The campsite's in the national park so there's no electricity or water. But there are kangaroos and bandicoots, fairy-wrens and penguins,' Susie amended, toasting me with her tea.

'Susie, camping doesn't make me want to get back to the land. It makes me want to get back to some posh hotel suite for a bubble bath.' I toasted her back. 'Nothing could induce me to go.'

Nothing except the unexpected appearance of my husband. Jasper sauntered into my kitchen the next night. I had just returned from swimming training, so had goggle marks gouged beneath both eyes, flat, damp hair and no make-up. The kitchen was in chaos. I was so focused on trying to help Ruby with her maths homework that the milk was boiling over and the burning chops had set off the smoke alarm.

Jasper surveyed the scene with a judgemental eye before urging the kids to go and wash their hands for dinner. 'I heard about the shoplifting,' he blurted, as soon as we were alone. 'And the impromptu party. Ruby told me. Lucy, I think it's clear that Tally is going off the rails. You must concede that the girls would be better off with me for a while. You obviously need some time to get your act together,' he said with synthetic sympathy.

'Um . . . And what act would that be?' I asked, dashing to and fro turning things off or over, mopping up spillages, sweeping dishes into the sink. 'The third act of the play where I stab my rival to death and throw myself from the parapet?' I tried to fluff the chlorinated tangle of my hair into something which made me look less like a Gestapo wardress.

'You see? Can you hear yourself? Tally told me about the drinking and the sleeping pills. You're obviously self-medicating. And look at the result. Tally's headed for juvenile court and Ruby's turning into a tearaway tomboy. You may be angry with Renée, but you can't deny that she is sophisticated and worldly. She'll be a very good influence on the girls right now. I mean, you obviously need a break.' His voice softened. 'I've been so selfish. Lucy, I'm offering to take the kids off your hands so you can get your life back on track.'

'The only track I know about is the one I'm tied to. You have no idea how tempting it is to tell our families and friends back home what an asshole you've been, and shame you into giving me more money. But it's too humiliating to tell anyone. I mean, who would believe it?'

'Look, Lucy. I know it's been hard for you, but money is tight right now . . . Haven't you been reading the papers? There's a recession. The stock-market's in free fall.'

'So, I'll just sell the children into slavery, shall I?'

'I'm just waiting for some investments to mature. I've told you.'

'*You* maturing would be a bloody start. I mean, what do you see in that maniac? She's over-dressed and under-educated. She's . . .'

Jasper bridled. 'Renée is a self-assured, independent, career woman . . .'

'Who has independently squandered our life-savings. Why give our hard-earned money to Renée when you could just flush it down the loo?'

'I did not come here to listen to you vilifying my girlfriend. I came to take the kids to town for the weekend. So that you can think about your future. We could leave right after . . .' he cast a disparaging glance at the burnt chops, '*dinner.*'

His audacity was so breathtaking, it almost induced an asthma attack. 'What? No way. You absolutely cannot take them this weekend.'

'Why on earth not?'

'Because . . . because . . . we're going camping.'

Jasper looked at me for a moment, before erupting into laughter. 'You? Camping? Where?'

'Jervis Bay National Park.'

'Don't be ridiculous,' he wheezed, catching his breath. 'Do you really want to overtax accident and emergency services? You'll all die of hypothermia. You'll starve. You'll be lost in the bush and eaten by dingoes.'

I squared up to him. 'I love the outdoors. I'm not the woman I was. I'm more capable now. I'm a self-assured, independent, worldly female.'

Who was I kidding? To have fallen in love with an idiot like Jasper, I obviously *had* been self-medicating. With Dumb-erol.

Australia contains large quantities of nature and we were about to be in a lot of it.

'I see you like to travel light,' Lockie drawled, having arrived to find me struggling to close the bulging boot of my Holden. Another of life's great mysteries is why the male of the species believes you can only start a holiday at six in the morning. He had appeared around dawn to pick up Matilda and Ruby, so they could ride south with Ryan in his weatherbeaten Kombi-van. 'Strewth, I don't know if anyone told you, but we're only going camping for the weekend. We're not actually embarking on a round-the-world nomadic pilgrimage.'

But whereas Jasper would have unpacked my car

with a martyred sigh, laying everything out on the pavement scientifically, and then repacking with the precision of a military exercise, tut-tutting the whole time, Lockie just smirked, before putting his back to the boot to squash the detritus in a little deeper.

'Is there a hotel nearby?' I asked, nervously. 'If, you know, I don't actually take to camping?'

'Sure,' he drawled. 'You can find it by the neon sign outside reading "Bates".'

Tally refused to come if she couldn't bring her latest boyfriend, Spike, a snarling skinhead with 'Made in London' tattooed on to his forehead, even though he was a local kid from Kirrawee. He was so revolting it made me wish Fang had not bitten the boyfriend dust.

'Spike's really nice. You just don't understand him,' Tally scolded, and with that pulled on Spike's leather jacket covered in swastikas and stomped in his borrowed storm-trooper boots to her bedroom.

An hour later, Tally clambered into my old Holden, with Spike in tow. Susie, who was explaining directions for the two-hour drive south, canted an incredulous brow.

'Whenever Tally's down in the dumps, she gets herself a new boyfriend,' I whispered.

'Oh,' Susie replied, briskly. 'So *that's* where she finds them.'

'Please, the obligatory fortnight and no more. Do you think it would be inhospitable to strap him to the roof racks?'

Listening to two hours of nu metal is a lot like having your eardrums shredded on a cheese-grater, which explained my mental exhaustion when I finally arrived at the turn-off. The majestic Jervis Bay, the size of Greater London, is surrounded by a national park with a naval base secreted in one sandy-coved corner. Because of worries about wartime bombing by the Japanese, the Aussies constructed the road on a wavy line, to make it more difficult for pilots to line up and strafe supply-trucks. Bumping along these corduroy roads, my over-laden car, flannelled with dust, rounded each corner under protest. We finally caromed over a eucalyptus-laden crest to find the bay, spread out like silver silk.

The campsite was a higgledy-piggledy, haphazard arrangement of tents scattered through the tree grove by the beach. The mystery of why the male of the species believes you can only start a holiday at six in the morning was solved when I swung the car into the only spot left – near the Portaloos. Lockie had the prime position by the beach and was already smoking bandicoot dung to deter mosquitoes. I noticed his modest backpack. I packed more clothes than that to walk to the letter box. Lockie sauntered over to watch me unloading. He wore an increasingly bemused expression, no doubt due to the fact that I had brought enough stuff to survive for a year while fleeing from Cossacks. Monopoly, Scrabble, Pictionary, duffle jackets, sun block, a library of classics . . . I'd even packed two flashlights. But the boot was so chock-a-block I'd need a flashlight to find them.

I was determined to prove that I could cope on my own, but the instructions for putting up the tent might as well have been written by a Martian. Or a government bureaucrat. The colour-coded chart for a step-by-step procedure would probably have proved helpful except that Ruby had spent her entire Kombi-van trip colouring over it in felt-tips.

The other campers were mainly parents from Nippers. About thirty in all. As if by caveman instinct, all the husbands had immediately set about making fires. As the kindling was damp, fathers were frantically blowing and rubbing and fanning, even sacrificing their socks to the pyre to get one-up on each other. There was only one man who could keep his fire blazing. The other blokes surveyed Lockie with slit-eyed envy. Their wives, however, desperate for a cup of tea, regarded Jack McLachlan with nothing short of adoration. The man could even make a fire without matches. 'You simply strike two small stones together over moss, lichen, dried grass and twigs, blow on it till it takes hold – then add more kindling,' he told the doting female gathering.

I struggled with the tent for at least an hour. When my head finally emerged from the canvas folds, gasping for air, I saw Lockie leaning on a tree, arms folded, a wry smile on his lips. 'Howzit goin'?'

'Fine. It's not that hard.' (Hard? Who was I kidding?

It was like assembling the Taj Mahal, single-handedly.)

'Um . . . I think your difficulty might be that you seem to have left behind the tent pegs.'

'Oh well,' I smiled through gritted teeth. 'Improvisation is all part of the fun, right?'

'Ah, yeah, sure.' He glanced around my disorganized campsite. 'But improvising water and food could be a little more tricky.'

The Esky! How could I have forgotten the coolbox? Oh what had happened to my IQ? Once upon a time I'd run my own practice with four employees. When had my frontal lobe shrunk to the size of a Smartie? I tried to reply calmly. 'Oh, I'll just catch something to eat. I am perfectly at home in the wild, thank you very much.'

And the wild, it would seem, was perfectly at home in me. When I saw the spider, the size of a cattle dog, gambolling across my feet, my scream could have been heard by the astronauts on the Mir space station.

'Lemme get this straight. You can take boiling-hot wax and pour it on your private parts then rip the hairs out by the roots and yet you're terrified of an insect?'

'Do something!'

'Um, being one thousand times its body weight should make you a little more secure, I would've thought?' He scooped the huge and hairy interloper onto a sheet of newspaper and shook it free, far into the bush. As I cowered I was sure I could hear it having a celebratory knees-up with all eight of its horribly hairy legs.

It was then Tally's turn to run screaming back into camp. She had just experienced the Portaloos.

'The toilets,' she gasped. 'They're beyond disgusting. They're, they're . . .'

'Long-drops,' Lockie explained. 'Never look down a longdrop dunny, love. You'll lose the will to live. One guy smoked inside and blew himself up because of the chemicals. Now *that's* toilet humour.'

'I'm not used to such disgusting horrors!' Tally hunched into her skull-and-crossbones-emblazoned Satanic-themed leather jacket. 'How could you bring me to this hideous place?' Next mood swing approaching. I winced inwardly. How to warn Lockie that we are now entering a hard-hat area? 10, 9, 8, 7 . . . 'That's *it*. I am not talking to you, Mother!'

'What? Again?' I sighed.

'But before I stop speaking to you,' my oldest daughter whined, the glaucoma of teenage disdain veiling her eyes, 'could you make Spike and me a bacon sandwich?'

I left Ruby with Ryan and Lockie before trudging across what felt like the width of, say, Belgium to Susie's well-organized campsite. It was while buttering bread for sandwiches that a creature more unnerving, more venomous and more deadly than any spider scuttled into camp. She was alighting in tight black shorts from Jasper's 4X4, her Pilates-flat belly displayed in a leopard-skin

196

tank-top, her teeth-bleached smile on high beam. An Akubra hat topped off her Competent Camper look.

My toes curling like Turkish slippers, I watched as my husband unloaded his state-of-the-art camping gear and set up a high-tech site, including a private Portaloo, in record time. Renée opened up their instant tent. It came flat-packed in disc shape. She simply threw it in the air and it unfurled into a canvas shell to sleep twenty. My mouth gormlessly ajar, I watched as she then unpacked her dry shampoo, waterproof socks and wellies. The woman had brought everything required in an apparel emergency. As well as designer lederhosen for hiking, she'd brought enough camouflage gear to enable her to commandeer an army rubber ducky inflatable and invade a small Pacific island. My arch-enemy had basically come as a Sindy doll with all of her accoutrements. They'd also nabbed a choice, creek-side position fortuitously vacated by a departing ranger. I wanted to leap on her and push her well-stocked Esky down her throat.

One-upmanship when it comes to gadgets is second-nature to men. And this was the camping version of the nuclear arms race. The other dads, who'd been competing for the biggest and best portable barbecue and miniature battery-operated fridge, underwent a collective spasm of male camp-site envy. Employing the nonchalant charm which he had honed on the football pitch, Jasper quickly defused their resentment by allowing them to play with his high-tech toys. When one of the mums recognized my husband from a guest appearance on a television sports quiz and asked if he'd pose for a photo, I heard him utter his practised, swoon-inducing line, 'So, how do you want me?'

When I regained the power of speech, I strode up behind Renée and jabbed her in the ribs. 'What the hell are you doing here?'

'Well, Jasper just wanted to keep on eye on you. In case you needed help. That's the kind of thoughtful man he is,' she simpered.

I could feel the muscles of my face tightening. 'I do not need any help. I am set up very nicely, thank you.'

'I've brought yoga mats, a massage tepee and mosaic-making for under tens, plus herbs and spices for a kiddies' barbecue cookery class, including a beginner's guide to thyme and parmesan baskets. I'm frankly surprised at your lack of organized play.'

I looked at her in equal measures of outrage and awe. 'Funny. But when you ask kids what makes them happy, a variety of learning experiences and IQ-enhancing toys is not usually one of the answers they volunteer.'

'Hello, darling.'

At the sound of Jasper's warm and loving endearment, I turned, expectantly. But it was Tally he was hugging. My husband was looking svelte and tanned in denim jeans and open-necked shirt.

'Camping just sounded so much fun, I thought, why not? I've also got a tent which has enough room for both you kids . . . Just in case.' He pointed to his aerated mattresses and weather-proofed sleeping bags. Oh great. While I was to sleep on the cold, hard ground, Renée was to slumber on a warmed waterbed – no doubt filled with Perrier.

'Where's Ruby? At your campsite?' Jasper looked around hopefully for what he ambitiously referred to as my 'campsite'. 'So . . .' he pressed, when I didn't answer. 'Where *have* you pitched tent?'

'Um . . .' I prevaricated. 'Um, I'm not 100 per cent sure . . .'

'You can't find your tent?'

'It's a camouflage tent, which is why I can't find it.'

'Oh, that gives me confidence. If you can't find your way back to your tent, what's going to happen if you get lost in the bush? It's just as well I came.' Jasper gave me a haughty look before striding off, calling Ruby's name at the top of his voice.

I scurried along behind, in a spasm of dread. My campsite looked like a battle scene from the Somme. Rounding the bend by the bottlebrush trees, excuses were on the tip of my tongue. But then I stopped in my tracks. I'd always thought a 'semi-permanent erection' referred to a priapic pop star. But my campsite suddenly resembled a proper home. Not only was my tent erect, but there was a fire blazing in a stone pit and a billy on the boil for tea. Mosquito netting was strung across the enclosure and air mattresses were laid out neatly in a row. A loaf of home-made bread and a tea cake sat on the portable table.

'Oh,' Jasper said.

But 'oh' didn't really cover it at all. 'Jack McLachlan, I want your love child,' was more my reaction.

After lunch, when Ruby and Tally were busily doing yoga stretches in Renée's tepee, I went to thank Lockie.

'Hey, it's nice to be needed. Life went bad for us blokes once they invented the wheelie bin. Since then we've been surplus to requirements.'

'Not to Renée the man-eater. Deep below the surface of that woman, it's all shallows. I mean, why? Why her? We're so different. I'm a total bookworm. Whereas she just reads until her lips get tired.'

Lockie stamped out his fire. 'Hey, life is like a big surf. There you are, happily paddling along, when a flash rip current, which you'll remember from class . . . ?'

'. . . results from a large build-up of surf in a short period and an intense pull seaward.'

'. . . drags you into deep water. Suddenly you can't touch the bottom. You need to learn to body surf.' He threw a towel at me. 'Come on.'

To me, body surfing is right up there with amateur leg-severing. But I owed him a look, at least. Beyond the sandy bush track, a blue cove beckoned. But Lockie trekked past the serene, sapphire pond. The track twisted and turned over rugged, eroded headlands, a geographical reminder of the vast land mass which once heaved up from the sea. This was an ancient place. And Lockie fitted effortlessly into it. He led me across the rocks, squelching through seaweed thick as risotto. The soft, percolating sound of the algae and weeds drying in the midday sun could be heard beneath the distant thunder of ocean waves. Atop the bluff, I looked down on big, confident creamy breakers rolling on to a three-mile stretch of silica sand. There was no other person in sight, just the immensity of sea and sky.

'Wow!' was the most inadequate response imaginable – but I said it anyway.

'The trick is to use the wave's energy for propulsion.'

'Wait. You don't think for a minute that I'm going in there, do you?'

But apparently he did, because fifteen minutes later he was holding on to my waist in the deep water. 'As the wave is almost upon you, push off the bottom and start paddling towards shore until you feel the water begin to carry you. Then just swim like buggery. As the wave breaks, take a breath and put your head down. Your feet should be together, your back arched slightly and your arms extended. As the wave becomes steeper, tilt forward and surf along its face. And kick like the blazes.'

I was about to ask him if he'd like me to find a cure for Aids or perhaps even something more difficult, say, Melanie Griffith's birth certificate, when he hurled me like a human javelin towards shore. I was starting to panic when I realized I was actually aloft, hurtling on the crest of the wave. I kicked, arched, threw my arms in front, dug into the water, tilted and – holy hell, I was flying.

I was squealing with delight when Lockie surfed to my side in the shallows in a spritz of spray.

'Not bad,' said Jack McLachlan.

Australian men are not good with praise. 'Not bad' is the equivalent of euphoric rapture in other countries. 'Not bad *at all*', well, you've basically won the lottery, Nobel Prize and an Oscar all in one.

'Thank you,' I beamed.

Later, while he snorkelled around the rocks to dive for abalone, I caught ten more exhilarating rides, my confidence growing each time, until I was skittering down the face of every wave, whooping.

My mood was light when we returned. Sea salt encrusted my eyebrows. I sauntered towards Susie's camp to retrieve my children only to be met by my husband's thunderous expression.

'I don't think the children will be rejoining you, Lucy. Teenagers are quite particular about food – there particularly needs to be a lot of it. And apparently you forgot the Esky.'

I held aloft my bucket brimming with fresh abalone. 'The reason I didn't bring a lot of food is because we're living off the land. I caught these while snorkelling.'

Jasper looked at me, gob-smacked, for once at a loss for a lecture.

★　★　★

After dinner, when the kids were all gathered around the communal campfire, raggedly harmonizing 'Waltzing Matilda', I went to find Lockie. He had a glass of Sauvignon Blanc waiting for me.

'I thought you might be in need of one of these.'

'Thank you,' I said. 'I mean, for everything.'

He passed me a plate of sizzling abalone. There was a richness in their salty taste, redolent of life. The hint of smoke in the flavour, mingling with the resinous aroma of gum trees, reminded me of sex. As the sun set, the bark of the trees began to blush pink, as though sighing with relief that the heat of the day was no more. The sweet surrender of the tough bush land to the moisture of the evening was intoxicating. We ate, licking our fingers with relish, as the twilight seeped away into night. Lockie stoked the fire into a full-throated roar and made our shadows entwine in a distorted dance on trees which seemed to be stretching in the moonlight. The bush was now murmurous with nocturnal life. The tremulous yellow beam of my torch picked out Lockie's strong face. Lockie was so good at being Lockie, he should be a verb, I decided. To McLachlan – to help gruffly.

'You know I'm not interested in other men, but I tell you what, if I wasn't still in love with my husband . . . all the kind things you've done for me, the car tyre, the fuses, the tent, not to mention saving my life on the odd occasion . . .'

'It's OK. I'm not interested in having a relationship, either.'

He said this, but I could feel a yearning coming off him in waves. He was obviously still raw with grief from his wife's death. Perhaps this explained our attraction? Two lonely people, each one grieving over a different kind of loss.

'Why?'

Lockie's eyes were now a burning blue, like a gas flame. I felt singed when he turned them on to me. I knew he hated to be asked anything personal, but the word was out of my mouth before I realized it. Lockie scratched at his ear, pulled a face, rolled his eyes, shuffled his feet and cleared his throat.

I thought it might help if I looked away so I bent down to relace my sand shoe. When this task was completed, I knotted my hair into a ragged ponytail. I was running out of distractions when he finally spoke.

'Well, it's been so long since I met a woman I have any feelings for, Lou.' I felt his gaze like a breath on my face.

Australian men are emotional bonsai. You have to whack on the fertilizer to get any feelings out of them. But I knew one thing for sure – the more an Australian shortens your name the more they like you. Embarrassed, now it was my turn to pull a face and shuffle my feet. I would have cleared my throat, except his tongue was down there already. It wasn't so much a passionate melting of mouths as drive-by kissing. It was one of those self-conscious, clumsy, first-time kisses where he got his tongue up my nose and my lips collided with his chin.

We stood apart for a shocked moment, then he kissed me again – long and luscious and slow this time. We ran our hands over each other's bodies, feeling the muscles tense and flex. It had been so long since I'd been held by a man. I savoured the length, strength and breadth of him. When I opened my eyes, slivers of light were crawling down the bay as the moon rose and I realized that a whole five minutes had elapsed when I hadn't thought of Jasper.

'Not bad,' Lockie said when our lips parted. 'Not bloody bad at all!'

It was the Australian equivalent of a Shakespearean love sonnet. He smiled at me with heat in his eyes.

'I'm not really ready for . . . you know. That was so delicious. But I'm still sort of . . .'

Lost for words, I resorted to the training Lockie had given me and executed the surf lifesaving warning signal for '*Deep Water*'.

Lockie kind of grinned and sheepishly raised one arm in the air which signified '*Shore Signal Received and Understood*'.

If only life could be all signals, I thought to myself later that night, as I lay in my tent, listening to Spike snoring, watching an aureole of insects around the lantern. How simple it would be. How wonderful to have no misunderstandings. Renée could do the '*Oops! It somehow slipped my mind to tell you that I'm sleeping with your husband*' signal.

And I could reciprocate with the '*I wish you no ill, except perhaps to see you destroyed by tactical nuclear weapons. Oh, and I just got a job as a US postal worker, so run like hell, bitch!*' semaphore in return.

But it seemed that someone was doing my dirty work for me. A shriek alerted the entire campsite to some kind of catastrophe. Disorientated by dreams, we all stumbled in the direction of the scream. It came from Jasper's camp, where others were already gathered around the private Portaloo. It had been tipped forward, barring the door – and some unfortunate was locked inside. Locked in an upside-down toilet cubicle. And it was a woman. My first fear was that it was Tally, but judging by the expletives emanating from the air hole, my wildest wishes had come true. The men put their backs to the Portaloo to upright it. They jimmied open the door. And oh, the joy of seeing Renée – who takes a shower after each individual push-up and whose preferred interior design decor is Early Disinfectant – covered head to toe in sewage. As she emerged, spluttering, from her private plastic sarcophagus and I heard Ruby and Tally join in the mocking laughter, I can honestly say I was, at that moment, a very happy camper.

CHAPTER 14

FISHING PERMITTED

Some decisions can be put off hundreds of times until they slip your mind. I was so indecisive I considered joining Procrastinators Anonymous, but I just kept postponing the appointment. Having failed once, I found endless reasons not to re-enrol for the bronze medallion.

'You're going to graduate on time, no matter how long it takes,' Lockie boomed laconically over the phone. I hadn't seen him since the carry-on camping trip and our aphrodisiacal abalone encounter. That kiss had certainly left something to be desired – the rest of him.

'I'm sorry I've missed training, Lockie.' I was talking fast to cover my blushing embarrassment. 'It's just that it's quite aerobic, you know, when your husband leaves you. All that pacing and angsting. Jasper is being very fair about the separation. He's letting me keep my own hair and teeth. Which means, until I get my Australian physio licence, taking part-time jobs. But having been out of the work-force for a decade raising babies only equips me to stitch footballs in the Third World until I go blind, apparently.'

'You're signed up for a refresher course,' said Attila the Coach, unmoved by my monologue. 'Be there.'

Susie and I were on an early-morning jog up the beach when I confessed about the kiss.

'You slut!' She punched my arm.

It had taken me a while to realize that all insults in Australia are actually terms of endearment.

'So?' she demanded. 'When are you going to jump the horn bag? I've heard Lockie's a real gentleman in bed. He takes the weight on his elbows!'

Romance, Australian-style.

'I don't need a real man, Susie. Not when sex with George Clooney is only the flick of a light switch away.'

'Tell me about it, darl. I've worn off a fingerprint. I could perform the perfect crime now. Bloody hell. I've got so many Rampant Rabbit vibrators they need their own warren.'

'Well, it's better than dating. I'm too embarrassed ever to date again. I'm obviously crap at sex. I mean, if vaginal orgasms are natural – why are there so many experts telling us how to have them?'

'Of course you don't know anything about orgasms, ya big dag,' Susie replied. 'You're married.'

Listing with laughter, our banter was lost in the wind as we turned at Greenhills and tacked back down the beach to Eloura. Clouds were sloshing across the sky like pegged-out washing.

'I know one thing for sure. If we don't have sex soon we're going to end up with a Barbie stump.'

I sidestepped a dog which was licking itself in a most unsettling area. 'A what?'

'That little bit of moulded plastic between the legs of a Barbie doll. That'll be you. You'll heal over, woman.'

I looked at my friend, appalled. 'I can't just have sex with someone else! I'm in love with my husband.'

'Why? You're completely incompatible. Your rising sign is Aquarius . . . and he's a complete bastard.'

'Susan, I'll have you know that I'm just one husband short of a very happy marriage.'

'Lucy, you know I'm very fond of you, but I think you've got kangaroos in your top paddock,' Susie sighed, tapping her temple. 'But if you're serious, what better than to make the boofhead jealous? Don't be so available.'

To be honest, since my clandestine campfire kiss, there had been a shift in my attitude to Jasper. It wasn't exactly seismic. It was more like the minuscule moves of a melting glacier, but at least it was movement. When he made arrangements to see the kids, I told him flat-out that it didn't suit me. I didn't return his calls, either. Sometimes for a whole day. And I'd been stern about access. Unless he put some money into my account, I told him austerely, he couldn't see the kids without a court order. I also rang my sister in London, confided in her about my marital meltdown and got her to sell my Mercedes saloon, which was parked in her driveway. There was ten thousand pounds – about twenty-five thousand dollars – in my account a week later. It just about paid off my overdraft.

'Jasper's agreed to pay me a monthly amount,' I told Susie as we grunted through our tricep-dips on the club steps.

'Did you get it in writing? My bloody husband gave me nothing in the divorce. Except syphilis. I'm, like – thanks for sharing.'

The cloudy laundry overhead had turned dark and dirty. Then the rain came, in thick, juicy drops. With it came Lockie, striding from the club with a mug of steaming tea. 'Don't want you coming down with a cold before class, you weedy Pom,' he added gruffly, to cover up his confusion over our vigorous exchange of saliva. (It had been the kind of kiss you could drown in. The kind of kiss, ironically, that you need a lifesaver for.) He thrust the tea into my hands. 'I've rescheduled your test for just before Christmas.'

'No. I'm not ready!' I could see my self-esteem bobbing away towards the white-capped horizon. 'I'll only drown again and make a total ass of myself.'

Lockie smirked. 'So? Hasn't anyone ever told you how beautiful you look coughing seawater up out of your lungs?'

Susie winked, cupping her hand over her pudenda to remind me of my Barbie stump. I shook my head but in truth I had found myself thinking of Jack McLachlan more and more. And often with the lights off . . .

The English do nothing spontaneous without a warning. Having a predilection for procrastination meant that I *was* actually contemplating doing something impulsive with Lockie – maybe in a week or so. But fate and a parked Ford Escort got in the way . . .

Susie and I were strolling to our first refresher class in the balmy evening air when I took all the skin off my shin on a bumper bar. How could I contemplate a walk on the wild side when I couldn't even walk in a straight line without falling over?

'Only *you* could get hit by a parked car, Lucy.' Susie laughed so hard she snorted. 'You nincompoop.'

The reason I had walked into a parked car was standing twelve feet away. Mid-twenties, with a schoolboy head of floppy hair which fell over his forehead in a sweep, he possessed a physique the like of which has always received rave notices from the romantic poets. Put it this way – the man looked out of place without a plinth. His creamy skin had been burnished to a smooth mahogany in the sun. And the eyes he turned towards me now were cut through with different colours. One of those highfaluting poets might remark that it was as though lightning had congealed there in a storm. Not being particularly poetic, all Susie and I could say was 'Yowzah!'

When we two middle-aged women saw the Greek god stroll into our surf club, Susie and I started frantically playing eye-tennis. If eye-tennis were

211

recognized by the Lawn Tennis Association, we'd have won the ocular doubles at Wimbledon.

We took our seats on the bench with the new recruits, only to see him saunter towards us. Whereas Lockie walked with a sturdy, weighty gait and Jasper moved with the silent, sinuous grace of an athlete, the newcomer had a cheeky spring in his step. I shifted to make room for him. Feeling the warm length of his thigh against mine I started calculating exactly how much self-control it would take not to lunge for his groin. I looked down at my surf life-saving manual with mock concentration.

'I'm so sorry to intrude but I couldn't help noticing your textbook. Would you mind if I had a quick glance?'

I had a drastic decision to make. Should I keep sucking in my cheeks all night and look younger? Or should I actually converse and sound intelligent? 'Book? This is not a mere book. It's a bible. Surfing is a religion in Australia. It's called sun-worship.'

'Ah, another Brit abroad.' The Love God smiled. 'Sebastian,' he said, in a polished upper-class accent, extending his hand. It was a formal gesture at odds with his casual, board-shorted attire.

Susie, sitting on his other side and so shielded from view by his half-turned back, mischievously flapped her arms out from her body as though she were flying, which is the surf lifesaving sema-phore for '*Pick Up the Buoys*'.

I was trying so hard to suppress a giggle whilst also holding my stomach in, that I nearly choked.

'So? How are you getting on with the natives? I find them frank, friendly and funny. They treat everybody the same, no matter where they've come from or what they've done. They're welcoming and warm, chock-full of optimism and have a gruff, gregarious good humour . . . Apart from that, they're right bastards.'

I laughed. He was so different to the men I'd been spending so much time with, who greeted each other with great bonhomie but said little. 'How's it hangin', Chook?' 'Low and lazy, Dingo.' 'Gettin' any, Wombat?' 'Jeez, I'm flat out runnin' tryin' to get away from it.' It was rather nice to have a conversation in English.

Having gratified Sebastian with a laugh, he took a mock-bow. 'Irony is only one of the services I offer.' A roguish grin split his face.

With pouty lips like those, I didn't want to think too much about what else the man could do. 'So, why are you in Australia? And Cronulla, of all places?'

'Travelling. Took a gap year after university. Looks as though it's going to turn into a gap life, the way I'm going. My father keeps lecturing me that hard work pays off in the future. But lethargy and slovenliness are paying off pretty well right now,' he smirked. 'Got bored with Europe. Did the whole Thailand thing. Travelled round Asia. And now I'm experiencing the delights of Cronulla with some Aussie lads I met surfing in Bali. I'd like to work up in North Queensland at the resorts, teaching watersports. But you need the bronze medallion to do that.' The sun was low in the west and shone through the window. A rhomboid of golden light lit up his perfect smile.

He was wearing a shark's tooth around his neck that he'd probably picked up in a market in Goa, and some crappy string bracelets next to a battered Rolex, most likely an old one of his father's. His Quiksilver board shorts and Ramones T-shirt were faded, no doubt from handwashing in fresh water outside some yurt.

'I'd hate to say that I'm "slumming it", but it's true that I'm of no fixed abode. Still, I'm not a waster. Had a slim volume of poetry published once. But in the poetry world, if you've got over six readers then you've sold out.'

The Poet on L-Plates picked up a stray patrol hat and tried it on. He was struggling to tie the bow beneath his chin, so I lent forward to assist.

'You must have gone to Oxford or Cambridge, as you have such a big head,' I joshed.

'Hey, the bigger the head, the closer to heaven,' the young man replied smoothly.

'Oh, I'm sorry.' I tied the strings way too tight, nearly garrotting the arrogant trainee. 'But you're exceeding the 100 per cent recommended daily allowance of Smug.'

Those eyes of his glistened like quartz, as he appraised me more closely.

Lockie called the class to attention to introduce himself. A curt nod of his head in my direction was the only acknowledgement he would allow himself in public. His rough-hewn voice was an octave lower than everyone else's and commanded respect.

'Today we're going to deal with a patient who's in shock. We'll be practising methods of revival on each other, so in a minute I want you to break into twos and choose whether you want to play the lifesaver or the patient.'

As Lockie listed the symptoms of shock – faintness, breathlessness, nausea, pale clammy skin, confusion – I ticked off the symptoms on my fingers. I was going to make such a good practice patient. I could go into a state of shock just by thinking of my husband and my ex-best friend entwined in wanton carnality. I developed crippling knots in the stomach, felt faint and had to put my head between my legs – which only made me feel worse when I realized this was no doubt exactly how Jasper and Renée were currently positioned.

'Do you mind if I ask, is everything all right?' said the posh-voiced stranger suddenly.

'Oh. Sorry.' I dabbed my tears with a tissue.

Sebastian, his eyes bright and playful beneath a Byronic flop of fringe, looked at me with open curiosity. 'Looks as though you need a little TLC.' And then, with no warning, he patted me someplace interesting.

When Lockie asked us to pair up, I looked towards Susie. But my best friend had turned to the Lebanese girl who had signed up to the new class. Meena was seventeen and self-deprecating. She'd told us her strict parents had only allowed her to join if she wore a waterproof burkha. These lycra ensembles, which cover a woman from the top of her head to her toenails, are nicknamed 'burkhinis'. While I'd been talking to Sebastian, Meena had been attempting to convert Susie into wearing one, as it was excellent for bad hair days.

'Darl,' I overheard Susie drawl, 'I'm Jewish. Every day for me is a bad hair day. The women in my family are so hairy that when I was born I got carpet burn from my mother's thighs.'

With Susie and Meena paired up, I found myself lying on the floor at the feet of this tousled-haired, piercing-eyed, heart-stopping combination of bronzed upper-class British youth.

'After an accident, it is vital that the surf life-saver does a full body check, working their way down the entire body checking for vital signs and broken bones,' Lockie reiterated, from the front of the classroom.

I gulped. Susie and I had practised this many times before and it is a very intimate once-over. Apart from the kiss with Jack McLachlan, it had been seventeen years since I'd been touched by a man other than my husband. Sebastian swept his honey-coloured hair behind his ears, then proceeded to mimic Lockie's instructions. He tilted back my head and opened my mouth. He ran his fingers down my chest and over my ribs, grazing my breasts and making out it was an accident. At such close quarters I could study his musculature. His shoulders were broad and strong. His skin was a baked crème brûlée. I tried to pretend that my interest in him was purely professional: his toned rectus abdominis, deltoids, lat dorsi and pectoralis muscles were in textbook condition. But as his fingers moved up my thighs, I astonished myself with an impulse to wrap my legs about his waist.

'If your patient has no vital signs and needs CPR, you need to find the heart. Place three fingers above the nipple to get the right distance,' Lockie instructed.

Sebastian, smiling wickedly, placed his hand directly on to my left breast.

'Hey, lover-boy.' The stentorian voice which rang out over the hall was Lockie's. I opened my eyes to see his inverted face above mine, thunderous as an English February. 'We don't actually touch the practice patient,' he admonished Sebastian sternly. 'Are you sure about this course, mate? Being loathed at high school for being a complete wanker is no just cause to take up surf lifesaving, ya know.'

'Oh ciao, chief,' Sebastian smiled impishly, by way of greeting.

'Ciao?' Lockie picked up the word with invisible, sterilized tweezers and examined it with distaste. 'People in my class are only allowed to say "ciao" if they know how to spell it. And then only if they actually live in Italy. Is that clear?' Lockie's eyes narrowed into crocodile slits. Any other male, sensing a top-order predator in his midst, would have pulled back. But later, during mouth-to-mouth resuscitation revision, the cheeky young man broke the rules again, removing the paper mouth-guards used for hygienic purposes, and brushing my mouth with his lips.

'What are you *doing*?' I asked, astonished.

'The chief just said to moisten the patient's lips without giving drink or food.' Sebastian gave me a rapacious look before wetting my lips again. 'I hope you really *do* know CPR, because you take my breath away,' he added playfully.

It struck me that I'd forgotten how to flirt. Who cared about the bronze? Advanced Flirting was the course I urgently required. The multi-coloured lozenges of Sebastian's eyes were upon me and I felt a hot pang of lust. For a fraction of a second I fell under his spell. A fan laboured away, turning its broad face this way and that. But nothing could cool me down. Then reason returned. Didn't he realize I was conceived during the Aztec empire? I pushed him away from me. The pasture may be greener on the other side, but I was way too old to get over the fence.

'I'll have you know I am married with two children.' I sounded like Queen Victoria. 'You obviously keep fit by doing bench-presses off your own ego,' I added as stoutly as I could without actually putting on a bustle and a bonnet. Mesmerized and irritated in equal parts, I stropped away from him back to Susie and Meena.

'Many bacteria and viruses, including HIV and hepatitis, tuberculosis, meningitis and cold sores, are present in human saliva. Did you know that, Lucy?' was Lockie's grumpy goodbye.

I did know. And so, for the next few days, I tried to put all thoughts of Sebastian out of my mind. But it's very hard not to think about sex when you live in a country where people take their clothes off most of the time. Poets have been curiously quiet on the subject of men's testicles – but you sure see a lot of them on Aussie beaches. Whether exposed by a slip of the towel as men execute the time-honoured beachside quick change from 'undies' to 'scungies'. Or during surf-boat drill, where the oarsmen pull their swimming 'cossies' up into the cracks of their muscly bottoms to prevent sliding on the wooden seats (which causes the nylon to heat up and toast the boaties' buns). Or under the open-air beach showers where Aussies sluice off the salt after a surf. When female visitors rave about those gorgeous Australian views, they aren't talking about the flora.

Light travels faster than sound. Which is why some people appear bright until you hear them speak. While taking a quick beach shower later that week after a surf with Susie, I hadn't paid much attention to the gang of youths positioned in their car opposite until one of them yelled 'Aussie slut'. Two other bikini-clad girls waiting for the shower told me that a carload of 'Lebbos' often parked here to watch the women washing. Susie reckoned

219

that such a car was the opposite of an echidna because 'all the pricks are on the inside'. But I wasn't sure if it was a car they were in or the Starship Enterprise, as the vehicle sported enough antennae to get to the moon and back.

I'd heard a gang of Australian boys berating Meena to 'show us ya tits' the day before, then calling her a 'todger dodger lezzo' for not doing so. A lot of boys at this age have the brain frequency of a lentil. And so I just stood beneath the shower stream, made warm from the day's sun, and tuned out their profane braying. Until I felt the pebble hit my leg. I wheeled around in pain.

'Sluts. Skips. Scrubbers,' came the predictable insults. Another rock twanged impotently off the road sign beside my head. The man who threw it had tattoos up both arms, which didn't do much to dispel his aura of menace. Before I could scribble down his number-plate, I heard a torrent of obscenities blurted out in cut-glass elocution. It was Sebastian. He kicked at the leering grille of the souped-up Mustang. I hadn't even noticed he *had* such powerful thighs until now. Great. Just what I needed. Something else to think about besides his eyes.

'Why don't you chill the fuck out?' he yelled as the car screeched off, spewing heavy metal music. 'Are you hurt?' There was a trickle of blood running down my leg, which Sebastian daubed with the end of my towel. 'Where's your husband?'

He flipped out his mobile. 'Do you want me to call him?'

'He's busy.' It was all I could think to say.

'Most husbands are so inattentive. You could leave them at the beginning of the football season and they wouldn't notice till the end, don't you agree?'

I crumpled into tears.

'Oh fuck,' the stranger said. 'He's left you, hasn't he?' He handed back my towel. 'My friends are quite disparaging about me, because just about everything I ever say is an irresponsible lie. But just for a change I'm going to say something from the heart. You are very attractive. And your husband is a moron for leaving you. Or possibly gay.'

I knew it was just a meringue of words, all sugar and air. But it tasted so sweet after all the bitter pills I'd swallowed.

'Listen, I don't know anybody locally, except these Neanderthals I'm staying with – they're half-human, half-Australian. Why don't you come out with me for a drink?'

'Because I've only just met you,' I said, towelling off, and surprised by the blush staining my cheeks.

'So what? Cinderella married her prince after only one date.'

'Tell me,' I said, regaining my composure. 'Don't your Narcotics Anonymous meetings somewhat interfere with your dating life? Because you are obviously out of your head to come on to me. I'm old enough to be your mother.'

Sebastian shrugged. 'I love my mother.'

'Really? Not in the manner of a Greek tragedy, I hope?'

Sebastian gave his wide, Cheshire cat smile. 'Besides, you're not old. You're ripe. Fine wine takes many years to mature. But what makes a vintage wine desirable is the quality of the fruit. And you are,' he looked me up and down in my one-piece, 'a Pétrus '82.' There was a sly gaiety about the man, which was quite unsettling.

'And *you* are a quality bullshit artist.' I looked at him with incredulous amusement. What did he want from me? A place to stay, perhaps? Some English cooking? Croquet? A morris dance? A little light fox-hunting?

'Do you know what I like about older women? Younger girls are constantly worried about what a guy's thinking. Older women never ask what you're thinking, because they don't give a toss.' He laughed. 'Can I give you a lift?' He gestured to a battered, tail-finned Chevrolet with surfboard racks.

'Where to? The fifties?' I said, in a hearty voice, to camouflage my bewilderment.

Susie walked up from the beach, the white towel knotted atop her head seeming to float there like a cumulus cloud. I told her what had happened as we power-walked home, concluding, 'I can't believe he asked for my phone number!'

'And I can't believe you didn't give it to him! Although, to tell you the truth, I think he might be strictly dickly. I mean, he must be gay. He's far too good-looking to be straight. And too buff. Also, have you heard the way he speaks?'

'That's just because he's a public school Pom.'

'That's private school, right? Oh then he *must* be a vagina decliner. The man can name non-standard colours and ordered a soya decaf in class. I rest my case. He's fagadocious, a player of the pink piccolo for sure. Believe me,' she said bitterly. 'I know the symptoms. My husband's motto is "Ditch the bitch and switch".'

Besides feeding and watering and prodding with a foot occasionally to see if it is awake, there's no fool-proof method of raising a teenager. When we got home to find Tally and her new beau, Stoner, flaked out on the couch, the kids they were allegedly babysitting for eight dollars an hour not yet fed or bathed, I turned to my more worldly friend.

'Do you think Tally's doing drugs?' I asked, nervously, after we'd shaken the teenagers awake and rescued the fish casserole from the oven.

'I reckon a pretty good indication that your kid is doing drugs is if she's jailed in Thailand for the term of her natural life.'

'Even if Tally's not doing drugs, I'm pretty sure her boyfriend is,' I said, chopping carrots for the hummus dip.

'Gee,' Susie said facetiously, 'what makes you think *Stoner*'s a drug addict?' She ran the broccoli under the tap.

'Gosh, I dunno . . . The fact that his nostrils are glued together?'

223

Since meeting her 'Goth' friend, Tally had taken to wearing a long black coat, even though it was summer. Her bedroom walls were now draped in black cloth and she was not meeting anyone's eye. The question on any mother's mind would be: is this just the usual aberrant behaviour of a rebellious adolescent – or the first signs of skunk-smoking-related schizophrenia?

Whenever Tally was at school I sniffed around her room like a dog, for clues that she was scrambling her brains with Ecstasy. Were those joss sticks she kept lighting in her room covering up the smell of hashish? During dinner, while Tally crouched over her plate saying nothing, I cautiously approached the subject of my own pot-smoking days. The huge silver cadaver suspended from one of the six holes in my daughter's earlobe jangled its movable bones. When she jack-knifed to her feet, the earring practically dangled lower than the hemline of her Lycra mini.

'I can't believe you would accuse me of using drugs! I'm not a loser like you, Mother.' A pirouette on her stiletto boot and I was speaking to air. I thought it best not to suggest at this precise moment that she was not allowed to go on Stoner's motorbike unless he added trainer wheels.

When I was saying goodnight to Tally, finding my way by Braille through her gloomy room which was glutinous with incense and teen angst, I tried to introduce the subject of her dermatologically challenged, glue-sniffing paramour.

'Stoner is nice, darling, but it won't last.'

'Why do you say that? You just don't want me to commit.' Her lips compressed to the width of a papercut and words scissored out. 'You probably feel safer with me in short-term relationships, because then I won't get dumped the way *you* were. But I'm not like *you*.'

I retreated to the hallway, the words having stung me once again. But then I rallied. The only place I intended getting dumped from now on, was in the big surf.

When hospitality tickets came next day for Mr and Mrs Jasper Perricone to attend the members' box at the cricket test in early January, I snaffled them up and accepted instantly. By the time the officials worked out that Jasper and I were separated, it would be too socially awkward to disinvite me.

Lying in bed alone as ever (hey, I was only two people short of a threesome), I convinced myself that divorce didn't have to be the future tense of my marriage. Maybe I couldn't make Jasper love me as passionately as he once did, but that didn't mean I couldn't stalk him until he became so freaked out, he'd finally break down and move back in. I determined to invite Lockie to go with me to the cricket, to make Jasper jealous. As a plan, it wasn't exactly Mensa-like in its brilliance, but it was better than nothing. Put it this way, on the other hand . . . I had five fingers.

CHAPTER 15

PICKING UP THE BUOYS

Cricket is like playing baseball on Valium. It's the sport's version of tantric sex – but the only thing which gets sticky is the wicket. But to the male of the Antipodean species, tickets to a test match are prized above, say, eternal life. When word got out that I had entrée to the members' pavilion, I became more popular than a packet of breath mints at an onion festival. Sebastian was on the phone daily, begging me to rethink my decision to take Jack McLachlan.

'We'll have so much frivolity between innings. We can play that favourite English parlour game of guessing who is gay in the royal family. Not to mention which one we'd most like to saddle up and ride around a Balmoral ballroom.'

Lockie was so grateful he could not do enough for me. 'Do you know how I overtake your car? I just walk a little bit faster. I reckon it might be in need of a tune-up.'

'It's true. I'm only getting about two blocks to the gallon. Whenever I look in the rear-vision mirror, I can see traffic backed up to, oh, the Queensland border.'

Lockie not only refitted new wing mirrors, but my tyres were suddenly pumped and the fan belt stopped whining. At home, my screen door was no longer wheezing. The kids' mobile phones were recharged via the Internet. Electrical appliances were humming, bikes free of rust-dribbles, light bulbs changed and drains unblocked. I've no doubt if he'd been a lifeguard at an aquatic centre, he'd have allowed me to go right ahead and pee in the pool if I'd wanted to.

If Lockie was all action, Sebastian was all talk. 'You are my dictionary. You add meaning to my life,' the cheeky chappie emailed me. I would have laughed at his corniness, except I didn't want to alert Tally to the fact that I was getting emails from a man. Man? Who was I kidding? More like a jock-strap-straining-love-bunny. 'Your lips looked so lonely today. Would all four of yours like to meet mine?' The inbox brought such mushy missives on an hourly basis.

The cricket-loving Lothario was relentless. In surf life-saving class there were whispered asides. 'Just where do those legs of yours end? Shall we find out?' During board training out at sea – 'You were fantastic on *Baywatch* last night.' Or 'What's got two thumbs, speaks French and enjoys cunnilingus?' He gestured with a thumbs-up. 'Moi!'

'Can you stop with the pathetic pick-up lines?' I cajoled.

'I don't use pick-up lines!' Sebastian replied

scandalized, before caressing my thigh and commenting, 'So, exactly how long have you been bathing in milk?'

Next Sebastian took to texting me on the school run. 'I bet you taste so good I'll want the recipe.' He even stalked me at the gym. When I saw him watching me, I lost concentration on the treadmill and ended up splattered against the wall like a squashed spider. In the hope of usurping Lockie for those seats in the members' box, Sebastian offered to train me, gratis.

A tanned young Adonis holding my knees while I grunted through my sit-ups in the local park was undeniably thrilling, but I was constantly worried that Tally would catch me. Guilty as a truanting teenager, I took to lurking behind shrubbery. The merest crackle of a twig and I'd lunge into shadows. When the noise turned out to be nothing more sinister than a falling limb, Sebastian quipped, derisively, 'Oh, look, it's Special Branch.'

When I chuckled, he added, 'I thought women rated men with a sense of humour as the most sexually attractive. So why aren't your clothes off?' When I laughed again, he added playfully, 'That's like a multiple laugh. Oh, you minx!'

But Lockie was an excellent trainer too. When the kids were having a sleepover at their father's, he took my mind off my miseries with a dawn kayak through sea as pale as milk. We ate the breakfast he'd packed at a perfect half-moon bay called

Wattamola. As we snorkelled, the trees above us were sprinkled with a confetti of cockatoos . . . And I found that a whole morning passed where I didn't constantly miss my kids.

'What about sharks?' was all Sebastian could say when I told him how we'd snorkelled beneath the pearly dawn sky.

'Well, apparently,' I parroted Lockie, 'seventy-three million sharks are lost to fishing and shark-fin soup every year but the number of people killed by sharks averages less than ten. *We* are more of a threat to sharks than they are to us.'

Sebastian's reply? 'But if you lose a leg, darling, it makes it so much harder to go dancing.' Which turned out to be *his* favourite contact sport. Something I discovered when he tricked me into joining him at a nightclub called JD's by telling me he'd seen Tally inside. At first I recoiled from the raucous, tortured music and the revellers jerking on the dance floor as if being electrocuted. It seems that the trick with modern dancing is to never tell your left buttock what your right buttock is doing, then tell the opposite to your feet. Actually, you don't really have to be able to dance. The best technique is just to hold on to a young stud muffin while *he* does. JD's, Sebastian told me, with one hand on my ass, stood for 'Just Divorced'. And even though I slapped his hand away, saying I didn't like the music, as I lay my head on my pillow that night,

I found that the tune was still warm in my ears . . .

Lockie relied on a different recipe for success. The instant coffee he'd heated by ping cuisine the day we met was a gastronomic aberration. He liked to cook what he called 'bush tucker'. At his weather-worn cottage on Bundeena Beach he served me up roolet mignon (which uses kangaroo instead of beef), tempura-battered crocodile, wallaby bourguignon, emu filet wrapped in prosciutto on a saltbush and potato tart, with a red wine and quandong peach sauce. He knew that the way to a woman's heart is through her stomach . . . that is definitely not aiming too high.

Sebastian thought 'bush tucker' a reference to colonial cunnilingus. When I shared a quick lunch with him one day after training, we ate at the cheapest Chinese restaurant in Cronulla. Not only were we probably eating bubonic beef but there was so much MSG in the food that I was wide-awake for the following fortnight.

Sebastian was also big on party games, like Scrabble, Monopoly or Twister. But only if you put the word 'strip' in front of them. 'You see? I'd be so much fun to take to the cricket.' He was a huge fan of skinny-dipping, too. 'It's the best way to stay young. Better than Botox.'

'So, you think I need Botox?'

'No, absolutely not. I like to read between your lines.'

While Sebastian couldn't wait to get his psychological kit off, Lockie found self-disclosure as alarming as I found being naked. Like most Aussie men, he kept his emotions fully clothed. Nor was he comfortable with public displays of affection. Susie said that the only thing she'd ever seen Lockie have his arm around in public was a beer glass. He was as emotionally self-sufficient as a Raymond Chandler hero. If Lockie was ever bitten by a snake, he'd just cut out the venom with his own knife, make the snake into a belt, then hike a hundred miles to the nearest shop to buy a pair of matching boots. Tough and ruthless when he had to be, I felt sure there was a romantic streak in him. Buried. Like a seam of gold.

When I asked him why he didn't show more emotion, Jack McLachlan replied, sardonically, 'Oh, you women. You want to be told how much we love you over and over again . . . At least three or four times a year. It's bloody exhausting.'

Sebastian, on the other hand, took to writing pithy haikus on the public noticeboard on the beach. This is a blackboard where warnings on surf conditions or the presence of stingers are chalked up daily . . . And now rhyming testaments to the attractiveness of my legs and, oh, also the poet's love of cricket.

231

Lockie, chalk duster in hand, was not amused. 'That kid didn't just kiss the blarney stone; he fucked it up the ass,' I overheard him say to his mates from the Last Man Standing Surf Team.

'Ah, I see you have no love of poetry,' Sebastian commented when he turned up for board practice half an hour late. 'Still, you're Australian. You can't help it, you're just not that high on the evolutionary scale.'

'Yeah, we Aussie blokes are inadequate Neanderthals, aren't we?' Lockie glowered, cracking his knuckles. 'Maybe our conversations aren't high-brow enough to make your ears pop. But at least we don't have bizarre fetishes. You can probably only get off by being touched on the genitals by a rubber-ized gardening glove. Am I right, mate?'

Sebastian took in Lockie's jogging shorts and damp T-shirt. 'Aren't you worried you'll have a heart attack, old boy? I'd give up jogging if I were you. You can't have sex after a heart attack, you know.'

'Is that right? I'd heard that it's OK to have sex after a heart attack, as long as you shut the door of the ambulance first.'

'To be fair, you do look pretty good for an eighty-year-old . . . Shame you're only fifty-two.'

'Shame you're still choosing your cereal for the toy.'

This exchange made me think about parenthood – another area in which Lockie and I could empathize, while Sebastian was still a big kid. The guy was so young he couldn't remember Michael Jackson before he was white. This is what I was thinking as I cooked pumpkin soup the week before Christmas. I was idly stirring in chives when, from outside, there came a great squelchy flipping and flopping and two flippered eleven-year-olds waddled in. Ruby and Ryan were as thick as, well, as the cream I was dolloping into the soup.

When Sebastian came to class that night and announced that he'd 'slept like a baby', I heard Lockie mutter, 'Really? That badly?'

Susie, Lockie and I shared a conspiratorial sigh.

Sebastian, sensing he'd lost precious ground, clawed back with the comment, 'Of course. It isn't easy being a mother. If it were, fathers would do it.'

'I do,' Lockie shrugged in reply.

And he did it bloody well. Lockie's image was misanthropic. But I'd seen him with his son at a local run in aid of a breast-cancer charity. He'd dressed as a giant lobster, a charity bucket dangling over one orange claw. The fastest runners had all finished before Lockie had even crossed the starting line. Lumbered down by the unwieldy suit, it took him about a week to complete the course. And, oh, how I warmed to him then. When Ryan got tired, Lockie carried him on one of his lobster feelers, an 'I Love Mum' sign draped over his other orange talon. I presumed it was breast cancer which had killed his wife, and my heart went out to him.

And I felt that Lockie grudgingly respected me, too.

233

'It's hard, being both parents,' he said one day. He didn't say much more, there was just an implied appreciation of my stoicism; a chummy camaraderie.

Having Lockie around would also be a good influence on my wild child, Tally. I'd seen her the day before, shimmering towards me in a diaphanous micro-mini and boob-tube, an angry red colour on her arm. From a distance she seemed to have contracted some kind of pestilence. As she got closer, the pestilence cohered into a tattoo of a boy's name.

'Tally!' I'd shrieked. 'How many times have I told you that a female shouldn't have any more holes in her body than are strictly speaking necessary? How many needles did you have?'

'You're really shocked, aren't you?' Tally seized on my comment with sour satisfaction. She smelt of lemon sherbet. The sweet aroma was so incongruous with her dark scowls and operatic gestures.

I ran through a few responses in my mind, finally settling on a comment which would be too innocuous to encourage her to repeat the parent-provoking gesture. 'Well, I wouldn't recommend tattooing personally, because of blood-poisoning potential, but still . . .' I leant forward to decipher the name distorted by the swelling of traumatized flesh, '. . . BYRON is a preferable name to Spider. Or Chook. You'll just have to get all your boyfriends to change their names by deed poll. Cheaper than having it removed.'

'Byron and I are never breaking up. Just because you couldn't keep your husband . . . You just don't get it. I'm *so* not like you.'

To keep from snapping back at her, I concentrated on the Asian symbol tattooed on her midriff. Although small and neat now, it would no doubt come to resemble a map of the Ukraine after she'd given birth to a few large kids later on in life. She claimed that the Chinese characters spelled out 'love, peace and tranquillity'.

'Oh yes. That's what the tattooist told you. In reality it probably decodes as sweet and sour prawns with bean shoots,' I joked. 'Tally!' I called out after her, but she just strode faster towards the house, taking the outside stairs two at a time. Then the screen door slapped between us.

When I told Lockie, he shook his head. 'Perhaps you should tell her the recipe for Progeny Pie. Take one daughter, boil down to size . . .'

The other person Lockie could cut down to size was Renée. I was at the salon helping Susie clean up one afternoon while waiting for Ruby to be dropped home after a night at her father's, when I felt the hairs on the back of my neck prickle. It could only mean one thing. 'They should use that tower on the beach to look out for real man-eaters like Renée Craven,' I moaned to Susie.

Hair freshly highlighted, tanned legs displayed in a designer dress, pedicured toes peeking provocatively out through the beads of her Manolo

Blahnik sandals, aura recently feng-shuied and chakras shimmering, in purple Prada, Renée was arriving. She'd come to inform me that she'd be picking Ruby up tomorrow after school for a shoot with a modelling agency. 'She's *per*fect.' Renée almost purred the word, her face luminous with excitement.

Ruby sauntered in behind her now, although it took me a moment or two to realize that she was actually my daughter. She was wearing a padded bra on her flat chest and clutching a doll which looked like a prostitute. She'd had a manicure, pedicure and an eyebrow wax, and was sporting a T-shirt which read '*Future Boy Magnet. Hands Off – For Display Purposes Only!*' A pink kiddy thong poked above her Juicy Couture designer tracksuit pants. She was also wearing St Tropez blusher, turquoise eye-shadow, mascara and lip-gloss. Her naturally wavy hair was dead straight, and spritzed and sprayed with gels.

'Ruby now has a cleansing, toning and moisturizing routine. Which I'd like her to keep up. Plus hundred-and-twenty-dollar designer ceramic hair-straighteners, which I don't want lost,' Renée instructed, patting Ruby's head as though she were a prized poodle.

I looked at her the way you'd look at a man on the tube who had fifty pounds of plastic explosives strapped to his body. 'Ruby's not a doll, Renée.'

'I'm grooming her for the Bondi Junior Beauty Pageant. It will do wonders for her confidence.

She'll win three thousand dollars plus a modelling assignment in London. I'll need to take her shopping for clothes before she shoots some photos for her portfolio. Say . . . after school Wednesday?'

My face in the salon mirror took on the pallor of a person who has just stepped off the Daredevil Thunder Mountain ride at a theme park. 'She's eleven years old!'

'Ruby is a tweenager.' Renée talked to me as though I were retarded. 'The ad's for a tweenager doll called Dollita. It's harmless.'

I'd seen the Dollita range. Each doll wears high-heeled boots, a mini-skirt that flicks up to reveal bikini briefs, gold earrings, a T-shirt labelled '*Pretty*' and streaked hair that falls to her knees. The dolls have bedroom eyes, pink, bee-stung lips and long, skinny legs so out of proportion to their torsos that in real life they'd keel over face-first and asphyxiate. The Dollita website encourages girls as young as nine to embrace cosmetic surgery and extreme dieting. 'No way.'

'You're just jealous that I can give her a mothering opportunity you can't,' Renée retorted, shrilly, the hard, bright light of the evangelical burning in her kohl-lined eyes. 'Jasper's really keen.' Straightening into the deportment of a department-store mannequin, she then snapped open her mobile and pressed her speed dial. 'Darling, as predicted, the shrew needs a little taming.'

Moments later, I saw Jasper, gliding through the

crowded shopping mall as easily as a knife through butter. I felt jittery in his presence, like a junkie needing a fix.

'Lucy,' he said, gently, all warm smiles and disarming charm. 'This could be a great start in a modelling career. Besides, with you only working sporadically . . . we need to be innovative.'

'A good mother would want to give her child an enriching experience,' added Renée superciliously.

'Oh, right, like divorce.' Susie, who'd been hovering protectively at my back, moved to my side, brandishing her hair-dryer like a gangster's handgun. 'Now *there's* an enriching experience. It seems to be making you very rich indeed.'

'Jasper,' I entreated him. 'This is our daughter you're talking about. What has happened to you? Why do you let this woman manipulate you?' My husband's brow wrinkled like cooling custard but he said nothing. 'OK. Why don't you get back to me after you've talked it over with all of your multiple personalities,' I concluded, angrily.

'It would be more honest to allow Ruby to decide,' Renée interjected unhelpfully.

Ruby looked from one parent to another, then raised her chin defiantly in an exact replica of Tally's standard sullen expression. Oh no. I would soon have teenage rebellion in stereo. 'I want to be a model,' she said with the obstinacy of a toddler.

I might as well have walked out there and then, found a chalked outline and lain down in it, because her words were a mortal blow. I had to haul Ruby out of the shop by her Juicy Couture designer tracksuit top. Renée and Jasper, making sympathetic noises to Ruby about her unreasonable mother, followed our zigzagging progress down the open-air mall.

Sweaty-faced, I looked up to see Lockie strolling down the pedestrian mall amidst a squall of raucous boys wearing ju-jitsu suits.

'Rubes!' Lockie raised an astounded brow skyward. 'What the hell happened to you, love? Looks as though you fell into a vat of paint. Where've you been? Haven't seen you at Nippers.'

'Ruby is following more feminine pursuits now,' Renée supplied. 'She was becoming way too much of a tomboy. Are you taking these boys to a martial arts class?' she demanded.

'Yeah. We do a bit of kick-boxing and karate. I was going to ask you to join us, Rubes.'

Renée recoiled. 'Isn't that irresponsible? Encouraging violence and brute force? It's so dangerous.'

Lockie shrugged. 'It's dangerous not to know how to look after yourself.'

'But you're equipping them to become violent killers.'

'That's not logical,' Lockie bridled. 'After all, you're equipped to be a prostitute, but you're not one. Are you?'

'That's debatable,' I snickered, overjoyed to see Renée blush a deep shade of furious puce beneath her foundation.

'You really should do something about those wrinkles around your mouth, Lucy,' Renée retaliated. Her voice had a nasal, brittle quality. 'They're really ageing.'

'They're called laugh lines and I got them from guffawing at the notion of *you* thinking you could be a good mother.'

The tension was all too much for Ruby, who dissolved into tears, making me instantly regret my outburst. She cried all the way home. The only way to win back my daughter's affections was to give in to her endless demands to have a pet. 'Just make sure it's flushable,' I whispered to Tally, who volunteered to undertake the trek to the pet shop before dinner. 'Like a goldfish or a stick insect or something.'

What she came back with was a diamond python snake named Fluffy. I made some whimpering noises associated with childbirth. I then tried to look innocent in an attempt to reassure the coiled creature that I had never, ever worn snake-skin high heels. Or handbags. That key ring was a gift!

'Best of all, Fluffy's free 'cause Ryan breeds them!' Ruby explained, her nose twitching with excitement. 'His dad said to tell you that snakes have had a rotten press since that business in the Garden of Eden. I've gotta get an animal licence, though, Mummy!'

Fluffy. Oh well. Looking on the bright side, not only was a snake the opposite of a Dollita doll but it also addressed Renée's problem with my wrinkles. I had accidentally discovered a homegrown solution to getting rid of laughterlines. Have a daughter who collects pet snakes, and, believe me, you will never laugh, smile or vaguely relax ever, ever again. Especially when the mouse she buys to feed it escapes. The *pregnant* mouse. Nothing like roaming your own home with a net and tranquillizer dart to take the joy out of life.

When Sebastian rang yet again to plead his case for tickets to the test match, I asked for advice on rodent-catching. His lame suggestion was that we should make love in my bed, then lie around saying cheesy things to each other to tempt the mice close enough to whack.

'Is sex all you can think about?' I asked him, tetchily.

'I like to have sex when I'm sad. I like to have sex when I'm lonely. I like to have sex when I'm happy. I like to have sex when it's raining. I like to have sex when it's steamy and hot. I like to have sex in the morning. I like to have sex in the evenings. I like to have sex in trains, planes and automobiles. I like to have tantric sex for hours and hours. I like to have quick-fix sex standing up backwards over the kitchen table. Otherwise, I don't have sex unless I'm really, really horny.'

'Oh,' I gulped.

After Lockie had caught the mice with his cat, we went for a walk along the bay, weaving down through the trees by the honeycombed sandstone rocks. The stillness of the bush before rain felt like an audience silently anticipating a performance.

'I heard that Sebastian is your personal trainer and I just wanted to say . . . A grown man has to have inspiration to make love to a woman. All a boy needs is a hard-on.'

'Making love? Oh my God! That's the last thing on my mind!' I laughed, my face staining red. 'My only attempt to find my G-spot led to a totally humiliating trip to the Accident and Emergency ward,' I blurted, which only made me blush more.

'*You* don't have to be good at making love, Lucy, because *I* am.' He gave me a look which I felt in my lingerie drawer. The air by the rocks was languid with moss and moisture. He nuzzled these words into my ear as he leant me back against the cool stone and pressed his body against mine, savouring my neck and throat, making the nerves there go wild. Lockie's musky smell – of boat petrol, fish and tobacco, with a tang of testosterone – kicked my pulse into double-time. The raw spicy scent of seaweed drying in the sun, the pungent aroma of male sweat and coconut suncream and the sigh of the sea on to the rocks below, combined into something disarmingly sensual. Lust spread across my skin, melting my thoughts in throbs. Just when I was feeling misty with desire, Jack McLachlan pulled away.

'You don't need sex, Lucy. You need tenderness,' he said in a low, plangent voice. And then he smiled at me, a sleepy, lazy smile just for me.

I *was* only taking Lockie to the cricket to make Jasper jealous. Wasn't I? I made a cursory stab at sorting my motives by consulting Susie. 'Lockie's kind of more handsome than he looks, if you know what I mean. I also like the way he's interested in big things . . . but happy in small ways.'

'What about Sebastian? And don't try to tell me you haven't had the hots for him. You've been moist with excitement since you first met in class. Put it this way, the chair got up when *you* did.'

'Well, not any more,' I said adamantly.

And yet in my dreams that night, Sebastian's smile floated like a little curl of seaweed on the foam . . .

A few days before Christmas I suggested Sebastian give me a lift home from class. At Shelly Beach, I asked him to swing in. After his battered old Chevy came to a halt, he kicked back and lit up a joint.

'So, you've finally realized that when it comes to charming the cricket board members I'm the man for the job,' he said cockily. 'I move in quite distinguished circles in London, you know. Which I would tell you about, except that it's crass to name-drop . . . as Prince William once advised me over dinner.' He grinned.

'Sebastian, I'm flattered, really flattered, that you would consider going with me to the cricket, but I am way too old for you. You're always going on about how old Lockie is; well, my birth certificate is written in Roman numerals.'

Sebastian raised one irreverent eyebrow, as he drew back on his joint. 'Easily fixed. I'll just make myself look more wrinkled. I'll fall asleep on my corduroy jacket.'

'You're not getting it, Sebastian. I don't go to the beauticians for a procedure. I go for a *quote*.'

Sebastian chuckled as he passed the joint my way.

I shook my head. 'You see? Yet more proof of our age gap. The hardest drug I do is evening primrose oil. The most reckless thing I'd ever done before my husband left me was to go to bed without flossing.'

Sebastian's fingers tentacled, enticingly, on to my bare thigh. 'Have you forgotten our mouth-to-mouth?'

I gnawed fretfully on the inside of my left cheek. 'Yes I have,' I lied. 'You see? I'm going senile. I am. No, really. I'm so forgetful that I only have a vague recollection of starting this conversation.'

'It's McLachlan, isn't it?' Sebastian said, taking another toke. 'He's trying it on. What's he got? The seventy-year-old itch? He's so ancient. I mean, how did you meet? No, no. Let me guess. You bid on him at an auction?' he taunted.

'Jack McLachlan's not old. He's distinguished and . . .'

'You mean extinguished. The man's geriatric. He should be wheeled into class sucking on an oxygen mask and clutching a brochure on cryonics.'

'Age has got nothing to do with it. He's

compassionate, caring, a conservationist. He saves whales . . .'

'Saving whales. Wow, if you accumulate the whole set can you sell them on eBay to an eccentric collector for a fuck-load of money?' Sebastian asked, sarcastically. 'Women hit their sexual prime in their forties and men in their twenties. It's a fact.'

'I'm sorry, Sebastian. But it's a fact that I don't sleep with people outside my species. You're too young.'

'Are liars your species? All that bullshit he goes on with about sharks being endangered by humans. He was nearly killed in a shark attack. Has he ever told you that?'

'This is just sour grapes. An entire vineyard.'

'But what does his hypocrisy matter when they're making such giant strides in the field of prosthetics? Still, out of curiosity, why don't you ask him what else he's lied to you about?'

'Sebastian, I realize that you're trying to put me off him, but I know what the man is made of by the way he parents Ryan. Lockie is a loving, warm and wonderful dad.'

'Really? Ha! Tell that to his wife.'

'I would if I could, but she's dead, sadly.'

'Dead to him, maybe, but nobody else.'

'What on earth do you mean, Sebastian?'

'She's in prison.'

My throat constricted and I couldn't speak for a moment. 'Who told you that?'

'I've had a snoop around. Giving up a high-powered job as a lawyer to save the planet and Do Creative Things With Play Dough? How sweet. My father's a lawyer in London. I got him to call some contacts in Melbourne. Jack McLachlan just sounded too good to be true. And guess what? He's not good at all. Word is that he's a womanizer. His wife hit the bottle, so he hit her. Then he burnt down their house to get the insurance.'

I refused to take him seriously. 'Blowing up the marital home! What a good idea. That's the housework done, then!'

'I'm only telling you this because I care about you. Then he framed his wife.' Sebastian's eyes were unreadable beneath his floppy fringe.

'This is nothing to joke about, Sebastian,' I swatted at him. 'This man works with children. If this ridiculous tittle-tattle got out, he could lose his job as a surfing instructor and his captaincy of the club.'

'He took their kid and got his wife sent to prison for insurance fraud so that he wouldn't have to give her anything in the divorce. Oh, except an orange dayglo jumpsuit.'

An intense throbbing in my temples told me that this insane conversation had reached saturation point. 'You are never to repeat this rubbish, do you hear me?'

'I feel totally remorseful – but I think I have the strength of character to fight it,' he concluded glibly.

I slammed out of his car before he could say another word, and jogged the rest of the way home, fuming. But, once the children had gone to bed, even though I didn't believe a word Sebastian had told me, I found myself trawling the net for old newspaper stories on shark attacks . . . And there it was – a report on a lawyer named Jack McLachlan, miraculously surviving an attack from a Great White. I then looked up the online registration of deaths. And couldn't find any trace of a Mrs Jack McLachlan.

After a fitful night's sleep, I was down at the beach by nine to find Lockie. As well as inter-beach competitions and surf carnivals, Nippers also get a Christmas treat – Santa in a pair of red board shorts and flippers zooming in over the waves on a rubber ducky, bearing gifts. The kids flocked around Lockie, bearded up as Santa, as he distributed toys and sweets by the edge of the sea.

After the mayhem had died down and the children were all on a dangerous sugar high, I watched as Lockie, sweltering in his Santa suit, slipped away to the club. I followed.

'I love Christmas. It's so much fun getting all those gifts you can't wait to exchange.' Lockie smiled at me.

I took a deep breath and leapt right in. 'Whether it's a consequence of careless exotic pet owners, Australia is alarmingly stocked with things that want to eat you, wouldn't you say, Jack?'

Lockie, stripping off his padded Santa belly and

red board shorts, turned to face me in his budgie smugglers. It reminded me of the first day I'd met him, right here, in this room.

'I've realized there are three stages of a man's life,' he chuckled, wryly, ignoring my question. 'You believe in Santa Claus. You don't believe in Santa Claus. Then you *are* bloody Santa Claus.' He dropped a hello kiss in the curve of my neck.

'Jack, you're not listening. Sharks are a little more frightening than your standard-issue squirrel, wouldn't you agree? Which is the only wildlife my kids and I are used to, coming from England. But you are always telling me sharks are harmless, right?'

'Well, yeah. Swimmers shouldn't worry about being eaten by a shark . . . Although a large number have lost weight as a result of an encounter . . .' He grinned.

'But you'd agree that you could truly claim to have had a bad day when part of it has been spent with your head inside the mouth of a Great White. Why didn't you ever tell me you'd been elected into this elite club?'

'Ah . . .' Lockie shrugged one bronzed shoulder. 'It was a one-off. A freak accident. Years ago. It was my own stupid bloody fault for diving in the wrong place. South of Perth. Seal breeding-ground. Suddenly, everything went dark without warning. The seabed disappeared. I seemed to be inside this eerie cave. I must have been in shock, because it took me some moments to realize that

I was caught in the jaws of a Great White. My head and shoulders and one arm were inside the shark's mouth. The long-sleeved, lead-lined vest I'd worn to keep my body from floating upwards saved me from being bitten in two. Even though the shark shook me like a cat shakes a mouse, I've only got a few tiny scars. I'm a lucky bastard, I know. Instinctively I clawed my free arm down the outside of its head and gouged at its eye-socket with the chisel I'd been using to prise free the abalone. The shark opened its mouth and I wriggled free. My diving goggles had been smashed into my face . . . That's how my nose got broken. Amazingly, I was still conscious. My lungs were bursting. The shark was swimming in ever-tighter circles around me. Its big, black eye was staring straight into my face without one hint of fear . . . I just bolted for the surface. Luckily the shark uttered a "No, thanks. I already ate." Or maybe I just didn't taste sweet enough.' He smirked. But I refused to be charmed.

'So, you tell people sharks are safe, but they're not. You lied to me. What else have you lied about?'

'Lucy, what's the matter?' Jack McLachlan looked up at me with such rumpled perplexity that it made my heart lurch.

'What about your wife? Was she wearing a lead-lined vest when you dumped her? Did she see you circling closer and closer? Was there blood in the water?'

Lockie's eyes were bright and he swallowed hard

several times. The muscles in his face knotted and flexed with emotions he couldn't or wouldn't express.

'There's a rumour, well, it's tacky, Jack, but people are saying that you had an affair. They're also saying that you wanted to get rid of your wife. I'm sorry to tell you, but the gossip is that you burnt down your house and then framed her so that you could get custody of Ryan.'

'That's not true. Who is the mongrel bastard telling you this crap?'

'Did your house burn down or not?'

'Well, yes . . . but . . .'

'Then where is your wife?'

Lockie looked at me the way a smoking beagle looks at a medical researcher – as though he knows that such experiments need to be conducted for the sake of knowledge, but is still pleading for release.

'What happened to your wife?' I reiterated.

The muscles twitched under the skin of his face but he remained silent.

'Why do you let people believe that she's dead? What have you got to hide, Jack?'

Lockie turned away. He seemed to be fighting off an emotion he did not want witnessed. Guilt, I deduced, for the way he had treated his poor spouse. Mr Rochester, that's who he was. Making me the gullible Jane Eyre. 'You're a wife disposer . . . Just like my husband.'

'No!' He recoiled from the accusation.

Cross-currents of feeling were pulling me to and fro. 'I let my guard down with you because I thought you were in mourning for your wife.'

Jack McLachlan's expression froze in a granite-like grimace. 'You're talking about things you don't understand.'

'Oh, I understand all right. You've done to your wife exactly what my husband is doing to me. Trading me in for another woman, starving me of money, then trying to get custody.'

'It's not true.' His eyelids pleated at the corners with pain.

'Then tell me, where is your wife?'

We stared at each other in misunderstanding, sensing that the empathy delicately forged between us was dissolving. All at once Lockie no longer looked handsome to me. His face, which I'd thought of as rugged, seemed merely weather-worn and leathery. His nose no longer Roman, but a wedge of cheese. The strong countenance I'd thought seamed in wisdom suddenly just appeared heavy and stern. Now I thought about it, there had always been too much join-the-dots perfection about Jack McLachlan. The books by Melville, the painting hobby, the Bach cello suites, the successful lawyer who downsized for the love of his son.

First my husband betrayed me, then my best friend, followed by Jack McLachlan. From this minute on I vowed to be suspicious of everyone. If I met the Dalai Lama I'd presume he was a closet Catholic, I'd assume Heather Mills had a full complement of limbs and Andre Agassi – hair.

Outside the club windows, the beach broiled in the glare of the summer sun. I turned on my heel and walked out into it. My last image of Jack McLachlan was of him standing, head bowed, arms hanging by his sides, palms open, red Santa hat askew, his cotton-wool beard at half-mast – a subordinate clause, I would have punned, if we had still been pals.

'Lucy . . .'

'Yes?'

'I'd like to tell you . . . but I can't.'

'Take a tip from Santa,' I called over my shoulder. 'Just visit me once a year, OK?'

CHAPTER 16

TREADING WATER

Over the next week, I seriously started to rethink the guppy approach to parenting – i.e., eating your young.

Boyfriends landed in Tally's life like sailors on the beach at Omaha, storming ashore and then, one by one, getting their heads blown off. We'd had to endure Tally's latest – the sort of guy who spent more on nostril-piercing than armpit hygiene – all through our first Aussie Christmas, only for them to break up by Boxing Day. All that remained of Byron was the tattoo. I researched laser removal. It would take five sessions, costing three hundred bucks each time. But Jasper was late **again** with his maintenance money.

'Money doesn't bring happiness, you know,' he'd texted.

I was on such a tight budget, I'd spray-painted old toilet-rolls and glued beads on to pine-cones to make festive home-made Christmas decorations. As I threw them in the bin I thought of Renée, burning through cash at the rate of a medium-sized space programme, and mused on the fact that I'd really like to see how miserable money could make me.

The day of the cricket, I'd planned to look sensational. But my preparation time was spent driving Tally down the coast to a girlfriend's house. For teenage girls, a sleep-over takes on more global magnitude than fatal illness or an impending terrorist attack. 'If you don't take me right now, I'll die,' she drama-queened, looking down from her bedroom window and pouting her pink-glossed lips.

'But I'm in a hurry myself.' I was hanging out the washing, lost amid the crisp white sheets undulating on the line.

'Thanks! Thanks a *lot*. I've blobbed now, thanks to you. Are you really determined to ruin my life?' She'd obviously been at a critical stage of mascara application.

Ruby too, engrossed as she was with Fluffy, seemed totally unaware that her mother was on the brink of a beauty break-down. When the wretched snake got loose in the house, the situation called for an adult to do something adult. As there was no man around, that adult had to be me. Any minute now I would have to put down my mango body-scrub and go out there and face that python. The situation seemed so surreal, it was tempting to re-name the creature Monty. This maternal chaos meant that I was left with about fifteen minutes to get ready. In a panic, I spritzed my underarms with a bleach spray which promised to remove all mould and shaved my legs with Listerine, which would keep them mint-fresh for up to ten hours. A spray of fake tan in my hair and I was a grooming sensation.

Once upon a time I used Crème de la Mer, which is as expensive as caviar – about a hundred quid per bead. But I was now so broke, I was using an old tube of foot cream on my face – handy for the woman with a tendency to put her foot in her mouth. After rummaging through the unironed laundry, all I could find in the clean underwear department were my airline anti-DVT socks with the grip of a boa constrictor. I slipped on a dress I'd bought at the Salvation Army second-hand shop. But did it matter that I looked as though I'd been dressed by Stevie Wonder, when I'd have the most glamorous human handbag? Glamorous, *young*, human handbag! Oh how eagerly I anticipated bumping into Jasper. 'Are you seeing a shrink yet, Lucy?' he'd ask. 'No, I'm seeing a toy boy, actually.'

Sebastian had just returned from a surf when I arrived at his apartment in a 1950s block of blond brick flats. His mates invited me in to wait. I picked my way over wetsuits and surfboards to the couch. At least I think it was a couch. It could have been a dead yak. The indistinguishable young men with their matted blond locks and gleaming brown torsos brought their dog inside to entertain me. Unfortunately, they were still at that age where they think it's funny to feed your pets beer, then watch them fall over. As hard as it was to tear myself away from this fascinating display, I took in my surroundings. The dripping tap, the piles of plates left 'soaking' in the sink, the mildewed dish-cloth half-submerged in soggy, filthy sink water, the walls seasick yellow, with lighter squares where other people's posters had been pulled down; it was so reminiscent of the flats I'd shared as a student, I gulped – *twenty years ago*. Good God! I was so goddamned old I could barely do that mental arithmetic without a calculator.

I excused myself and knocked on Sebastian's bedroom door, before pushing it open. The man had a beanbag instead of a chair, a futon instead of a bed and old wine bottles as candleholders. The decorations stretched to a batik sarong curtain and a stolen street sign. 'Go Back, You Are Going the Wrong Way.' Any art was hung on the wall with Blu-tack. (When I told Susie later she just shook her head and said, 'Darl, if I go out with a bloke and he has Van Gogh's *Sunflowers* on the wall, it had better be because he paid thirty bloody million bucks for it!')

Sebastian was half-dressed in tight black trousers and thick leather belt, his toned torso about to be worshipped by the white cotton of a clingy T-shirt. Sebastian caught me looking at him and shrugged on his shirt with a grin. 'You know, celibacy, if caught early, is curable.'

'Hurry up. We'll be late.'

'Apparently, 50 per cent of married people are having affairs, and the other 50 per cent will no doubt be looking for one as soon as they read that statistic. It's no big deal, sweet cheeks.'

'This is the day I make my husband jealous. Remember?' I handed him an Armani jacket, crisp white shirt and Versace tie that Jasper had left behind.

We parked the car and followed the flow of Akubra-hatted cricket lovers into the ground. Lockie had once explained that the Akubra is the 'lid of choice' for both real Aussie men and those 'pretentious soft cocks' who want people to *think* they're real Aussie men. But we followed a panama-hatted brigade up the wood-panelled staircase to the prestigious private members' room. What, I wondered, was the collective noun for prime ministers? An oration of? An ego of? Because there were at least four of them here today. Present, past, future . . . complemented by a whole bevy of cricketing greats, famous actors and TV personalities. Michael Parkinson was trading anecdotes with Russell Crowe; Shane Warne with Hugh Jackman. After aperitifs and nibbles, we chosen few moved out to the shaded seats in the grandstand to watch the start of play. But my eyes were on the door, awaiting Renée and Jasper's appearance.

I wouldn't say that her dress was scanty, but I've seen more silk on a worm. Renée's frock was so flimsy it seemed to be made of a soluble material, possibly the same stuff as those translucent breath-mint strips that dissolve on your tongue. I jabbed Sebastian in the ribs and he kissed me, as planned, full on the mouth. Oh, the sweet revenge of your estranged husband seeing you running your hands over the taut musculature of a tawny love god half your age.

Renée immediately moved towards me through the members' room with the hungry, predatory look of a piranha in Prada.

'Oh, I'm so sorry. Someone told you it was fancy dress!' she meowed, looking my second-hand frock up and down with contempt.

'Isn't it time you went to the vet's and got your claws done? Besides, I think *you're* the one in fancy dress . . .' I indicated her sun hat, which was effectively shading her eyes from my scrutiny. When I say sun hat, it was more as if a small flying saucer had got lost and was pausing for reconnaissance upon her cranium.

'Aren't you going to introduce me?' Renée purred.

'This is Sebastian. My . . . *boyfriend.*'

Her eyes bulged. 'Wait. *You're* going out with *Lucy*? Gosh, what's that sound? Oh, it's just the bottom of a barrel being scraped.'

'A sound you recognize, because that's where Jasper got *you* from.'

'Isn't he a little too young for you, Lucinda? There are three signs of senility, you know: memory deterioration and . . .'

258

'The other two have slipped your mind, right?'
I lashed out, reverting to the puerile bitchery of
the school playground.

Renée feigned injury. 'Even though you insist on
bad-mouthing me to everyone you meet, I still
have affection for you, Lucy. For old times' sake.
And so, senile or not, it didn't slip my mind to
come and tell you that Jasper and I won't be here
today. We've had a better offer, actually. Cruising
on Jamie Packer's yacht. Cruising, literally, as Tom
Cruise is going to be there!' she trilled. 'What a
fabulous way to celebrate our engagement.'

The noise I emitted sounded similar to a rhinoc-
eros being fed into a food-processor.

'Engaged? You and Jasper? Actually, I don't think
that's possible. His family totally object.'

'His family?'

'Yes, his bloody wife and children!'

Renée's new-found radiance was as flashy as the
diamond ring I now noticed on her finger.
'Speaking of which . . .' She extracted some legal-
looking papers from her bag and laid them on the
table next to me. 'It's a petition for dissolution.
Pleadings, I believe they're called. Divorce papers,'
she explained to my perplexed expression. 'The
solicitor wanted to post it but I thought it im-
polite not to deliver it in person.'

My whole world imploded right there and then.
But as I'd rather eat my own pancreas than break
down in front of my arch-enemy, I forced myself
to stay intact and aloof. 'Why get married and

make one man suicidal when you could stay single and destroy thousands?' I taunted.

'It's painful, I know,' Renée conceded. 'But, like ripping off a Band-Aid, the quicker the better, no? I suggest you instruct a solicitor.'

'Gee, I'll have to think of a congratulatory present, won't I? But what do you give the woman who's had everyone? Herpes? The clap? A case of genital lice, I guess. Oh, and please tell Jasper from me that your wedding ceremony will have to be held in an accountant's office, because all you want is his money. Our money.' But I was talking to the back of her Philip Treacy hat as she hip-wiggled towards the stairs.

'What a cunt,' Sebastian concluded, with just the warmest hint of admiration in his voice.

Any person with an IQ, even a moderately sized amoeba, would know that alcohol and heartbreak don't mix. But the booze was flowing freely. It had been ages since I'd had a drink, but when a bottle came my way I dived right in without armbands. I savoured the throaty richness of the Sémillon and the smoky, burnt flavour of a Chardonnay. A bottle later and I was asking people what sex they were, and then laughing hysterically when they answered.

'Wine really does improve with age,' I slurred to Shane Warne over lunch. 'The older I get the more I adore wine!' I think I was sitting on his lap at the time. As the afternoon wore on, I was on more laps than a serviette. With Sebastian preoccupied with the cricket, I was indulging in the kind of drinking that can lead to thinking that tongue-kissing a major Hollywood actor you've never met before, then cackling maniacally until you pee your pants, is a fun and desirable thing to do.

Just to top off my stunning debut in Sydney society, during afternoon tea, I think I may have put my tongue in a prime-ministerial ear. 'I actually hate cricket. I've had marriages which have lasted less time than a cricket match,' I said to the PM flippantly, before shattering into great, gut-wrenching sobs which distorted my lipsticked mouth and smeared make-up all down his sleeve.

'My husband's getting married again. And even though I won't be invited to the engagement party, I feel no jealousy or bitterness towards Renée, who is a syphilitic slut,' I explained to the Minister of Defence.

'So, how have you enjoyed your move to Australia?' one of the ex-Prime Ministers asked in a desperate attempt to distract me with a change of topic.

What I would have said, although I was now sobbing too hard, is that I'd thought I was moving to Australia. But what I'd actually moved in to was a castle in the air.

CHAPTER 17

WOMAN OVERBOARD

Next morning I just wandered around in a daze, clutching the divorce petition and lurching from one emotion to another. I would cry and rage, then withdraw into a foetal curl of self-loathing. I was totally exhausted, yet couldn't sleep because of a dull ache in my chest.

As Tally was on a sleep-over, at least she wasn't hogging the phone because she hadn't talked to her best friend in, oh, say, *twelve seconds*. But it dawned on me bleakly that there was nobody I could ring. Normally, if I were ever in a state of despair, I'd ring Jasper.

I was so upset I forgot it was my forty-third birthday until Ruby burst into the kitchen while I was taking down the final Christmas decorations. She was balancing a bunch of hand-picked wild flowers and a cup of cold tea and soggy toast.

'Shall we get your party ready? Is Daddy coming?'

A good indication that your marriage is over is when your husband proposes to your best friend. I felt like the food on the supermarket shelf, with my obsolescence date stamped on my forehead.

How to tell my daughter that her mother was little more than a brood mare, put out to pasture?

'Sweetie, Daddy is . . .' it was better she heard it from me, even though the Rules of Disengagement forbade me from trashing Renée to my children, '. . . living with Aunty Renée because they are in love. Isn't that exciting?' The words singed my lips on the way out.

'Oh,' she said, not taking it in. 'Does that mean I can go modelling?'

What a Christmas and birthday it had been. When Tally arrived home from her sleep-over to find me slumped across the table, laced in Christmas lights, with holly in my hair and tinsel tassels on my earlobes, she rolled her eyes. 'Shall we wait till New Year's Day before we take you down?'

I was crawling into my clothes when the mail-man came with birthday cards from London, which made me throb with loneliness. But amidst the London mail was also my Mastercard statement. I dissolved into tears. I owed seven thousand pounds and couldn't think of a way of paying it back without selling the house in Hampstead, but that was in Jasper's name. When the doorbell rang and I saw the packages in the courier's truck with Jasper's name on them, I thought for one irrational, euphoric moment he'd had second thoughts and was atoning by showering me with gifts. But the parcels turned out to be merely possessions that had come by sea mail. I stood, transfixed by all the unpacked boxes in the hall. I spent the rest of the morning unpacking my husband's belongings and sobbing uncontrollably into his jumpers and socks and Rolling Stones CDs. If I didn't get a grip I was going to end up as one of those women on a confessional daytime telly show called *I Chopped Up My Husband's Lover and Fed Her to Him in a Lovely Tasty Casserole.*

And so I opted for the time-honoured female response to all moments of emotional chaos. I went to the hairdresser's. The salon is the new confessional. Women, with their hair turbaned with tinfoil, make a clean breast of it all to their stylists. Cocooned by female camaraderie, life just seems more cosy and cosseting.

'I'm too young to be this old,' I snivelled to Susie. 'I'm forty-three. I'm older than most of the *buildings* in Australia.'

'The secret of staying young,' Susie comforted, interrupting her energetic floor sweeping to administer chocolate to me in large chunks, 'is to get off the booze, only eat organic food, hit the sack early . . . and to lie your tits off about how old you are.' It was New Year's Eve and Susie's salon was buzzing. Despite being flat-out, Susie led me to a chair, sat me down and started brushing my hair in big, soothing strokes. 'I too am going to turn forty, Lucy . . . any decade now,' she added, drily.

'Next time I'm going to marry an older man with a heart murmur so that "till death us do part" takes on a much shorter connotation,' I addressed her in the mirror.

Susie laughed richly above the fffttt of hairsprays, but then her hair-brushing strokes became more gentle. 'Next time?' she probed.

I showed her the crumpled divorce petition in my hot, sweaty hands. 'I'm going to get a gun and kill her.'

'That's a beaut idea. Then, when you get sent to prison for the rest of your natural life, you can take up macramé and make me a nice pot-holder.'

'They'll never know it was me. I'll kill her in a drive-by shooting.'

'What in? You car is about to be towed away by the cops because you didn't turn up for that court hearing about your rego. So, what are you gonna do? A drive-by shooting *on a bus*?'

I sank my head down on to my folded arms and let out a desolate sob. Women immediately gathered to soothe and pet. Half-dyed clients in foils, some with dripping locks, others curlered or creamy with treatments, interrupted their perms and blow-dries to bring tea, tissues, photos of celebrities looking fat in magazines, and to administer various versions of 'You're better off without him'. They layered on kindness and comfort and morale-raising compliments, plus satisfyingly bitchy barbs about the Other Woman.

'Try to concentrate on small, everyday tasks.' Susie placed a gentle hand on the nape of my neck. 'There's no short cut, darl. One day you'll just wake up feeling stronger and start picking up the pieces of your life. But the best thing you could do right bloody now is to go and get laid. Birthdays are nature's way of telling a woman to get a toy boy.'

The middle-aged women in the salon nodded, their multicoloured heads moving in unison like a bunch of poppies in a breeze. They all joined in to play a game called 'How Low Can You Go?' There was no actual limbo involved, but a lot of bending of birth dates to a more desirable digit to hook a younger man.

'Can I get away with 40? . . . 35? . . . 32?' Susie asked, pouting into the mirror. 'Hey, the sun is going down so we'll soon have nature on our side,' she chortled good-naturedly.

I daubed at my eyes with a tissue. 'The only way I could ever have sex with another man would be to have a fantasy.'

'Really? Why? Sebastian is a total spunk rat. Believe me, girls, he looks as good close up as he does through the binoculars . . . Why would you want to pretend *he* was someone else?'

'No! What I mean is, I'd have to fantasize that *I* was someone else. Say, Cameron Diaz or Angelina Jolie or some supermodel or other.'

Susie threw back her head to emit one of her raucous guffaws. 'You kinky devil.'

She then urged me to stay for a cup of tea. But as she was frantically busy, I left the salon and walked along the beach so the briny breeze could clear my head. Toes sinking into wet sand, I pondered what my friend had said. Surely, orgasms, taken in moderation, couldn't hurt anybody? The worst thing about being abandoned is the marital bed – cold as day-old porridge. Sebastian was twenty-five. Surely, at my age, I should have childproofed my love life? But I found myself dwelling on his velvet, sun-kissed skin. Hell, women my age would *pay* to have sex with a man like that. And he'd driven me home drunk from the cricket, so he'd seen the worst of me.

The coast was creamy with mist and the sea lapped like a cat at the shore. The air in January is thick enough to brush against your face. The heat beat on to my arms and legs. My skin tingled and ached to be touched. When I looked up from my feet, I found myself outside the North Cronulla surf club. Lockie's car was nosed up against the kerb. Sebastian was desirable, yes, but he'd flirt with an inanimate object. Lockie was just the opposite. The man should have had a doormat which read, 'Fuck off. Not welcome.' Whereas Sebastian was all charm and witty banter, Lockie's succinct sentences had no room for wasted words. I was still angry and confused about him, but I hadn't really given Jack an opportunity to defend himself. He was full of mystery and secrets, a little like the signal he'd taught us in class. '*Investigate Submerged Object. Proceed Further Out.*'

Susie had once explained to me that a 'spunk rat' is a man you notice . . . but a 'stud' is a man who notices you. I had paid drooling attention to Sebastian. (Who wouldn't? With that ice-cream-cone-shaped torso?) But Lockie had been attentive to me. And loyal. It hadn't been fair of me to dismiss him so brutally after all he'd done for me. (Under my cross-examination, Lockie had reluctantly confessed that he had been the one who'd tipped over the Portaloo, ensuring it was Renée in the shit for once.) The poor man was probably wounded and withdrawn. I wanted to give him one more chance.

I creaked open the clubhouse door, worried that Jack McLachlan might be holed up in the dark, spooning cold baked beans straight out of the tin while listening to *The Death March*. I was pulled up short to find him with a big-breasted blonde. And she was all over him like a fake tan.

Lockie's eyes jumped to mine. His greeting was one of pained geniality. 'Oh, g'day.' The expression in his eyes was baffled disappointment.

'Gee, it obviously took you a long time to get over me,' I faked a casual comment, to distract from the blush which was staining my face.

Lockie stood up from the couch with slow dignity. The bimbo, whose age was hard to ascertain due to Botox and collagen, eventually put out her pink, manicured paw.

'I'm Chardonnay,' she chirped pertly. 'Chardonnay Chappell.' She wore a low-cut top revealing melon-shaped breasts which didn't move when she did, and low-rider jeans with a cherry-pink satin G-string peeking provocatively above the leopard-skin belt. I glanced down at my faded tracksuit pants with embarrassment. She smelt like frangipani. After a day and night of drinking, I was sure my breath alone could immobilize a charging water buffalo.

'I got the sack as a bar maid. I have this rool good trick of crushin' beer cans between me boobs and hanging spoons off me nipples. The blokes loved it an' that. But apparently, it's in breach of hotel bloody licensing laws.' Her sentences went up at the end, as though everything she said was a question and not a statement. It made me yearn for a conversational cadence. 'So, I'm gonna be a surf lifesaver. It's gonna be just like *Baywatch* an' that.' Chardonnay's mouth was so full of silicone the woman could undertake a surf rescue using her own lips as the inflatable raft. 'And best of all, Jackie-boy's not gonna charge me, are you, love?'

Jackie-boy? I winced.

'Any fool can apply to join surf lifesaving and many of them do.' Jack McLachlan gave me a flat, measuring look in which I saw his opinion of me shift. 'But few of them have what it takes. Chardonnay, however, is very . . .' he chose his word carefully, 'persistent.'

I stared at Lockie, aghast. How could any man go to bed with her? She was model thin – a human thermometer in high heels. I could use her to take my temperature – which was actually very, very high all of a sudden. Judging from the bimbo's

269

conversation, her mind was obviously as empty as her refrigerator. If Chardonnay were an actual beverage, she'd be alcopop – sweet, cheap and quickly intoxicating. There was only one explanation for Lockie's attraction to her. The woman must wear beer-flavoured lip-gloss.

'I'm gonna get me bronze thingy and then I might even get a job at some posh resort someplace, doin' water sports,' she giggled. 'Though I'm already pretty good at that, aren't I, Jackie-boy?'

I watched her slink across the room to apply more lipstick, straining into the mirror with savage concentration. If only it were possible to harness the static cling in her synthetic clothes, it could power the whole of the Cronulla peninsular. I turned towards Jack to whisper a thin-lipped aside. 'So, tell me. When Chardonnay was filling in the consent form, where it said "sign" did she write Pisces or Aquarius?'

'She's straightforward.' Lockie shrugged, crossing to his desk to irritably attack his paperwork. 'Which is better than being a braggart. That metrosexual knob and total toss bag you're so keen on swaggers while sitting down. Quite a feat. So, what did you come here for?' His fury was tight but monumental. He flexed one muscled forearm by his side.

'I . . . ah . . . I came to . . . I felt bad that I didn't really ever give you a chance to explain yourself . . .' I said to the trophy cabinet above his head. 'To put forward your side of the story,' I amended. 'I . . .'

'Doan worry about it. I was only being nice to you for the cricket tickets. That was it. That was all.'

Oh, happy birthday to me, I thought, winded by his words. 'Right. Yes. I realized that. You know, it's the constant brag of the Australian male that you never brag. But you seem to be pretty confident that I fancied you. Well, guess again. Hell, I wouldn't give you mouth-to-mouth resuscitation if you were Jesus himself.'

'If I were Jesus I'd be walking on the water, not teaching whingeing Poms like you how to avoid drowning in it.' He put on his Stonehenge face. 'Now, if you'll excuse me, I have a class to attend to.'

'What? Now?' Storms descending from the north had whipped the seas into a huge creamy swell with meringue-like peaks. From Palm Beach to Cronulla Point, all Sydney's beaches were closed to swimmers. I looked below to see a group of Lockie's trainees staring nervously out at the ocean as though it were a growling beast. The boom of the waves cannoned against the rocks. A few surfies had braved the elements but their boards just kept flipping skyward, riderless.

'You shouldn't send the boys out in that big surf. It's too dangerous.'

'Funnily enough, that's just the time people *need* rescuing.'

'You just want to kill all other men.'

'And why would I want to do that?'

'Because you think all those women were joking

271

when they said they wouldn't shag you if you were the last man on earth.'

'It would be so bloody nice if you had an occasional flash of silence,' Jack McLachlan said, pushing up on to his feet. 'That would make talking to you so much more interesting.'

I was out the door and sprinting down the road before my legs let my brain know where they were carrying me. I didn't knock, but pushed straight in through the fly-screen door. I ignored the young men and their teenage girlfriends sprawled around the living room, smoking joints and swigging beers. Sebastian was lying across his bed with the blinds drawn wearing nothing but a towel, hands lazily laced behind his head as he watched the cricket on a small flickering television screen in the corner. His chest was the size of a South American country. A slanting tongue of lamplight lit up his lap and I could see the outline of his large appendage.

After agonizing for, oh, about two-fifths of a second, I straddled him on the bed, pinning his arms beside him with all my body weight. 'Remember what you said about chastity being curable if caught early enough?'

I kissed his mouth ravenously, devouring his neck, earlobes, chest. He broke free with muscular ease, unhooked my bra with composed expertise, found my nipple and flicked his tongue back and forth until it went hard. His towel fell away. Sebastian's erect member was so big I mistook it for some sort of monument in the centre of a town. I almost started directing traffic around it. He rolled me sideways on to my back and, in one flowing motion, my tracksuit and panties were down, lassoing one ankle. His fingers edged up my thigh and then plunged inside me. My legs yielded to the weight of his body and I wrapped them around his hips, tugging him against me with a pang of hunger I hadn't felt for so long.

It was New Year's Eve. My life was so dull, I'd been toying with a resolution to take up a new vice – internet dating, cocaine, even lesbianism (hey, it was only a slip of the tongue), indoor competitive nude badminton . . . I was so inexperienced, not only had I never joined the Mile High Club, I'd never even joined the *Foot* High Club and made love in the back of a car. I'd never read the *Kama Sutra*, let alone tried all the positions. What if I'd been doing it wrong all these years? But I suddenly found I didn't need advice on vice because I was pulling him into me with an animal force I didn't know I possessed. I'd been parched for so long, and he was the long, cool, sensual drink I'd craved. I twisted under him, caught in the heat and the slide and the thrill of it. There was nothing but obliterating sensation as we contorted like origami creations for the next hour, until a sweet and inward rapture spread through my thighs, leaving me tranquil, calm – serene at last.

I lay on his sculptured pectoral and waited for

my endorphin high to be replaced with embarrassment and mortification. How had I allowed
myself to be led astray, off the path of virtue? I'd
obviously been guided here by twatnav . . . But no
guilt gland throbbed. In fact, all I could think of
was the erotic encore. And if there's one thing a
twenty-five-year-old can do, it's more. There was
nothing for it but to give the guy a horizontal
ovation.

CHAPTER 18

MASS RESCUE

I slammed Susie's back door behind me as though a wild pack of foaming-jawed dingoes was pursuing me at pace.

'What?' It was nearly midnight and Susie was in her nightie making cocoa in the kitchen.

'I've done something terrible!' I panted.

'What?' she yawned. 'Hacked into the Pentagon and set off a missile? Gone on the game to fund a drug habit?'

'Had sex with a twenty-five-year old.' I beamed euphorically.

Susie zapped to life. She excitedly poured another cup of cocoa for me and slammed a muffin into the jaws of her metallic toaster. 'Oh my God! How do you feel? Is remorse eating you alive? Sit! Tell me *every*thing. Do you think you should have a big A for adulteress branded on to your dirty, naughty little forehead? How do you feel?'

'I feel . . . like a bloody idiot that I waited so long. I feel liberated. In lust. As if I'm being tickled from the inside with feathery fingers. The air tastes sweeter,' I gushed. 'I'm the effervescence in the champagne bottle, the froth on the wave, the phosphorescence in the water . . .'

'That bad, eh?' Susie said, drily.

'It was paradisiacal.'

'You mean aphrodisiacal.' Susie rescued the muffins and slathered on honey and butter, greedy for detail. 'So, I gather he was good in the sack, then?'

'You know what? I always thought sex with Jasper was so fantastic. But Sebastian doesn't just have sex. It's like playing twister in the nude.'

'Yeah, I shoulda guessed there was a little something wrong with *my* relationship when my ex-hubby started flossing during foreplay.'

'I know. Jasper once corrected my grammar when I was talking dirty.'

'No!'

'Yes. In the last year, he practically smoked *during* sex. And do you know what else? For the first time, I feel that I just don't need a husband. No more sulking and pining. I'm going to get an exotic pet, dye my hair fire-engine red and wear nothing but leopard-skin.'

'Happy New Year, darl.' Susie hugged me warmly.

Susie was, without doubt, the best friend I had ever had. When Jasper left me I'd felt like an astronaut who'd crash-landed on an unexplored planet. If it hadn't been for Susie, the highlight of my day would have been inhaling Ruby's Pritt Stick homework glue. 'I owe you everything, Suze. A kidney, at least. I just hope one day I can repay you for all your kindness.'

'You can right now, ya big dag, by making me another cup of cocoa while we watch the fire-works.' She flicked on the television to watch Sydney Harbour exploding with colour.

'Well, that pretty much sums up my sexual encounter,' I boasted, beaming.

'Male mystique,' Susie mused. 'That indefinable something about a hot-to-trot young spunk rat with a huge cock.'

The mood of a middle-aged, first-time adulteress is one of enchanted contentment, enhanced by the anticipation of there being more where that came from. I was tingling with excitement. Even Visa-phobia – the fear of unexpected credit card termination – couldn't stop me feeling that fizz of exhilaration through my veins whenever I thought of Sebastian naked.

Over the next week, I kissed him so much I thought my lips would require a splint. Best of all were the stolen moments before the afternoon school run. I began to think my headboard should have come with an airbag. It was a waste not to construct a hydroelectric dam to utilize the flow of bodily fluids between us. I became the kind of frisky, quirky, kooky girl who dyed her snatch to match (Susie called it a fanicure), and hid straw-berries in her pussy for dessert.

I was now working part-time as a waitress for a local restaurant. But even all those tedious hours of carrying round glass window-panes balancing

277

roasted vegetables with pesto canapé hats, which the guests were too fashionably thin to eat, couldn't dampen that feeling of giddy abandon.

I was not even put off by Sebastian's bedroom, which was so rancid even the dust-mites walked away with disdain. The shambolic tip became totally romantic to me. Sebastian's pillows often had no cases, and the only beverage on offer was out-of-date juice drunk straight from the cardboard carton. His flatmates blew their noses in the shower and flicked the phlegm drain-ward, shaking their knobs and making woo-woo noises as they made their way back from the bathroom. Under normal circumstances I would have demanded medical benefits before entering such an unsavoury environment, but not when my loins were throbbing. Lying there amid the surfboards, wet towels and bacteria big enough to saddle up and ride home, I would sink into the most deep and untroubled sleep.

Tedious refresher classes in physiotherapy, helping Susie with mundane chores at her salon, even having to feed Ruby's pet snake a defrosted rat: nothing could rain on my euphoria parade.

Even Tally's excesses failed to make me lose my footing on cloud 9. The change in my personality (I'd always liked to go out to breakfast, but now I was getting home just in time for it) made her suspicious.

'You're dating someone, aren't you? That's disgusting,' she said when I answered with a satisfied smile. 'You're just attention-seeking. Ugh. You are just so immature!'

'But isn't "immature" just another way of saying "young"?' I replied, contentedly. 'If so, I look forward to a continued state of arrested development.'

But while I became more and more like a teenager, having sex in alleyways, smoking dope in bed, skinny-dipping at dawn, Tally turned more and more serious. My once-gregarious daughter became suspicious and furtive, like a kicked dog. She stopped eating 'processed animal corpses' and became an animal rights activist, liberating lobsters from restaurant tanks. She became politic-ally correct. People were no longer handicapped but 'physically inconvenienced' or 'cerebrally chal-lenged'. Her friends were no longer unemployed, but 'involuntarily leisured'. The illiterate yob she brought home for dinner was just 'alternatively schooled'. And anyone who disagreed with her was 'ethically disorientated'. Tally could give integrity to any fashionable thought just by adding an 'ism' to the end of a word. Everything in her conversation was ism-ized. Fat-ism, age-ism, height-ism, look-ism, aroma-ism. She wouldn't even describe me as a bad dancer any more. She'd just say I was overly Caucasian. She blamed white supremacist males for all the world's ills. 'They rape forests, just as they rape women. They have an "ego-*testical*" world view.' Tally preferred the words 'enclosure' or 'engulfment' to the word 'penetration', which she now saw as phallocentric.

After months of hideous males cluttering up my house, Tally announced that she no longer wanted a boyfriend, but a 'non-heterosexist, non-patriarchal, non-hegemonic, gender-free relationship'. Wives she saw as unpaid sex workers, while I, apparently, was a survivor of 'domestic incarceration', which is why she had stopped visiting her father.

The Sydney summer was so hot, it was like being in a Tennessee Williams play, especially with Tally's politically correct histrionics. As Lockie would have said (if I were still talking to him), one fart would start a bush fire. It was hot by eight in the morning, with the syrupy sun shoving its way through the slats in the blinds and under the door-frames. Susie and I were still turning up to the North Cronulla surf club so that we could escort Ruby and Matty 'out the back' on our boards, but our main motivation was to time our trips to the club showers to discover if Chardonnay was what Susie called an aeroplane blonde: 'Yeah, blonde hair with a black box.' A curmudgeonly Lockie made Susie and me paddle boards that were cruddy and scratchy, with straps which didn't grip, to rescue beefy, beer-bellied men. Not only did this mean slipping a disc trying to haul all that dead weight on board, but then having to lie with your face wedged between their huge and hairy butt cheeks for the long paddle back.

'You two were pathetic out there,' Lockie would invariably snap upon our fatigued return. 'You were bobbing around like a couple of barium turds in a toilet bowl.'

Chardonnay, meanwhile, was allowed to simply breast-stroke out with a flotation tube to rescue slim girls and underweight boys.

'It's Pearl friggin' Harbor out here today. There's a real nip in the air,' Chardonnay chatted as she watched Susie and me crawling, exhausted, up the beach one Saturday morning after our mammoth practice rescue. 'So many Jap tourists,' she elaborated. 'And what's bloody Meena doin' tryin' to be a surf lifesaver?' She pointed to the only Muslim female in our class, who was waving goodbye as she jogged up to the car park. 'Only Anglo Saxons should apply. Real stail-yans, j'know?'

Susie and I looked at each other from where we lay at her feet. It no longer mattered if Chardonnay was a natural blonde or not, because she definitely had a platinum blonde brain. I'd learnt in life that a blonde bimbo's conversation is always compelling to men, no matter how inane. But I couldn't believe even Lockie would live down to the male stereotype. Yet Chardonnay was always with him. She was like a devoted dog.

'Yeah, but a really dumb dog,' Susie expounded. 'She probably sticks her head in the glove box instead of out the window.'

I obviously hadn't really known the man at all. I stood up to face Chardonnay. 'Once you qualify, you should get a job as a lifesaver at a sewage plant because you talk such shit.' Chardonnay

281

flicked her hair and started to flounce off. 'The person you choose to go out with says a lot about you, and the fact that Lockie is going out with a racist like *you* says he's had a DIY lobotomy.' She tossed her hair again. The woman tossed her hair so much I thought she might be half-horse. I was tempted to hold out a sugar cube on my palm to see if she'd count with her foot.

Five minutes later Lockie stomped towards us. He kicked the surfboat, making the wood wince and creak. His face was Easter Island statue stern.' "The person you choose to go out with says a lot about you,"' Lockie parroted. '*Your* boyfriend says that you are sexually naive and, frankly, desperate. I mean how old is the poncey prick? I bet his pyjamas have little feet.'

'Show me a bloke who's a good loser . . . and I'll show you a man who has hidden all his money before divorcing his wife.'

'Push-ups,' Lockie ordered the class. 'Up, down, up, down,' he shouted with drilled belligerence. His voice was as deep as a holler in a cavern.

Susie was momentarily rescued by her son Heath bounding down the beach. 'Mum!' he exclaimed. 'Catch ya later. Me and me mates are off to a demo Tally just told us about.'

'Oh God, what is it this time?' I groaned. 'Empowerment to one-legged Lithuanian lesbians?'

'Pesticide plant. At Bate Bay.'

'Don't tell me those bastards got planning permission?' Susie seethed. 'They want to put in a Private Ocean Outfall – the acronym of which is, appropriately, POO.'

'Yeah, well, there's this bikini protest demo. To show that the sea's for swimmin' and not for toxic shit. Everyone's there already. Cops, TV cameras, company heavies. And we're all goin' – to check out the chicks. Apparently, they're gonna streak.'

'I'm so glad to see you care about the environment with such passion. You're positively David-bloody-Attenborough,' Susie said sarcastically, before elaborating for my benefit, 'A sea-horse colony is threatened. As well as flying-fox habitat.'

'And Tally's there?' I interrupted, alarmed.

'Everyone's there – surfies, clubbies, westies . . . Tally got a lift with that chick in the burkhini. From the club.'

'Meena?' Chardonnay chipped in, uninvited. 'J'know how to chat to a Muslim woman? Through the letterbox, so then she'll know what it's like.'

If only they'd invent a pesticide strong enough to eradicate Chardonnay – because the woman bugged everyone. Whenever she opened her mouth I was tempted to commit insecticide. She was such a genuine pest, if I looked at her through a magnifying glass on a sunny day, she'd probably burst into flames.

'Can I come with youse?' Chardonnay pouted.

Susie rolled her eyes. 'It's amazing how much you love nature, Chardonnay, considering what it's done to you.'

But Heath's seventeen-year-old eyes leapt out of

his zit-encrusted skull at the prospect. 'Oh, no worries,' he drooled.

In Australia there should be at least one day a week when no one is allowed to say 'no worries'. Because I was worried. I was, in fact, running up to the car park, water flying off me with each squelchy footstep, Susie in soggy pursuit. On the Parental-Angst scale, the prospect of your naked daughter surrounded by a pack of aggressive, baton-wielding males comes top – with the possible exception of abduction by aliens. As I gunned the engine, I tried to think what was security-guard jargon for 'Relax, boys. This rally's just a youthful, light-hearted jibe at the over-zealously capitalistic.' But I was pretty certain that a peaceable security guard is one whose battery has gone flat in his cattle prod.

Ten minutes later we jack-knifed the car to a halt off Captain Cook Drive, near a construction site cut like a scar into the bush. The disputed area, bristling with barbed wire, was ringed with thick-set, private security guards, many of whom were wearing visored helmets to maximize their intimidatory tactics. To maximize publicity, facing them were rows of bikini-clad females, waving placards. There were halter-neck bikinis, tankinis, monokinis, burkhinis, microkinis, bandinis, beaded, faux-fur, crocheted, rubber, lace, leather, leopard-skin, polka-dot, paisley and PVC. The younger girls were parading past in G-string bikinis, which were comprised of a few threads held together by a worried look. One false move and they'd be exposing parts of their anatomy only a gynaecologist should see.

Thickening the throng were squads of sun-scorched, board-shorted young blokes wearing T-shirts with such politically committed slogans as '*I drink till she's cute*'. But it wasn't just locals who'd come to fight for the beach. I recognized the tattooed macho man who'd thrown the rock at my leg that day at the showers, outside the surf club. I was about to say, 'Hey, haven't you hurled sexist abuse at me somewhere before?' But I then noticed that he was joining in a chant about saving the sea-horses from pesticide pollution. The protesters, arms linked, formed a writhing grid-lock with the police. Nobody was moving anywhere and everybody was shoving to get there. I'd seen more civilized rugger scrums.

I pushed through the rows of jeering kids and leering media, my eyes raking the ranks of scantily clad females. And then I saw Tally. Her iridescent green bikini was small enough to clothe an anorexic mosquito. One gust of wind and she'd be wearing nothing but a pint of fake tan.

A gaggle of Greenpeace protesters, their faces concealed by animal masks, lurched forward. When a metallic twang alerted me to the fact that they were tossing rocks at the bulldozers, I blew my piercing patrol whistle and the immediate crowd parted like the Red Sea.

Tally was mortified with embarrassment. 'Mother,'

she hissed at me, blushing, 'I can't believe you came here in your patrol uniform.'

The contemptuous look she gave me said, 'Can we just be friends? I'd like to start seeing other mothers now.'

'Tell me, Tal, do Prada make a bullet-proof bikini? Because I don't think it's a sensible fashion choice to attend a violent demonstration without one. Let's go before things get ugly.'

'No way.' Tally stuck her chin out nobly.

I was just about to tell Tally that I hadn't gone through twenty-five hours of labour to see her flattened into roadkill by a steamroller, when a firm hand on my arm made me wheel around defensively. I sighed with relief to find it was only Jack McLachlan and Ali, better known as Al-Qaeda dot com.

'What are *you* doing here?'

'I just wanted to make sure there were no kids from the club caught up in anything nasty. I'm not interfering.' He put his hands up as though under arrest. 'I'm just keeping a low profile.'

At six foot two, Lockie trying to keep a low profile was like King Kong trying to lie low in New York. Right on cue, he was forced to place a restraining arm on a quarrelsome surfie boy who was shoving Ali and saying that 'bomb chuckers' weren't welcome.

'Leave it out. My Muslim mate here believes in full integration to the Aussie way of life . . . Luckily his harem disagree with him, right, Ali?'

'Yeah, ya gotta feel sorry for us Lebbos, man. Multiple wives means multiple mothers-in-law,' Ali bantered in return.

There was defusing laughter, and for a moment things seemed to simmer down. Which is what made the following fracas so surprising. I'm not exactly sure what happened. I know that I heard Ali suggest to Susie that they should go and get some 'gloriously martyred chicken parts' from the fast-food shop for lunch. To which Susie laughingly agreed, as long as they were kosher. And I know that some of the adrenaline-frenzied private security guards started to call crude remarks about 'white pointers' and it being a bit 'nippley'. I was also aware of a blond-haired boy nearby accusing a rather swarthy security guard of being lazy and fat.

'I can't help it. It's your mother. Every time I fuck her she gives me a biscuit.'

To which the surfie replied, eloquently, 'Why don't you get a furry dog up ya, ya towel-head.'

The guard stuck to his guns. I just hoped they weren't loaded. 'I'm Greek,' the bouncer replied, with equal articulacy, 'you knob-jockey,' before landing a surreptitious punch on the head of his teenage tormentor.

To kids, this type of protest is intense and exhilarating, but, like a freak wave, the crowd can surge and you can suddenly get out of your depth. Which is exactly what happened when the protesters hit back. I tried to grab Tally's hand, but she slipped from my grasp. My daughter came to the surface and went under again, just like Ruby in the big surf that day. My foot came out of my sandal and, as I staggered, I glimpsed Chardonnay surreptitiously ripping off her own bikini top then crying out, topless, to the television news crews, 'My top!' She pointed to the security guard who'd thrown the punch. 'That mad Muzzie tore my bikini off! Dirty perv!'

'You took it off yourself,' I called to her. Tally bobbed up nearby and I immediately pulled her to me. 'And he's Greek, you idiot.'

Caught out, Chardonnay's face puckered as if she'd licked a wasp's nest.

There was some urgent shoving and wordless yelling, then raw panic as the crowd heaved up and pitched forward. My arm was protectively around my daughter's shoulders when I heard the phlegm gurgle in the back of a throat and then the ominous ripping sound as the globule landed on the face of a policeman.

'What bastard did that?' another policeman bellowed.

'She did.' Chardonnay, her huge breasts 'accidentally' exposed, nodded toward Tally, a glint of malice and revenge in her eyes. A moment later, my daughter had a handcuff glistening from her wrist.

'It wasn't her,' I shouted.

'One of them two done it,' a topless Chardonnay cheeped, sashaying towards the TV cameras in a way she no doubt thought suggested seductive femininity, but looked to me like a bad case of thrush.

'You're busted,' the policeman announced to Tally as though they were both in an episode of *The Bill*.

Had I packed my daughter to the gills with IQ-enhancing fish oils her whole life to end up with a criminal record? No, I had not. I also didn't want Tally to undergo what would no doubt be a semi-gynaecological level of scrutiny at the police station. Chardonnay was their witness. And Chardonnay's answers would be about as straight as Elton John in a tutu. 'It was me,' I said.

And so it was that I found myself charged with affray and assault on a police officer.

At the police station, when the officer ran my details through the police computer, they discovered that I had not turned up to court on a driving charge after being bailed on my own recognizance. It was then that things began to look a bit more serious. Apparently I had what is known as 'form'.

'The car insurance matter! Oh God, I just forgot. I'm sorry. I just haven't really been feeling myself since the baby was born.'

The police officer softened for a moment. 'Oh, I see.' A note of sympathy crept into her voice. 'And how old is the baby?'

'Nearly sixteen.'

The woman police officer gave me the kind of look you'd give if you found out that the person with whom you were stuck in an elevator was a scientology recruitment officer. She explained that because of the seriousness of the offence of assaulting a police officer, and the fact that I was living in rented accommodation and was transitory, with no real ties to Australia, and as it was the weekend, I would have to stay in jail till Monday when the magistrate would make a bail determination.

I gazed at the shift supervisor, dumbfounded. 'Your witness lied. Why would I spit on a policeman? Look at me. I'm a timid, middle-class mum. Has someone spiked your tea urn with hallucinogenic drugs?'

This went over so well I could see myself stamping due dates in the prison library for the rest of my natural life. 'But I can't stay locked up all weekend. I have two children who depend on me.' I gestured to Tally who was sitting in the waiting room, still only wearing her bikini. 'Surely there must be an alternative? I'm begging you.'

'Well,' the officer conceded, 'we could bail you this afternoon but you'd need to give us five hundred dollars bail money as a surety.'

When Susie didn't answer her mobile, I had no choice but to call Jasper. Another lecture from Renée. Oh joy! And in front of Ruby, who was with them. With any luck the police would forget to take away my belt and shoelaces and I'd be able to hang myself from my cell door before they got here.

As I waited in a tiled box which had the same ambience as a public toilet, I wondered where it had all gone wrong. Nobody had warned me that raising a family was on a par with an SAS commando course. All I'd wanted to do was bring up two happy kids and love my husband till death do us part. If it had been nail-biting, death-defying, action-packed adventure I'd craved, I would have taken up volcano-hiking, tornado-chasing or jumping over the Grand Canyon on a motorbike.

Jasper bailed me out an hour later. When I was led up from the cells, there he was, all dishevelled and distraught, reminding me of the day he'd rushed to the hospital when my waters broke with Tally. I was immediately ambushed by feelings I'd long forgotten. Perhaps seeing me in peril would snap him out of his self-centred fantasy? But when I glanced across at my husband to gauge his reaction, Jasper was looking at me as though I was the organic beet salad his doctor had made him order, instead of the carb and full-fat burger he really pined for. Lockie, on the other hand, swallowed hard several times. He was trying to organize bail for a junior surf lifesaver who'd been caught up in the melee. The muscles in his throat tensed and knotted as he glared at Jasper and Renée.

'Do you know what Jasper's nickname is for you?' Renée was moving her mouth in an exaggerated way, like a facial exercise. '"Jigsaw", because you're always going to pieces.' She was holding Ruby by the hand. Ruby turned her face up to me, the long, down-turned mouth a mask of dismay.

'What on earth were you thinking, Lucy? Allowing Natalia into such a dangerous situation?' Jasper rebuked, placing his sports jacket around Tally's shoulders. He was talking with the same deeply concerned voice reality chat-show hosts use to persuade you of their serious journalistic side.

'It wasn't Mum's fault . . .' Tally began, but Renée interrupted.

'A child's formative years are an opportunity to instill responsibility, a sense of discipline and self-reliance, by role model. What kind of example do you call this?' Renée was positively dripping with moral righteousness.

And then I heard Jack McLachlan's voice, as rich as liqueur. 'If you think Lucy had anything to do with this, mate, you're obviously swimming with one flipper. I was there. Tally didn't spit on anyone, either. They were just in the wrong place at the wrong time.'

Renée sent Lockie a slit-eyed look, which practically accused him of cannibalizing his young. 'The children would be better off with us full-time, Lucinda.'

'So, how are things going with your team?' Lockie asked Jasper. 'I hear they lost six-nil. And they were lucky to score nil.'

Jasper flinched, clearly wounded, and turned his back on the big Aussie. 'Renée and I just want what's best for the children,' Jasper addressed me in his soothing voice, the one he used to calm feral dogs and traffic wardens. His arm was around Tally's shoulders. She looked cold and lost and very confused. As did her little sister. When it came to mothering, why did I always feel as though I was testing the depth of the water with both feet?

When Jasper dropped us home, lecturing me the whole way about what a bad mother I was, Jack McLachlan was waiting on the porch steps, prowling up and down like a caged panther.

'This *Sebastian* of yours,' he launched in, once Tally and Ruby had gone inside. 'You think you know all about the bloke, but what you *don't* know about him would make a search-engine to rival Google.'

'Your point?' I said, wearily.

'He wins the Dropping In Award on every wave.'

Surfie etiquette requires that you never drop down the face of a wave on which another surfer is already riding. 'Some people call it a manoeuvre,' I said in Sebastian's defence.

'Last week he dropped in on a cripple. The little toe-rag could talk the flies off a shit wagon. I don't trust him. And nor should you.'

'Funny, he said exactly the same thing about you, Jack, but in a more couth way.'

'I'm sure I saw him in the crowd. Behind you. But he had one of those animal masks on. Still, I reckon it was him who spat at the cop. What

I want to know is, what was the mongrel even *doing* there?'

'He's a stirrer, that's all. He's always skating on thin ice.'

'I just hope I'm there when it breaks and the bastard falls through and drowns.'

'Spoken like a dedicated surf lifesaver.'

Lockie gripped me a little too hard, the muscles along his forearms fanning out with tension. 'The little public school prick is an inferior species. In his science lessons at that posh pommy school, the bloody *frogs* would have dissected *him*.'

'You're hurting me.'

'Yeah, well, he could hurt you more. I don't know how to word it so that you'll listen. When they circumcized this guy they threw away the wrong part.'

'Charming. It's time the Australian government enacted strict Macho Posturing Control. Of all men, despite religion or race,' I said pointedly. 'And another for bull-shitting bimbos. It was your girlfriend who pointed the finger. After lying that some security guard pulled off her top to get on TV. What an actress. *And best supporting bra goes to* . . .' I waited for Jack McLachlan to revile Chardonnay . . . And waited. 'Well?'

Falling back on his famed verbal dexterity, Jack McLachlan remained silent.

My lifesaving assessment had required me to demonstrate that I could use signals to communicate to fellow lifesavers and members of the public. But there was only one signal I wanted to communicate to Jack McLachlan right now. I gave him the finger.

'Oh, that's a great way to ensure that you get your bronze.'

'I don't want my bronze. I quit the club.'

'Well, that's just fine with me. You'd have to bloody well beat me over the head with a club before I'd let you stay in it.'

As I watched Lockie stride off, the sunset made orange welts on the horizon.

A part of me knew that Lockie was right, that my relationship with Sebastian was an illusion, a sexual chimera. But the other part of my brain scoffed at that notion. It wasn't a mirage . . . It just looked like one. Still, I knew deep down that I was in the middle of a fantasy. I lectured myself to stay grounded. But there was another voice in my head. And what it said was: 'Show me a woman with both feet planted firmly on the ground – and I'll show you a girl who can't get her knickers off.'

CHAPTER 19

PROCEED FURTHER OUT TO SEA

Ahealthy relationship is all about telling the truth . . . If you can *pretend* to tell the truth, you'll have a very happy union. Talking to Sebastian was like being in the sun. To a woman with self-esteem lower than a rat's rectum, the words were an elixir, even if his flattery was insincere.

'Supposing neither of us had a birth certificate and so couldn't do this calculation of the differences in our ages? I believe that love transcends calendars and clocks. It resides in the moment, that shared breath or well-placed touch . . .'

A mute nod of the head was about the best I could come up with as he was caressing my inner thigh at the time.

'We have a real connection, Lucinda. There's a natural rapport that doesn't exist with women my own age. In an older woman, you get intellectual as well as physical maturity, and, believe me, it's a sexually powerful combination. You're my Madonna, Demi Moore and Sharon Stone.' The fact that he was wont to say these things as I basked in the rich after-scent of love-making, that spicy, sweet and sour mix as pungent as pipe tobacco, made it even more persuasive.

It was as if I had suddenly found myself in one of those subtitled European movies. The man made love to me as though I were an endangered species.

'Show me a sexier woman than Charlotte Rampling, Catherine Deneuve, Helen Mirren or Isabella Rossellini. Girls my age starve themselves, mentally as well as physically. Whereas *you* have an appetite for life.'

Lines like this definitely whet my appetite – for him.

'I'm, like, a man when I'm with you. The lads I live with earn money by taking piece-of-shit cars and customizing them. My flatmates' only goal in life is to save up for a plasma screen TV. They also exaggerate the number of women they've slept with. But nothing makes your mates look at you with greater awe than dating a bona fide woman.' Sebastian smelt of cocoa butter as we lay naked in a velvet torpor. 'Mmm, your breasts are so soft and creamy,' he said, nuzzling them appreciatively.

An unhappy marriage creeps up on you. Like bad underwear. I hadn't realized, until meeting Sebastian, just how unhappy I'd actually been. When he bought Japanese take-out, then ran around me with the plate so that we could pretend we were at Yo! Sushi, I laughed so hard tears fell down my face. Happy tears. I was having so many flights of fancy that I needed to file flight plans.

'All aboard. Your flight of fancy is approaching take-off. Your exits are . . .' But hey? Who would want to leave?

Sebastian even adored the baby stretch-marks on my belly. When he first kissed them, I felt a twinge of unease and embarrassment. But then he said just the right thing. 'Proof that you've lived and experienced. It shows me that you're a real woman.'

Growing old is compulsory. Growing up is optional. This is what I told myself as I responded by running my hands over his satiny, bronzed skin and kissing his dreamy, creamy eyelids.

'When can I meet your kids?' Sebastian pestered me on a daily basis. 'I want to play a bigger part in your life.'

'I'm not sure . . . My daughter might take you aside and ask what your intentions are.'

But what were *my* intentions? Did I still love Jasper? I'd stopped crying at our song whenever it came on the radio. I'd stopped driving past his apartment and checking his bank statements. I'd actually started to think that there must be something good about divorce or why else would so many people do it? I began using my maiden name, signing forms as Ms Lucinda Quirk. I'd also started to wonder if what I'd thought of as love had been nothing more than the terror of being alone. Had I only stayed with Jasper because I was not sure what the three remote controls for the television actually did? Now that he'd left me,

I had one remote, and total control. No more random flicking just before *The X Factor* winner is announced – to go to an unknown football team scoring a try in some remote outpost of civilization. And there were other benefits. No more wincing every time he picked up the phone and said, 'Yel-lo'. No more lying about how much the shoes cost in the sale and hiding the receipt. For the first time in my life I found myself thinking, What are capital gains? And how can I tell if I have them? I no longer thought that 'stagflation' was some beast hunted by the Royal Family. Or 'growth recession' a slang term for male baldness. When Susie found me a job I actually liked, it jumped into my mind, like a fish on to a hook, that I no longer needed my husband. Suze had detected a niche in the business world – nit-combing. Mothers waste months of their lives washing their kids' scalps with chemicals. I became part of her Lice Squad, with Ruby as my able assistant. I drove from house to house, armed with bottles of conditioner, combing vermin from the offspring of frustrated, busy, wealthy parents. For a little extra cash, I would also drop kids at the dentist's or football practice and pick up the weekly shopping. In short, I was a wife. But with a wage, for a change.

I had a feeling that once Jasper saw me standing on my own two slingbacks, he'd find me attractive again. And, oh, how I fantasized about him begging for forgiveness – so that I could ruthlessly reject him. As the father of my children, I would eventually wish him well . . . straight after I put his nuts through a garlic press. The vow 'in sickness and in health' had become 'in sickness and remission'. For the first time since Jasper left, I felt a fledgling sense of hope.

Tally, too, had turned a corner. All through January and February, she'd used every shock tactic to upset me. One after the other, she joined Amnesty International. (I read the prison memoirs of Nelson Mandela and Oscar Wilde.) The PLO. (I made hummus.) Then she swung over to Friends of Zion. (I made chicken soup with matzoh balls.) When these phases failed to faze me, she then took up the cause of Sinn Fein. (I started eating potatoes, wearing green and talking Gaelic.) She next embraced Catholicism. ('A fascinating and important theology' was my non-confrontational response.) Susie agreed that a teenager needs understanding and support – or a kick up the butt with a pointy boot. If a rabid teenager gets loose in your home my advice would be: do not under any circumstances approach it. This creature is armed and dangerous. It has teeth. Back slowly out of the house and sleep on the nature strip.

But just when I was beginning to wish I'd raised orchids instead of children, Tally stopped plotting the order in which to pierce her body parts and the best capitalist regime to overthrow. She started eating meat again and wearing deodorant.

She stopped ism-izing everything. She spoke to me civilly and in whole sentences. The first time Tally was up before lunchtime on a Saturday, I nearly dialled emergency services because I thought her mattress must be on fire.

This was all to do with a new mystery boyfriend. He was a twenty-year-old uni student, but the effect he was having on her was so good I turned a blind eye to his age. Besides, she was nearly sixteen. They'd met at the demonstration. He wasn't her normal type but feelings for him had crept up on her, which is why she called him her Stealth Boyfriend, or SB for short.

'I'd really like to meet him, Tal,' I said one night as I was writing nit-combing invoices on the kitchen table. 'I've been planning a little beach barbecue for your birthday next Saturday. Why don't you ask him?'

'Maybe. But what will you do for me in return?' she asked, kissing me lightly on the cheek. It had been so long since my oldest daughter had shown me any affection that I was dumb-founded with gratitude. I was the emotional version of a famished beggar, pleading for the odd crumb. I was so excited that she was actually going to share something about her life with me after all these months that I would have agreed to anything.

'OK, you can meet my boyfriend . . . But only if you invite Dad.'

I retreated so fast it felt as though my bra strap was caught in a train door. 'No way.' But then

Tally sat on my lap and put her arms around my neck. It was something she hadn't done since she was a little girl, and it filled me with an inexpressibly poignant joy. 'Oh, OK darling. If it's what you really want, of course Dad can come.'

'That means you'll have to ask Renée for lunch too, Mum. As a gesture of good will.'

I wanted to say, '*Why bother asking her for lunch? She'll only throw it up again later.*' But I said, instead, 'Of course, Tal. If it will make you happy. And you're right. It's time we all moved on. I'm seeing someone now, too. He's a little younger than me . . .' I looked at her but lost my nerve, 'He's thirty-five.'

'That's great, Mum. Now I can give *you* advice and lecture *you* until your ears fall off.'

I was shimmering with pleasure. Ruby passed through the room then, like a tidal wave, leaving a flotsam and jetsam of half-eaten apples, wet towels, books, flippers.

'Rubes, guess what? Dad's coming to my birthday on Saturday.'

Ruby reversed her high-speed tracks and, squealing with excitement, leapt on to Tally's lap, who was on mine. My thighs groaned with the combined weight, but a surge of affection for them both kept me buoyant. I buried my face in Tally's hair and inhaled the lemon-scented, sunny aroma. I would ask Jasper and the She Bitch from Hell because Tally thought it would be a 'nice gesture'. There was only one kind of gesture I really wanted to make to Renée, but that involved hiring a hitman.

Tally's birthday would be a wonderful opportunity to bond with the family – which was why my husband was bringing his girlfriend and I was thinking about bringing my toy boy . . . And why we'd all be bringing our food tasters.

Gullible and green as I was, what I hadn't realized is that when a teenager starts helping around the house without being asked, and making meals unaided and stops standing in front of a fridge groaning with food whining that 'there's nothing to eat' – that is the signal for parents to call the police.

CHAPTER 20

BEWARE UNSPECIFIED HAZARDS

Mothers have a lot of arduous responsibilities – birth, breast-feeding, speech days, late homework assignments – and being civil to their husbands' mistresses. This is what I told myself the day of the beach picnic. I also administered a lecture that just because parents are at war it doesn't mean they should conscript their children.

I would say that in *The Good Friendship Etiquette Guide*, there couldn't be a more delicate chapter than the awkward moment when your best girlfriend has to inform you that she's marrying your husband. You could only feel for such a woman . . . feel like killing her, that is. But, packing the picnic, I reminded myself that dignity is a superfluous emotion for mothers. Like styling mousse for bald men.

I'd been up since dawn trying to arm-wrestle naked chickens into the gynaecological position so that I could stuff them with vine tomatoes and pine nuts. All Renée had had to do was turn up with a bag of cashews and yet she started whining the minute she flumped down next to Ruby on the picnic rug.

'Oh, the flies,' she moaned, ignoring the dazzling turquoise sea and tangy salt breeze. She immediately became engaged in some kind of entomological semaphore, waving the air around her with increasingly frantic gestures.

'Ryan puts poo on the tail of his shirt so the flies are all attracted to that instead of his face,' Ruby giggled.

'Oh, this country!' Renée flinched. 'Rugby is called football. Dinner is called tea. Making love is called a 'root'. An indepth conversation is a three-grunt vocabulary. A near-death experience is called a 'fun run'. Their only culture is to litter their highways with giant fibreglass prawns and sheep and bananas. You're forced to swallow insects via your nose on a daily basis. And the children put faeces on their clothing to divert flies.' The woman was positively itching with cultural impetigo. 'Oh dear God! It's happened to *me* now!'

She brushed at the small pellet of possum poo which had lodged itself on her white linen trouser cuff. 'The whole of Australia is just one big animal toilet. Oh and wouldn't it just be on my Versace!'

'Wearing Versace trousers on a picnic is the universe's way of telling you you're making too much money,' I deduced coolly.

'Flies, snakes, convicts – it's just too, too much,' Renée said, dabbing at the sweat shimmering through her facial foundation.

'Aussies are just Poms who are optimistic, happy and have sunny weather. I think the real motivation

305

to create an empire, hitherto overlooked by historians, was the desperate desire for a tan,' I said, cheerily, desperate to create a happy atmosphere on Tally's sixteenth birthday.

'Tans cause cancer. I mean, who in their right mind would want to live here? It's all just melanomas, shit and criminals.'

'You know what, Renée? In my experience, a criminal is a person with predatory instincts who just didn't have sufficient capital to set up a corporation. How *is* your new company going, by the way? The one you funded with my life-savings?'

Ruby's face was clouding over with anxiety. Her habitual gap-toothed grin was gone. She started sucking her thumb – not a good look on an eleven-year-old. If Jasper hadn't strolled towards us, having finally parked his armoured tank, otherwise known as a 4X4, on someone's nature strip, Renée and I would have been sharpening our claws on each other's jugulars.

'Hello, Lucy. You look great,' Jasper said blandly, pecking me perfunctorily on the cheek. He gathered Ruby up into a bear hug, the storm on her face immediately breaking into sunshine. He then lay supine on the rug, his arms casually knotted behind his dark head. It was a gesture which reminded me of him naked on our bed, post love-making, and I had to look away. He still had this ability to hijack my hormones. And just when I'd thought I was cured. The problem was what to do with the love I still felt for him. Where did I put it? In the freezer? In the bank vault? In a re-cycling bin?

Renée was examining my coleslaw salad as though it was an unexploded bomb. 'I suppose I should have brought a food taster,' she sniffed, poking with a plastic fork at the tabouleh and tzatziki in their Tupperware containers.

Jasper peered dubiously into a bowl of potato salad. 'I think it best if you don't jeopardize the success of your luncheon party by actually serving any food, don't you?' He chuckled. 'Lucy tends to use the smoke-alarm as a timer, don't you, hon?'

His attempt at bonhomie made my stomach churn, as did his casual use of our old endear-ment – did he mean anything by it? Possible and improbable interpretations whirred in my head – but for the sake of my girls I managed to keep smiling. I smiled until my gums dried out.

Jasper tore off a chicken drumstick and gnawed on it. 'Oh well, why let the threat of a painful death by salmonella poisoning get in the way of a good time?' he half-joshed.

I was beginning to wish I *had* stuffed the chicken with plastic explosives. As I poured champagne into a plastic tumbler for Renée (in lieu of the E.coli Colada I'd like to have served her), Jasper unscrolled his arms and leant up on one elbow. 'Well, I'm certainly looking forward to meeting Tally's amazing new boyfriend. Does he have a name?'

'She calls him SB. Her Stealth Boyfriend.'

'Are you sure it's a boy?' Renée contributed from behind her massive Chanel shades, as she buttered a brittle triangle of toast for Jasper.

'Renée's convinced Tally's . . .' Jasper covered Ruby's ears and mouthed the word, '*lesbian* . . .' He uncapped Ruby's ears and patted her affectionately on the head. 'What with all that politically correct, anti-male sloganing, environmental protesting . . .'

'And not wearing any make-up!' Renée shuddered.

'Knowing Tally, he or . . .' Jasper mouthed the next word, '*she* will be some kind of unemployed tofu farmer, or a misunderstood Taliban extremist or something.' He munched happily on the food Renée prepared for him.

'Well, all I know is that Tally has abdicated from her role as Princess Bitchface. She's been so much more reasonable and focused of late,' I amended Jasper's harsh remarks. 'She's even talking about university again. I'm so relieved.'

'I'll tell you what's a relief,' Jasper interrupted. 'It's a *he*.'

I turned, a warm and welcoming smile on my lips. But the image before me was so surreal that I lost the power of speech. I sat, welded to the spot. My mind rejected what I could see so clearly. I gaped incredulously and groped for the table-top so as not to overbalance from my portable picnic chair. The moment was frozen in a horrifying snapshot: Tally, my darling daughter, her fair skin turned a light copper colour from the summer, her lips ripe and smiling . . . with her arm loosely draped around the waist of . . . my lover. Sebastian stared at me, eyes wide, like a schoolboy caught smoking.

'Mum,' Tally beamed coyly, 'this is Sebastian. Sebastian, this is my mum and dad, Jasper and Lucy. And Aunty Renée. And Ruby, my little sister.'

My tongue felt suddenly swollen and unyielding. Words came out, but they sounded foreign in my mouth. 'Hello, nice to meet you,' I ventriloquized.

My heart was like a heavy-metal drummer in my chest. The force seemed to shake my whole body. Put it this way – if I'd been a nuclear reactor, I'd have been going into meltdown. I glanced frantically to my left and right to see if anyone else had noticed my dismay, but they all seemed oblivious to the cataclysm unfolding before them. My eyes darted to Renée's face, but to my astonishment she didn't show a flicker of recognition. Sebastian had cut his hair since the cricket and was wearing board shorts and baseball cap, not jacket and tie. If I kept my cool, perhaps we could just sit around and exchange pleasantries about the taramasalata?

Sebastian shook hands with everyone, including me. I drew my hand back from him as if he were a live socket.

'Sebastian, would you help me fire up the gas barbecue?' I asked as nonchalantly as I could, considering my throat was on fire with misery.

'Sure.' His smile was as varnished as his surfboard.

By the blond brick barbecue – free to the public for all picnickers – I feigned a fiddle with gas knobs as I looked at him, stupefied. 'When you said you wanted to show more interest in my family, I didn't know you meant date my daughter!' I was squeaking like a stuck drawer.

'Hey, we never said we'd be exclusive. How was I to know Natalia is your daughter?'

'Just don't let on, for God's sake. Renée doesn't seem to have recognized you. We've never met, OK? You told Tally that you're twenty!' I seethed, thin-lipped. 'I also thought you didn't like younger women?'

Before he could answer, Tally was at his side, lacing her arm through his and brushing hair from his lying eyes, in a proprietary way. A lobotomized grin was the best I could manage.

For the next excruciating hour, all through the games of tag and the Frisbee-flinging, all through the boogie-boarding and rock-pooling, I held my smile in place as if waiting for an invisible photographer. I tried to feign nonchalance and calm, but it's hard to be calm and nonchalant when you're spooning hummus into your ear because your head is jerking around like a hooked fish in an effort to read every facial expression.

Sebastian finally made noises about having to leave early. He had just disentangled himself from Tally's besotted embrace when Susie arrived. She had just finished work, and breezed in with baskets of food. In all the Grand Guignol confusion,

I'd forgotten she was coming. 'Susie, have you met Tally's new boyfriend, Sebastian?' I said, hurriedly, trying to catch her eye. But Susie was too busy unpacking prawns and oysters as she prattled on about perms and parking and surf conditions to hear me.

'Susie, could I talk to you for a minute?'

'Sure. Let me get something to eat first. I'm starving.'

Oblivious to my frantic eye signals, Susie plonked down on the picnic rug and drank in the unusual company of my husband and his mistress, plus my younger lover. 'What a happy little family gathering,' she said, facetiously, between bites. 'One of the women in the salon read this article to me today about older women who date younger men. They're called urban cougars. Not bad, eh?' she enthused, clawing the air and growling.

'Fascinating,' Renée said in a bored voice.

Telepathically begging her to shut up, I tried to change the subject. 'Without wanting to create undue alarm for the kids present, do you think that global warming means an end to the future of the world as we know it?'

'Well, Jasper, why should you and Renée be the only ones to get any love action,' Susie blundered on, ignoring my conversational bait. 'Taking the old phallic cure! It's just so great to see Lucy happy for a change.'

Horror was more the emotion asserting itself on my facial features. I felt a flicker of a migraine

311

forming in my left temple. 'Have something to drink.' With shaking hands, I poured a glass of champagne and, as I shoved it into Susie's hands, half-turned my back to the others so that I could desperately mouth the words 'shut' and 'up'.

'No, I won't shut up. I'm proud of you. I mean, a younger man with an older woman makes sense. He can enjoy us, as we're in our sexual prime.' She executed a little shimmy to emphasize this point. 'And we are old enough to enjoy his ingénue charms. Actually 80 per cent of women are now against marriage. Hey, why buy the whole pig just to get a little sausage?' she laughed, pinching Sebastian's posterior.

'Susie! That's enough,' I pleaded. 'Tally doesn't like it when you manhandle *her boyfriend*.'

'What are you talking about? If Jasper can flaunt his lover, you should be able to flaunt yours,' Susie insisted, missing my point. I locked my eyes straight ahead as though driving through heavy traffic on a wet and treacherous night.

'Wait,' Renée probed. 'You're saying that Sebastian and Lucy know each other?'

'Oh, give the woman a PhD in The Glaringly Obvious. How long have you and Lucy been lovers now, Sebastian? Six weeks? He's madly in lust with her, aren't you, possum?'

Tally's head was tilted in that hyper-alert way, like a bird sensing danger. 'You know each other?' she asked me, wide-eyed.

I gazed at my daughter, dumbstruck. She looked

pensive and delicate in the buttery light, except for the big childish mascara blobs on her eyelashes, and the low-slung jeans barely clinging to the ridge of her slim hips. I knew one thing for sure: the family who picnic together gets dyspepsia, heart-burn and a bad case of poisoning. 'Oh Tally . . . I had no idea.'

A fly crawled across Sebastian's sleeve. He was too dumb-struck to strike it as it wiped its front legs on his elbow.

'Wait!' Renée's voice was like a wasp in a jar. 'I thought I recognized you. You're the lothario from the cricket.'

'You're wrong. All of you,' Tally said, her voice quavering with emotion. 'Mum is going out with a guy in his late thirties. She told me all about him yesterday.' Tally turned to me, ashen-faced. 'Didn't you, Mum?'

'And you told me you were going out with a twenty-year-old,' I said, mechanically. 'Sebastian's not a student. He's twenty-five.'

We stood speechless, frozen in our private tableau. When I turned to confront Sebastian, he was moving so fast in the opposite direction that he left a vapour trail. I could vaguely hear a low painful moaning and realized absently that this disembodied cry of anguish was in fact my own voice.

'Oh, give the woman a mother medal.' Renée's voice was dripping with sarcasm as she paraphrased the expression Susie had used earlier. 'You wouldn't let Ruby undertake a lucrative modelling job and enter a beauty pageant. Yes, you mounted your high horse on that one, didn't you? But it's OK for *you* to have sex with your daughter's boyfriend. Paging Dr Freud to reception.'

'I had no idea Sebastian was going out with Tally. I'm horrified.' I floundered. 'Tally, darling, I'm so, so sorry. This is just awful. A nightmare. You know I would never, ever do anything to hurt you.'

My older daughter's face had become pale as skimmed milk. Her thin cotton top slipped, revealing her frail shoulder.

'This just proves once and for all what a bad influence you are on your girls, Lucinda,' Renée said with acidic satisfaction.

'You don't think I did this on purpose, do you? And anyway, don't you judge me. What would *you* know about raising children? The heaviest burden you've ever borne is the latest Hermes handbag.'

'I'm calling the modelling agency tomorrow to sign you up, Ruby,' Renée decried. 'Modelling is a wonderful lifestyle choice for you. Luckily we disobeyed your ridiculous orders, Lucy, because Ruby won the Bondi Junior Beauty Pageant, you know.'

'What! You enrolled her behind my back? You just want to live vicariously through my daughter. But children are not a lifestyle choice, Renée.'

'I love Ruby and Tally. Anyone can see that. Don't I, Ruby?'

314

Ruby's face burned in confusion. She sucked her thumb. It looked as though the bed-wetting was not going to abate in the foreseeable future.

'Love?' I seethed at Renée. 'Love is not something you out-source to nannies and au pairs. Which is exactly what you would do. Ruby's just an accessory to you. Something which makes you look more human.'

'Shagging your daughter's boyfriend is not human,' Renée retaliated. 'It's monstrous.'

In a divorce scenario, lunging at your husband's mistress with a bread knife is a pretty accurate sign that things are not going smoothly. Luckily Susie was quick enough to knock the knife from my hand before it actually became airborne. Renée's nails were in my hair, yanking hard and, faster than you can say 'cat fight', I took a fistful of her sleek black bob in my own hands and tugged. We were locked, antler-like, both squealing in pain. Ruby burst out crying, 'Mum, Mum!' Susie hit Renée over the head with a breadstick while Jasper forced my arms into the air.

'Stop this unseemly circus!' he yelled. 'How could you, Lucinda?' He confronted me, as I stood dishevelled and panting before him. 'With a man nearly half your age. Didn't you stop to think how this would affect Tally?'

Tally! I ached for her then. I turned to look for my darling daughter. And my heart caught in my throat. 'Stop. Where is Tally? Tally?'

My head swivelled frantically, eyes ransacking

315

the few gawping picnic groups who were all focused on us. And why wouldn't they be? My life had suddenly taken on all the lurid banalities of a television soap-opera. It was off the scale on the Oprah-ometer. 'Tal?' I shouted. 'Tally?' Then more loudly, my hand cupped to my mouth: 'Tallleeeeeee!' I strained my eyes until they stung.

I punched her number into my mobile. No answer. I rang the house phone. Nothing. I rang Sebastian's mobile. It went straight to messages. It was daylight and she was capable and independent, but I had a portent of danger in the pit of my stomach. 'Spread out,' I ordered our deranged gathering.

'She can't have gone far,' Susie placated. 'I'll drive along to South Cronulla and check the mall. You drive around to Gunnamatta Bay.'

Ruby shattered into tears – great heaving sobs complete with gulping and hiccoughing. I hugged her to me.

'Jasper, I need you to pack up the picnic and take Ruby back to the house. I'll look for Tally – I know all her haunts. Call me if she turns up. You still have your keys, don't you?'

For the next two hours I drove to all Tally's favourite places – beaches, friends' houses, cafés – even to Sebastian's flat. Sick with nausea, I clambered over the old surfboards and shopping trolleys piled up down the side of the building and forced myself to peer through his bedroom window. But nobody was there either. By the third hour, all

I could smell was the warm, spicy scent of my dear daughter's skin. How I longed to hold her tight to me. By the fourth hour, I rang the police. They asked me Tally's age. When I told them sixteen, they enquired if she had 'special needs'. When I said no, the police officer pointed out that teenagers run away all the time. It was a family matter. She would not be seen as officially missing until twenty-four hours had elapsed. 'Come in tomorrow and bring a photo.' Twenty-four hours? He might as well have said twenty-four years. Tally may not have had special needs, but I did. I had a special need to see my daughter. Now.

And so I kept searching. As I frantically rang around to Chook, Fang, Spider, Spike, Stoner, Byron . . . I felt as if some terrible fate was gathering, like a storm far out to sea. On cue, it started to rain. From nowhere a summer storm burst open. With the day dying in the wet car window and still no word, the silence thickened like curdled milk. I got out of the car and searched restaurants and shops along the ocean front. A couple of cats skulked from the shadows and executed a complicated minuet around my legs. The wind was gusting in alleyways, tormenting treetops, roaring around street corners. Lightning tore open the sky. My Tally was nowhere to be seen. My darling daughter was gone. And it was all my fault.

CHAPTER 21

EMERGENCY EVACUATION ALARM

Which way had she run? The brutish flow of cars sped by, oblivious to my distress. The southerly wind was in full force now. Rain shuddered against my face. Under frugal street lighting, I stabbed Tally's number on my speed dial over and over. No answer. Silence fell like a guillotine. The heels of my sandals rang on the naked paving stones and echoed down the empty alleys.

There are certain warning signs that your teenage daughter hates you. 1) Sullen silences. 2) Locking the bedroom door. 3) Leaving home with no forwarding address. Where was my baby? What if she'd gone swimming? Had she been sipping on the champagne? Lockie's stern warnings about combining the two came back to me. 'Swimmers who have been drinking alcohol are more likely to vomit and inhale the contents of the stomach into their lungs and then drown.'

Yesterday I'd read a news report from the UK Foreign Office, which stated that fifty-nine Britons had died in Australia in the last year alone, making it the second most dangerous holiday destination for tourists, second only to Afghanistan. From deranged murderers of backpackers, to flotillas of anaphylactic-shock-inducing jellyfish, crocodile attacks and snakes' envenomed fangs . . . in Australia you can die in more ways than in any other country on earth.

My mobile shrilled. I broke a nail in my haste to answer it. It was Jasper. He told me that he was going to search the inner city around Central Station and King's Cross in case she'd really run away. Renée would wait at home with Ruby. 'OK,' I muttered, my nerves stretched to twanging point.

The wind keened as I walked the length of the boardwalk, peering desperately into café windows. With each step I thought of all the things I hadn't told my darling daughter. Like – never to eat at a place called Squat and Gobble, as I gawped into the gloomy interior of a gastro-pub. Or to dine anywhere which revolves or floats. That she should always choose a table near a waiter. But who would she be dining with? I tortured myself with all the vital information she would need in the world, and which I had failed to give her. Like the fact that men only grovel at your feet so they can look up your dress. And that if one did, she should attack his testicles with a taser gun. Come to think of it, had I warned her never to go out with any man who combs his hair sideways over a bald patch? And never to trust a man who says 'trust me'? Did she know that condoms are not 100 per cent safe; that there's still danger? *For example,*

Tally, your father was wearing a condom when he fell off the bed and sprained his ankle . . . Another thing I hadn't told her was that people use humour as a defence mechanism to disguise their terror.

I'd reached the main street again now. My feet beat time with my maternal mantra. *Don't run while holding scissors. Check each tin of canned salmon for dents which cause botulism.* Dear God! Did she even know what botulism was? *Always shower with the curtain on the inside of the bathtub to avoid flooding the floor. Never use an electrical appliance near water.* I pressed the traffic-light button. *And be decisive. There's nothing in the middle of the road but splattered animals.* I pushed into a pub on the opposite side of the street and scanned a crowd unmoved by my plight. No doubt the place was staffed with sex offenders, working off their community service by counselling runaway teenagers. I walked into the leathery dark, still talking to my daughter in my head. *Don't marry your future. Make your own.* I'd learnt that the hard way. *Never marry for money, either, Tally. Your wedding vows should be to: 'Love your husband, respect your husband – but to get as much as you possibly can in your own name.' Wear the pants if you can, dear daughter, after all, you'll be washing and ironing them.* Marriage, I wanted to tell her, is not the answer. It's only the beginning of a million more questions, like, what did I ever see in that schmuck?

I was crying now. Huge, great, wracking sobs.

With a sickening lurch in my stomach I realized I'd been a total failure as a mother in the last year. Hijacked by my own traumas and dramas, I hadn't trusted my mothering instincts. I'd let my daughter down. And now I'd lost her. My precious darling.

In a dangerous surf situation, the emergency evacuation signal is to hold both arms vertically above the head and to raise the red and white chequered flag. The radio call is 'Rescue, Rescue, Rescue'. More than ever now I needed to swim between the flags, because I was seriously in danger of drowning.

I slammed through the surf club office door, drenched and wild-eyed. Lockie was sitting at his desk, in an illuminated pool of light among the crowding shadows. He looked up, aggressively, brandishing his pen like a dagger. But when he saw my harrowed face, he shot to his feet, poised and alert. 'I've lost Tally,' I cried in a voice suppurating with panic.

I told him quickly what had happened, including the humiliating detail of mother and daughter sharing the same boyfriend.

'Do you have a photo of Tally?'

I produced one from my wallet and he scanned it on to his computer. Lockie then stabbed the number of a key club-member into the phone. This set off a chain reaction, as that particular member then rang other members who rang others. The photo was emailed to them all. Soon there would be search parties all over the Shire looking for my daughter. I was shaking uncontrollably now, shivering with fear not cold. Lockie thrust dry clothes and a towel at me, as well as hot, sweet tea – just as he'd done the last time he'd rescued me.

When I'd changed and calmed down a little, he took me by the shoulders and talked to me slowly and clearly. His voice was clipped, reminiscent of a wartime commanding officer who has to inform a wife that her man has died in the line of duty.

'I've been sniffing around that bloody Pom for weeks now. I thought it odd that he was living so well with no visible means of support. I tracked down a few of the places that lousy low-life said he'd worked, hotels and the like. Seems that Sebastian sheds identities like a snake, leaving them shrivelled and withered behind him, just like the people he's duped. Today I went through the file to see who had paid for his bronze medallion fee – it was done by cheque. The cheque was in the name of a company called Lifestyles. Does that name mean anything to you?'

'No.'

'Well, I got a solicitor mate to look into it. It's a fitness and beauty organization. The main shareholder is one Renée Craven.'

'What?' The enormity of what he'd just said forced me back into the chair. 'That can't be right! Renée didn't even know him. I mean, today she didn't even recognize him at first . . . She . . . He . . .'

My stomach was churning and my heart accelerated once more. The blood raced through my veins so fast I could feel the friction on my arterial walls.

'As a lawyer I'm a great believer in the integrity of the justice system – even if we have to bloody well bribe and cheat our way to victory,' Lockie said. 'A mate of mine works at the local bank. I got her to do a bit of illegal checking-up for me. It would seem that Ms Craven has been putting money into Sebastian's account at various intervals for the last three months. Looks like Renée and Sebastian are in cahoots.'

'Ruby!' I gasped then. 'Ruby is with her now. At my house. Alone.' If I'd had a spine, a shiver would have been running up it. But of course, I had no spine, as it had turned to jelly.

That was something else I would have to teach Tally. The difference between a rat and a toy boy. One is hairy and lazy, grazes on leftovers and brings home disease – and the other is a rodent.

Lockie grabbed my arm and we bolted for the door.

CHAPTER 22

ASSISTANCE REQUIRED

My house was in darkness. There was a note on the table from Renée. It said that she had taken a cab to her apartment so Ruby could watch movies and have makeovers to take her mind off her 'poor, traumatized sister'.

I showed the note to Lockie. It was now 10 p.m. I rang Jasper's apartment. No answer. I fired off a frantic call to his mobile. It was turned off. But wasn't he supposed to be looking for Tally? I voiced my concerns to Lockie.

'There are hundreds of people all over Sydney looking for Tally now. I think it's Ruby we should be worried about. Renée is up to something,' Lockie deduced. The trip to the city lasted forty minutes, but if you were actually there, racing to find your missing daughters, *three and a half years*. It seemed to take so long, I was amazed not to see the seasons changing out of the car window. To lose one child may be regarded as misfortune; to lose both looks like carelessness. What kind of mother was I? My children would soon be writing the sequel to *Mommie Dearest*.

At the end of Wunulla Road, I leapt from the car, leaving the door swinging, and leant on the bell so hard it roused a neighbour.

'They left for the airport,' a woman in satin pyjamas and pearls informed me, gin and tonic in hand. 'Oh, hours ago. For London I believe, lucky sods. We go to Wimbledon every year, you know.'

London. It had a dull, final sound to it, like a lead door closing.

'Who? Who left for the airport?'

'Jasper and Renée and that dear little girl. She's so pretty. No wonder she won that junior beauty pageant. And what a prize. A modelling assignment in London!'

A sense of foreboding as heavy as a winter coat pressed down on me. In all the chaos I'd forgotten that Renée had let slip that Ruby had won some pageant. On the divorce hostility index we were now off the chart. Something cracked open in me, and fury welled up out of dark, hidden places in my soul, and I thought about killing Renée Craven.

'Get in,' Lockie ordered, spearing the key into the ignition. We tore away from the kerb on two wheels, missing giving a rich banker in his Porsche a cardiac arrest by half a centimetre.

As we belted away from the harbour and towards the airport, the impact of what had happened slammed into me so hard I expected the driver airbag to balloon out to cushion the blow. Caroming towards the expressway, city buildings cast long shadows which fell upon me like a net.

Renée and Jasper had tricked me, and now I was trapped.

I rang the police on speakerphone, screaming about abduction. I explained that my estranged husband had taken my eleven-year-old daughter out of the country without my knowledge or permission. Once the policewoman had ascertained the facts, she explained as calmly as she could that it wasn't abduction as Jasper was the father, he held Ruby's passport, and England was her principal residence. This was a family-law matter. I just stared at the phone, a cold chill settling on my bones. I was beginning to rethink my attitude to gun laws.

When we got to the airport, Lockie's wheels throwing up noisy gravel, we abandoned the car illegally at the kerb and sprinted inside. The check-in desks were closed. I grabbed hold of an official's sleeve, babbling at him. 'London. The last plane to London. Has it gone yet?'

He cast a bored eye to the departure board. 'Yep. Via Melbourne,' he said, before trundling on, unaware of the quicksand he had opened up beneath me.

A shuddering swoop of anguish made my knees give way, as though full of marbles. Despair welled up in my chest. 'But why, Jack?'

Lockie, despite his discomfort with displays of feeling, wrapped his sturdy arm around my crumpled shoulders.

'Lucy, if you ever meet someone who says

they've overcome their materialistic desires, that's a euphemism for 'just divorced'. Jasper wants you out of his life. But he wants custody of your money. And he's using Ruby to do so.'

'How?' Monosyllables were about all I could manage.

'When you go to court, which is basically a big building where judges sleep between golf games, whoever has the kid gets the house. Whoever has the house gets the dough. Although they don't call it a house any more. It's a domicile . . . Your "domicile" is the place you used to call home before your lawyer took it. English divorce is favourable to women, but I suspect they've been building up quite a case against you. Tally's sixteen and old enough to leave home, so she's out of the picture. Ruby's the key.'

'Plus they can make money out of her through modelling,' I added, dismally. 'But what has Sebastian got to do with it all?'

'Let's find out, shall we?'

Lockie set his chain in motion once more and soon had his surf lifesaving pals combing Sydney for Sebastian's Chevy. It was located in the airport hotel car park, and fifty minutes later Sebastian was waiting for us at Burraneer Bay where Lockie moored his boat. When we reached the secluded jetty, four of Lockie's friends stood waiting. They were impassive and menacing at the same time. Despite the fact that they looked like the type of muscle men who chewed on raw steak washed down with the blood of their underlings, Sebastian was sitting on a dock bollard between them, one leg crossed cockily atop the opposite knee, apparently without a care in the world. Until he saw me, when his deceptive eyes jumped nervously.

'So, all those things you said to me, they were all lies?' I blurted.

Sebastian shrugged, insouciantly. 'Listen, cupcake, when we first met I told you that just about everything I ever said was an irresponsible lie. Ninety per cent of all lies are made up on the spot, you know.'

I noticed for the first time that Sebastian had the big, ready smile of a professional – all mouth, no eyes. We'd both had sex, but obviously I was the only one who got screwed.

'Why was Renée paying you?' I demanded. 'What did she pay you to do?'

'Ah, if I told you that, I'd have to kill you,' he said in a James Bond accent.

'And if you don't tell me you'll soon be singing in the Vienna Boys' Choir.' Lockie's muscles popped from his arms like grapefruit, then he thumped Sebastian in the stomach where it wouldn't show. 'Feeling more chatty now, mate?'

'It's such a joy to see Darwin vindicated,' Sebastian wheezed. 'We really did evolve from apes.'

'Yer fulla shit, j'know that?' Lockie gave a harsh chuckle. 'Boys, I think His Lordship and I need to have a more indepth chat.' Lockie leapt aboard his boat and fired the engine.

'What a simply charming offer, but I'm afraid I

won't be able to take up your kind invitation to go boating, owing to an unavoidable diary clash with a nap I was planning to take.' Sebastian made a dash up the dock for freedom, but was seized and unceremoniously dumped on to the deck of the fishing-boat. He feigned unconcern, and merely sprawled on some canvas bags like a Turkish emperor awaiting his concubine.

Lockie turned the boat towards the open sea. I felt the swell running under the hull and could soon hear the seabirds wheeling. Lockie kept me beside him. The familiar scent of his leather jacket mingled with engine oil and greasy denim. Once we were out to sea, Lockie cut the engine and the boat coasted silently in the milky water.

'J'know where we are?' Lockie asked Sebastian, as he tipped a bucket of fish heads and bloodied guts into the water. 'Beyond the shark net.'

On cue, Lockie's mates picked Sebastian up by one leg each and dangled him over the side, where the bloodied guts were floating on the surface. My face took on the sick green glow of the navigation instruments. I had to remind myself that Sebastian was a barracuda – all silvery and lean on the outside and mean and predatory on the inside. And it was Tally he'd taken into his snapping jaws. I hit her number on speed dial. Nothing. And Susie still had no news. A hot spasm of hatred for this charlatan prickled my flesh, and I steeled myself for whatever was to come.

'What do you say when a toffee-nosed Pom is

in a shark's mouth, up to his waist? Get a bigger shark.' Lockie nodded and the boys dipped Sebastian's head into the sea. He came up spluttering. It only took two more dunkings for the Hero of the Hour to cave.

'All right! All right!' he gasped, still upside down. 'I met Renée Craven at our gym in west London. We were intimate for a while. When we met up here in Sydney, she offered me money to sleep with her boyfriend's wife. Then seduce the daughter.'

Lockie motioned for his mates to bring Sebastian back aboard. Seabstian's speckled eyes no longer seemed like warm quartz, but cold, hard marble.

'But why?' I gasped.

'To make you look untrustworthy and unsuitable in the eyes of the law. During the custody case.'

'Custody case?' I recalled how I had scoffed at Jasper's half-arsed threats about wanting custody. But now the words were like an ice pick shoved into my brain.

'Renée said she'd make a much better mother than you.'

I felt a surge of queasiness. Once Renée got tired of picking the peas out of the fried rice, cleaning the Polly Pocket pet boutique, and finding the lost glove (allow at least twenty minutes for this), she would realize that motherhood didn't suit her self-centred lifestyle. Ruby would be like one of those unwanted puppies at Christmas time. She'd get dumped down a dark alley. Or packed off to boarding school. Which amounted to the same thing.

When I'd first met Renée she'd commanded my grudging admiration. She was self-obsessed and ambitious to a fault, but carousing with her had been great fun. Basking in her limelight had made me feel taller, stronger and more important. She could dish it out but she could take the punishment in return, thanks to her hide of a rhino. (No doubt designed by Louis Vuitton, with Filofax and briefcase to match.) On the surface Renée possessed an aloof self-assuredness that was so convincing others mistook it for sanity. Even me. Long tremors shook my legs and my belly roiled – and not from the rocking of the boat.

'You lousy bastard.' Lockie punched Sebastian in the stomach again, just for good measure.

'Shit, what's that noise?' Sebastian spluttered, trying to maintain a veneer of cavalier composure. 'Oh, don't worry. It's just the sound of my spleen rupturing.'

'J'know what, mate? I don't think your long-term health is a major concern for you right now.' Lockie cuffed him across the chin.

'Thank you, sir, please may I have another?' Sebastian said in a mocking echo of a public-school beating from a prefect. But as Lockie drew back his fist he dropped all pretences. 'Fucking hell, who are you all of a sudden?' he exclaimed. 'Vincent Fucking Price? Can we go back to shore now? After all, I am on a penitential knee. And I have a plane to catch to Fiji.'

'Really? What do you use as a passport photo? Your police mug-shot?' I asked, bitterly.

Lockie got up close to Sebastian's face and lowered his voice to a menacing baritone. 'What I wanna know is why you were so interested in little old me.'

Sebastian gave a small, sphinx-like grin. 'I know no more.'

'Oh really? So you don't know who this is, then?' Lockie asked, indicating one of his muscular mates. 'This is Chicken Wire Charlie. You see, the trouble with disposing of bodies in the sea is that they usually get eaten by a shark. The sharks are caught by fishermen. They slice them open and there's an arm with a wristwatch or ring, complete with fingerprints. But Charlie here had a brain-wave. He wraps the body in chicken wire, then weights it down with lead. So your corpse sits on the bottom of the sea, getting nibbled at by little fish, until all the evidence is eaten. No one will suspect a thing. Australia's number one industry is losing tourists. On the reef while snorkelling, in the outback while backpacking, in a rip while swimming. Even Lord bloody Lucan is lost here someplace.'

Sebastian eyeballed the swirling, murky water, where fish of all sizes had gathered in a feeding frenzy. 'When you put it so eloquently . . . Renée hired a private detective to find some skeletons in your closet. So you'd not get in the way of my seduction plans.'

'And the demo?' Lockie demanded, grimly. 'She hired you to make trouble there too, didn't she?'

'Oh, no shit, Sherlock, or rather *Mr Holmes*,' Sebastian said with feigned reverence.'Renée suggested it would be advantageous if Lucy or Tally got into trouble with the law. Especially Lucy, as she already had a previous conviction. The protest offered a perfect opportunity.'

My mouth dropped open. Renée had arranged things with more painstaking care than the hair strands of a balding newscaster. Extreme sports obviously have got nothing on extreme divorce. *The Renée. Comes in Regular, Lethal and now More Advanced Lethal!*

When the crashing in my ears had faded, I faced him once more. 'Why, Sebastian? Why did you do it?'

'I'm a poet. Renée is my Medici. My patron.'

'In other words, you needed the money for your coke habit,' Lockie translated, extracting a packet of white powder from Sebastian's jeans pocket where it was rashly lodged.

Sebastian shrugged. His serrated smile was sharp as a razor. 'Ah well, planting drugs on Lucy was a part of Renée's plan . . . A coke-fiend mother rarely gets custody. But I just had to sample them for authenticity. I mean, fuck it. I've always loved drugs, so why wouldn't I? And, well, when it's in free supply, it's rather hard not to get a taste for it. I'm afraid Renée found out and we, ah, parted company. She bought me a ticket to Fiji as a farewell gesture. This is good shit, by the

333

way. It's not cut with any crap. I can get a good deal on a few grams if you're interested.'

Once more my powers of perception amazed me. I hadn't realized Sebastian had been born with a silver coke-spoon in his nose. As the man also spoke with a forked tongue, I really should have kept him in the cutlery drawer. I was flabbergasted that he'd planned to plant drugs on me. All that physical passion we'd shared wasn't proof that Sebastian felt anything for me. It just proved that he had an over-abundance of testosterone and an under-abundance of cash. It meant no more to him than exercise. Naked yoga. A jog he didn't have to go outside for. It was no more intimate than, say, a Pilates class for two.

'If you slept with my daughter, I will kill you in the most painful way possible,' I threatened him, bracing myself to hear the worst.

'Relax. I didn't sleep with her. I just made her fall in love with me. Of course, it will take her some time to get over me.'

'Yes, how will she ever find another man to fill your *shoe*,' I spat scathingly.

Lockie punched him before I had to ask him to. One thing was clear, Sebastian wouldn't be putting anything up his nose for a while, except cotton-wool.

Lockie then switched back into lawyer mode and extracted a whole confession in writing, witnessed by Chicken Wire Charlie. We then motored back to the jetty and Lockie tossed Sebastian on to the shore like a bit of driftwood the sea had spewed out.

My phone was vibrating. In all the commotion I'd missed two calls and a text from Susie. 'Come home. Tally found safe.'

When I saw my darling daughter again, I hugged her with a relief that was painful in its intensity. What a sweet reprieve in my misery. 'Tally! Where have you been? I've been sick with worry.'

'At a friend's house. I told her not to tell you. But her mum's one of Susie's clients, so she dobbed on me.'

'It doesn't matter. You're safe.' While I crushed her to me, Lockie explained Renée's deception. I felt an electric shiver go through Tally's body. Her mouth fell open. At the sight of my daughter's pale face, drained of all artifice, her mascaraed lashes claggy from crying, I felt a subtle wave of nausea – and a flush of prickly heat which made my temper boil.

'Tally, you know since your father left I've been at pains not to say anything negative about him because all the psychology books say not to undermine the other parent? Well, screw that. Your father's a bastard!'

I felt as though my destiny had been on hold to one of those call-centres in India, listening to mangled versions of all my old favourites. 'Your call is important to us, but we're putting you on hold for the rest of your natural life.'

My brain was now miraculously clear. When I picked up the phone I was extremely precise about what I had to do. A ticket for London.

CHAPTER 23

TRAPPED BY THE TIDE

With my cheek mashed against the cool glass of the plane window I tried to fathom what had gone wrong in my life. A treacherous toy boy, a kidnapped child, a deranged husband . . . These things didn't happen to an ordinary woman like me. It was as if my life had become a teenage delinquent. Maybe I could just pretend it wasn't mine. It was as though in the last year I'd been reading and lost my place. But Ruby and Tally were my bookmarks. It was time to solve the plot.

My thoughts turned to my home country. The chief products of England are pessimism, sexual perversions, gardening programmes, TV murder mysteries set in Oxford, epigrams, puddings and pinstripe. The chief products of Australia, on the other hand, are optimism and mateship. Which is why Susie was seated next to me in row 38 of economy. We were travelling on my air miles. But Susie was keen to fly by the seat of her pants. 'If Ralph Fiennes is on this flight I'll be in that loo as soon as they turn off the "You May Now Unfasten Your Pants" sign.' Susie was so excited at the prospect of seeing London that she wasn't even perturbed when the huge man in the row in front put back his chair during mealtime, ensuring that the snack-tray embedded itself into her abdomen for most of the flight. Susie's gay ex-husband, Arron, had moved in to keep an eye on all three of our kids. 'Heath will be a fully paid-up member of the Kylie Minogue Fan Club, and Tally and Matilda will be in an Abba tribute band by the time we get back. But hey, he owes me, like, ten years of child-care! As long as he doesn't spend all the housekeeping money on lubricant,' she laughed.

I tried to sleep, but anxiety and remorse thickened the darkness of my dreams so that I jolted awake, my teeth locked solid, jaw muscles bunched and aching. And I remained so until touchdown.

A wan light seeped in through the smeary train window of the Heathrow Express. After all that Aussie sunshine, I'd forgotten the murky, sepia light of Europe. I'd also forgotten London's despondent grandeur. The rows of grand Georgian houses I'd always found so charming now seemed down on their luck. For centuries they'd had to get by on drab economies, and now seemed inward-looking, dark and brooding. Susie saw it differently. As the train sped past vegetable allotments and tense tenements, she thrilled at the amber lights glowing warmly from lichened cottages, older than any structure in Australia. While I thought the polluted air as thick as broth

337

and the city grimed with existence, she thought the whole country smelt like a beautiful old church, the air languid with antiquity. Susie thrilled to be in a place which haemorrhaged history. She wanted to sniff under every sofa for the host of ghosts who'd been lurking there since the days of Henry the Eighth.

She was enchanted by all the buildings, with their pudgy domes, curves and cupolas, their frosted glass giving them the appearance of giant puddings. She squealed with glee at the black taxi, which she said looked like a four-wheeled bowler hat, as it whisked us from Paddington station to Knightsbridge. She was charmed by the quaint little arcades with the toy-sized shops which glimmered invitingly in the gloaming. 'Wow. Look at all this stuff!' She gestured at Harrods and Harvey Nichols in awe. 'I never knew there was so much stuff I didn't want!' She didn't even mind the cold. 'The blokes here must cuddle up to the sheep, but for their *wool*,' was how she put it. '. . . But oh, that sharp, green smell after rain.' The relentless rain pattering on windowpanes only added to Susie's sense of cosiness. She even delighted in the big, empty bendy buses trundling over potholes, searing pedestrians with their petrol breath. The throng of London seemed to be exclaiming all around her – the clanking radiators wheezing emphysemically, the shriek of cars, the shouts of pedestrians, who seemed to me to hurry neurotically like caged mice. While Susie was captivated by the way the light dwindled, I now found the low, thick sky, bulging with dampness, claustrophobic. Europe seemed all used-up – the air full of other people's breath. I missed the salty tang of the wind, fresh from tousling the heads of the trees in the national park. While Susie delighted in the cool wintry light, crisp air and stark parks, to me the leafless trees seemed dismally denuded. All I could think of was Sydney, lush and green and drunk on its own juice.

We bunked down at a bed and breakfast in Earls Court. The next morning, a few phone calls to mutual friends and family, and I had tracked Renée down. Pieces of information jigsawed together. Renee would be on a boat all day on the Thames, revealed one pal. Modelling assignment, confirmed another. This was the prize Ruby had won at the Bondi Junior Beauty Pageant. The one I'd forbidden Renée to enter my daughter in. I kept my rage reined in – like a fuse burning in the direction of a bomb. The morning was chilly; bitter inside and out. But I would always be in bleak winter without my two darling daughters.

As Susie and I submerged into the dank-smelling tube, I warned about pick-pocketing, advising her to strap her shoulder bag across her body. 'Crime here is so bad, there's a six-week waiting-list to mug a tourist. And try not to inhale until we get to the Embankment. That sound you can hear is the bunged-up noses of people desperately expelling mucus clots.'

'Ah, so that's what they mean by the "congestion charge". You pay to drive into town so you won't catch a cold in the tube.'

I laughed, despite my fretfulness. After locating the boat which had been hired for the Dollita ad campaign, Susie and I darted aboard at the last minute. The old tug was named after Neptune . . . the ancient god of seasickness, I realized, when I saw Ruby's green complexion. Locating her in the galley, I felt a bright, white-hot joy. I was awash with relief. I felt elated – helium-filled. In fact, I was so high, I should have been frightened I'd exceed the prescribed altitude and get shot down by a fighter jet as a UFO.

When Ruby saw me, joy bubbled into her eyes. She displayed her picket line of perfect teeth. 'Mummy!' She flung herself into my arms and clung to me as though she were drowning. I squeezed her little body to mine. She smelled sweetly of soap and minty toothpaste, but her skin, varnished to a violin shade after a summer of sun, was goosepimpled from the cold. 'Mummy! I'm so sorry I didn't tell you about the tweenager pageant. Renée said it was our little secret. She said you needed the money and would be so grateful and happy. But then they wouldn't let me say goodbye and . . . well, I don't like it here. I thought it was going to be like *America's Next Top Model*. But it's freezing! Aunty Renée says I have to wear these stupid clothes and stop whining. She pinched my cheeks too, to make them rosy!

340

It really hurt! I don't want to be a model, Mum! Who is looking after Fluffy? I want to go home!'

Home, I noted, was Australia. 'It's all right, darling.' My daughter was dressed in a ridiculously skimpy mini-skirt outfit to advertise Dollita tweenager dolls. She was corralled with seven or eight other girls, similarly attired. As I wrapped my coat around her delicate shoulders, a young woman with a clipboard, who was officiously ticking-off names, confronted me.

'And you are?' the clipboard Nazi demanded in a nasal, Estuary accent.

'Ruby's mother. And I am withdrawing my daughter from this contemptible ad campaign.'

'Zat right?' Her tone was as arch as her eyebrows. 'One click of my fingers and three hundred other brats'll come running to take her place.'

'Really?' I growled, no longer the timid, brow-beaten woman of six months ago. 'Instead of clicking your fingers,' I covered my daughter's ears, 'why don't you click your heels together three times and go fuck yourself.' I squatted down beside my daughter. 'Where is your father?'

Ruby pointed to the lounge, where the parents of the models were gathered, drinking Irish whiskies to keep warm. 'Ruby, listen to me. I want you to wait here with Susie. Do not let go of her hand.' The way I spoke made each word capitalized. 'WE'RE GOING HOME.'

★　★　★

When Renée saw me she started making the noise of a sink backing up. Jasper's face twitched as if the nerves were jumping beneath the skin.

'What the fuck are you doing here?' The boat bar was crowded with make-up artists, stylists and other flotsam and creative jetsam. Renée's voice cut like a buzz-saw, and heads spun to look.

'Let's talk on deck,' Jasper ordered, under his breath. I followed them on to the icy upper deck, the London Eye looming cyclopically over us.

'Ruby is staying with us. It's the best solution.' The thin smoke of Jasper's breath steamed skywards. 'Otherwise I'll fight you in the courts. And do you really want the spilled contents of a failed marriage exposed: your alcoholism and arrest for assault on a police officer, fines for failing to turn up to court, not to mention sleeping with your own daughter's boyfriend? Do you really want all that to come out in public? I'm trying to help you here, Lucy.' Jasper had the synthetically sympathetic countenance of a funeral director.

'And I can offer Ruby so much,' Renée patronized, tapping the deck with her collapsible umbrella in irritation. 'I know you think of me as super bitch. But just because I'm a woman who knows what she wants doesn't make me evil. It makes me a wonderful role-model for Ruby. I would stop at nothing to get the best for her.' Renée was clinging on by her lacquered, acrylic nails to the idea of motherhood. 'The best schools, the best friends, the best clothes . . .'

'You allowed your house to become mouse-infested, true or false?' Jasper said, stonily. 'How will a judge look upon that? This is not an environment in which to bring up a child.'

I looked at the man some evil fairy had substituted for my husband. 'Jasper, the only can of worms that will be opened in court is Renée's employment of one Sebastian Ponsonby – ponce by name, ponce by nature – to frame me. And don't bother trying to deny it, Renée. I have it all in writing.' As the whole story tumbled out in one go, I pulled Sebastian's affidavit from my jeans pocket. 'But who am *I* to judge you? That will surely be up to a jury when you're arrested for supplying Class A drugs.'

If Renée had had any wrinkles they would have creased.

'Drugs?!' Jasper's tone was so shrill bats would have winced as they winged by.

'If you read on you'll see that Sebastian has given us every sordid detail. You could throw yourself on the mercy of the court – but does the word *splat* mean anything to you? I think a better option would be to give me sole custody and the deeds to the house, and to get the hell out of our life.'

Jasper's Adam's apple zoomed up and down his neck like a little elevator. 'I didn't want to take Ruby. It was Renée's idea.' Jasper was backing up so fast he should have emitted warning beeps. 'And I knew nothing about any drugs. I hope you believe that.'

'What I hope is that you get the upper prison bunk.'

Renée gave me the look of somebody who has just had their life-support system removed. Medusa-ish, her windswept hair writhed on her head. Her eyes flared with a napalm burst of wrath. Then she swooped down on me, like a vulture settling down on a corpse. There was something unhinged and lunatic in her laugh. The boat was cruising towards the Tower of London. In the shadow of Traitor's Gate she grasped me by the throat. I felt my face swell like a cartoon character, my eyes squeezed out of their sockets. Letting go, she fired the barrel of her collapsible umbrella in my direction, knocking me backwards. Apparently the boat railing was designed by the same person who had decided how many heat-shields there should be on the Apollo 13 space-shuttle, because it snapped like a twig. The skin on my back tore in a rip of fire as I toppled past the splintered rail. Instinctively I flung my arms forward, seizing Renée's fur coat with both fists. Overbalancing, she, in turn, groped for purchase – and the nearest thing to her was Jasper. And then the boat lurched to the left as it rolled from the wake of a passing barge.

Viewed from the safety of Tower Bridge, the whole catastrophe must have unfolded with sinister slow motion – the woman falling over-board and taking her assailant with her, who, in turn, toppled a third person water-ward. But if

344

you're *in* the Thames in early March, all you can think is: Hello, Hypothermia. My skull chimed from the cold. My lungs filled with damp air. The rapidly flowing, swollen tide bumped our bodies downriver. We were swept towards the architectural priapism of Canary Wharf. I'd given Ruby my jacket, so all I had to do was shuck off my trainers to swim easily. I saw Jasper and Renée floundering in their big coats, then they disappeared into a trough.

The question is, if you saw your husband and his lover drowning, would you have a glass of champagne or go shoe-shopping? Dear God. I was going to have to rescue the woman I most loathed in the world, placing myself in direct personal danger of winning a bravery medal from the Queen. But what of Jasper? I couldn't save them both. People often ask, how can you tell if your marriage is truly dead . . . ? Well, I think a pretty good indication is if you're in a morgue identifying the body of your spouse.

And so, I dug my arms into the icy water and stroked towards my husband. Of course, I would torture myself with the memory of those alarmed eyes as Renée went under. Yes, I would punish myself with the image of her hands clawing at the surface of the water. I would have to endure this feeling for . . . oh, about *five minutes tops*, I thought, as I saw her body whoosh by towards Dartford.

I could hear Lockie's voice in my head. '*Identify*

345

the hazards. Decide on course of action. Retrieve and secure patient. Return patient to shore.' I used the technique he'd taught me for rescuing without equipment. 'Move to the rear of the patient. Blood circulation is vital. Administer five quick breaths then proceed back to shore for cardio-pulmonary resuscitation – thirty compressions / two breaths.' Jasper's lips were thin and papery, the colour of wet cement, the eyes pellucid as the eyes of a fish. But he was still breathing. One arm was out of his heavy coat and I tugged the other free. Put your preferred arm over the patient's corresponding shoulder, across the chest and under the armpit, clamping the patient to you. Use side strokes, with your hip close to the small of the patient's back. Don't let your emotions wash you away. I discerned a wharf up ahead to the left, and kicked towards it. It was a little hazy with distance, but at the speed we were travelling we would be adjacent in less than a minute. When I stretched my legs downwards and felt the Dickensian slime, I was shaking with adrenalin, but the pure rush of survival was exhilarating. I clung to Jasper on the slimy planks of the dock steps and performed mouth-to-nose rescue-breathing. The whine of a powerful motor-launch engine alerted me that real rescue was at hand. The water police wrapped us in blankets and took us upriver to St Thomas' Hospital to check for hypothermia. It wasn't until we were safely in casualty, waiting to be interviewed by the police, that Jasper spoke to me.

346

'I nearly died,' he said blearily as the shock wore off. 'You saved me.'

'You should have died months ago, really, crushed by the Mount Everest pile of unpaid maintenance money you've accumulated.'

'Lucy, darling, listen, I didn't know that Renée had hired Sebastian.' Jasper looked at me in a wild-eyed parody of disbelief. 'When I think of her paying him to seduce you and, oh my God, Tally, I could kick myself.'

'Why waste time? Judging by your team's goal rate you'd only miss . . . Speaking of which, once I leak this sordid story to the press, you'll never work as a coach again . . . Unless you cut me a deal, that is. As you stole our life-savings, I think it only fair that our house is put in my name. And that you only see your children under my supervision.'

I find that a husband's opinion of his wife is greatly influenced by whether or not she is holding a gun to his head – and I had come armed with copies of the sworn statement Lockie had extracted from Sebastian.

Jasper descended into snivelling. There were a lot of 'I didn't mean to hurt you's, and 'I don't know what came over me's, and 'I was obviously having some kind of breakdown's. You would have to have a heart of stone to listen to a husband's apology for adultery – without laughing your head off.

'But I still love you,' he said with all the genuineness of a used-car salesman.

Love is like a tide. When it's in, everything looks beautiful and inviting. Only when love recedes can you see the debris beneath the surface – the old bottles, the rusty prams, the sewage pipes, the bloated cats and dogs weighted down to drown. The man I had once loved so passionately I now saw as weak, gutted like a fish.

'Let's forget divorce. Let's pick up where we left off. Our marriage wasn't that bad, you know, Lucy.'

'That bad? The marriage wasn't that bad?' I took a sip of hot, sweet tea. 'Gee, let me think about that. Other than the infidelity, the psychological abuse, the mental torture, the shrivelled bank accounts, the domestic blindness, the emotional amnesia and the manipulation of our children, yes, I've yet to notice any downside,' I replied sarcastically, picking clumps of dried weed out of my hair. 'I now pronounce this relationship dead, Jasper.'

'I deserve it,' he said, suddenly.

'If you don't sign over the house, I will also tell the police that you pushed me into the river in an effort to kill me, so you could run off with your mistress. I left all my worldly goods to you, which makes killing me a dead giveaway.'

'But . . .' he quavered. 'But the kids . . . They're everything to me . . .'

I no longer cared. 'I'll let you know when they're graduating. Have a nice life.'

CHAPTER 24

INVESTIGATE SUBMERGED OBJECT

I n Australia, people are frank and plain-spoken. If a street is called Brookside, it will be by a brook. If some place is named Buttercup Way, it will be amid fields of buttercups. In England, if a place is called Buttercup Way, it will be over-looking a housing estate, sandwiched between a scrapyard and a brothel and practically on the tarmac at Heathrow.

I returned from England with Ruby and Susie a few days later to find a 'For Sale' sign on Lockie's house. He'd also taken leave of absence from the North Cronulla surf club. When I still couldn't locate him after two days, I followed Chardonnay's BMW to La Perouse. Even though I kept a couple of car lengths behind, there was really no need. Chardonnay had her rear-vision mirror pointed permanently downwards, for the sole purpose of make-up application. At every intersection she coated on more lip-gloss and mascara. The street she eventually turned into, Ocean Cliff Road, ran along a cliff overlooking the ocean, as advertised. She pulled into the car park of a modern, beige, official-looking building. It had electronic gates and the perimeter fence bristled with steel spikes. Perhaps she was undergoing counselling for lip-gloss addiction? Intrigued, I pulled into a wedge of shade and waited. Chardonnay parked in a disabled zone because it was closer to the door, and checked her frosted pink lipstick one more time.

When I saw Jack McLachlan emerge, my pulse skipped a beat. He was dressed in khakis, elegantly faded, shirtsleeves rolled to the elbow. A conniving Akubra kept his expression from me. I felt anticipation and elation at the thought of seeing him again, but also apprehension. There was still so much he hadn't explained. But the thought of his smile held me like an embrace.

Chardonnay pranced towards him in her tight pink mini-dress and gold sandals. I watched, miserably, as she kissed Jack on the cheek, and I felt a keen stab of jealousy. His back was to me so I couldn't read his face but I did see him flip open his wallet and strip some notes from a wad of cash. Chardonnay took the money, laughing flirtatiously, then wiggled back to her car, no doubt off on a lingerie shopping-spree for their next liaison. She peeled back the roof and exited the car park to the strains of Amy Winehouse. At least the open-top sports car explained why the woman had no brains. They'd obviously been dashed all over the roadside one time too many.

'Jack.'

He reeled, startled, car door gaping, key in hand. Lockie stared at me for a moment as though I were some rare aquatic creature which had washed up on the beach. Then his face clouded over with anger. 'What the hell are you doing here?'

'I'm fine, thanks,' I replied, sarcastically. 'And how are you?'

'I'm still on the right side of the grass, if that's what you mean,' he said, thinly. 'What the bloody hell are you doing here?' There was a funereal droop to his shoulders and his flesh appeared more seamed than I remembered.

'I was worried about you. I thought you'd want to know that I got Ruby back. And that Jasper's resigned from the Australian Football Federation. He's off to coach a soccer team in Columbia – where crime really pays, the hours are good and all the judges are dead. Renée, I think, might have drowned . . . Although Susie did find an article in *The Times* about a woman plucked alive from the Thames.' I prattled on, nervously. 'It could have been Renée. But I guess we won't really know for sure until we hear about a deranged interior decorator taking over some small, defenceless country in the near future.'

Lockie's eyes swivelled to and fro, not really listening. 'You didn't bring anyone with you, did you?' he asked, guardedly.

'No.' The March air sat still and gauzy, leaden with humidity. In the heat, his shirt stuck like a khaki skin. 'Where are we, exactly?' I asked.

His eyes grew distant. They were fixed on horizons far away. 'It doesn't matter.'

'Jack,' I interjected tentatively, 'what's going on?'

Lockie canted his chin towards the ground to avoid meeting my eye.

'I don't believe anything Sebastian ever said, obviously . . .'

'That fuckwit couldn't tell the truth. You just couldn't tell the difference.'

'I'm sorry, Jack. Why don't you tell me the truth now?'

Lockie surveyed the asphalt with optometric attention to detail.

'In class you taught us to demonstrate mature communication skills, remember? Talking to a lost child, dealing with aggressive board riders, advising the public about blue-bottle jellyfish . . . Active listening, you called it. *"Those things on the side of your head?"'* I imitated his voice, *'"they're ears. Use 'em."* . . . Well, mine are all yours.'

The muscles bunched and slid under the tanned skin of his forearms as he clenched and unclenched his fists. The man was definitely fluent in body language. And what he was saying loud and clear was 'Go away.' But his reluctance to show emotion only made me feel more tender towards him.

'"Communication is vital." That's what you taught us in class,' I persevered. 'Communication between lookout towers, beach-patrols, jet rescue boats, helicopters and, most of all, people.'

But Lockie was on a difficult frequency. He was harder than ever to reach. It was all static. I needed to change bands.

'That damsel-in-distress routine of mine has really annoyed you, hasn't it? Well, I've changed. As have my light bulbs. Last night. By myself. From now on I'm going to fix everything that boils over, blows up, leaks or fumes. I've been reading up on DIY. And I've learnt so much. I've learnt that as soon as your hands become coated and icky with grease, your nose will begin to itch and you'll suddenly be desperate to pee.'

A chorus of kookaburras chortled raucously, but Lockie refused to be amused. Nervous, I just kept talking. My lips seemed to be on an aerobic assault course, up, down, up, down, words pouring out.

'Of course, as I'm now doing my own DIY, phone calls have started coming through on the waffle iron, and when I turn on the television, the shower runs. But it's a start, right? And I'll never need Jasper again.'

Lockie looked at me properly for the first time. 'So you finally saw through the bastard?'

'Yeah, well, nostalgia isn't what it used to be . . . Looking back over the decades, I can't help but wonder . . . what the hell was I thinking?! I've had to face the cold hard truth that if it wasn't Renée, it would have been someone else. I thought my husband had abandoned me, but really he set me free. Free to have feelings for someone else . . .'

I sensed him stiffen but pushed on.

'The best revenge is to make a new life for me and the kids and to be happy.'

353

There was a new-found wariness in the man's gaze, but he said nothing.

'You make me happy, Jack,' I added, pointedly. He stood, imperious as a lighthouse. 'What do you need? A PowerPoint presentation? Put it this way, you big, idiotic, Aussie surf life-saver, if I can't have you, life isn't worth guarding.'

Lockie glared at me gruffly. 'You English girls read too much Jane Austen. It is a truth universally acknowledged that I must be in want of a partner. Well, get this, I'm not.' His voice see-sawed with emotion.

'There are good things about being in a relationship,' I heard myself stuttering. 'Companionship, shared housing costs . . .' *Shared housing costs!* Puh-lease. *Was this the best I could come up with?* 'Childrearing convenience.' *Oh, shoot me!* 'Occasional sex . . .'

'When you've been around as long as me, Lucy, you'll know that there are three types of sex.' Lockie counted them off on his calloused fingers. 'One – brand-new, kitchen-table sex. Two – bedroom sex. Then number three – hallway sex, when you pass each other in the hallway and say "Fuck you".'

'But aren't you even curious to find out if English women really do wear triple-breasted, tweed lingerie?' Personally I hadn't been able to stop from wondering how Jack McLachlan would move in bed, how he'd sound, what he'd say, how he'd smell and taste.

Lockie narrowed his eyes at me. 'I don't get you, Lucy.' His face was naked in its hurt. 'First you treated me like dirt. Then you were sweet to me. Then you treated me like shit again. And now you're being all lovey-dovey once more.'

'So, haven't you ever been out with a female of the species before?'

Lockie pulled off his Akubra, as if he couldn't bear the weight of it on his head any longer. 'Sure, being in love is bliss. Just don't recommend it to single people,' he said wearily. 'Not unless they want to *work on it*. Oil rigs you work on. Key accounts. Yachts, as a deck-hand. But a relationship should be a retreat from all the things you work on.'

That hot spasm of jealousy shot through me again. 'It's Chardonnay, isn't it? You're just putting me off because of her.'

Jack McLachlan drew himself up to his full six-foot-two height and turned the beam of his anger down upon me. 'How can you think that I'd be attracted to a lousy leech like her?'

'It's just . . . you're always with her. And the free lessons. And then after the police station, you sided with her . . .'

'There's a reason.'

I looked at Lockie now, genuinely worried. He seemed sand-scoured, like pieces of glass on the beach – his rough edges worn down.

'What reason? Jack . . . You know everything about me. Can't you take off your Ned Kelly

355

armour for once? I know there's a beating heart under there, but you're so strangely reluctant to hand anyone a stethoscope.'

Lockie's eyes were now a faded blue; the once-warm expression, cold and suspicious.

'Just tell me! Unless it involves you being a cross-dressing Klingon, in which case feel free to save that for your shrink.'

'She's been blackmailing me. About my wife.'

He spoke emphatically, as though every word wounded his tongue. I kept very quiet so as not to deter him. 'I'm only telling you because it doesn't matter any more. My wife is, well . . . *was* sparkling. And clever. She was working as a parole officer when I met her. But some of those crims are very charismatic. After Ryan was born she started spending too much time with one in particular. He gave her cocaine. Friends told me to work on my marriage, but they didn't know that the drugs were working their poison on her. They warped her. She was in denial. Like most addicts. *"Cocaine's not addictive – I've been doing it for years! Nor is there anything wrong with my one remaining brain cell,"'* he mimicked. 'Then he got her using smack. She got more and more crazy. And in debt. I filed for divorce. It was like some tawdry bloody soap-opera, just one drama after another. No kidding, if it had been raining palaces, I would have been hit by a dunny door. I was fighting for custody of Ryan, who was only three, when she burnt down our house. Smoking crack. The house

I built from scratch. Only, she was so out of her skull she forgot Ryan was in it. I only just saved him in time. I only just saved her in time, too. Her beautiful red hair was on fire, Lucy.' His voice caught in his throat. He drew in a deep breath, then continued, scathingly. 'Chardonnay was one of her druggie mates. I moved up here from Melbourne. To rebuild our lives. But that junkie tracked me down looking for moolah. I've been paying her to keep her mouth shut about my wife. I don't want the poor little bugger ever to know that his own mother nearly killed him.'

I was stupefied. It had all come out in a torrent. Nothing, and then this deluge. We stood still, looking at each other, silenced by all we might say.

'So, what is this place?'

'Loony bin, I believe, is the colloquial expression. I come to see her once a week. There's a very fine line between madness and mental illness, you know,' Lockie concluded bitterly.

Bloody hell, I gulped. Jack McLachlan really was a romantic hero, I realized, complete with crazy wife in the attic. I was suddenly in a novel – a tragic novel. All the literature I like abounds with mentally unhinged women. Mrs de Winter, Mrs Bertha Rochester, Lady Macbeth, Miss Havisham . . . The works of Shakespeare and Dickens would be nothing without them . . . Virginia Woolf, Sylvia Plath . . . It wasn't something to be frightened of. 'I should be committed too, for ever committing to Jasper,' I bumbled, jet lag making me stupid and inadequate. 'But what about Ryan?' Beads of sweat were breaking out on my upper lip and not because of the sun.

'It's for the best that Ryan thinks his mother's dead. Even if it means paying off Chardonnay. There. Are you happy now I've confessed to you? Does it make you feel better?' he asked sarcastically. I felt the warmth leave his voice, like the cold drop in a summer's night.

'We're leaving, Ryan and I. For FNQ.' His words vibrated like a plucked string.

'Far North Queensland? No. When?'

'As soon as I organize shipment for my boat and tie up a few things.'

But it was me who was tied up in knots. He cared more about his bloody boat than me. Running away wasn't like him. Jack McLachlan barrelled against every challenge. His body was corded with muscle and sinew. The man may not have been lying face-down in the water, but he was obviously in distress. It was clear to me that Jack McLachlan was drowning.

'But when I thought there was absolutely no problem which was too complicated or too daunting that it couldn't be run away from, you made me stay and fight my fears. It's not like you to be so cowardly.'

'Why is it that every time I talk to you I get an overwhelming desire to be alone?' he growled. 'We're all better off being alone.' Like a sailor in

358

a storm, his signal was getting weaker. 'That's how I want to be buried. In my Last Man Standing boardies.' He peered over the cliff at the sea hurling itself on the jagged rocks below. 'If you took a tumble from up here your clothes would be out of date before you hit the rocks,' he commented, mournfully.

Australia is the world's largest island. Lighthouses are strung around the coastal cliffs, like a glittering necklace. I tried to make some analogy about lighthouses being alone, but still signalling each other, but Lockie had already beeped his car door alarm.

'But, Jack . . . I care for you. I . . . You're the only man I trust.'

'You lose a lover and the sun still comes up in the morning. The stars still come out at night. Life goes on. In my experience only dolphins ever die for love.' I thought I sensed him lean into me a little, sensed his warm breath on my skin – but then he was gone.

CHAPTER 25

RESUSCITATION

Surf lifesaving changes your attitude to life. It teaches you about the benefits of having established goals. It helps you identify tasks which have to be done. It encourages participation in activities from all members of the group, and instructs you how to allocate specific jobs to individuals.

I came downstairs to find a chaos of dirty dishes and piles of washing, and my children sprawled across the sofa like sultans awaiting a peeled grape. 'Right.' I zapped off the Saturday morning television. Both girls looked up at me aggrieved and started whining in stereo. I silenced them with a hand, like a policewoman stopping traffic. 'If you two don't start pulling your weight, things are going to get very Oliver Twistian around here. Spanking, flogging, washing of the mouth out with soap, beating with red-hot pokers, banishment to orphanages . . .'

They were thunderstruck.

'Yes, I used to be a laid-back, unconditionally loving mum. But that was before I worked out that a mum who is laid-back and unconditionally loving ends up with snapped heels on her stilettos, or just one lone shoe, laddered pantyhose, missing make-up, and a self-esteem lower than Paris Hilton's bikini line. Not to mention her fridge being raided by the entire population of men under twenty in the southern hemisphere. The Mummy Hilton is now closed.'

I handed out a dishcloth and a feather duster. 'Now I've got my Australian licence, I'll be working as a physiotherapist full-time. So, we are going to have rules. And if you break them you are grounded.'

Tally looked at me inquisitively. It was a look which said, 'Could this be my mother?'

'These are your new commandments. Thou shalt eat broccoli. Thou shalt honour thy mother's sleep needs and be home before midnight. Thou shalt never have sexual relations with anyone whose name is Chook, Fang, Spider, Spike, Stoner, Byron . . . or Sebastian. In fact, thou shalt rejoice in celibacy until thou meets a kind, literate, domestically trained male, preferably in full employment. Thou shalt not covet thy mother's one cashmere sweater and only pair of Jimmy Choos.'

Eleven-year-old Ruby, already displaying mild symptoms of early-onset teen malaise, started to whinge. So I confiscated the TV remote. 'If you keep that up, there will be no television for the rest of the day. Now, where was I? When I shout up the stairs that it's time for school, I want you

361

both to leap into action like a precision-drill marching-band instead of deciding that this is the perfect time to disappear into the bathroom with a bottle of hair dye and a self-waxing kit.' Both girls were looking at me as if I was one of their school science projects gone wrong. But I persevered.

'In the event of missing designer clothes, jewellery and silverware, a mother has the right to search and seizure. Boyfriends left in the kitchen longer than one week must have a forwarding address. No more tattoos or multiple earrings, either. The only thing you can pierce in this house is the can of tuna, which you will open every morning to make your own school sandwiches. There's to be one hour of television a night, then study. Tally, you're allowed out once a week only, on Saturday nights. Curfew is midnight, no later or no pocket money. Not only that, but if you upset me in any way, I will pick you up from school and hug you in front of all your friends. Possibly wearing hot-pants. What's more, if you ever again have a party without my permission, I will not only dance badly while lip-synching the lyrics but I will also *act out the song with hand-puppets*.'

Tally, mortified at the image, tried to protest, but I drowned her out.

'Ruby, as for your pets, I don't want anything else in this house which has a mouth. Or a gill. Or anything that needs to be kept alive by me.

I am over mothering. If you forget to feed Fluffy one more time, he's going to be made into a marinade. Oh, and you're both going to take up lessons in a musical instrument of my choice and play for the whole family every Christmas. Is that clear? Now look! Over yonder is a dish-washer and, miracles of miracles, you have hands with which to stack it! Praise the Lord! And finally, I'm a bloody good mother. So, if you even think about putting me in a nursing home in forty years' time, I will personally haunt you both.'

Ruby was scandalized and stropped from the room. But, to my amazement, Tally smiled. Her smile widened until you could have hooked it over her ears like a stethoscope. I then watched in wonderment as she pulled on the rubber gloves and started stacking the dishwasher and filling the sink with suds for the bigger pots. Her long blonde hair, caught into a shining ponytail with an old rubber band, reminded me of her younger self. Before my eyes she seemed to revert to the placid, open countenance I remembered from the days before her father had left us.

'Tally,' I asked, pouring myself a coffee from the plunger. 'Why have we been fighting so much this year, do you think?'

'Because I know you can handle it. You have to. You're my mother.'

I took it as a compliment.

'And because we're so alike,' she postscripted.

That I really did take as a compliment. And I smiled back at her, our love miraculously intact.

I glimpsed Susie crossing the back garden, a little unsteady on her feet, and went out to meet her with hot coffee.

'Hangover,' she muttered.

'What the hell are ya? A bowling ball? Then I suggest you get up out of the gutter, girl.' I echoed the first words Susie had ever said to me.

'Ha ha.' She put a hand to her head to ease the throb. 'You're not going to believe this . . .'

'Believe me, after what I've been through this past year, it's got to be pretty damn amazing for me to be shocked.'

'Ali kissed me.'

'Al-Qaeda dot com?'

'I know. We were at a party at JDs nightclub and danced till dawn. He's so gentle. And those chocolate eyes. I think I could fall for him, Lucy. Except it will never work out. I wear a Star of David necklace. He wears a Koranic leather pendant. If we go out together the crops will fail, the planets will stop revolving around the sun, everybody's penises will fall off, and the world will stop existing as we know it.'

'It might work out. I mean, miracles can happen. Look in there.'

Susie lifted her sunglasses on to her head and peered through my open kitchen window, her eyes widening in disbelief. 'Is that your daughter doing the dishes?'

'Then she's going to put on a load of washing and help with the ironing.'

Susie turned to me with admiration and formally shook my hand. 'Well done,' she beamed. 'You are now officially no longer in mummy martyr mode. I mean, why would any woman want a halo? It's just one more thing to polish, right?' She slurped gratefully on her coffee. 'What about Lockie? Did you tell him how you feel about him?'

'I'm afraid he's committed to his boat, in sickness and in health, for as long as he can afford petrol and fishing-nets. Till death do them part. He can't have feelings for a woman.'

'I did warn you, Lucy-Lou.'

'I think when the kids leave home, we should sell our houses, combine our dosh and buy our own boat, Susie. We'll call it HMS *Pantyliner*. And we'll just go cruising with all our girlfriends.'

'It'll be our Aqua-disiac.'

And we cackled along with the kookaburra cacophony in the trees above us. Not at sea any more. But two single mums, taking on the world. And just for a gloriously indulgent moment or two I believed the adage – 'What do you call a husband who has lost 95 per cent of his brain capacity, sensitivity and warmth?'

Divorced.

CHAPTER 26

THE BRONZE MEDALLION

The ocean was liquid turquoise. On my last attempt the sea had been turbulent and terrifying. Today the wind had dropped and the water had taken on a look of blank innocence. Poised on the starting line, I glanced at the others attempting their bronze medallion swim. Australian boys are a hardier species. They seem taller, healthier and happier, with huge flippers for feet. Amidst this masculine throng was Chardonnay. And she was pointing at me.

'Oh God. Look who's here. The blow-in. She's Pom-golian,' Chardonnay contemptuously informed the acting club captain.

I ignored Chardonnay and concentrated on the buoy, way out the back beyond the breakers. When the whistle sounded and the stopwatch clicked, I torpedoed ahead. The water felt so warm and silky that progress was easy. This time I allowed the rhythm of the waves to lull me into a meditative state, arms and legs in harmony, my body and spirit in perfect synchronicity. Out by the buoy there were no menacing shadows looming in the depths, just sunlight reflected and refracted upwards in millions of silvery shards.

I ran the four hundred metres and swam the two hundred metres in under eight minutes. My next arduous task, rescuing a fifteen-stone drowning man on my board, I executed with text-book precision, a thrilled rush of adrenaline propelling me to shore.

Waves of amusement were rolling out from inside the cancer council sun-tent where Susie and Al-Qaeda dot com were waiting in the shade for me near the shore. I jogged up the beach and collapsed, panting, at their feet. I teased Susie about wimping out of her test but she and Ali were too busy diving into a different kind of deep end.

'Ali's going to give me some private tuition,' she flirted, breaking free of their besotted clinch. 'Don't you think he looks like my second husband?'

'How many times have you been married?' Ali queried, kissing her nose.

'Just the once . . .' Susie grinned.

As I lay in the sun and caught my breath, I watched Chardonnay floundering in the water until she was ignominiously rescued by the Clubbies in the inflatable.

'It doesn't matter about the stupid test,' she spat at me as she minced by, unknowingly crowned in seaweed. 'Lockie's gonna make sure I pass. That man would do anyfink for me,' she crowed.

'Only 'cause you open your furry pink cheque-book,' Susie surmised sardonically.

Half an hour later, the club president handed out the bronze medallions and certificates of achievement. I clutched my award proudly. But there was only one person to whom I wanted to skite. Clambering into Susie's car, she didn't even have to ask me where I wanted to be dropped.

The air was fragrantly charged with the scent of the frangipani which swung in the breeze, tickling my legs as I walked – well, winced my way – through the secluded river cove. My hair was flat and salt-encrusted. My nose was running. My skin was speckled aubergine with bruises. It hurt to laugh, which meant that I'd probably cracked a rib. I was grunting in pain – yet had never felt so elated. The brightly coloured fungus decorating the trunks of the trees along the water's edge of Burraneer Bay was like bunting.

'I'm absolutely dead. I must be the only person in the world to have received a posthumous award in person.'

Lockie stood up. He'd been oiling the wood of his old boat. His wet shirt stuck to the dark curls on his broad chest. He glanced at the medallion around my neck and I saw his estimation of me rise meteorically. 'Well, I'll be buggered. You went and bloody did it!' I was rewarded with a hearty slap on the back.

'Don't touch me!' I winced. 'My shoulders are sore from paddling. In fact, don't touch me anywhere. My calves are aching from running in the sand. My wrists are sore from flipping the board over. My fingers are crimped from gripping on in big seas. The tendons in my arms feel torn. My back's strained. And I have nipple rash from wetsuit friction. My hip bones are bruised from banging up against the board, and my pelvic bone is black and blue from the board whacking into me. I think I have swimmer's ear, too, so don't even *think* about whispering sweet nothings. The only part which doesn't hurt is one eyelash and a nostril.'

Lockie's eyes lit up mischievously. 'Surely there's some other part of you that's safe to touch?'

'Believe me, if I ever break up with you, the whole surf lifesaving ordeal will be the first incident I'll mention to the lawyer who'll be handling our separation.'

Lockie raised an eyebrow. 'And I'll explain to the lawyer that making you take up surf lifesaving is what kept you from drowning in your own sorrows.'

'Well, I don't need rescuing any more.'

'You're right . . .' Lockie muttered, softly. 'I, on the other hand . . . I, ah, I think I owe you a slab of beer.'

'But isn't that the standard fee for saving someone?'

He mumbled and grumbled and scuffed his feet. 'Ah, yeah.'

'And what exactly have I saved you from?'

'Myself. Because of you, well, I've decided to be

honest with Ryan. If only for the deep satisfaction of being able to tell Chardonnay she's corked.'

For once in my loquacious life I didn't paper over the awkward silence with nervous chatter.

'You know how I wanted to be buried in my Last Man Standing board shorts? Well, it struck me that you really do need someone there to know you're the last man standing, otherwise, what's the bloody point?'

The breeze played through the sun-sequinned gum leaves. The pulse of late summer murmured all around us, the tide hissing percussively on the rocks, the cicadas thrumming. Sea mist embroidered the air with satiny threads. Jack McLachlan didn't, perhaps couldn't, say the word 'love', with all its transforming nuances. But his eyes spoke for him. As did his body. I watched, amazed, as he raised one arm and waved it slowly. '*Assistance Required.*' That was the signal.

I signalled back '*Transmission received.*' And laughed. 'Ouch. Ouch. Don't make me laugh. It hurts to laugh. I think I've strained an intercostal.'

'Crikey. Maybe you've cracked a rib, Lucy.'

Lockie helped me lie down and knelt beside me. The rising warmth from the long grass felt like a friendly embrace.

'Look. Listen. Feel.' A wash of sunlight illuminated his face. 'You know the drill. First look at the chest for movement.' I felt his gaze slide across my breasts. 'Next, check for any movement of air from the patient's mouth or nose, on your cheek.'

I felt his warm breath near my mouth. 'Check pupils for size and ability to fix and follow.' I gazed into his sea-blue eyes and felt the centre of my world shift. 'Next, examine the patient all over for lacerations or wounds. You're looking for soft-tissue swelling, indicating fractures. Then move back to the chest to check breathing.' He ran his hands lightly over my bare skin. 'Next, examine the pelvis area for fractures.' He gently stroked my belly and I stretched and arched like a cat. Aqueous sunlight rippled over our bodies. 'This is indicated by pain on movement.'

'That's a very abnormal movement,' I said, indicating the bulge moving in his board shorts. 'Looks like the surf isn't the only thing that's up.'

'Of course, an erection is a sign of a spinal injury . . .'

'Well, you have been a bit spineless letting Chardonnay walk all over you for so long.'

'But now I've decided to tell her where to go . . . my spine is fine.' He gave me a wicked smile.

'Jack McLachlan, I'm shocked.'

'Treatment for shock – raise the patient's legs, but keep head level with heart. Protect patient from extremes of temperature.' He pressed his warm legs up against mine, then leant down and kissed me. 'Mouth-to-mouth resuscitation should be accompanied by compression. Cardio-pulmonary resuscitation, otherwise known as CPR,' Lockie said. With one adroit movement he unhooked my bikini bra.

'What are you doing?'

'External chest compression, a procedure requiring rhythmic strokes . . .' As he tenderly caressed my breasts, he kissed me again, and I began to live in the heat of his mouth and the rhythm he was building in me, and the shudder and the shake of my breath as the tension inside me twisted tighter.

A magpie carolled in a long, melodious coruscation. 'Jack.' I whispered his name with the deliberation of a child trying out the distinct sound for the first time. But a delectable moistening in my general groin area told me that talking was really quite superfluous at this point. When I curled up against him, he bit my neck, not quite playfully. When I didn't pull away, he kissed my mouth harder. His hands were in my hair, tugging my head back, which raised my breasts – breasts which he tongued, ravenously.

And so, hidden in the sunny cove, the balmy afternoon dissolved into heat and soft laughter. As Jack McLachlan slid into me every nerve in my body became incandescent, and in that moment of seamless happiness I forgot all my aches and pains.

Love is like drowning. A very nice sensation once you stop struggling.

CHAPTER 27

RESCUED

*L*ike all prisoners, she feels the presence of her captor like tentacles reaching down to where she's cowering at the bottom of the stairs. The house is hushed. She takes a deep breath, like a diver going under, and peeks down the hallway. Empty. A rustle of leaves outside the window startles her. The nerves in her body contract as she moves gingerly towards the door. She bumps into something in the dark and jumps as if bitten, but it's only the fronds of a pot plant she's forgotten. She waits an agonizing eternity to see if she's been detected. She shuffles forward, apprehension dogging each tentative step. Finally, she can see the outline of the front door, but the sensation that she's being watched intensifies. Goosebumps rise on her neck and arms. Adrenalin slams through her. She tells herself to breathe, then inches, one painfully slow tiptoe at a time, towards liberty. The door handle is almost within reach when a mutinous floorboard creaks. She hears the running thud of feet and fright licks like flames all over her. Trapped, she wheels around to face the furious countenance of her captor. The hall light snaps blindingly on.

'What on earth do you think you are wearing? You are not going out dressed like that. Go back to your room and change immediately!'

She glances down at her denim mini-skirt, vertiginous stilettos and the Wonderbra-ed cleavage semi-draped in a sequinned tank-top.

'I mean look at yourself! You're sixteen. Not thirty-six.' Her voice is metallic with anger. 'When are you going to start acting your age, Tally?'

Tally gangles in the half-open doorway, all lithe limbs and loose hair. Then she turns to me and laughingly unzips my top to expose some cleavage. 'Oh, come on, Mum. Live a little.'

Tally's smile is vivid. A hazy vanilla light seeps into the hall from the street lamp and I notice for the first time that my daughter has ripened and grown more luminous of late, like rock-hard butter which has melted into fair spreading consistency.

It's eight o'clock on a Saturday night. The air is warm and the sky above the sea is a deep, darkening blue.

'After you've changed into something that makes you look less like a crack whore . . . where are you intending to go, exactly?'

'Out.'

'Out where?'

'Just out.'

'Out is obviously a most desirable destination, as you are always going there.'

'You've got to let me come home a bit later,

Mum. I'm, like, the only one of my friends who has to be home at midnight. We're going to try to get into this club . . .'

'The only thing you'll get into at that hour is mischief. So, no, absolutely not.'

'You are soooo mean,' she sulks, but there's no anger in it. She is beaming, in fact.

A five-foot bonsai exocet missile in a Ju-jitsu suit shoots through the door and nearly knocks me over. 'I'm zorsted!' Ruby's eyes are summery with happiness. 'And guess what? I thrashed Ryan at karate!' she laughs delightedly. As I bend to kiss her, the smell of her hair is like daylight.

In the past month, Ruby has stopped wetting the bed and Tally has stopped cooking cakes. Even so, I am under no illusion. I suspect that the last forty years of parenthood are always the hardest.

Suddenly Tally whirls around and crushes me into an unexpected bear hug. 'Mum,' she says, before raiding my purse. 'When I was younger, like when we first moved to Oz, I just couldn't believe what an idiot you were. But now that I'm sixteen, it's incredible how much you've learnt in a year.' My oldest daughter smiles, knowingly.

Motherhood, I realize, is like a beanbag – easy to get into, hard to get out of, but has its cosy moments while you're down there. I execute a little dance down the hallway, much to the scathing derision of my two daughters.

Lockie always says that change is inevitable. Except from a bloody vending-machine. And for the first time in my life I'm no longer frightened of the prospect. It looks like constant change is here to stay.

In the kitchen I glance at my bronze medallion pinned on to the noticeboard among the shopping lists and yellowing art homework and dental appointment reminders, and feel a swell of pride that I survived the rough seas of the past year.

And now that I've won the bronze . . . all I can think about is going for gold.

ACKNOWLEDGMENTS

Writers make a living out of lying. But for injecting the fact into the fiction I would like to thank the following people:

My sister Elizabeth and her best friend, Tassia Kolesnikow, for enduring the bronze medallion on my behalf, ensuring that it was them and not me who suffered bruised thighs and cracked ribs. Thanks also to my Cronulla pals, Toni, Wayne and Bianca Moon for introducing me to the Last Man Standing Surf Team. (Motto – 'The older you are, the better you were'.) And Martin Dillon, the former president of North Cronulla surf club, for explaining to me, amongst other vital information, why Australian men tuck their cossies up into their bottom cheeks. For letting me into the secrets of the Advanced Padi, heart-felt thanks to BOD. And to Billy Connolly for giving me the Bush Tucker quip.

For vernacular veracity, thanks to Nick Henzell (physio-therapy), Guy Vesey (Etonian), Robbie Amhaz (Lebanese), Jane Belson (divorce details), Jamie, Danni and Ali Felber and Penny Mortimer (teenage). For snake-rearing tips I'd like to thank, at a safe distance, my herpetologist sister Jenny. (My third sister, Carolyn, offered no help at all, using the feeble excuse of a new baby. Where are the woman's priorities?)

My gratitude also to my publishing team – the perspicacious Francesca Liversidge, literary love god Larry Finlay, Margie Seale, Karen Reid and Laura Sherlock; my agents, Ed Victor and Grainnie Fox; and my home-grown commentator, Geoffrey Robertson who, along with Penny Cross, were very sound sounding-boards on all those early drafts. And to Natalie Perricone, who bid a generous amount to the Institute of Contemporary Arts for her name to appear as a character in this novel.

To my dearest girlfriends, The Gerts, see you on HMS *Pantyliner*.

And lastly, thanks to my darling children Jules and Georgie for not putting yourselves up for adoption.